more ...

"Ms. Becnel spins a fascinating story of customs, marriage, and love in twelfth-century England. Her characters are intense and vibrant, their lives complex."

—The Time Machine

Heart of the Storm

"Great characters, a riveting plot and loads of sensuality . . . a fabulous book. I couldn't put it down!"

—Joan Johnston, author of Maverick Heart

"Well-written and enjoyable."

—Publishers Weekly

"Tempestuous and seductive, this winner from Rexanne Becnel will enthrall from the first page to the last."

—Deborah Martin, author of Stormswept

Where Magic Dwells

"A passionate, compelling story filled with engaging characters."

—Library Journal

"Rich settings always bring Becnel's medieval novels to life."

—Publishers Weekly

"Enthralling . . . Another irresistible medieval romance from one of the best."

—The Medieval Chronicle

A Dove at Midnight

"A non-stop read. Rexanne Becnel understands the Medieval mind-set, and beguiling characters' passions and adventures will hold you enthralled. Once more, Ms. Becnel demonstrates that she is a master of her craft."

—Romantic Times

St. Martin's Paperbacks titles
by Rexanne Becnel

The Knight of Rosecliffe

REXANNE BECNEL

St. Martin's Paperbacks

THE KNIGHT OF ROSECLIFFE

Copyright © 1999 by Rexanne Becnel.

Excerpt from *The Mistress of Rosecliffe* copyright © 1999 by Rexanne Becnel.

All rights reserved. No part of this book may be used or reproduced in any manner whatsoever without written permission except in the case of brief quotations embodied in critical articles or reviews. For information address St. Martin's Press, 175 Fifth Avenue, New York, N.Y. 10010.

ISBN: 0-312-96905-8

Printed in the United States of America

St. Martin's Paperbacks edition/June 1999

10 9 8 7 6 5 4 3 2 1

For my Brian and my Katya

You're grown up now
but you'll always be the children of my heart.

Author's Note

In my previous novel, *The Bride of Rosecliffe*, an excerpt appeared under the title, *Mistress of the Wildwood*. That book has since been retitled *The Knight of Rosecliffe*. I hope you enjoy Jasper and Rhonwen's story.

The Knight of Rosecliffe

When stones shall grow, and trees shall no',
When noon comes black as beetle's back,
When winter's heat shall cold defeat,
We'll see them all, ere Cymru falls.

—*anonymous child's verse*

Prologue

Northern Wales, between Carreg Du and Afon Bryn
May, in the Year of Our Lord 1139

Rhonwen spied the rabbit and froze. Why didn't it run? Warily she peered about, scanning the quiet glade for some predator, whether man or beast. When she spied nothing she turned her narrowed gaze back to the rabbit and slowly set her willow basket down. The hare made a little leap, then thrashed madly about in the bed of newly unfurled ferns, before coming to an exhausted halt.

It was caught in a snare.

Again Rhonwen glanced around. Stealing from someone else's trap was never right. In these lean times it was a crime. But it wouldn't be the first time she'd done it. Nor, she feared, would it be the last. There were times when honor came in a poor second to hunger.

She approached the rabbit slowly, murmuring soothing words. "Come, now, brother rabbit. Let us see what has hold of your foot." You shall make a very good stew, she added to herself, and her stomach rumbled agreement. It had been a long, lean winter, and she'd forgotten how it felt to be fully sated with food, especially good food like rabbit stew.

With deft hands she released the hare, then tucked it into her basket. She would take care of it elsewhere. For now she must slip away before whoever trapped these woods caught her.

The sun was hidden behind a layer of slate-gray clouds, yet she knew it neared the western horizon. She'd gone farther afield than usual today, and it was getting late. Down one rugged hill she went, half-running, half-sliding on the dark grit stones. She would cross the river on the fallen tree, then head straight for Carreg Du, and with any luck, she'd be home well before dark.

But luck was not with her. She was almost to the river when a stone whizzed by her left ear. "Return my rabbit, else the next one lands on your head!"

A child's voice. He was angry, but he was only a child. She didn't slow down.

The next stone grazed her shoulder. Still she ran, across a rocky clearing, through a stand of pale green willows, dodging and twisting, then straight for the river. She had nearly reached the crossing.

Then her foot slipped, she fell, and when she scrambled up, a rock caught her squarely on the cheek.

"Ow! Oh!" She lost her footing and fell again, this time in the rock-strewn shallows of the frigid waters. Her basket went flying and in a moment the rabbit was freed. As it dashed away, tail flashing in fright, the boy ran up, panting and cursing all at the same time.

"That's my rabbit!" He flung one last fruitless stone at his disappearing dinner. "That was *my* rabbit and now it's gone— and all on account of you!"

He glowered down at Rhonwen, a ragged scruff of a boy, dirty-faced and with the look of a wild creature. Rhonwen's heart thudded from her exertions as well as from guilt and fear. Then her fear eased and frustration set in. She'd been caught red-handed. The rabbit had escaped. Her cheek hurt terribly, and the cold water was chilling her to the bone. This skinny boy had best not anger her further, else she would drown the nasty little beggar.

Suddenly her eyes narrowed and her nose wrinkled. "Don't tell me," she said, rising to her full, fourteen-year-old height. "You're Rhys ap Owain, aren't you? I'd recognize your filthy

face and nauseating stench anywhere.'' She shoved past him.
''Get out of my way.''

He was shorter than she, and slighter also, for he was a
mere child while she was nearly a woman. But he was no
more intimidated by her now than he had been as a foul-
mouthed little boy.

''And you're the bitch Rhonwen,'' he spat. ''The thievin'
bitch of Carreg Du.'' Before she could grab it, he snatched up
her basket. ''You took my rabbit, so I'll have this basket in
payment.''

''That's mine! Give it back.''

When she ran at him he danced away. ''Give me back my
dinner and I'll give you back your basket.''

''You filthy little bastard,'' she swore. ''I'll teach you to be
careful who you throw stones at!'' But try as she might, she
could not quite catch him. He dashed and whirled along the
brown riverbank with her in close pursuit, but always just a
hairbreadth behind him. Once she caught the tail of his tunic,
but it ripped, leaving her with a handful of filthy wool.

She glared at him, her chest heaving with her effort. ''You
haven't had a bath since the one I gave you five years ago,
have you? No wonder you live in the woods. No one could
bear to have you under the same roof with them!''

''I live in a fine house. A fine, snug place,'' he countered.
He waved the basket at her. ''Meriel will be glad to have this
basket. But she'd rather have had the rabbit—''

Suddenly he looked off to the right, and Rhonwen made her
move. She launched herself at him and, with a grunt, he went
down. Using her greater weight to advantage, she grabbed for
the basket. But he was stronger than he looked. Though he let
the basket go, he rolled over and pinned her. She tried to knee
him in the groin, but he evaded the blow.

''Be still. Be still!'' he hissed, catching her hair in a painful
grip. Rhonwen yanked a handful of his hair and tried to shove
him off her, but her wet skirts tangled in her legs.

''Stop it, Rhonwen! There's English upon us. English soldiers!''

English soldiers.

With those two words everything changed. Of one mind the two of them scrambled backward, into the meager shelter of a stunted alder tree growing beside a jagged black boulder. Though they considered one another enemies, when it came to English soldiers, the Welsh always stood united. So they huddled together, as still as the rabbit had been in the snare, and stared at the group across the way. They could not run, for the Englishmen would see them and five of them rode massive steeds that could trample two children to pulp.

Worse, Rhonwen knew she was old enough that enemy soldiers might devise a very different fate for her. Her newly budded breasts, of which she was so proud, would be her undoing should the English vermin spy them. So she pressed herself against Rhys's side and ordered her racing heart and trembling limbs to a calm she did not feel.

The soldiers paused on the opposite side of the river. Men and beasts alike availed themselves of the cold, refreshing waters. Their voices carried but fitfully across the rushing stream.

" 'Tis him,'' she heard Rhys mutter.

"Him? You mean Randulf FitzHugh, Lord of Rosecliffe?''

"Nay. His brother. Jasper FitzHugh. The one 'at killed my da.''

Rhonwen glanced at Rhys. Like him, her father had also been killed by the English. But her father had been a good, hardworking man. By contrast, Rhys's father had been every bit as awful as the English. Though a staunch Welsh loyalist, he'd been greedy and cruel, neither a good leader nor a particularly good father to Rhys, as she recalled.

But this was not the time to point that out. Jasper FitzHugh was their mutual enemy and, though she'd not laid eyes on him in several years, she had no trouble picking him out now.

He was tall with longish brown hair and the handsome face of the devil come to lure the unsuspecting to sin. All the women of the village spoke of him, but only when their menfolk were not around—and when they thought no children could hear. But Rhonwen made it her business to know everything about everyone, and she knew enough about Jasper FitzHugh to damn him in her eyes forever.

Bad enough that he was English. They were all monsters.

Bad enough that he was a man. They were all bullies.

To be fair, however, neither of those facts was entirely his fault. God had made him English and a man.

Beyond that, however, he was the worst sort of man, hard-drinking, wenching, gambling. Some said he'd been meant for the Church, but that the good fathers wouldn't have him. His soul was that black. He outfought both Englishmen and Welsh, and he was indiscriminate in his use of women. Mostly Welsh-women, as the few Englishwomen at Rosecliffe were married.

She studied him, trying to understand why any Welsh-woman would stoop so low as to cavort with an English knight. A Welshman, even one as ill-humored as her stepfa-ther, was always a better choice than an Englishman, no matter how comely his face and finely formed his body.

"One day I'm going to kill him," Rhys swore.

"I'll help you," she murmured. Then she added, "But only if you take a bath."

"I don't need a bath. And I don't need a girl to help me neither."

Down at the riverbank Jasper FitzHugh scanned the rocky valley. He was anxious to return to Rosecliffe Castle. He'd heard that Sir Lovell, the master builder for Rosecliffe, had two daughters soon to arrive. Jasper hadn't had an English-woman since the feast of St. Crispin's, six months previously. Of course, he'd have to be careful. Rand wouldn't look kindly on him deflowering a young virgin. But surely one of them would already be experienced between the sheets.

He lifted a wineskin from his saddle and took a deep draught of red wine. But as he wiped his mouth, his eyes narrowed. Someone was watching them, someone hiding be-side a jagged boulder halfway up the hill.

Casual in every movement, he angled away from the others as if to relieve himself. When he glanced at the boulder again, however, he made out two heads—but not men. They were too small. Children?

He bent over to scratch his ankle and picked up a stone. Then, with a lightning move, he heaved it at the hidden pair.

They scattered like hares, a boy and a young woman. A girl, judging by the dark, unbound hair streaming down her back as she scrambled up the hill. His men whooped and laughed at the sight.

"Shall we nab 'em?" Alan, one of the knights, called out.

Jasper shook his head. "There's no reason. They're just children and harmless enough."

Alan snorted. "They won't always be children."

No, they would not. But in this Jasper agreed with his brother: As frustrated as he was by the boring routine of his life, only a fool would make war purely for the thrill of it. "There's naught to be gained by terrorizing Welsh children, save to stir up their elders. And that is not our aim. Enough of this," he added. "Let us be on our way to Rosecliffe. I'm heartily tired of the company of men. I want a woman."

Book One

I crowned her with blisse, and she me with thornes.
I led her to chambre, and she me to dye . . .

—anonymous medieval verse

One

Jasper FitzHugh sat in a high-backed wooden chair with his legs outstretched and his booted feet crossed. He was biding his time, sipping but sparingly of his wine, as he played a halfhearted game of chess. But he kept a close watch on his brother Rand. A messenger had arrived shortly after the midday meal. A messenger from Simon LaMonthe.

Jasper knew that Rand did not trust LaMonthe. But a summons by a representative of old King Henry's daughter Matilda was not easily ignored. Matilda wanted the support of the Marcher lords against her cousin, King Stephen, who she said had stolen the British crown from her and her young son.

How would Rand respond?

Jasper watched his brother pace the width of the great hall, passing in front of the massive carved fireplace. His shadow fell, dark and long, across his children who played on a rug near the warm hearth. But they were unfazed. To his men Rand was a formidable knight. To his adversaries, a fearsome foe. But his three children saw him only as a warm and loving father. They did not pause in their game of Odd Man Throw, save to glance up with a grin.

Jasper sighed and drank from his pewter cup. Ten years now he'd been at Rosecliffe Castle. Ten years laboring in the long shadow his brother cast. And though he knew he was Rand's equal on the field of honor—and perhaps even better—that no longer satisfied him. He was restless. Of late he'd become more and more unsettled. He had a home for life; he had women enough when he wanted them. He had good hunting and plenty enough victuals, and Rosecliffe's alewife was a magician with hops and malt and barley. But it was no longer enough to content him.

"No, no!" Gwendolyn's shrill cry broke the evening quiet. "Mine," the three-year-old asserted.

"Begone from here," Gavin ordered, blocking his younger sister's access to the game he and Isolde played.

"Mine!" Gwen demanded. She shoved him but the seven-year-old boy only scowled and held his ground.

"You cannot play, Gwen. You're too little." Then, turning to Isolde, he said, "It's your turn."

"Mama!" Gwen began to wail. But Josselyn was upstairs helping one of the maids restring a loom, so baby Gwen turned to her older sister.

"Come here, Gwennie," Isolde said. She held out her arms, then settled the pouting child on her lap. "You can help me play, all right?"

Jasper studied the scene, which was restored again to harmony. When his brother stooped over and ruffled the baby's riot of dark curls, then murmured a few words to each of his children, Jasper frowned. Rand was truly blessed: a loving wife, adoring children, and a sturdy castle that had become a warm and welcoming home, a haven from the trials of the world. Though Jasper might equal his brother in physical prowess, he had none of the rest.

Not that he'd ever wanted a wife and children in the past. But sometimes . . . He turned away and quaffed the rest of his wine. It was long past time for him to seek his own place in the world, he realized. For Rosecliffe no longer was it. It never had been. His brother's castle was meant only to be a way station for him—but on the way to where?

He pushed to his feet and crossed to where Rand stood. "I would go to Bailwynn in your stead."

His brother looked up. "You wish to parlay with Matilda's representative?"

"Why should I not? I'm as like to fight for her cause as are you."

Rand's dark features darkened further still. "I would rather not be drawn into either Matilda's cause or Stephen's."

"You cannot avoid the conflict between them, brother."

"Mayhap not. But I can work to delay any battle that might involve mine own people." One of his hands swept the room. "I do not labor daily to build Rosecliffe Castle in order to foster war. I do it to maintain peace."

Jasper shrugged. "You cannot alter the whims of royalty."

Rand shook his head. "Mayhap I can. 'Tis the reason I must be the one to attend Simon LaMonthe's gathering."

He tossed LaMonthe's missive on a table and turned toward the stairs. But Jasper caught him by the arm. " 'Tis plain you do not wish to go. Meanwhile I am more than eager. Why will you not trust me to do this?"

" 'Tis not an issue of trust."

Rand met Jasper's angry gaze without any returning anger, but that only served to anger Jasper all the more. Was Rand patronizing him? He poked a finger in his brother's chest. "I want to go. You do not."

Rand shoved him back. "You misunderstand my motives. LaMonthe cannot be trusted except to yield to a greater strength than his own. I am Lord of Rosecliffe. I am the one to remind him of that fact."

"And what am I to do here? Ride these hills, chasing the damned elusive Welsh rebels through the woods, startling hunters and wood gatherers and Welsh brats at their play—"

He broke off, but not soon enough. Rand's gaze had turned to frost. "I meant no insult," Jasper swore. "You know I meant no insult, Rand, least of all to mine own nieces and nephew. I care for them as deeply as if they were mine own."

Rand nodded curtly, accepting Jasper's apology. "Do you never wonder whether those Welsh brats you refer to are not your own? In the past you have been known to spread your seed far and wide." He shook his head, returning to the subject. "No, brother. You will remain at Rosecliffe Castle. I trust you to protect Josselyn and the children from any harm. I place them in your care because I know the affection you have for them—Welsh blood or no. I trust you as I trust no other. Do you understand?"

Jasper did, though he resented his older brother's reference to his profligate ways. Would Rand never see him as more than a foolish younger brother? Still, he was mollified by the sincerity of Rand's words. Rand loved his wife and children with a ferocity Jasper could only marvel at.

Would he himself ever feel such a deep and abiding love for anyone—for a wife and babes of his own? There were times when he wanted to. And yet he feared he could never find one woman to bind him that dearly.

There were other times, however, when he was grateful for the freedoms of his bachelorhood.

Rand slapped him on the back, then looked up when Josselyn descended the stairs. Jasper saw the appreciation in his eyes, the love that had grown ever stronger in the ten years of their marriage. That Josselyn returned his love was no secret, and when she smiled at Rand, Jasper felt a stab of jealousy.

He wanted what they had, he admitted to himself. He wanted it. It was plain, however, that he would not find it in the hills of northern Wales. He knew all the women of these lands—and had sampled more than his rightful share of them. Yet not one of them had laid a claim to his heart.

For now he must perform his duty: protect Rosecliffe and the people of the demesne during Rand's absence.

But upon his brother's return he would discuss this matter further with Rand. Perhaps he would visit their brother John at the family estate in Aslin. It had been ten years since last he'd seen him. Or perhaps he would take service elsewhere, in a place with heiresses who owned lands aplenty.

No matter where he went, however, the change would be for the best.

*   *   *

The next morning, as the chapel bells rang prime, the whole of the castle folk turned out to bid Rand farewell. The meeting of the border lords was to take place at Bailwynn, Simon LaMonthe's fortress on the Divernn River, fully three days ride south. The contingency from Rosecliffe included eight mounted knights and a dozen foot soldiers.

Josselyn held Gwendolyn in her arms as she hugged her husband close one last time. "Give me your solemn vow, Rand, that you will be careful. LaMonthe is not a man to be trusted."

"You have my vow," he assured her. Then he turned to Jasper. Nine-year-old Isolde clung to her uncle's arm. Gavin straddled his shoulders. Rand grinned at his brother. "I see I need not request that you have a care for my family."

"Gavin and I will guard Rosecliffe from any blackguards who dare venture near, will we not, Gav?" He jiggled the boy, making him laugh.

"We will slay any knave who threatens," Gavin crowed, waving his wooden sword about.

"You, my boy. Look to your sisters. And do as your uncle bids you."

"You may count on me, Father."

Rand hesitated a moment, glancing at his wife before addressing his son once more. "While I am away, 'tis my plan to inquire after a suitable household where you may be fostered."

Gavin hooted with delight. But when Jasper glanced at Josselyn, he saw she was less pleased. The Norman custom of fostering their sons in the households of others did not appeal to her Welsh sensibilities. It was one of the few matters she and Rand disagreed on. Over the years Rand had made many concessions to the Welsh residing within the limits of his demesne, and all on account of his Welsh wife. But it appeared that on this particular issue, he would stand firm.

Rand kissed his girls and solemnly shook Gavin's hand. His last words before parting, however, were for Jasper. "You should get you a wife to give you babes," he said. "Methinks you have a talent for it."

Jasper watched, bemused, as the column of men rode over the bridge. Bright and warm, the day was filled with the cries of choughs and woodcocks. The brilliant morning light glinted on harness and weapons, but the heavy thud of the destriers' hooves was a somber reminder of the seriousness of the men's mission.

The masons hanging upon the sheer stone walls of the castle paused in their labors as their lord departed. But from the quarry beyond the western walls, the sharp tap and crack of the stonecutters carried on the wind. "Let us climb up to the wall walk," Isolde suggested. "We'll be able to follow Papa's progress past town. Past the *domen*, even."

Gavin was off in a flash, racing to get there first while Gwendolyn trundled in his wake. Isolde went slower, walking in the ladylike manner she'd begun to adopt. As Jasper watched her go, Josselyn put words to his thoughts.

"Rand plans also to make inquiries regarding a husband for her." Josselyn's pretty face settled in worried lines.

Jasper shrugged. "Eventually she must wed. It is not too soon to consider her choices."

"She is but nine! I do not understand your bloody English customs."

Jasper circled her shoulders in a brotherly manner. "You may not like our bloody customs, but you certainly like our bloody curse words."

That drew a reluctant smile from her. "I never said the English were completely bad. I wouldn't have married your brother if I thought such a thing." Then her smile faded. "It's just that I cannot bear the thought of her leaving here. Of any of them leaving."

Jasper tightened his grasp. "Gavin will return and one day he will be lord of Rosecliffe. As for the girls, they must eventually be wed. 'Tis unlikely they will find acceptable husbands at Rosecliffe."

"Rand says that Gwendolyn may wed a lesser lord, the son of one of his knights, or what have you. But as for his eldest daughter—and eldest child—he insists that Isolde must marry well. But I will not let her go too young. Nor too far," she added. She sighed, then tilted her head to look up at him. "Methinks Rand would be better served putting his efforts toward finding a suitable mate for his brother."

"Oho. You're that anxious to be rid of me?"

"There's nothing to say you must leave us when you wed. You can bring a wife here to live at Rosecliffe."

"And how is there a benefit in that? I am a landless knight. If I must shackle myself to a woman she might at least be an heiress."

She studied him a moment, then shook her head. "Ah, you English. I had hoped you'd been long enough in Wales to learn that the choice of a wife—or husband—need not be dependent solely upon politics and property. You are not content, Jasper. I see that very well. Have you not considered that it may be love more so than land which you need to soothe the restlessness in your soul?"

Love? Jasper was saved defending himself against that remark when Gavin shouted down to them. "I can see Father! He approaches the *domen*. I can even see Newlin!"

"God shield me, child! Do not lean out so far!" Josselyn called back to the grinning, waving boy so high above them now. "Oh, that rogue," she muttered. "He will not rest until he turns every hair on my head gray."

"Once he is fostered out you will not have to worry so."

Josselyn shook her head and shot him an exasperated look. "You do not understand a mother's heart. If anything, I will worry more. Is he mistreated? Is he well fed? Is he lonely for his family? No. Fostering Gavin away from his home will break my heart—as will pledging Isolde to some distant lord. Were the decision mine, they would all wed people from Rosecliffe—or Carreg Du," she added, referring to her home village not two miles away. She sighed. "I had better fetch them down, ere one of them tumbles over the side."

Jasper watched her go. She was still nearly as slender and youthful as when she'd wed Rand. Rand had done well with a Welsh wife, and yet he preferred his children wed English citizens. But that was only practical, since league by league, it was the English who controlled Wales. Even Jasper, who found Welshwomen a handsome, lusty lot, was not likely to marry from among them.

Then he ran his hand roughly through his disheveled hair. What had caused all these maudlin thoughts today? Why did he moon over the idea of marrying and settling down? It was plain he needed something to lift his spirits, something to remind him of the pleasures of bachelorhood.

Leaving orders for the guard, he filled a wineskin from the cellar, fetched his horse, Helios, then rode out into the little town slowly growing below the castle walls. In the past, Maud the blacksmith's daughter had always been good for a tickle and a laugh. And if she could not slip away, Gert the dairy maid might be available.

Blood rushed to his loins at the thought of Maud's lush breasts and Gert's pink, rounded bottom. Two lusty wenches, one English, one Welsh. Yes, he'd been far too long without a woman. As he urged his horse on, he wondered if there was a way to have the two of them, both at the same time. Now, wouldn't that be a night to remember?

Though small, the town of Rosecliffe was busy. Three women, their heads covered with *couvrechefs*, gathered at the well, drawing water. Two old men basked in the sun, whittling arrow shafts as they talked of times past. A dog loped by, then ducked around a newly built waddle-and-daub house, with a pack of urchins fast on his trail.

The children skidded to a halt when they spied Jasper, and they stared curiously at him, so tall astride Helios. There was no fear on their faces, though, and Jasper knew Rand would be pleased by that fact. His brother's plan to build a fortress that promised peace to all, both English and Welsh, was working. But though some Welsh people had moved into Rosecliffe village, living side by side with English settlers, they remained in the minority. For the most part, the warlike Welsh still harbored the hope of expelling the English from their borders.

Jasper knew, however, that it was a fruitless hope. The English were too strong and too organized for the fractious Welsh ever to defeat them. The change to English rule might come slowly across Wales, but come it would. Rand's marriage to a Welshwoman had begun the change in northern Wales, and there had been several subsequent intermarriages since then.

Should he consider doing the same?

The answer was simple: Not if he wanted lands of his own.

He found Gert at her churn with her mother. The mother handed him a jug of buttermilk, then crossed her thick arms and watched him with narrowed gaze until he departed.

At the smithy's open-fronted shop, Maud worked the bellows while her father and brother labored painstakingly, beating out points for new lances. Her arms were bared in the heat of the fire. Her magnificent bosom bounced and jiggled every time she leaned forward shoving the bellows up and down. Her skin glistened with sweat and her thin blouse, damp with the heat, clung to her breasts, revealing enough to torture even a blind man.

Her father looked up at Jasper, glanced at his daughter, then grinned. The man was not above tempting his liege lord's brother with his enticing daughter. But Jasper knew he was holding out for marriage. He had one son and seven daughters. Maud was only the first whom he must find a match for.

He handed a finished point to Jasper. " 'Tis fine and hard, milord, and still warm to the touch. Here, feel it.''

Jasper did not linger there. He didn't want to marry Maud, just bed her. Only that was proving more and more difficult to do—and he was getting hard just remembering the pleasures of the doing.

Who else? But there was no one else, not at midday. Though he was restless and in dire need of some distraction, it was clear that today, at least, a woman would not be it.

He ought to return to the tilting yard, he told himself, and work out his frustrations with lance and sword. But no one gave him adequate contest save for Alan and Rand, and they were both gone to parlay with LaMonthe.

So he turned to the third choice left him, and rode to the alewife's brew shed. Between the jug she provided him and the generous wineskin already tied to the saddle, he was certain to drown his woes.

He urged his mount through the village and past the town

gate, waving to the watchman who sat in the sun, twisting twine that later would be braided into rope. He followed the hard-packed road down the hill. Below and to the left the shepherd boys trailed behind their woolly charges. To the right the cool woods and the River Geffen beckoned. Between him and the river stood only the *domen*, the ancient burial tomb avoided by most of the Welsh and all of the English, save for Rand.

True to his poor luck this day, Jasper spied the little bard Newlin. The deformed old man sat on the flat stone that topped the *domen* and stared fixedly at Jasper. Or at least he seemed to stare at Jasper. His eyes did not always focus in the same direction, so Jasper could never be certain where the odd little fellow was looking.

Though he was not in the mood to parry words with the strange old man, Jasper felt keenly his responsibility now that Rand was gone. He would speak to Newlin briefly, then be on his way.

Newlin rocked back and forth, a slight movement, both mesmerizing and irritating. His beribboned cloak wafted and billowed about him as if some mystical breeze cavorted about the man. Jasper halted beside the stone, eye to eye with the ageless Welsh bard.

"Ah. The young lord." Newlin spoke softly, in English today. "Surveying your lands."

"They're not my lands. They never will be."

The bard smiled. "Perhaps they already are."

Jasper shifted in his saddle. Osborn, Rosecliffe's captain-of-the guard, and most of the rest of the English, were afraid of Newlin—or at least viewed him with a superstitious eye. Rand and Josselyn, by contrast, often sought his company. Jasper himself neither feared the man nor found his obtuse maunderings particularly interesting. "Unlike you Welsh," he replied, "we English have clearly defined lines of inheritance. These lands will go to Gavin, not to me."

Newlin smiled, the sweet, gentle smile of a simpleton. Jasper knew, however, that he was anything but simpleminded. "Who shall keep the order in these hills may change," Newlin said. "The wind blows, sometimes from the south, sometimes from the north. We Cymry, we endure. As for this land, it shall ever remain in the possession of those who are, in turn, possessed by it."

"I keep the peace in my brother's absence. That is all. I am neither possessor or possessed. Soon enough will his son perform that task."

"His son," Newlin echoed after a moment. "The sons of sons haunt these hills. And their sons too. Have you a son?"

"You know I do not."

"Perhaps soon you will." He stared off toward the forest as if the conversation were finished.

But his last remark had caught Jasper's interest. Though he did not credit visions and predictions, he couldn't help asking, "Am I soon to wed and have a son?"

Newlin's interest remained fixed on the horizon. "The day will come when you will teach a child the chant of these hills."

"The chant?"

This time Newlin did not answer. He closed his eyes and his rhythmic swaying deepened. No music played, and yet the wind seemed to chant through the trees.

When stones shall grow, and trees shall no' . . .

Jasper remembered bits and pieces of the song the Welsh taught their children, reassuring them that no English would ever rule Wales. There were three predictions, but he couldn't recall the other two. Not that it mattered what sort of foolishness the Welsh chose to believe. The stones had grown. Rosecliffe castle was proof of that. Nothing else the Welsh might predict concerned him overmuch.

He stared closely at the bard, but Newlin had retreated into his own visions. Jasper stifled a curse and wheeled his horse about. Enough of this. These damned Welsh and their damned country were supposed to have provided him with adventure and opportunity. He'd left the smothering life of the Church only to find life at court boring. When Rand had needed his help in Wales, he'd come willingly. The Welsh were said to be a fearsome lot, and he'd looked forward to testing his mettle in battle against them.

But after only one troublesome year, there had been little enough excitement, only the occasional raiding of some disgruntled Welshman or two. And now, when King Stephen and Matilda, the old king's daughter, promised some sort of confrontation, he was left here to the unchanging boredom of Rosecliffe.

He reached the river and dismounted, letting Helios browse freely while he took both ale jug and wineskin and clambered onto a boulder. The only good thing in the whole of his brother's considerable holdings was the quality of its ale and wine, he groused. He took a deep pull of the wine and settled onto the boulder. Being left behind by Rand was the final indignity, he told himself. The river rushed by, dark and cold. A perch broke the surface with a silvery flash. A crow's raucous cry echoed; another answered it. And all the while Jasper brooded and drank and subsided into morose daydreams of adventure denied and daring suppressed.

When his brother returned, Jasper knew he must leave. He would attach himself to Stephen's army—or Matilda's. He didn't care which. He would fight battles and win rewards, and if he died, he didn't care about that either.

He drained the wineskin, then tossed it aside. What was a knight but a noble warrior? What was a man but a creature of blood and bone? He would fight with honor; he would win with honor; he would die with honor.

So he drank and he dreamed and the sun moved across the sky. It lit the opposite riverbank and cast him into shadow. He needed to relieve himself but he could not move. He was too relaxed. Had the rock not been so hard, he could have slept.

He squinted at the diamond reflections on the river. If he kept his eyelids half-closed, one of the twisting willow trunks on the opposite bank very nearly resembled a woman. Slender and strong. Supple in the breeze.

Then the tree stepped nearer the water and into the sunlight, and Jasper blinked his eyes. The tree *was* a woman. A woman.

He pushed up onto his elbows and tried to focus. At his movement she looked up and spied him. He froze, praying she would not flee. A woman, and alone as far as he could tell.

His head began to pound from the effort of staring so hard. But he remained still, sprawled upon the boulder, no weapon in his hands. Perhaps that was what reassured her, for after a moment she advanced farther into the sunlight. Her hair was long and dark, as black as a raven's wing. It gleamed in the waning sunshine. And she was young. Her waist was narrow and her breasts high and firm. Jasper felt portions of his own anatomy begin to grow firmer too.

She saw him and yet she did not shy away. Fifty paces and an ice-cold river full with snowmelt protected her. It emboldened her, it seemed. As he watched, she put down the bundle she carried, then began to remove her dark green mantle.

Slowly Jasper sat up.

She stretched her arms high to let down her hair, then shook it out and began to finger-comb the thick, luscious length of it.

He was mesmerized. Was she real, or was she a lovely dream, some fanciful conjecture created of wine and ale and restlessness?

Then she removed her short boots, and tucked her skirt up, baring her pale ankles and legs. His heart stopped, then started again at full force. She waded into the water. Did she mean to cross over to him?

He jumped to his feet—an unfortunate movement, for he'd consumed more spirits than he realized, and on an empty stomach. But he refused to succumb to his spinning head or to his traitorous stomach, for her breasts were such lovely thrusting things, and her legs were long and shapely. She wanted to wrap them around his hips. He was convinced of it.

God, but he must have her!

Across the river, Rhonwen was shocked by her own daring. Baring her legs to a hated Englishman! But it had caught the scurvy knave's attention, for he stood now on the flat rock that jutted into the river. He stood there swaying and she thought he would lose his balance and topple over. What was wrong with the man? Though her feet were turning numb from the ice-cold river, she squinted at him. Was he drunk?

Suddenly she gasped. It was *him*! Brother of Sir Randulf. Jasper FitzHugh, whom she'd first laid eyes on when she was but a child and he a newly dubbed knight.

At the time, he'd been the captive of Rhys's father, Owain. Now, ten years later, Owain was dead by Jasper FitzHugh's hand, and Rhys had become the scourge of the English. Meanwhile, Jasper FitzHugh had no claim to fame, save as English sot and despoiler of Welsh womanhood.

She'd seen him once or twice in the intervening years, but only from afar, like now. But there were few as tall and broad-shouldered as he. Even from this distance, she could see the square jaw and straight nose that lent his face a comeliness no man should possess. Especially an Englishman.

Yes, it was Jasper FitzHugh. Would he recall the wild little girl who had stopped Owain from severing his hand? He'd lost only a finger instead, but he'd lived though the ordeal. Would he remember her?

She snorted. Not likely.

Had she the opportunity to do it all over again, would she save him a second time? Absolutely not!

Ten years ago she had saved him but only so he could be exchanged for her friend Josselyn, who'd been taken hostage by Randulf FitzHugh. But Rhonwen's efforts had all been for naught, for Josselyn had eventually wed her captor. Jasper FitzHugh had recovered from his wounds and stayed to become one more Englishman oppressing her people.

Across the river, FitzHugh raised a hand to her in drunken salute. Rhonwen frowned. The past was past. She could do nothing to change it. But the present . . . the present demanded that she act. So she waved back at him, all the while wondering what Rhys would do were he here.

The answer was uncomfortably clear. Rhys passionately believed that Wales should be purged of the English by whatever means necessary. Those who would not leave willingly must be killed.

The FitzHughs had long ago made it clear that they did not intend to leave.

So she steeled herself to do what she knew any true Welsh loyalist must do. Slowly she reached back for the small hunting bow she carried. Carefully she eased an arrow from the quiver that hung at her waist.

Then, not allowing herself time for doubt, she swung the bow into place, notched the arrow, and let it fly.

Two

When Jasper slammed into the frigid river, the impact sobered him at once. She'd tried to kill him! That vision beside the river, that siren with the curvaceous body and black silk for hair, had tried to kill him.

Had her arrow struck home?

He took quick stock and realized it had not—but only by chance. God protected children and drunkards, he'd oft heard said, and he believed it must be true. For his bleary eyes had not registered the siren's murderous intent until too late. It was not self-preservation that had protected him from her deadly arrow. His drunken swaying and a stray gust of wind had tilted him off balance, and in the process saved his life.

But for how long?

The water dragged him along, pulling at his tunic and braies, sucking him down into its icy depths. The urge to swim toward the shore was overwhelming. But somehow he beat it down. If the wench thought she'd succeeded, she would not pursue him. Not that he feared her. But she might not be alone. Once he was far enough downriver, he could double back and trap the devious bitch.

The river was stronger than he'd thought, and it carried him a goodly distance before he could escape its hold. When he finally clambered out on the opposite bank, his teeth were chattering and his entire body shuddered with the cold. He was drenched, chilled to the bone and a long way from home. Added to that, once he caught his attacker, he would have to cross the river again to reach his horse.

His horse!

The Welsh were notorious horse thieves and Helios was as fine a piece of horseflesh as could be found outside of England. Rage burned off Jasper's chill and, despite his exhaustion, he began to run, dodging willows and holly bushes, sometimes slipping but never letting up. She would not have Helios. He refused to let a mere woman best him.

But best him she had.

Jasper arrived at the place on the river where she had been. Across from him rose the great boulder he'd sprawled upon. What an arrogant idiot he'd been to sit exposed upon the most indefensible spot along the river. And now Helios, who'd foraged in the meadow just beyond the boulder, was gone.

Rand would be furious.

"Hell and damnation," he swore. She'd even taken his wineskin. "Bloody hell and damnation!"

But cursing did him no good and after a moment reason took charge. He shoved his hair back from his brow and considered his situation. If she'd crossed the river to steal Helios, she would have to cross back again in order to return.

Return to where?

Where was she from?

Not the village of Rosecliffe. He knew all the women of Rosecliffe. Perhaps Carreg Du, or even Afon Bryn, though that was a fair distance for a woman to travel. In order to escape capture, she would have to take Helios far from Rosecliffe.

Afon Bryn it was, he decided. And he must intercept her before she reached that village and its hostile populace.

He started off at a steady pace, scanning the riverbank for signs of a horse, and a hundred paces upstream he was rewarded for his efforts. Hoofprints in the muddy bank, then clear signs of a large creature headed south through a stand of arrowhead.

Jasper felt for his daggers, the large one in its hip sheath, and the smaller one inside his boot. She thought he was dead and would be careless in her escape. He gritted his teeth and pressed on faster, ignoring the stitch in his side and the dull thud in his head. She would not escape him, this devious wench. She might be exquisite in form, and deadly in intent, but she was only a woman. He would capture her and he would make her pay.

One way or another, she would pay dearly for this day's foul work.

Rhonwen trudged through the forest, leading the destrier. She'd struck a blow for Cymry this day, and she should be consumed with joy. But she didn't feel joy. In its stead she felt a miserable guilt. She'd killed a man—killed him!—and even though he was an Englishman, she felt terrible.

But there was no undoing what she'd done and so she pressed on toward home. At least the beast was docile and followed her reasonably well. It refused to let her mount him, however, adding further to her guilt. As if the animal knew what she'd done, it rolled its eyes when she approached, and sidled away. He was too tall for her to jump on, and anyway, she was not so used to horses as to be that confident of her riding skills.

But she had no intention of losing such a valuable prize, so she led the animal toward the campsite between Carreg Du and Afon Bryn. Rhys would be there and he would know what to do with the Englishman's destrier. And he would be elated to hear she'd killed the man—except that he'd wanted to kill Jasper FitzHugh himself.

Then again, had she really killed the man?

Rhonwen gnawed her lower lip. She'd shot him and he'd collapsed into the river, so she must have struck him. If the arrow hadn't killed him, surely he had drowned. She'd watched his body catch in the current, then careen down the swollen river. Yes, he was dead. He must be. But she could not be glad for his death.

She trudged forward, up an embankment, following a dim trail through the newly budding forest, and with every step guilt plagued her. She'd never killed anyone before. She'd hunted, of course, and killed fish, fowl, and small game animals. But that was for food. That was for survival.

Then again, her people were fighting for survival against the English, and he *was* an Englishman.

But she couldn't put him out of her mind. Had he died easily or not? Had the arrow quaffed his life quickly, or had he slowly bled to death? Or had he drowned, desperately sucking in water instead of the blessed air?

She paused on the narrow trail and inhaled great breaths of the cold spring air. Death by drowning. She shuddered at the thought. Somewhere above her a crow let out a raucous cry. She looked up, startled. The horse behind her blew a hot breath onto the back of her neck and she jumped. Then it nudged her with its nose, nearly knocking her over.

"Stop that, you great, overgrown beast," she swore in a shaking voice. She tightened her fingers on the reins and twisted the leather around her hand. She was behaving like a frightened child, starting at shadows. Let her mother fret and worry; Rhonwen was made of sterner stuff.

"Come along," she muttered, starting forward again. Rhys's rebel camp was not too much farther. But the horse had turned balky. It started forward, then stopped. "Come along!" she repeated, yanking on the leather reins.

The animal only eyed her, staring down his long nose from his superior height.

What if he refused to go any farther? How was one to bully so large a creature?

"If you come along, there will be cool water and a lovely meadow waiting for you," she said in Welsh. Then, realizing he was a Norman lord's horse, she translated the words to the best of her ability.

The destrier stared at her with dark, intelligent eyes. His ears pricked forward and she could almost believe he understood what she'd said. Once more he blew out a hot breath. Then his ears flickered backward, heeding the soft call of a wren.

All at once Rhonwen's skin prickled. A wren? Wrens were

not found in these parts until midsummer. Something was not right.

At once she backed up the path, tugging for the horse to follow. But the huge animal did not move. The reins tightened around her hand, nearly jerking her off her feet. Then, before she could free herself from them, a man burst out of the woods. A tall, wet man with murder in his eyes.

He wasn't dead!

"No!" Rhonwen grabbed for her dagger with her left hand, but it was too late. He caught her wrist in a harsh grip and, with a jerk, ripped the reins from her other hand.

She struck at his head with her fist, then tried to claw his eyes, to no avail. She could not best him physically. He was too big, too strong, and too furious. Yet she could not let herself acquiesce. So she twisted and kicked, and tried to knee his groin. She bit him and clawed him and screamed curses with every breath.

"Plague among men! Scourge of the earth!"

He grunted when her elbow caught his chin.

"Snake!" she screeched. "Coward! Impotent bastard!"

"Not hardly," he muttered in her native Welsh. Suddenly he lifted her off her feet, then threw her up into the air.

Rhonwen shrieked—was he mad?—and braced herself for a painful landing. But he caught her and before she could react, he had captured both her wrists and twisted them behind her back. Then he pulled her hard up against him, holding her so tight she could barely breathe.

Her face was smashed into his padded wool tunic. Her breasts flattened against the studded chest piece, and her thighs felt the muscular weight of his legs.

"Give in, vixen. You have been caught, and in a trap of your own making."

His smugness enraged her, but she could not free her hands no matter how she fought. So she fought him with the only weapon left to her. She bit him.

She got a mouthful of wet wool, but he jerked just the same. "Damnation, but you're a feisty one." He caught a handful of her hair and yanked down so that she had no choice but to look up at him. It was a terrifying experience.

His eyes were gray. Not blue, but a true gray. Like wet slate. Ten years ago he'd been captured by the Welsh and she'd seen him up close. But he'd been too concerned with his own survival to notice a little Welsh girl. She'd not actually looked into his eyes that time, and since then she'd kept her distance from him.

But there was no distance between them now.

She stared up into those gray eyes, and she remembered the whispers of the women at the well. Even the devil could not best him when it came to the pleasures of the flesh, they said.

Then he smiled and she began to shake.

"I'm neither a bastard," he said, his low voice rumbling from his chest into hers, "nor impotent." As if to provide proof of that, he shifted his hips and she felt the unmistakable outline of his manhood.

"My mistake," she muttered. "I should have called you a coward and a rapist."

He laughed. The sound was ludicrous under the circumstances. But whether furious or amused, he was dangerous. Rhonwen did not delude herself on that account.

"Pray tell, wench, what are you called?"

Rhonwen did not answer.

Holding her gaze, he shifted again, and she felt the strength in his hard warrior's body. If he meant it as a threat—a reminder of her vulnerability—he succeeded very well. She swallowed hard.

"What are you called?"

"Rhonwen ap Tomas," she spat.

"Why did you try to kill me, Rhonwen ap Tomas?"

"You are English," she replied. Was he a simpleton?

"I am English, so you would kill me and steal my horse and consider it a good afternoon's work. Where were you taking Helios?"

Rhonwen glared at him. She could do little else. How long did he mean to continue this ridiculous conversation? How long did he mean to hold her crushed to him?

The answer was obvious and her heart sank: Until his arousal was complete and he could begin raping her.

She tried to look away. She didn't want him to see her fear. But he moved his hand up to the back of her head and made her face him once more. "Where were you taking my horse? Afon Bryn?"

"Yes. What difference does it make?"

" 'Tis always wise to know where my enemy sleeps."

She laughed. "Your enemy sleeps all around you. Even in the village beneath the castle walls."

"So you know I am of Rosecliffe."

"Jasper FitzHugh. Brother of the man who styles himself lord of these lands."

"Brother-in-law to Josselyn. Yes," he added when her eyes clouded over. "I know you once were friend to Josselyn. I know who you are, Rhonwen ap Tomas. And I know also the debt I owe you." Then, to her utter surprise, he loosened his hold on her and stepped away.

Rhonwen stumbled back, bewildered by so abrupt a change in her circumstances. She shivered with the sudden cold, for she'd grown warm in his embrace.

Across the narrow path they stared at one another. He was tall and well formed. His thick brown hair had begun to dry, but his damp clothes clung to his shoulders and arms and legs. Yes, he was well formed. Straight and strong, with comely features and all his teeth. And those intense gray eyes. She hated him, yet she was a woman and she could see now why women flocked to his side.

Was he fool enough to think his magnanimous gesture might win her over? Was he fool enough to think he might lure *her* into his bed?

She crossed her arms over her chest and backed farther away. "You are letting me go?"

He lifted his right hand, the one missing a finger. "My hand is attached to my arm still, thanks to a brave little girl named Rhonwen. So this once I will let you go. But only once. Of course, if you would like to linger with me awhile . . ."

He approached her and, though she should have run, she

did not. He stopped but inches from her; then, reaching slowly forward, smoothed a tangled strand of her hair back from her cheek. "You have grown into a beautiful woman, Rhonwen."

"We are enemies," she answered. But her words sounded mild when she meant them to be accusing. She frowned. "It was not for your sake that I convinced Owain to spare your hand."

"Yes, I know. Josselyn explained everything to me. Who you were. How you held the boy Rhys captive so that his father, Owain, would not kill me. And all to save Josselyn from Rand's clutches. No matter your reasons, I am grateful for the results. So, Rhonwen, wild creature of the wildwood, I give you your freedom in thanks for the boon you did me ten years past."

Rhonwen could hardly credit it. He was serious, even though she had just tried to kill him. Her brows drew together in a V. "This changes nothing. We are still enemies, and I will do everything in my power to drive you from these lands."

"You've made that abundantly clear."

"I would do it again," she warned.

His eyes narrowed. "I see no reason for us to battle one another to the death. No good can come of it."

"You are English. I am Welsh," she said, and in her mind that explained everything.

"I am a man. You are a woman," he countered in a voice so low and warm that Rhonwen felt it in the center of her belly. It was like nothing she'd ever felt before, a melting feeling, a sucking away of her will to reveal a completely illogical, completely mad desire to linger awhile with him.

He was a man and she a woman. She was old enough to make her own decisions regarding men and certainly old enough to have lost her innocence. But she hadn't because no man had attracted her in that way. How could it be that this man—this Englishman—did?

"Nay," she said, sidestepping him. "We are enemies. We can be no more."

He caught her hand before she could flee. "Have you a husband?"

"Nay."

Perhaps if she'd lied and said yes he would have let her go. But she didn't say yes and he didn't let her go. Instead he pulled her toward him and when they were face-to-face he said, "Before we become enemies once more, I would have us see whether we ever could have been lovers."

Rhonwen gasped. "I don't think—"

"Don't think," he commanded. "Just feel." Then he bent nearer, slowly, keeping their gazes locked until their lips met.

Only then did Rhonwen's eyes close. She could not escape him, she told herself. This was merely an experiment, she rationalized as his warm mouth moved over hers, merely an exercise in curiosity.

But her body deemed otherwise. Her insides melted. Her limbs trembled, and her skin prickled. Fire raced over her and yet she shivered.

He slanted his mouth over hers for a closer fit, and his teeth plucked at her lower lip. Then, when she took a breath, his tongue stole between her lips, strange and yet wholly seductive.

So this was why the village women gossiped about him.

She tried to pull back, for she could feel her body succumbing to him. But the wretch would not let her go. His arms came around her, gentler than before, but no less binding.

Though she should have, she did not fight him. He had charmed her with his unlikely sense of fair play and his hypnotic eyes. And now with his kisses. She knew it and yet she could not prevent it. If she'd known kissing could be like this, she might not have avoided the several fellows who'd tried to steal a kiss from her in the past.

"Ah, sweetling," he murmured, moving his clever lips in a trail down her throat, then over to her ear. "You taste like salt and honey."

"And you taste of wine," she murmured without artifice.

A harder kiss, forceful and demanding, put an end to further conversation. This time his tongue slid deeper into her mouth, possessing it in a way that seemed to scorch her from the inside out. She pressed up into him and felt his arousal, bigger than before, and though it still frightened her, it was now a different sort of fear. She did not fear rape any longer. But loss of control? Suddenly that loomed dangerously real and even more terrifying than the threat of rape.

"Nay. Stop." She twisted away, panicked by the strange emotions he'd roused in her. He'd nearly seduced her with the promise of pure physical pleasure, just as the village gossips whispered he could do. But she would not allow it. She could not!

She faced him, hugging her arms about herself, afraid of him but for entirely different reasons than before. "We are enemies, you and I. Nothing has changed."

He smiled and she could see the heat of desire in his eyes. She could feel it as his gaze ran over her. "Everything has changed, Rhonwen. We were meant to be lovers. We *will* be lovers. If not today, then sometime soon enough."

"No, you are wrong in that."

"I've never been more right."

Rhonwen refused to bandy words with him any longer. It was far too dangerous. Slowly she backed away, keeping her eyes on him. "We are done," she whispered, though the words were more for her benefit than his. "We are done."

He grinned, a wicked, knowing grin, and raised his hand in farewell. "Till we meet again, fair Rhonwen." Then he blew her a kiss.

Rhonwen didn't wait. Ludicrous as it was, she could not let that kiss land—that gesture of a kiss, of affection. So she turned and she ran, and she did not stop until she reached the safety of the rebel camp where Rhys and the others would drive thoughts of Jasper FitzHugh clean out of her head.

As for Jasper, he shook his head as she fled, amazed at what had transpired. So that was Rhonwen. She'd been but a girl he hardly recalled, save that she had inadvertently protected him from Owain's vengeance. On occasion he had wondered about her, especially at Josselyn's sorrow for having lost the child's friendship. But the years had passed and the little

Welsh girl had lingered in his mind only as a story to be told when the hour grew late and the wine flowed long.

But today all that had changed. When he'd first spied her alongside the river, he'd thought her an erotic vision—a drunken erotic vision. Then in short order she'd gone from temptress to murderess to horse thief, then back to temptress once more. She'd used no artifice to attract him, only the natural beauty of a fair complexion, a voluptuous mouth, and luxuriant masses of exquisite hair. And her sweetly shaped body—he could not forget that. Her simple garments could not hide the perfection of those curves.

He wanted her, more now when he was sober than before when he'd merely been drunk and horny. "Damnation," he swore, astounded by what had transpired between them.

He whistled for Helios, who grazed alongside the narrow trail. He could not ride the destrier, however. Not just yet. He grinned to himself as he caught Helios's reins and headed on foot back toward the river and Rosecliffe Castle. The feisty little wench had left him with an arousal that might take miles to walk off.

But the next time they met—and there would be a next time, he vowed—she would not leave him in this same wretched state. The next time he saw her, he would finish what they had begun this day.

He would have the unruly vixen in his bed and teach her that it was far more pleasurable to make love to your enemy than to wage war.

Three

Rhonwen speared a haunch of roasted venison with her dagger and grabbed a horn cup of ale, then retreated to a crude bench propped up beside a twisted old oak. Rhys was not in the transient rebel camp, but that was just as well. She needed time to think how best to tell him of her little adventure with Jasper FitzHugh. One thing she knew, however. She would not reveal to Rhys—or to anyone else—that she'd kissed the Englishman.

She bit into the overcooked venison and stared around the temporary campsite. The accommodations were rude: five lean-to huts, a central fire pit with a poor excuse for a spit. No pots or bowls. Even her mother's household was better equipped, and it was mean indeed.

Just once she would like for her mother, Gladys, to live in a comfortable house with a chimney so the smoke would draw properly, a raised hearth so she need not stoop to prepare the meals, and private sleeping quarters. It wasn't fair that the English lived in such a spacious abode as that castle they'd been building for the past ten years, while the Welsh eked out their harsh existence in tiny cottages.

Not that all the Welsh lived that way. But many did. Certainly her family had, especially since her father, Tomas, had died. Unfortunately, her new stepfather, Cadoc, was a good-for-nothing layabout and their living accommodations had not much improved. It was for that reason Rhonwen stayed away so often.

She sighed and slowly chewed the stringy meat. She was more than weary of this nomadic existence, sometimes in her mother's household, sometimes at the rebel camp. What would it be like to have a home of her own to tend?

The answer was simple. Whether spacious or cozy, a cottage of her own would be truly divine. But she would never possess such a home unless she wed.

For the first time ever she allowed herself to imagine what it would be like to take a husband, to let him hunt and fish while she cooked and gardened—and raised their children.

Unaccountably she recalled the kiss Jasper FitzHugh had given her, and she felt her cheeks grow warm. A husband would want to kiss her and make use of her body. That was how a woman got with child. Only Rhonwen had never particularly wanted to do that with a man.

You wanted it today.

Her face grew warmer still. She swallowed the tasteless meat, then washed it down with ale. She hadn't *wanted* to do anything with him. She'd simply been curious. And even if he had made her desire him a little, at least she knew now that she could desire a man. Perhaps it was time for her to get herself a husband.

Perhaps she should consider the possibilities around her.

Across the clearing, Oto hawked, spat, then scratched his crotch and belched. Rhonwen grimaced.

Fenton limped up with firewood. He was gray-haired and toothless, too old to father any children.

Garic tore a piece of red meat from the roasted deer, cursed when he burned his hand, then grabbed the hot meat again. Rhonwen blew out an exasperated breath. He was too simple-minded.

Rhys and his rebel band harried the English, foraged the wildwood, and lived as best they could. But the fact was, all of the men were misfits. It was no wonder she spent so much time among them; she was as much a misfit as they.

She set down the meat, dismayed. Was this to be her life, then, hoping to kill enough Englishmen to drive them from her homeland, meanwhile never finding a husband and the love and joy which should go along with marriage?

The hoot of a long-eared owl sounded from the woods. "Aye, and it's Rhys!" Garic cried, though his mouth was stuffed with meat.

"What ho, friends," Rhys called as he and Daffydd strode into the clearing. Like a magnet the handsome young man drew all the others to him, and Rhonwen was no exception. There was an intensity about Rhys, an energy. A fervor. He hated the English with a violence that made everyone else's hatred pale. Through a harsh childhood and an even harsher adolescence he'd thrived so that now, though three years her junior, he seemed years older. He was taller than her now and stronger too. More importantly, though, he thought like a man and fought like a man. In truth, though he was now but six-and-ten, he'd been an old man since he was a lad of six or seven.

Still, she'd always considered him a child and lorded her advanced years over him. She was nineteen and he but sixteen. Yet now she stared at him differently. Twice in the past she had rebuffed his clumsy advances toward her. The first time he'd been three-and-ten, gangly and curious about women. The second time he'd been five-and-ten, still gangly but old enough to be horny too. Now, though, he was more sure of himself. And not entirely unattractive.

Her brow wrinkled as she studied him. His tunic was too small for his wide shoulders. His strong thighs filled out his braies, and his calves strained the limits of his threadbare hose. But his well-worn and patched garments did not lessen his rough appeal. Could he make her body tingle in the same way Jasper FitzHugh had?

Rhys must have felt the weight of her scrutiny, for after a moment his black eyes fell upon her. Though she should not, she couldn't help comparing him to Jasper FitzHugh. He looked nothing like the Englishman. Not as tall, nor as powerfully muscled. Nor as virile. Then again, Rhys was not fully grown. But there was more. Their eyes. Their hair. Even their attitude. Jasper was all confident charm and easy smiles. But with Rhys, nothing was easy.

Since she did not want a man like Jasper FitzHugh, however, perhaps it behooved her to look at Rhys in a different light.

He grinned when she did not look away, and once he'd given the deer carcass he carried to Fenton for butchering, he sauntered to her side.

"So. What brings you out into the wildwood today, Rhonwen? Your stepfather does not still harass you, does he?" he added, raising a knotted fist. "For if he does, I will swiftly cure him of the habit."

Rhonwen stared steadily into his eyes and, though it was uncomfortable, refused to look away. "You would do that for me?"

She saw the exact moment when his awareness of her changed.

"I would kill him if you asked it," he earnestly vowed.

She looked away. "That is hardly necessary."

"I will decide that. Has he bothered you again?" He caught her arm. "Has he?"

"No. That is not why I came here today." She pulled her arm from his hold, then frowned at the dirty imprint he'd left on the faded plunkett cloth. "Look what you've done now!" she exclaimed. "Go wash yourself, Rhys. You're still bloody from the hunt."

He backed away, a confused expression coming over his face. And why shouldn't he be confused? She usually treated him like a younger brother, and he accepted the role. Now, though, with her deliberately long eye contact she'd changed the rules. Should she try to change them back?

She wanted to, but she forced herself to wait. She took a slow breath, then looked up at him again. "Would you like a cup of ale?" she asked in her sweetest tone.

"Yes. Ah, no. That is, yes. But . . . but let me go wash and . . . ah, perhaps we can sit and sup together."

She smiled at his returning eagerness. He was not gone five

minutes, but during that time he scrubbed his face and hands, slicked his hair back with water, and changed his tunic. He even cleaned his nails, and Rhonwen was touched by his efforts. She was also amazed that one lingering gaze on her part could effect such a transformation. Were all men so easily controlled? Was it a weakness peculiar to them—or a power peculiar to her? Or perhaps a little of both?

She needed to find out, and Rhys was the only man she could experiment with. She fetched him a cup of ale and presented it to him with a half-smile and that same steady gaze. "Here you are. You must be so weary after such a long hunt. Garic said you left before dawn."

"Me, weary? Nay. I'm not in the least affected. I could have hunted all night. It was Daffydd who wanted to return. But I'm glad now that we did," he added. "Otherwise I might have missed you. How long will you stay with us this time?" He stared at her, handsome and hopeful in the waning light of the forest clearing.

She shrugged. "I'm not certain. I had not meant to come today, but . . . well, something happened."

"What? Is it Cadoc?"

"No. He's harmless," she said with a dismissive gesture of her hand.

"Then what?"

She looked away, then gritting her teeth, met his concerned gaze. "I came upon Jasper FitzHugh today."

From fumbling suitor to dangerous hunter, Rhys's transformation was instantaneous. "You came upon him? How did you happen to come upon *him*?"

"In the woods. By the river below the log crossing. I shot him with my bow, then tried to steal his horse."

She explained everything—everything but how she'd finally escaped from him. But Rhys had cast aside his starry-eyed reactions to her. His expression was grim as he stared at her. "Why did he let you go?"

"I escaped. He was still drunk and I escaped."

Rhys shook his head. "No. There's more. Did he make any untoward advances?"

A blush crept over Rhonwen's face. She could feel the heat and knew he must see the color. "No. He did not," she lied.

He caught her chin in his hand. "Do not lie to me, Rhonwen. Don't ever lie to me. I know what the women say of him. He has a talent for charming wenches."

"How would you know what the women say of him?"

He hesitated, then cleared his throat. "I have my ways."

"Your ways?" She planted her fists on her hips and studied him through narrowed eyes. "You question the women who have shared his bed?"

He looked away, reddening with guilt, and the truth suddenly hit her. "You have lain with the same women he has. Do I have the right of it, Rhys? You have, haven't you?"

His expression turned belligerent and she was reminded of the stubborn little boy he'd once been—and still was. "That's none of your affair, Rhonwen. But even if it's true, what of it? He spies on us. I spy on him."

"And what of the women? While you two do whatever it is you do with these women, I wonder what it is the women are doing. Perhaps comparing the two of you?"

He bristled. "They have their fun, which is more than they deserve. Any woman who cavorts with the English is a harlot. And a traitor."

"I see. Well, I believe I shall ask some of those traitors how you compare to FitzHugh." She turned to leave, but he caught her by the arm.

"What does that mean? What did that damnable Englishman do to you?" He caught her other arm and gave her a harsh shake. "What did he do? What did *you* do?"

The rest of the men in the camp had begun to stare at them, but none came to Rhonwen's aid. They all feared Rhys's temper and she knew she should fear him too. But she was too angry to be afraid. She glared up at him.

"He tried to seduce me, and he nearly succeeded. But when I asked him to release me, he let me go."

Rhys shook his head in disbelief. "Why would he do that?"

"Because I did not let your father cut off his hand all those years ago. He remembered and he thanked me for it."

"You bitch. You should never have done that. My father would be alive if you hadn't done that."

"Now, now, lad. That's old history," Fenton put in, though from a safe distance away. "You was both children an' then there was Josselyn's safety to consider."

"That bitch?" he swore.

"We are all bitches to you, aren't we?" Rhonwen tried to pull away from him but his grip was merciless. She glared at him. "Let go of me, Rhys. You're hurting my arm."

He was so enraged she thought he might strangle her. His frigid black eyes bored into hers but she didn't look away. "Let me go," she repeated, and with a string of foul oaths he did.

"Begone from here and never come back! Crawl into his bed and become sister to those other . . ."

"Bitches?" she furiously prompted.

"Harlots," he finished. "Whores. They are whores to the English, as you too will be."

His words were awful to hear, but Rhonwen had never been one to suffer in silence. "You have no reason to speak so cruelly to me, Rhys. I have done nothing wrong—except to miss my shot. I thought you would be pleased that I struck a blow against the English. But no, you are so consumed by your hatred that you strike out at everyone, friend and foe alike. But I am *not* your enemy!"

She stormed away, not waiting for his response. Nor did she want him to see the tears that stung her eyes. She was not prone to weeping. She'd learned very young that it did no good and, worse, revealed weaknesses which should remain hidden. But she could not hide her emotions today. They were too muddled, too perilously near the surface.

So she hurried through the wildwood, wiping the tears from her cheeks and muttering angrily to herself.

"Unfeeling brute. He's nothing but a stupid outlaw anyway. He's always been a single-minded, thick-skulled fool. I never should have expected anything better of him."

Then she heard it, the almost undetectable sound of someone trailing her, and she froze. Nightfall was imminent, but not complete. The forest was still, as if holding its breath for the advent of the night predators. Keen-eyed owls. Wildcats. Wolves. Rhonwen held her breath too. Who was stalking her?

She pulled her dagger and crouched down with her back to a hazel tree. Pray God it was old Fenton, wanting to see her safe to Afon Bryn. She saw a movement and her stomach tensed. Her palm was damp around the dagger and her nails dug into the flesh of her palm. Then the man paused and she knew at once who it was.

"'Tis I, Rhonwen. Rhys. You needn't fear. I . . . I've come to make peace with you."

She shuddered with relief. Still, she was not ready to make peace with him. Not yet. He'd mistreated her too badly. "Begone from here, Rhys. I am well able to make my way though these woods without your aid."

"I know that."

"So leave."

But he did not. He came nearer, straight to her as if the dark were no impediment at all to his movements. She'd always marveled at his ability to see in the dark like the other forest hunters. Today, however, she wished he were less talented.

When he reached her, he crouched down to face her. "I had no cause to abuse you."

"No. You did not."

"I sometimes go a little mad at the mention of those two. Those two English bastards."

"I *tried* to kill him for you!"

"And I thank you for your efforts on my behalf. But you must leave him to me, Rhonwen. The day will come when he and I will face one another. I need no one to fight my battles for me, least of all a woman."

"Least of all a woman," she mimicked him. "You forget that I have bested you before."

"We were children then." He reached out through the darkness and touched her hair. "But we are children no more."

The change between them was abrupt, from bickering friends to tentative lovers, and it frightened Rhonwen anew.

He had not forgotten the flirtation she'd initiated. Now she would see where it might end. So she waited, as still as a wild hare poised before a snare, wary and yet undeniably curious.

When she did not resist, his hand moved behind her head, tangling in her hair. He drew her forward until she felt his breath warm on her face. Off balance, she braced her hand on his leg. He groaned and swiftly caught her mouth with his.

He was rough and eager, and she knew he did not mean to hurt her. But he hardly gave her time to breathe. Then he pushed her backward onto the damp ground and covered her body with his, and she'd had enough.

She twisted her face away from his. "Rhys! Stop it."

"I've wanted you forever, Rhonwen." One of his hands grabbed her breast. "Do you like that?"

"Nay, I do not! Now stop it!" She squirmed, kicking and pushing until he finally realized she was serious.

"What's the matter with you? I thought you wanted this."

She shoved his shoulder, then scooted back from him. She had wanted it, but it hadn't turned out the way she'd expected.

"No woman wants to roll around in the dirt like a pair of weasels or stoats," she muttered as she rose to her feet.

He stood as well. "Very well. We can go back to the camp, then. But I thought you would want to be away from the others."

"What I want..." she exclaimed, exasperated that he could be so obtuse. "What I want is one man—any man—who knows how to treat a woman. And I don't mean how to poke his ... his thing in her and consider it a job well done!"

"And what is that supposed to mean? If you would just relax—"

"Just relax? I will not play the mare to your stud, Rhys. No woman will long be content with that."

He glared at her. Though she could not see his features clearly, she nonetheless felt the angry weight of that glare. "Is that what you told FitzHugh? Is that how you put him off too? I caution you, Rhonwen, to have a care. No man will long countenance a woman who entices him, then pulls away. Who teases him."

"I did not tease—" She broke off, for she knew he was right. She had teased him.

She wrapped her arms around her waist. "I'm sorry. I . . . I thought that we . . . that you and I—" Again she broke off, shaking her head. "You're too much like a brother to me."

She heard his harsh exhalation. Somewhere nearby an owl hooted. The wind moaned through the still-barren trees and she shivered in the night cold. Her cloak had come loose while they wrestled on the ground. He picked it up and tossed it around her shoulders. She stepped back when he tried to fasten it, though, and finished the task herself.

He cleared his throat. "Perhaps it is too soon for such a decision between us. We have been friends many years. It is bound to take a little time, Rhonwen. But we can change the bond that connects us from friendship into something more."

"I don't know."

"There's no need for a decision now. We will see what the days ahead bring."

Rhonwen nodded. There was no other response to make. He was being so logical now, like a reasonable man, not an impulsive child. And yet she knew, without any pretense to logic, that he and she would never—could never—

Unaccountably an image of Jasper FitzHugh rose in her mind. He'd been dangerous and rough with her, then charming and honorable. As had Rhys. But one's kiss had thrilled her, while the other's had been vaguely distasteful. And though she didn't think Rhys would make a very good husband for her, she knew the Englishman would be far worse. Not that either of them had anything more than a swift tumble on his mind.

Agitated by her confusing thoughts, she turned and left. She did not respond to his call of farewell. Nor did she complain when he silently trailed her to within hailing distance of Afon Bryn.

Something had happened today, something she'd not expected and never predicted. She was more like the women who gathered at the well than she'd ever thought possible. For her curiosity about men had been roused—and by the English enemy, of all men. He hadn't behaved like her enemy, though.

But that meant nothing, she reminded herself. It mattered nothing that the Englishman had not been particularly oppressive, as some of her own people were wont to be. The truth was, the English generally kept to themselves, laboring on their castle and constructing their town. They'd improved the main roads and kept a loose sort of peace in Carreg Du.

But by their very presence they oppressed the Welsh. For ten years now, Randulf FitzHugh, Lord of Rosecliffe and brother to Jasper, had chipped away at Welsh solidarity, seducing the people in the same way he'd seduced her friend Josselyn. He'd gotten himself Welsh lands and a Welsh wife, and children that were half-Welsh.

Now his brother chipped further, beguiling the women of the castle, then of the village. Now he was chipping at her. But Rhonwen knew she would not succumb to his blandishments. She understood what he was about, and that knowledge would strengthen her resolve.

She crept into her mother's tiny cottage and found her pallet. But in the dark, with her stepfather's erratic snoring, her mother's softer breathing, and her siblings curled like puppies in their shared bed, Rhonwen could not sleep.

The facts were plain: She needed a husband. She did not want to live in her mother's household any longer. Besides, she was old enough to wed, and if today's reaction to FitzHugh was any indication, she was more than ready for it.

The trick would be to find the right man. Jasper FitzHugh certainly was not him, nor was Rhys. The former appealed to her body, the latter to her head. It was unfortunate that she could not make one good man of the two of them.

When sleep finally came to her in her narrow bed with its thin straw mattress, it came with dreams of men. Tall men, then short. Young men, then old. One after another she tried to avoid them. But no matter how she ran, they each managed to catch her. Even the old, bandy-legged ones. She could never quite escape, and though she fought them and struggled to be free, invariably they pinned her down, then stilled her with kisses.

Through the long hours of darkness they paraded through her dreams, kissing her into complacency.

And in her dreams each of them held her with strong arms, wet with cold river water.

Four

Jasper settled himself in his favorite chair, positioned near enough the fire for warmth, but far enough removed to distance himself from the bustle of evening domesticity in the great hall. He'd partaken but sparingly of the supper. White bread and hard cheese and a gravy made of the meat left from dinner had not held its customary appeal. His earlier-than-usual bout of drinking, coupled with the icy swim and the long chase through the woods, had left him with a throbbing head and a chill that would not relent.

It had also left him in a state of semi-arousal every time he thought of the elusive Welsh maiden Rhonwen.

Nevertheless, it was thoughts of her he wished to savor now.

He signaled a passing boy to refill his cup, then groaned when he spied Josselyn studying him. The several knights in the hall might have been warned off by his brooding silence tonight, but Josselyn had never feared his ill humor.

She paused near the massive carved stone hearth and filled her own pewter cup with heated wine, then moved gracefully his way. Though Jasper did not relish her probing this evening, he couldn't help admiring her. She'd made this raw castle a home for his brother and their children. Ten years had only increased her beauty, softening her figure and polishing her style. But it had also sharpened her intellect—and it had not blunted her manner.

"So," she began, pulling a cushioned stool beside him and settling herself upon it. "You return late and alone—and wet. You miss dinner, then eat but little of your supper. Is someone feeding you elsewhere, Jasper, and bathing you fully clothed?"

He shrugged and gave her an offhand grin. "I fell in the river, though I would prefer you not announce that fact to everyone."

"I see. Did you perchance swallow a fish while you were underwater? Or did you dislike Odo's efforts in the kitchen today?"

"You know that's not it, and God help me if you imply as much to him, for he will sulk. You know what a peacock he has become." He met her steady gaze, then looked away and blew out an exasperated breath. "How I spent the day is of no moment. The fact remains that I should have gone with Rand."

She sighed. " 'Tis a serious business. Simon LaMonthe is not a man to trust, and his allegiance to Matilda is not entirely to be trusted either."

"And that means I cannot accompany Rand, because it is serious business?" he raised his cup and angrily downed its contents.

"It means no drinking—at least not to excess. It means no womanizing either."

Jasper shifted in his seat and did not meet her gaze. It was one thing for her to chide him for his prodigious drinking. But his activities with women? That was a subject he was loath to discuss with his sister-in-law. "I would not have jeopardized Rand's mission," he grumbled.

She was silent a moment. Then, "Who did you meet today? And where?"

He scowled at her. "Leave off such questioning, woman. It is none of your affair."

"I beg to differ. You were left to safeguard Rosecliffe, yet Rand is no sooner gone than you disappear."

"It was not to find a woman." Then, annoyed by that dishonesty, he threw his hands up in disgust. "All right. All right. I was angry at Rand and sought solace with a woman and a wineskin. There is no news in that."

"You were not with Maud. Nor with Gert."

He stared at her in horror. "You searched for me there?" Though he'd not blushed in years, he felt hot color creep into his face. "How did you . . . that is . . ."

"I have my ways, and I know you were neither in the village nor at Carreg Du." She folded her arms over her chest. "So, where were you?"

"By the rood," he swore. "Rand should have sent you to Bailwynn. You'd ferret out the truth about LaMonthe in far less than a fortnight."

She only smiled, sweet but expectant still. Again he swore, then straightened up and gestured for a boy to refill his cup once more. Across the hall one of his men crowed at a lucky turn of the dice. The torchères hissed in their brackets and one of the hounds idly scratched his ear. In the comfort of the hall there was no reason not to discuss Rhonwen with Josselyn. Perhaps he'd learn something useful.

He looked at his sister-in-law. "I did not just fall into the river."

She leaned forward, her brows arched with curiosity.

"I was avoiding murder at the hands of one of your old friends."

"Murder?" She gasped and one of her hands went to her throat. "Oh, Jasper! You see? You should not go off alone. You make too easy a target, for everyone knows who you are. Did you recognize the fellow? I vow, he cannot be a friend of mine if he seeks to harm my brother."

"No, I did not recognize her—at least not at first."

"Her?" Josselyn pulled her stool closer to his chair. Gone was her amused, meddling manner. She was intent now, and rightly concerned. "A woman tried to murder you?" Then she drew back. "I hope you are not making some coarse joke at my expense, Jasper. For I warrant, if you are—"

Jasper shook his head. "I wish I was. No, your old friend—

and mine—tried to put an arrow straight through my heart.''

"What sort of friend would do that?"

Jasper grinned at her impatience. "A little girl, grown into a woman. A raven-haired warrior woman who—"

"Rhonwen." Josselyn stared round-eyed at him. "Rhonwen. Are you certain it was her?"

"She boasted of it," he ruefully admitted.

"But I do not follow your tale. If she missed you and you fell into the river . . ."

"She stole Helios but I caught up with her."

"You did not harm her, did you?"

"Surely your sympathies cannot lie with that devious wench. She stole my horse and tried to kill me. Or have you already forgotten that?"

"What happened, Jasper? Tell me everything."

He launched into his tale, though he had no intention of telling her *everything*. "When I realized who she was, I released her—unharmed—in thanks for the service she once did me." He flexed his right hand, short one finger. He did not miss his little finger, not when he recalled how near he'd come to losing his entire hand.

"How did she look?" Josselyn begged to know. There was a wistfulness in her tone and Jasper understood why. Her marriage to Rand had alienated her from many of her people. Not all of them, but many, like Rhonwen, avoided the English with a vengeance. He gave a one-shouldered shrug. "She is a comely wench. And spirited."

"Is she beautiful?" Then she frowned. "Did you try to bed her?"

"By the rood! That is not a matter a man discusses with his brother's wife!"

Her blue eyes glittered smugly. "Aha. So you *did* try. Did you succeed?"

Jasper swore and surged to his feet. "Enough of this."

This time she laughed. "So you did *not* succeed." She grinned up at him, clasping her hands over her knees, and for a moment she appeared as young and merry as nine-year-old Isolde. "Tell me about her. How does she look? How did she react to your honorable gesture?'' Then her expression sobered. ''Did she ask about me?''

Jasper knew Josselyn well enough to know she wanted only the truth. ''No, she did not ask about you.''

''I see.'' She looked away, silent a moment. ''What of Rhys ap Owain? Did she mention him? I understand they have mended their differences.''

''Rhys ap Owain?'' Jealousy sprang fully formed into Jasper's heart. ''Is she *his* woman?''

''I'm not certain. There is talk in the village, but gossip is not always reliable. Did she fail also to mention him?''

Jasper's fingers tightened around his cup. ''Ours was not a lengthy conversation,'' he muttered in response. Inside, though, his gut knotted. He'd had Rhys ap Owain's woman in his arms and in a moment of foolishness he'd let her go. Honor and lust had blended to make him behave like an idiot. He'd held the means to lure Rhys ap Owain in, to capture the troublesome young Welsh outlaw and thereby prove himself to Rand. But what had he done? He'd tried to seduce the woman, then allowed her to get away.

When Rand heard of this he would be more convinced than ever that his younger brother was unsuited for any real responsibility. And Jasper could not blame him for it.

''Bloody hell!'' he swore and pushed to his feet. ''If you will excuse me?'' Then he stormed away.

Josselyn was not perturbed by the sudden turn of his temper, however. For a long while she sat as she was, her arms wrapped around her knees while she stared unseeingly toward the remains of the evening fire. One of the maids banked the blaze for the night, piling the embers, then burying them just so with ashes. The hall had begun to thin of people. Yet Josselyn remained where she was.

There had been an attraction between Jasper and Rhonwen. She was convinced of it. No matter that Rhonwen had tried to kill him, Jasper had been smitten with the girl. Except that she was no longer a girl. She was a woman, and a comely one, at that. Yes, Jasper had been intrigued by Rhonwen, but had Rhonwen been equally intrigued by Jasper?

Josselyn gave a wry chuckle. Unless Rhonwen was blind, she would have to be intrigued by Jasper. The man possessed a lethal charm. Tall and straight, with the natural arrogance of a confident man, he was blessed also with a pair of clear gray eyes that could coax a smile from a stone wall. She'd seen the effect of those eyes often enough: Every woman in the castle, from toddler to crone, jumped to do his bidding.

Still, he was English, and Rhonwen despised the English. She'd tried to convince Josselyn not to wed Rand, and when that had failed, she'd withdrawn completely from Josselyn's life.

But Josselyn knew Rhonwen, and she knew the girl possessed a well-developed sense of integrity. She was brave and often impulsive, but she was honorable. Jasper's gesture might have surprised her, but it also would have impressed her.

Josselyn smiled and pushed to her feet. Well, and well again. This had been a most interesting evening. She would have to think how best to encourage Jasper's interest in Rhonwen. And perhaps she'd yet see him settled down with a good Welsh wife.

Isolde waited outside the great hall. Jasper would have to come this way eventually.

She was supposed to be asleep in the cozy nursery she shared with Gwendolyn. But once the younger girl had fallen asleep, Isolde had slipped away. She was too old to be confined still to a nursery. Too old to be sent to bed directly after supper. Why, in five years she'd be old enough to wed away from Rosecliffe. She'd overheard her father telling her mother that while he was at Bailwynn Castle he hoped to arrange a betrothal for Isolde.

If she was old enough to be betrothed, it seemed only right that she was old enough to linger in the hall after supper.

Her mother, however, did not agree. So here Isolde sat, huddled in the shadows, waiting for Jasper and hoping for the chance to share a few moments with him.

One of the heavy oak doors swung open. Pale light streaked

across the three stone steps, then shrank away when the door shut.

It was one of the other knights, not Jasper. The man ambled across the yard toward the stables and the barracks above it. Isolde sighed. She was sorry her father was gone, but thrilled that her uncle had remained.

If only he were not her uncle.

Marrying a member of your own family was forbidden, she knew. But cousins often wed one another. First cousins, even. So why could a girl not marry her uncle?

The door again swung wide and her heart began to pound. It was him! No one else in the castle was as tall and handsome as Jasper. She jumped up, eager and hopeful.

When Jasper spied her, he paused, but she could see he was distracted. He always had a smile and a joke for her. But tonight his smile was little more than a grimace.

"You'd best be forewarned, your mother is still about. Should she find you out here . . ."

"Mama is not nearly so strict as Father. She'll fuss, but little more."

His grin increased a fraction. "So, you have everyone figured out, do you?"

With damp, nervous fingers she smoothed the front of the new kirtle of holland cloth which she had just completed. "I had hoped to speak with you, Jasper. To tell you how glad I am that Father left you here to protect me—I mean to protect the castle. To protect us all."

He reached out and patted the top of her head. "You needn't worry, poppet. No harm shall befall anyone at Rosecliffe while your father is absent. Now go on. Be off with you."

He steered her back to the hall, much to her dismay, then pushed her inside and closed the door behind her. Though she wanted to follow him, she realized that it would be pointless. He had something else on his mind.

But at least he'd called her poppet. She smiled and hugged that knowledge to herself. He called Gavin, Gavin, and Gwendolyn, Gwen. But he called her poppet. She was special to him, and though she was only nine years old, in a few more years she'd be old enough.

She looked down at her chest and smoothed her hands over it. Nothing. Not even a hint of the breasts that one day would appear. Frowning, she made her way to the stairs that led up to the nursery. Maybe she wasn't putting on enough of the ointment she'd gotten in the village from Enid. She didn't like its foul odor, nor the way it caused her chemise to stick to her skin.

But that wasn't important, she reminded herself. Jasper liked women with breasts. The sooner she got hers to grow, the sooner he would see she wasn't a little girl anymore.

Rhys stood at the edge of the forest. Beyond him the fields unfolded, their boundaries marked with low stone walls. It was dark and he could see little, for the moon was but a thin crescent low in the chilly midnight sky. Still, he'd studied Rosecliffe Castle and the village beneath it so many times from this vantage point, he could map out the scene in his sleep.

The town wall was taller than those marking the fields, though still incomplete. He could gain access into town easily enough. But it was the castle he wanted. And though its walls appeared impregnable, he knew they were not. There was a way to take Rosecliffe Castle; he just didn't know what it was. At least, not yet. But he would.

He would rout Randulf and Jasper FitzHugh and make Rosecliffe Castle a Welsh stronghold. That had always been his goal, but now it held a new urgency. He needed to show Rhonwen that he was a better man than Jasper FitzHugh. Something had occurred between her and that Englishman. Rhys was certain of it. But he would prove to her that he was the right man for her. The only man.

A light flickered in the dark village, drawing his attention. It moved slowly through the streets. Someone carrying a lantern. The late walker disappeared into a stone cottage where a considerable fire had been built, judging from the plume of smoke escaping its squat chimney. Perhaps someone was ill, or the midwife had come to tend a childbirth.

His hands tightened into fists at that thought. Eight Englishmen had taken Welsh wives. Fourteen of their bastards peopled Rosecliffe village. Would tonight see a fifteenth added to their number?

God, but he must eject these English from his lands!

Behind him one of his men shifted. Dried leaves rustled. A twig broke with a brittle snap. Then someone cursed and the night silence turned to hysteria.

"God help us!"

"Sweet Mary!"

"Beware—"

Rhys spun around, his short sword at the ready. Had they been found out? Was this his night to finally meet his enemy in battle?

But it was not Jasper FitzHugh or any of his men who panicked the Welsh rebels. A short shadow trundled into their midst and Rhys let out a low, vicious curse.

"Damnation! Are you a pack of gutless cowards?"

Newlin, the deformed, walleyed seer, made his way through the chagrined Welshman with a benign expression on his deeply lined face. Though he had never been known to harm a soul, he nonetheless inspired considerable fear among the superstitious. Rhys, however, had never been superstitious. He did not hold with spells or magic—nor with the power of prayer. A man accomplished as much as his brain and body allowed, nothing more. If he had a strong will, he made the most of what he was born with. If his will was weak, he died young—and along the way lived a wretched life of cold and hunger.

Rhys had been cold and hungry as a child, and his life had been wretched. But his will had overcome that. He didn't intend for his life to be wretched much longer.

So he gave Newlin an annoyed glance. "Do you take a great pleasure in terrifying simpletons?"

The ageless little bard smiled. "To terrify simpletons requires no particular talent. But to terrify a man of intelligence—now, that would be something, indeed. Still, I am not come here to strike fear into the hearts or heads of anyone."

"Then why come you here?" Rhys snapped.

Newlin gave him a bland look that managed, nonetheless, to chastise him for his unnecessary rudeness. "I but make my way home."

He pointed to the ancient *domen*, the huge stone balanced above three lower ones. It stood outside the town, near the forest and the fields. The Welsh respected it as a holy site; the English gave it a wide berth. But Rhys knew that Randulf FitzHugh spoke often with the bard. Perhaps he might learn something of the English lord's plans from the bard.

"You saw FitzHugh off?"

Newlin shrugged with his one good shoulder. "I know that he is gone."

"Do you know why he left? Do you know where he went and how long he will be away?"

Newlin stared up at Rhys with his odd, unfocused eyes. "I know, as do you, that there is trouble among the English. Two of them would rule where only one can. I know, as do you, that he is gone to Bailwynn Castle in the south, to parlay with the other English lords. I know also, as do you, that he will not wish to long be absent from his wife and his children. Is there anything else you know that you wish to ask me?"

One of Rhys's men snickered, albeit from a safe distance, and Rhys's anger rose. "He takes you into his confidence and yet you refuse to provide aid to your own countrymen." He advanced on the bard. "Mark this, old man. I plan to attack the British stronghold. I plan to take Rosecliffe Castle and hold it for the loyal people of Wales." He stepped aside and made a sweeping gesture with his hand. "Go on with you. Reveal to your new English friends what the last true Welshman plots. I will not prevent you from your traitor's mission," he finished with a sneer.

Newlin stood utterly still—save for a faint swaying forward and back, forward and back. "The stones of these lands grow. They sprout tall and sturdy, into fortress along the shores and rivers, even as the forests shrink away. 'Tis not for me to say if it is good or no. The world turns. Change comes."

"The world turns? The world—this world—in not turning.

And if there is to be any change, it will only be that as pro-scribed by nature," Rhys countered. "An old man dies. His grandson is born and takes his place. The English think their grandsons can take the place of the Welsh who die here, but they are mistaken.

"I know well the remainder of that superstitious chant," he continued. "A fool might believe that the stones have grown, but darkness at noon? And heat in the winter?" He stared belligerently at the bard. "Not this year. The sun hangs as it always does. And the winter to follow the coming summer will be as cold a one as this year past. I've lived all my life in these wild woods. I know the signs. The English will not prevail. I will see to it."

Newlin sighed. "As you say, young Rhys. Your father fought this battle and now you do the same. But do you truly know your enemy?"

"I know my enemy is just a man, and that he bleeds and dies like any other man."

"And loves like any other man."

Rhys made a sound of disgust. "But he does not love us. Begone, old man. This battle is for younger men than you. Braver men."

After a moment the bard shuffled away. Behind him, Rhys heard the nervous mutterings of his men. They might be afraid of Newlin, but he was not. Still, the bard had left him uneasy. What did he mean, that the English loved like other men? They loved to steal other men's lands. Other men's women. They planted their seed in Welshwomen's bellies and peopled the land with their English bastards.

Then he sucked in a harsh breath. Their English bastard! Suddenly he knew his way in. Randulf FitzHugh's bastards. The man had sired three of them, and it was said he was a maudlin fool over them.

They were his weakness and it was at that weakness Rhys must strike.

A surge of power swept over Rhys. He would take Fitz-Hugh's children hostage. They were Josselyn's children too, but he would not let that deter him. Still, a fragment memory

of the first baby—a little girl—stole unwonted into his mind.
She'd been bright-eyed and merry, and though he'd been but
a lad himself, Josselyn had encouraged him to play with her.

It had been such an oddity to have a woman fussing over
him. He'd been a motherless child with an unfeeling father,
so Josselyn's affection had drawn him like a flame draws the
moth.

But that had been another time, he reminded himself
harshly. Before Josselyn's betrayal had led to his father's
death. Before the English stranglehold had tightened. If he was
to defeat his enemies, he could not let that sort of foolish
sentiment distract him. He must use whatever tools he found
in this war for survival.

Even little children.

Five

It was a good plan, Rhonwen conceded. In a head-to-head battle the Welsh could not defeat the English protected behind the stout walls of their fortress at Rosecliffe. But kidnapping, using hostages to force the English to abandon the castle—that might avoid bloodshed altogether. Still, Rhonwen listened to Rhys's plan with mounting dismay.

"They are but children," she protested. " 'Tis not right to use them so cruelly."

"Do you forget, Rhonwen, that I was but a child—that you were but a child—when the English came here?"

"But they never used us poorly. They never kidnapped us."

"They used me," Rhys muttered. Abruptly he turned away and Rhonwen frowned.

"Randulf FitzHugh may have tricked you, Rhys. But he didn't hurt you."

"My father died because of his trickery! My father was slain by his brother—" He broke off, his jaw clenched in fury.

Rhonwen could not contradict his words. She and Rhys had never discussed that subject before, though everyone knew what had happened. A six-year-old child, anxious to prove himself to a cruel and unfeeling father, had inadvertently provided the information that allowed the English to defeat the man. She knew Rhys shouldered a terrible guilt for that innocent mistake. It was, no doubt, what fueled his violent hatred of the English—and especially of the FitzHughs.

Still, she was more than uneasy about this plan of his. She needed to be clearer about her role. "You want me to go to the castle village and learn what I can of the children—when they come and go. But do you promise if you capture one of them that you will not allow the child to be hurt? You must promise me that, Rhys. The child must *not* be hurt!"

He kicked over an oaken bucket, then glared down at her, his fists planted on his hips. "Do you think so little of me, Rhonwen? Do you truly believe I would murder helpless babes? Jesus, God," he swore. " 'Tis their father I want— and their uncle." His eyes narrowed in suspicion. "Is that the source of your hesitation, that I will kill Jasper FitzHugh at the first opportunity?"

Rhonwen shot to her feet. "I tried to kill him for you. Why would I balk at your finishing the deed?"

Fortunately Rhys did not seem any more eager than she to pursue that subject further. With a terse nod, he acknowledged her words, then turned to his men.

The plan was simple. Rhonwen was to visit Carreg Du, the Welsh village nearest Rosecliffe, and ingratiate herself with Josselyn's Aunt Nesta. As a child Rhonwen had briefly resided in her household. Old Nesta was a direct line to Josselyn and her children, and it should not take long for Rhonwen to learn enough to put the plan into motion.

Rhys, meanwhile, would muster aid from among Carreg Du's malcontents, and when the moment was right, he would strike.

The only problem was in knowing how long Randulf FitzHugh would be away from Rosecliffe. Which brother was more likely to relent and open the castle gates to the Welsh, the children's uncle or their father?

That tricky point was a question only time would answer. But as Rhys reasoned to his men, it did not matter. If Jasper FitzHugh would not surrender, when Rand returned he surely would. He would not allow his beloved children to disappear forever.

Rhonwen listened and she appreciated Rhys's plan. But it nonetheless left her exceedingly uneasy. What if, while she was at Carreg Du, she came across Jasper? What if he should hear that she was near to the castle and sought her out?

As Rhonwen prepared to leave the rebel camp, Rhys finally addressed that subject. "Jasper FitzHugh will seek you out," he stated. "When he learns that you are at Carreg Du—and mark my words, he will learn of it—he will seek you out. You will have to gird yourself to resist his blandishments."

"It will be no difficult task to resist him," Rhonwen vowed. "Indeed, he may prove to be our best source of information." She gave him an arch look as she wrapped a *couvrechef* around her neck and head. "'Tis said a man's brains reside in his braies. If that is so, I will have no problem with him."

She gave Rhys a smug smile, then left. He hadn't liked that last remark at all, judging by the scowl on his face. Good, she thought as she followed a deer trail through the dense woods. Still, she was no more comfortable with the idea of Jasper pursuing her than Rhys was. How *would* he react to her appearance?

How would she react to his?

The little shiver that snaked down her back sent an alarming answer. Though she hated to admit it, even to herself, the truth was, she found the man sinfully attractive. Because of him, she finally understood the priests' admonitions against lust, for these inappropriate longings she felt must surely be lust.

But lust or no, the facts remained the same. He was her mortal enemy, and he always would be.

By the time she neared Carreg Du she had decided that all she could do was live for the moment. She would deal with Jasper as circumstances demanded, and she would not think about the future. Rhys and Jasper were bound to meet in battle someday, and one of them would not survive. She had no control over the outcome of that battle, therefore she must put it out of her head. If Jasper tried to woo her, so be it. No matter her response to him, she would remind herself that there was no future to be had with him. That way she would not care who won or lost.

She would do her duty to her people, and she would provide Rhys with the information he required. But she would not let herself become personally involved in their conflict.

And even if she should somehow become physically entangled with Jasper FitzHugh, she would never allow her emotions to become entangled by the man. No, never.

Jasper groaned and rolled over. His stomach clenched and bile rose in his throat. At the same time his head pounded like Scottish war drums.

In a long line of drunken nights and miserable mornings, surely this one must be the worst. He'd sworn off such overindulgence months ago. Yet here he was, wanting no more than to roll over and die and be done with this misery. No, he amended. First he wanted to puke his guts out. Then he could roll over and die.

But before he did that, he needed to relieve himself.

He opened one eye and stared blearily about. Where was he? The roof above him looked new. No smoke had stained the freshly hewn rafters. Light seeped in from somewhere, but he was afraid to turn his head to seek out the source. He closed the eye and tried to listen past the ungodly thudding inside his skull. He was not in the castle. That much he could tell. The sounds were wrong. But where?

He tried to think. Last night, after checking the watch, he and Uric, one of the few unmarried knights left at Rosecliffe, had gone down into the castle village. Ever since his confrontation with Rhonwen he'd been hungry for a woman. So they'd searched out a friendly wench or two.

Then it hit him and he winced at the memory.

They'd found a friendly wench, all right. Two of them. The widow Ellyn and her cousin come to visit. Two full wineskins and the offer of a silver denier apiece had convinced the giggling women. The nearly completed chandler's house had provided the privacy. But something had gone horribly wrong.

"Son-of-a-bitch," he muttered. He rolled over, groaning at the sharp stab of pain. But he pushed up onto all fours despite it. He stayed in that position a long minute, squatting back on his heels, braced on his arms, and fighting the spinning sensations that made him want to lie down again. But shame forced him on.

He had to get away from here. He'd made a fool of himself last night—a bigger fool than he'd ever done before. He'd paid the bouncy Welshwoman for sex and she'd been more than willing to provide it.

Only *he* hadn't been able to do his part.

She'd giggled and stroked and tried everything she could to coax him to attention, and he'd almost made it. But every time he'd look at her, at her fair hair and lush body, his desire had waned. He'd wanted a dark-haired woman of more petite proportions. The buxom woman's pale eyes had gleamed with lust, but he'd wanted flashing, dark eyes that glared with mistrust.

"Jesus God," he swore. He'd had a warm woman, willing to thrill him the whole night long. But instead of enjoying her, he'd mooned over a woman who'd spurned him!

"Damn the bitch," he muttered, dragging himself to his feet. Damn Rhonwen ap Tomas. She'd made a fool of him twice now—once at the river, and again, to his everlasting shame, last night. Would he be cursed like that every time he tried to frolic with another woman?

He shuddered with real fear. God shield him! He should never have let the vicious little wench go free. He should have taken her then and there, and been done with it.

Somehow he made it upright, swearing off drink as he did so. Somehow, despite the brilliant sunlight that blinded him, he located Helios. How he mounted, he did not know. Where Uric was, he did not care. He only knew that he needed a bath to sober him, and the solace of his own chamber to contemplate the sad state he'd sunk to.

Unfortunately he arrived at the castle gate to find Josselyn facing down the gatehouse guard. When she spied him approaching, she gestured him over. "I wish to walk into town. Remind your guard here that he does not have the authority to stop me."

"Be reasonable, Josselyn," he began, wincing at the boom

of his own voice inside his head. " 'Tis for your own good."

"My own good? Pray tell, explain to me how being denied the company of my people—good, honest Welsh people—is for my own good!"

His head felt ready to explode. He pressed one hand to his temple. "I would rather hold this conversation inside—and later."

She cast an assessing eye over him. "I have no doubt you would. But I have business to attend now, and I will not be hampered by your . . . by your ill health," she finished in a tart, knowing tone. "Seek you your bed, Jasper. Isolde can prepare a tisane for what ails you. As for me, I must be off."

She strode across the moat bridge and Jasper muttered a curse. "Go after her, and stay beside her no matter what she says," he ordered the befuddled guard. "I'll send someone else to watch the gate."

Josselyn did not suppress a grin as she made her way into town. She knew her husband had left strict orders that everyone must keep to the castle while he was away. He worried about attacks on Rosecliffe while he was not there.

Then again, he was always worried about attacks. He worked tirelessly to improve the castle's defenses. It amazed her, the amount of construction he'd managed in ten years.

Still, Jasper had left the castle last night. She saw no reason why she should not be allowed to visit among her own people in broad daylight. Poor Jasper, she thought. He was not accustomed to women who could not be manipulated by his handsome face and charming manner. Not that he looked particularly handsome and charming this morning. He'd clearly had a hard night and too much spirits. Again.

Her smile faded. He hadn't done that in a long time. She'd noticed the change in him over the past six months or so. Less carousing. Less wenching. But more restless than ever. So what had caused him to revert to his old ways? Was this perhaps due to Rhonwen? She sighed. Jasper needed a wife. Rand worried about a good match for Isolde, but Josselyn thought Jasper's need far more pressing.

Footsteps sounded behind her, but she didn't look back. She

could manage with Gregory trailing her. It wasn't as if she had any secrets to hide. Perhaps, however, while she was in town she might ask a few questions and try to determine who her troublesome brother-in-law had spent his night with.

"Here," she said, thrusting her willow basket at the man-at-arms. "Make yourself useful."

Rhonwen walked alongside Nesta's horse, leading the gentle mare. She'd arrived at Carreg Du to find a small party preparing for the ride to Rosecliffe. Nesta had welcomed her with a glad cry, and Rhonwen had been ashamed that she'd stayed away so long. She'd not seen Nesta in the two years since her husband, Clyde, had died. Nesta had behaved as a mother to her in the past, and now, as if no time had gone by, she was assuming that role again.

"No particular fellow, you say? Ah, but you are far too pretty not to have suitors."

"I've had a few," Rhonwen had admitted.

"But not the right one, eh? Never mind," Nesta had said. "Come along. We're off to the little market at Rosecliffe. P'rhaps you'll meet yourself the right fellow there."

So here she was, heading for the English stronghold far sooner than she'd expected. It was, perhaps, not a wise thing to do, considering her brief yet volatile history with the lord presently in command of the castle. But she did not think he would harm her. If he'd wanted revenge on her, he would have taken it then. But instead he'd kissed her and released her.

No, the danger Jasper FitzHugh presented came from within herself. He might try to seduce her. And she might let him.

Then again, she realized, that might be her best entrée to the castle. If she took advantage of his attraction to her, he might relax his guard.

"Look. There it is," Nesta called, breaking into Rhonwen's somber thoughts.

Rhonwen looked up and halted in her tracks. There, through the uneven stand of firs, loomed Rosecliffe Castle. She'd heard it was huge. Rhys railed about it all the time. But she'd not seen it herself in many years, not since before the completion of the two gate towers. Prior to that it had just been a wall, built tall and strong to keep some people in and other people— her people—out. But the towers . . . the towers lent the structure a majesty, with their completed crenellations and pennants fluttering above all. The sight took her breath away.

The English were a blight upon the land, she reminded herself. Their giant fortresses were an insult to the wild Welsh countryside. And yet the mighty stone fortress before her, gleaming white in the bright spring sunshine, was still magnificent to behold.

Was it any wonder that Rhys plotted day and night how he might make it his own?

Nesta leaned down from the mare. "I know I'm s'posed to hate it, it being a symbol of English oppression and all. But another part of me says it's a pretty sight. And inside, oh, inside 'tis fine indeed."

"You've been inside?" Rhonwen asked, still staring at the two round towers. She could see a guard making a circuit of one of them.

"Josselyn may have wed an Englishman, but she nonetheless remains my niece," the old woman explained. "Indeed, she is like my own daughter, and her children like grandchildren to me."

Her children. The thought of those children brought Rhonwen back to her purpose. She urged Nesta's mare forward. "I hear Josselyn has three children now," she said, following the other villagers as the narrow road dipped down the hill. The towers retreated behind the tall firs, but that did not erase the presence of the English.

"Ah, yes, and every one of them dear to my heart—despite them being half-English." She paused before adding, "For all that he was born an enemy to our people, he's a good father to his children."

There was no mistaking who "he" was. But it was not Randulf FitzHugh who interested Rhonwen. It was his brother—*and* his children, she reminded herself. But she had to proceed with caution. Nesta would not condone drawing those three children into a political battle.

"Well, I'm glad he's good for something. How fares Josselyn as the grand lady of Rosecliffe?"

"She is well. And happy." Again she hesitated. "She would welcome a visit from you."

Rhonwen shrugged, determined to appear disinterested. "Do you think so? We have not been on good terms in many a year."

"You were but a child when she wed Rand. Your anger was that of a child. She would not hold that against you now." Nesta reached out a hand and unexpectedly stroked Rhonwen's hair.

It was a gentle gesture, meant to reassure. But Rhonwen was not reassured. If anything, it increased her agitation. "I should not be accompanying you now. I meant to visit Carreg Du. Not Rosecliffe."

" 'Tis an open town. Both English and Welsh reside there, side by side."

"In peace?" Rhonwen scoffed.

"In peace."

Rhonwen was silent as the town wall came into view. Beyond the simple stone barrier the rooftops showed, some thatch, some slate. All new. A pair of red pennants fluttered above all, signaling the market day, and it was to the open square in the middle of the town that the small contingent of old women made their way. The streets were neatly lined with stones, even the ones not yet graced with structures. Buildings clustered together around the main square and its well, and also along the main street that led from the town gate to the castle.

Everything was neat and orderly, and the gardens lent it the air of a well-established village. But it was decidedly English in form, with houses as tall as they were wide, and most of them washed with white. Rhonwen doubted any Welsh citizen could truly be content there. Plus, there were English men-at-arms everywhere. At the town gate, in the market, and on the castle walls, watching over everything.

She felt for the slim dagger she kept sheathed at her hip. Though she knew she had nothing to fear, she was nonetheless reassured by its presence. Rhys might be pleased she had gained access to the town of Rosecliffe so swiftly, but she was not.

She helped Nesta down, then stood quietly while the group of women from Carreg Du arranged their stall. They brought cheeses and candles, pots and baskets to sell, and with their earnings they meant to purchase wine and fine thread. This was a routine the old women knew well. Even their arguments over where to place their goods, and who was to mind the stall when, sounded well rehearsed.

Nesta patted Rhonwen's shoulder. "Go, child. See what there is to be had. There is no need for fear, no cost for looking. After a while Josselyn will come down to make her purchases and I will reacquaint the two of you. Maybe she will bring the children. Isolde especially enjoys the market."

Isolde. The child must be nine or ten by now, Rhonwen thought as she wandered away. She tried to picture the baby she remembered as a half-grown girl now. Did she favor her mother or her sire? Was she more Welsh or English?

She began slowly to stroll the square. Everyone looked prosperous and fat. And better dressed than she was, she realized when three women passed in front of her. They each boasted close-fitting kirtles with slashed sleeves to reveal their chemises.

She frowned down at her old kirtle. It was clean and in good repair, made from sturdy green kersey. But it was simple in design, with no braid or buttons or embroidery to flatter her. Compared to the other women she looked plain indeed.

And their hair, the plaits bound with colorful lengths of Saracen cloth. She caught the end of her own single plait and fiddled with the faded bit of ribbon tied at the end, feeling more and more out of place.

The savory scent of something cooking caught her attention and her mouth watered. A stout fellow tended an open fire, tossing small rounds of sweet dough into a hot pan. He grinned at her hungry gaze.

"Sweets for a sweet lass. What will you have?"

Rhonwen shook her head. "I have no coin to pay you."

His gaze darted about, then came back to rest on her. "There are other ways to pay."

Rhonwen knew that leering look, and with a sneer of disdain she turned away. Revolting knave. It seemed her shabby clothing was no impediment to that sort of crude behavior. Still, though she knew there was no reason for it, she expected better from one of her own countrymen. But it seemed that men were men, despite their nationality. Every one of them was ruled by his cock instead of his brain.

She spied a pair of giggling girls just a few years younger than she. They whispered and pointed at a comely young man unloading a cart, then burst into giggles again. Were women any more ruled by their brains than men? she wondered. Until her meeting with Jasper FitzHugh she would have answered yes. Now, however, she was less sure.

As she watched, the lad looked over at the girls and grinned. The youthful pair flung their aprons over their heads and fled, laughing, and suddenly Rhonwen felt so much older than they.

Bleak as it had been, her life had nonetheless been easier when she was a girl. But she was a woman now and everything seemed infinitely more difficult and complex. Who to trust; who to doubt. What was right; what was wrong. If you struggled for the greater good, did that forgive the small wrong you did? She simply did not know.

Then a frustrated voice broke into her thoughts. "... But he said I mayn't leave your side. Please, Lady Josselyn ..."

Rhonwen did not hear the rest of the English words, for she fixed on the last two. Lady Josselyn. *Lady* Josselyn. So Josselyn affected the style of an English lady now. As if in confirmation, a woman's voice answered in cultured English tones. "Then make arrangements to have someone else deliver the goods. You have my leave to hire a lad or two, Gregory. 'Tis not so complicated a matter as all that."

With equal portions of curiosity and dread, Rhonwen scanned the crowded square, searching among the milling throng for *Lady* Josselyn. Her eyes passed over a slender dark-haired matron before jerking back again.

Josselyn.

But she was not garbed as an English lady. Rather, she looked like any Welshwoman, with a *couvrechef* holding her thick hair back, and a Celtic clasp on her cloak. The *couvrechef* was made of silk, though. And the cloak was a fine red stamel with gold edging the front.

As Rhonwen stared, Josselyn leaned over a table laden with baskets of berries, and fingered the merchandise. "How have you priced these?" she asked the vendor in her native Welsh. "Keep in mind that should the price be agreeable I will take the entire stock."

Rhonwen continued to stare as vendor and shopper haggled back and forth. Gone was the English lady Rhonwen had imagined, replaced instead by the same woman she'd admired so much ten years ago. When the deal was finally struck, the two seemed equally happy. But Rhonwen was more confused than ever. Then Josselyn turned to speak to the restless guard who trailed her and spied Rhonwen. Her gaze narrowed a moment in curiosity, then her expression froze.

"Rhonwen? Are you Rhonwen?" she asked, skirting the guard to approach nearer.

Rhonwen straightened to her full height. "I am. Hello, Josselyn. Or am I now to refer to you as Lady Josselyn?"

Her haughty tone had no effect on Josselyn, however. In a moment Rhonwen found herself swallowed up in a heartfelt embrace, and when the older woman finally held her at arm's length, Josselyn's smile was huge.

"Rhonwen. Oh, my, but you have grown into a beauty. I am so pleased to see you. So very pleased!"

"I had hoped to see you here," Rhonwen confessed, as her emotions got the better of her.

"Am I to understand that you had no plans to come up to the castle?"

A cloud settled over Rhonwen, reminding her of all the complications separating her life from that of her old friend. She stepped out of Josselyn's embrace. "I came to Carreg Du. Nesta convinced me to accompany her to the market here, but I did not intend—" She broke off, crossing her arms across her chest.

"I see." But even that could not discourage Josselyn, it seemed, for she grinned. "Well, now that I'm issuing an invitation to you, I hope you will reconsider. It would please me to show you my children."

Rhonwen shook her head. This was an ideal opportunity to put Rhys's plan into effect, but somehow, she did not want to take it. "I cannot."

"And why not? Is it because of Rand? For if it is, you should know that he is not presently at Rosecliffe. So you see, it's perfectly all right. You won't have to pretend a friendliness you do not feel."

"What of his brother?" Rhonwen blurted out.

"Who, Jasper?"

Rhonwen saw the precise moment when the surprise in Josselyn's eyes gave way to curiosity, and she could have kicked herself. Why had she brought him up? Had he spoken to Josselyn about her? If he had, how much had he told her?

And if he hadn't spoken of her, why not?

"Jasper is not feeling very well today," Josselyn said, her eyes twinkling. "He will not disturb us, I think. Come," she continued. "We will find Nesta and she can accompany you."

It was too easy—and much too hard. Josselyn hooked her arm in Rhonwen's and, with Nesta's promise to join them once her duties in the stall were done, they made their way though the busy little town and up the road to the castle.

The guard who trailed them was not happy. Rhonwen was not particularly happy either. But Josselyn's happiness overshadowed their lack. She chattered on, in both Welsh and English, asking about Rhonwen's mother who had remarried, and her younger siblings, Davit and Cordula.

"Davit is taller than I am," Rhonwen admitted. "Though that is no particular accomplishment."

"And have you a husband?" Josselyn asked as they crossed the bridge that spanned the moat.

Rhonwen shook her head, staring distractedly at the two huge towers. They were even more massive up close, with a stout iron-strap gate stretching between them and a monstrous chain to draw up the bridge. Rhys was right. They could not hope to rout the English with a frontal attack.

She hung back, hesitant to enter the castle. For if she entered she'd have to tell Rhys everything, and though it made no sense, that suddenly felt like a terrible betrayal.

"Come along, Rhonwen. I know you are curious about the castle, so you needn't pretend otherwise. I remember when you were a little girl heaving stones at the rising walls."

Rhonwen smiled tautly. "It did no good, did it?"

"No. Nor did my own opposition to Rand. But I cannot be sorry that he came here, nor that he built Rosecliffe Castle." She caught Rhonwen's hand, forcing her to meet her sincere gaze. "I love him. He is a good man who has worked hard to keep peace in this part of Wales."

"He is still English."

"So he is. But there is more to a man—or a woman—than the place of his birth. Come, let us find the children."

Rhonwen had never before been inside a castle, and as they crossed the bailey, she stared wide-eyed about her. The two-story great hall. The stone stables and barracks. The kitchen. She remembered the kitchen, for it had been constructed even before the walls.

Behind them someone called to the guard who'd accompanied them and he trotted off in another direction. Then as they went up the four broad steps to the main hall, she spied a page grooming a muscular horse and she nearly tripped. Jasper's horse, the one she'd tried to steal.

Without thinking she made a swift sign of the cross. *Please don't let him discover me here*, she prayed. Please let Josselyn be right when she said Jasper was too sick to be about this day. For she did not know what she would do if she were confronted by Jasper FitzHugh.

Six

The tapping came from inside his own head, hesitant at first, then more insistent. Jasper groaned and pressed his palms against his skull. If it didn't stop, his head would surely split in half.

But it didn't stop. He grimaced and only then realized the painful sound came from the door. Some fiend was pounding it down—

"Uncle Jasper? Uncle Jasper, Mother says you may not sleep the day away. We have a visitor. Uncle Jasper!"

"Enough, Gavin! God's bones," he added, groaning again. He rolled over and cautiously opened his eyes. How much had he drunk last night, that he was still so miserable at—what—midafternoon? If Rand should hear of this . . .

That was a dire enough happenstance to push him up from the bed.

"Uncle Jasper?" Gavin's voice came again, but meekly.

"I'm up. I'm up. And I'll be downstairs . . . eventually." Jasper sat on the edge of his bed, his elbows propped on his knees and his head resting in his hands. Then Gavin's original words finally registered and he looked up at the door. "A visitor? Who is it has come to call at Rosecliffe? Not a message from Rand already?"

"Nay. 'Tis only some woman. A friend of Mother's."

Jasper straightened up. "A woman? Who is she?" His pulse began to rouse from its sluggish pace. "What is her name?"

"She's someone Mother knew from before, I think. Her name is Rhonwen."

It was amazing how swiftly his body shed the rigors of his excesses. Jasper surged to his feet, his aching head clear and his roiling stomach forgotten. Rhonwen was here, at Rosecliffe. Rhonwen of the deadly bow and shapely body. Rhonwen, who despised him and yet had kissed him like a courtesan.

Rhonwen, who had consumed his thoughts last night and thereby ruined his rendezvous with another, more willing woman.

He shuddered at the shame of it.

It made no sense for Rhonwen to be here now, for she'd avoided Josselyn and Rosecliffe Castle for years. But she was here, and to his mind it could mean but one thing: She'd come to seek him out.

Masculine pride pushed back the memory of last night's humiliation. Instead he focused on a new truth: It had been but three days since their meeting, and she could not bear to stay away from him a moment longer.

Grinning smugly at himself in the polished steel mirror, he cleaned his mouth and bathed as swiftly as he could, washing the sleep from his eyes. He donned a fresh chainse and a studded leather tunic, and smoothed his unruly hair. Then, willing himself not to reveal his eagerness, he buckled on his best girdle, adjusted his dagger sheath, pulled on his boots, and hurried across the yard.

Gavin had not lied. Not that Jasper thought he had. Still, he could hardly credit his great good fortune. Rhonwen come to Rosecliffe Castle, sitting with Josselyn in the great hall. When he entered the spacious hall, lit by high windows on the east and south, the two women sat in a beam of sunlight. Josselyn looked up and smiled, and when she did, Rhonwen turned to see who'd entered.

Her shocked expression was clear, even from across the wide chamber, and it killed Jasper's hasty assumption that she'd come to see him. Her cheeks colored, her gaze swung accusingly to Josselyn, and she clenched the arms of her chair until her knuckles turned white. But she did not flee.

He took what satisfaction he could from the unpleasant fact that at least she did not flee.

He advanced into the room, not so confident as before, and well aware that Josselyn's machinations were somehow involved. Indeed, Josselyn's satisfied smile when she rose confirmed his suspicions.

"Ah, you are here, Jasper. I am so pleased, for I am anxious to acquaint you with a friend I have long hoped to entertain at Rosecliffe." She turned to Rhonwen, who now stood as well. "This is Rhonwen," she said, although she knew very well Jasper had already met her. For some reason she was pretending she did not know—probably for Rhonwen's sake. But Jasper was willing to play along with her farce. For now.

"You will remember," Josselyn continued, "that Rhonwen was my friend before I wed with Rand. Rhonwen, this is Jasper FitzHugh, whom you too will remember from that unpleasant incident with Owain."

Through the introductions Jasper and Rhonwen stared at one another. She was even more beguiling than he remembered, at once wild and earthy and delicate. Her hair was so black, and though her eyes were nearly as dark, they were also warm with amber lights in their depths.

No wonder the woman last night had paled next to her. Desire struck him now with renewed intensity, but her expression remained determinedly blank. Apparently she preferred to pretend they'd not met so recently. He decided to humor her.

"Welcome to Rosecliffe Castle." When she did not extend her hand, he reached for it, bowed, and kissed her bare fingers.

Rhonwen did not know how to react. From the moment he appeared, she'd frozen in shock. He was too tall and vital and unforgivably handsome. If he'd been attractive while wet and furious, he was ten times so now, with his fine clothing and his hair combed in place.

When he bowed over her hand she felt like an awkward

child, devoid of any manners. When he kissed her hand, she went from frozen to scorched.

She wanted to snatch her hand back, but he held it firmly in his larger, stronger hand. Then he kissed each knuckle, one at a time, and fire shot up her arm. With a little gasp she did snatch it free.

With just that faint touch of his mouth her entire body burned with awareness! Was she perverse? She needed to get away, and yet like a hunted hare, she knew her safety lay in stillness. She must not run. She must not react. Most of all, she must collect her wits, else he would surely devour her. As it was, his hungry stare already seemed to consume her.

She tucked her burning hand inside the folds of her skirt. "My visit was . . . um . . . not planned." She stifled a groan at so inept a response. Not only was she dressed like a drudge, but she also sounded as stupid as one. "I . . . um . . . met Josselyn in the market. In the village. She . . . she invited me here."

"I had to plead and cajole before she would agree," Josselyn added, smiling benignly at them both. "She only agreed because Rand was gone away, and also, I think, because I reassured her that you were taken sick."

Again Rhonwen could have groaned.

"You look much better," Josselyn blithely continued. "Was it the tonic Isolde made for you?"

"No doubt it was," Jasper answered. But there was something in their exchange that prickled the skin at the back of Rhonwen's neck, something in the look they shared. When it hit her, she was appalled at her own stupidity. Josselyn was playing matchmaker. And the match she hoped to make was between Jasper and Rhonwen!

Panicked, she hugged her arms over her chest and blurted out the first thing that came into her mind. "I must go."

"No, no. I forbid it," Josselyn cried. "You haven't met the girls yet."

"I'll do that another time." Rhonwen edged toward the door.

"But what of Nesta? She expects you to await her here."

"I'll find her at the market."

But it was too late for Rhonwen to flee. With a triumphant grin Josselyn said, "Ah, here are the girls now. Isolde, my eldest, and Gwendolyn, my youngest."

The two little girls skipped into the room and stopped beside their uncle. The elder had fair hair, though with gray eyes like her father, and was as pretty as a picture in her pale blue kirtle. The younger was plump and rosy, with dark curls framing her sweet little face.

Jasper squatted down beside them. "This is Rhonwen ap Tomas," he told his two nieces. "She's a friend of your mother's—and a friend of mine. Go ahead and greet her."

They made their curtsies to Rhonwen, two perfect little girls who clearly adored their uncle, and Rhonwen could hardly ignore them. Josselyn beamed her approval and when they were finished Jasper hoisted Gwendolyn onto his shoulders while Isolde hung onto his arm.

Rhonwen remembered Isolde as a baby. She was not much younger than Rhonwen's brother Davit. Though she was not eager to have children herself, seeing Jasper, a powerful man of war, handling the children so gently roused unexpected feelings in her chest. Her father had been that gentle. She'd forgotten that, but she remembered it now. But he had died so long ago. Only now did Rhonwen have a hint of what she might have missed.

She turned away, for it was all too much. Unsettled emotions careened through her—desire, sorrow, and a perverse sort of jealousy. But Josselyn was watching her and it was all Rhonwen could do to mask her feelings behind a false smile.

"Your children are a handsome lot, and well mannered," she said. "You must be very proud."

"I am. And happy too. Marriage and motherhood agree with me very well," Josselyn answered. "I hope someday you too will find that sort of happiness."

"I hope so," Rhonwen murmured. She cast about for some way to excuse herself, but before she could, the boy, Gavin, dashed breathlessly into the hall.

"Aunt Ness is here!"

At once the littlest girl scrambled down from Jasper and toddled off in her brother's wake. The older, Isolde, leaned against her uncle and took his hand. Jasper tugged on one of her long shining curls. "Go along now, Isolde."

"But I hoped we could play a game of chess. You said we might."

"And we will. But not this very moment." He chucked her under the chin, gave Rhonwen a deliberate look, then turned when Nesta came into the room, a child on each side.

Rhonwen saw Isolde's eyes gaze up at her uncle, then slide back to fasten upon Rhonwen. At once the child's mouth turned down and her young gaze hardened with dislike. But why? Rhonwen wondered.

When Isolde smiled back up at Jasper, the answer became obvious. The girl was possessive of her uncle's attentions. She clearly had a childish infatuation for him and viewed Rhonwen as a competitor for his affections.

How ridiculous, and what a disaster, Rhonwen thought. But there was no longer any hope of a quick escape. In the ensuing minutes Nesta settled into a chair near the hearth, a maid brought hot mulled wine and ginger biscuits, and Josselyn forced Rhonwen to sit beside her again. Little Gwen climbed up into Nesta's lap, Gavin played with a small ball and a half-grown pup, while Isolde settled herself next to Jasper.

The conversation, at least, was harmless. Josselyn asked Nesta about several of the villagers, of Dewey's rheumatism and Baran's gout. They discussed the day's market and the warming weather. But they did not speak of Rand's journey to meet with the other English lords, nor of anything at all to do with politics.

Rhonwen wondered if that was due to her presence in the hall. If Nesta had come alone, would they be freer with their subjects? She supposed she would never know.

And all the time that talk circulated, she was acutely conscious of Jasper's presence. Her skin tingled. Her entire being was aware of him, as if he projected some aura that only she sensed. It was madness, and yet she could not make it cease. Had the bard Newlin given him some love potion that made him attract her so? Or had he, perchance, cast a spell upon her?

She'd never heard of Newlin dabbling in such matters. Yet what else was she to think when her English enemy drew her and her Welsh compatriot did not?

Blessedly, the thought of Rhys dragged her back to her purpose at the English stronghold. She'd come here at Rhys's behest, on a mission of his devising. She needed to focus on that to the exclusion of everything else. She still had not overcome her distaste for taking one of the children captive, but as she observed them, she began to see a way to safeguard them.

She would not let Rhys take Gavin. As the only son, he might be treated too harshly. The temptation to be rid of him would be too high. Nor could she allow Isolde to be captured. She was too pretty a child, and too near the budding of womanhood. While she trusted Rhys not to harm her, there were others in his band who were less trustworthy. And even Rhys could be pushed to the breaking point.

That left Gwendolyn, and Rhonwen's gaze shifted to her. The youngest child, Gwendolyn was a sweet-faced cherub. No one, English or Welsh, could possible harm a baby like that. Besides, she would be the least likely to try to escape, and therefore would be guarded in a less oppressive manner.

Yes, Rhonwen decided. If she must help Rhys to take a hostage from among these children, it would be the youngest girl—and she herself would see to Gwen's well-being.

Bolstered by her decision, she moved to sit beside Nesta and smiled at the now-drowsy child. "How old are you?" she asked.

The girl held up three widespread fingers.

"And have you any of your teeth loose yet?"

Gwen straightened up. "I don't know. Do I?" With one chubby finger she waggled one of her lower teeth.

"I can yank one out for you," Gavin called from his spot on the floor. "With only a bit of string—"

"No!" Gwen clapped her hands over her mouth.

Rhonwen patted the child's knee. "You mustn't worry

about him. Like you, I also have a brother, and I've found they're never as mean as they pretend to be."

"But your brother is younger than you," Jasper put in. "Gwynnie and I know what it's like to have older brothers, and you may trust me in this: They can be unruly devils. But I'll protect you, Gwynnie. Come, sweetheart." He opened his arms to her. "You look ready for a nap."

"No. I don't want a nap."

"I'll give you a ride on my shoulders," he said, cocking his head and arching one dark brow.

A ride on his shoulders? Despite herself, Rhonwen was fascinated by the interplay between the little girl and Jasper, and she watched as Gwen slid down from Nesta's lap and climbed into his. He put her on his shoulders, but when he stood to take her up to the nursery, she reached out to Rhonwen. "You come too," she ordered. "You can tell me a story."

"I can tell you a story," Isolde offered, coming to stand beside Jasper.

"I know all your stories," the younger child said. "I want a new one."

"Isolde, you stay here and visit with Nesta," Josselyn put in. "Let Rhonwen go up with Gwen this time."

And with Jasper.

Rhonwen heard the unsaid words and her flesh prickled at the prospect. Jasper said nothing, but his dark-lashed eyes managed nonetheless to transmit a message all their own.

Come upstairs with me, if you dare. Be alone with me, if only for a few, brief minutes. What have you to fear?

What indeed? Rhonwen did not want to think about that. Instead she bravely answered his challenge. "I believe I do know a story or two."

The walls of Rosecliffe Castle were so thick that as they ascended the main curving stairs, the sounds of the great hall were quickly muffled. Though unnerved by Jasper's nearness, Rhonwen managed to keep her wits well enough to observe her surroundings.

On the second floor an open balcony looked down on the hall. A door standing ajar revealed a sleeping chamber with a massive curtained bed. The master's chamber, Rhonwen assumed. The third level held three smaller chambers, one of them a nursery, and it was there Jasper headed. The stairs led farther, to another level above them—probably the roof or a wall walk. There were arrow slits and narrow shuttered windows at each level, but that could be observed from the outside too.

She committed everything to memory, though she wasn't certain how helpful it would be. Then Gwen giggled and Rhonwen returned to the situation at hand.

Jasper sat Gwen upon a bed covered with a soft green woven blanket and a pair of plump pillows. Goose down. What a luxury, Rhonwen thought while the child removed her shoes. There were pegs on the wall holding fresh clothing, and a corner cupboard as well. Then Rhonwen felt Jasper's steady gaze upon her and her eyes returned warily to him.

"She likes stories of dragons," he said, studying her with undisguised warmth.

"So did I when I was younger."

"And princesses. I like princesses too," Gwen cried.

Grateful for the distraction, Rhonwen tore her gaze from Jasper's compelling eyes. "Dragons and princesses. Let me think. Do I know such a story? Oh, I believe I do." She smiled and sat down, then pulled then soft blanket over the child. "Once, long ago, in a faraway kingdom alongside a distant sea . . ."

Within minutes Gwendolyn was fast asleep. Rhonwen let her voice trail away, then for a long moment just sat there on the bed, gazing upon the child's innocent face. Rosy cheeks, long fair lashes, and baby curls at her temples. She was so lovely Rhonwen's heart ached. She'd known the child less than an hour, and yet her heart was already captured. How intensely Josselyn must love her!

"And then what happened?"

Rhonwen started at that low, masculine tone. When she turned her head, she realized Jasper was much nearer than before. "What do you mean?" she murmured, her eyes captured by his.

"What happens to the princess? The dragon has caught her fast in his clutches. What happens next?"

"He . . . he's not really a dragon."

"No?" He moved nearer still. His knee brushed hers. She felt the warmth of his body across the scant inches that separated them.

She shook her head. "No."

"Does he ever turn back into a man?"

Of course he did. And they both knew how. But if Rhonwen answered him . . .

The moment stretched out. Rhonwen stared into his eyes, so dark and yet so bright with promises she should not want to see. "How does she free him from his curse?" he persisted. "Show me, Rhonwen."

She couldn't show him. But neither could she turn away. Hating her weakness—and yearning for his strength—she closed her eyes, and when she did, he kissed her.

Somewhere beyond the window, a curlew called, its cry faint and poignant on the wind. Inside the chamber the only sounds were their breathing and the creaking of the bed as they shifted together. In Rhonwen's head, however, her heart thundered, her blood roared, and alarm bells clamored their warning.

Stop! Beware! Take care!

Too late.

His mouth moved over hers as it had before, only this time he was more sure of himself. He'd learned how to please her that one time, and now he built upon that knowledge. He slid his lips back and forth, and when she arched against him for more, he nibbled on her lower lip. That made her want even more of the wonderful, terrifying sensations he roused in her.

As if he knew what she wanted, one of his hands curved around the back of her neck, tangling in her hair. The other slid around her waist, pulling her fully against him. And in the midst of all that, his tongue slid between her lips.

She was utterly lost.

Was this how it was meant to be between a man and a woman? This wonderful drowning, this exquisite fire? She'd heard women whisper about it, of course. How exciting. How thrilling. But there were other women who were not so eager. For them it was cruel and hurtful, and they dreaded it. But who could dread this?

Wrapping her arms around his neck, Rhonwen capitulated fully to the kiss. Her breasts flattened against his solid chest. Her lips fitted closer to his. Her arms filled with him, yet still she wanted more.

Then his tongue found hers—and pulled away—then found it again. The rhythm began, the erotic slide of his tongue seducing hers, an in and out that fired her blood to new heights. When he eased them back onto the bed alongside Gwen, she followed him down. When he thrust his hips up against her belly, she moaned.

Had that wanton sound come from her? Was she actually laying beside a man she hardly knew—an Englishman—and behaving like a harlot?

She tried to push away, but he rolled her over onto the thickly padded mattress—and nearly crushed Gwendolyn.

"Shh. Shh." He hushed her protests before they began, pressing a finger to her lips. "Be still. We don't want to awaken her."

"Get off me," she hissed, humiliated by her outrageous behavior.

"I will, I will," he said. But instead of moving, he kissed her again, a hard, insistent, demanding kiss that robbed her of her breath and what little good sense she still possessed. Only when she was reduced to a puddle of heated emotion did he relent. He pulled back and stared deeply into her eyes. His voice was hoarse, but unlike her, he could at least still speak.

"Were we not chaperoned by this sleeping child, I would not release you, Rhonwen. I should not have released you before." His breathing was labored. "Is that why you came here today, to finish what we began beside the river?"

Was that the reason? Rhonwen shook her head. Dear God, but she hoped not. " 'Twas Josselyn insisted I come here. She implied that you would not be present."

He chuckled. She felt it in every portion of her body. He

didn't believe her! "I did *not* come here to see you, you great lummox." She shoved at him but he did not move.

"Someone sent Gavin to fetch me."

"Well, it was not I—Oh, no. She didn't."

"Josselyn." He put the word to her thoughts, then laughed again, deeper this time. "Josselyn has deliberately thrown us together. Now, why would she do that?" He lowered his head as if to kiss her again, but she tilted her face aside.

"Let me up. Now."

"One more kiss."

"No."

"Why not?"

To answer that would be to reveal too much. "What will Gwendolyn think if she awakens to find her beloved uncle attacking a woman in the nursery?"

He did not move, not for the longest time. She felt her heart thudding in her chest. Or was it his heart? She saw desire in his eyes and had to fight an answering desire in her own. Then slowly he pulled back and rolled to his side.

She lurched away from the bed, but stopped at the door. He lay on the bed watching her, a man in repose, yet still the most dangerous man she'd ever seen. How was she to deal with him and the way he made her feel? Denial seemed her only choice.

"This should never have happened, and were it not for Josselyn's interference, it would not have," she vowed. Nervously she smoothed the front of her kirtle. "It will not happen again."

"You think not?" He sat up; she backed up until she hit the door. But their eyes never broke contact. "The pull between us is a powerful one, Rhonwen. The day will come . . ." He let the rest trail away and Rhonwen shivered—in fear or awareness? She did not want to know.

"I bid you farewell." She turned to go.

"When will I see you again?"

"Never."

"What of your story? Gwen will want to hear more of the dragon and his lady."

Gwendolyn. In the panic—and passion—that had gripped her, Rhonwen had completely forgotten her purpose here. Rhys was counting on her. She must not let him down even if her task grew more odious by the minute. "I will visit Gwendolyn again. But not if you are here," she added. Then, like the coward she was, she fled.

Downstairs in the great hall, Nesta took one look at Rhonwen's face, frowned, and stood. "P'rhaps we'd better be on our way. The . . . ah . . . the weather is turning, and anyway," she told Josselyn, "the others will complain if I am not there to unpack when they return to Carreg Du. Are you ready, child?" she asked Rhonwen.

"Yes."

"But you've just arrived," Josselyn protested. Her gaze flitted from Rhonwen to the stairwell, then she smiled and looked back at Rhonwen again. "You must promise to return, Rhonwen. Now that you've seen how pleasant Rosecliffe Castle is, you must say you'll come back."

From the corner of her eye Rhonwen knew Jasper had entered the hall, but she refused to meet his gaze. "Perhaps I will," she answered. Anything to speed her departure!

It was impossible to avoid Jasper, however, for he strolled along behind the group of women, then helped Nesta mount her horse. Before the two women could leave, another horse was led forward by a young page, a horse Rhonwen recognized.

"I'll accompany you to Carreg Du," he said. "It will be faster that way, and safer." He held out a hand to Rhonwen. "Here, let me help you mount."

"That's . . . that's not necessary," she stammered.

"I wish to do this for you. It would be rude of you to decline."

"Oh, do take him up on it," Josselyn whispered in her ear. "Nesta will be beside you."

Rhonwen shot her a baleful look. "Leave off this matchmaking, Josselyn," she whispered. "It ill suits you and it will lead nowhere." She turned her scowl on Jasper. "I'm walking."

So she walked, leading Nesta's horse, and beside her Jasper walked, leading his own. When Rhonwen was not forthcoming, he switched the focus of his conversation to Nesta. But his sidelong glances were at Rhonwen. His easy smiles were for Rhonwen, and though she tried to ignore them, it was hard.

"Dewey's chest is constricted?" he asked Nesta.

"He complains, but it will improve when the days warm."

"How does he find the new hound Rand brought to him?"

"Ah, that hound. He works with her daily." The old woman chortled. "He is like a new mother with her first babe."

Rhonwen knew what Jasper was trying to do. He meant to prove to her how solicitous the English were, how generous to the people they thought they had conquered.

"Enough of this," she muttered in Welsh.

"I have not begun to have enough of you," he answered, too low for Nesta to hear. Rhonwen wished she had not heard either, for the heated undercurrent in his voice was unnerving. That he used her own language made it doubly so.

Muttering a curse, she halted and turned to face him. "Go away, Englishman. You gain naught by pestering me with your attention. Now that we are beyond your town gates, we have no need of your company. Begone from here."

"P'rhaps . . ." Nesta began, in a nervous, placating tone. "P'rhaps 'twould be for the best, Sir Jasper. Come along, Rhonwen. This old mare can carry your slight weight the rest of the way home."

Rhonwen feared Jasper would try to stop her and she wasn't at all certain what she would do then. When he dropped his horse's reins and closed the distance between them, she fell back a step. But when he knelt on one knee and offered her the other as a step up, she realized he meant only to help her mount behind Nesta.

She did not want to accept his aid, though, for that meant taking his hand and placing her full weight on him. Were it any other man she would not have hesitated. But this was Jasper FitzHugh, the man she'd tried to kill and meant still to drive out of northern Wales.

He waited, and Nesta waited, and in the end, Rhonwen let

out a frustrated breath. She took his proffered hand—it was too warm. She stepped up on his knee—it was too strong and steady. She was about to push up behind Nesta when Jasper suddenly caught her about the waist and lifted her onto the horse.

His large hands nearly circled her waist, and though he held her suspended for a scant second only, the gesture seemed incredibly intimate. Erotic, even.

Then he released her and sanity blessedly returned. By St. Agnes's bones, was she losing her mind?

Angry and frustrated, she kicked the horse and with a grunt of surprise it started forward. She did not thank Jasper. She did not explain to Nesta. She only dug her heels into the disgruntled mare's sides and sped them on their way.

She must put as much distance as possible between her and Jasper, and as quickly as possible. The man was a threat to her well-being in a way she'd never anticipated. But she would not underestimate him again.

Nor would she underestimate the depths of her own insane desire for him.

Seven

"But I cannot like it that you will be alone," Nesta protested, when Rhonwen dismounted not three minutes later. The old woman stared down at her. "Why won't you ride the rest of the way to Carreg Du with me?"

Rhonwen rubbed her palms up and down her arms. "I need to climb a tree and be alone," she answered. "Please, Nesta. Just let me be. I will be safe enough. I spend most of my days alone in the forests near Afon Bryn. These at Carreg Du are no different."

Nesta studied her a long moment with sad, worried eyes. "Do you go back to seek him? For if you do, I caution you not to be free with your—"

"I do not seek *him*! Anything but!" Rhonwen swore.

"Humph. Do not pretend that you are oblivious to him, child. I am not so old that I have forgotten what passion is."

Rhonwen started to protest that Nesta was mistaken, but the knowing gleam in the old woman's eyes stopped her. Was every woman in this place drawn in by these Englishman? Josselyn. The women at the well. And now Nesta.

What of yourself? an uncomfortably honest voice whispered.

"I need to be alone," she muttered. "Alone."

Nesta shrugged. "As you wish. But I will expect you for dinner. Do not make me worry."

"All right." Then, knowing she sounded like an ungrateful child, she reached up and covered Nesta's hand with her own. "I am troubled and . . . and I need time to think. That is all."

Nesta smiled. "I understand."

No, she did not, Rhonwen decided as Nesta's mare started forward again. How could she? Nesta's life was so simple. She'd met a Welshman, married him, and been a good wife to him for thirty years. She'd never been seduced by her own enemy. She'd never been kissed into submission by a man she'd sought to kill. She'd never been betrayed by her own body into desiring a man that she ought to hate.

That she *did* hate.

Rhonwen stood on the muddy path, watching through forlorn eyes the side-to-side sway of the other woman as she and her horse departed. What is wrong with me? she wondered. Carreg Du had been the home of her childhood, but she didn't belong there anymore. Afon Bryn had become her home, but there, too, she did not fit in. Rhys and his rebels of the wildwood offered some respite. But she felt like an interloper among them.

She knew her mother's solution—and probably everyone else's too: Find a husband and make a home with him. But if she'd been unenthusiastic about that possibility in the past, she was doubly so now. And all on account of Jasper FitzHugh.

A curse upon his head! she swore. A thousand curses! She snatched up a stalk of bog grass and, slapping it restlessly against her leg, waded through the dried field of wild wheat and winter scarlet, kicking angrily at the bent-over seed heads as she went. He'd robbed her of what little certainty she'd had in her life, hatred of the English.

She slumped against a linden tree. She still hated the English, she reassured herself. It was only that she hadn't known any Englishmen before, so it had been easier to think of them as ogres with no redeeming value whatsoever. Now, though it was painful to admit, she knew better. Jasper was her enemy, but he was also charming and beguiling, just as his brother was probably a good husband to Josselyn and a good parent to his three children.

But that changed nothing. She still must fight Jasper and all he represented. And she still must make young Gwendolyn her hostage.

Rhonwen sat a long time beneath the linden, mired in unhappy thought. The sun shifted nearer the horizon. Riding the wind, an occasional sound from the English village wafted to her ears. A dog's barking. A woman's shrill call to her child. Though out of sight, the town and the castle beyond it were inescapable.

Then she heard another sound, and her senses sharpened in alarm. Someone was approaching, not along the road, but through the woods behind her. On silent feet she rose, flattening herself against the tree trunk. Her hand stole to the dagger on her hip and though the feel of it in her hand was reassuring, it did not ease her fear. She was too close to the English settlement. She should have gone on with Nesta.

The sound grew nearer. A twig snapped. Some tiny forest creature scurried away. Rhonwen peered cautiously in the direction of the intruder—and was stunned by what she saw.

Isolde, Josselyn's eldest child, picked her way warily through the wildwood. When she spied Rhonwen, she went still.

It took but a glance to determine the child was alone. But on the heels of relief came exasperation. Rhonwen sheathed her dagger and advanced on the girl. "What are you doing out here alone? Does you mother know where you are? No, of course she does not." She crossed her arms and stared sternly at the young girl. "What were you thinking, Isolde? What were you thinking, to leave the castle unchaperoned?"

Isolde's guilty expression turned mulish. She glared up at Rhonwen. "I might ask the same of you. Why are you sitting out here all alone? Who are you waiting for?"

"Waiting for? Why, no one—" She broke off, for suddenly she understood. Her voice became caustic. "I'm not waiting for anyone, most especially not for your uncle."

Isolde's chin jutted forward. "I saw how you looked at him.

You can't fool me. But you're wasting your time if you think his attentions to you will amount to anything. He acts that way with all the women he meets.''

"I'm sure he does," Rhonwen muttered. "But you're wrong if you assume the man impresses me, for he does not." She gestured toward the road. "Get yourself back to Rose-cliffe, Isolde. Go home before your absence is noted and a search party is formed."

The nine-year-old hesitated, and on her face Rhonwen read uncertainty. "You say you don't want him, but how do I know you're telling the truth?"

Losing patience, Rhonwen snapped, "You don't. The fact is, you have no control over his behavior. Nor over mine. Nor over any other woman's who might attract him. Besides, why should you care whom he chases after? He is a man and you are still a little girl. He's your uncle, Rhonwen. You and he—"

"No!" Isolde clapped her hands over her ears and clenched her eyes shut. "I'm not listening to you. I'm not! So you can just cease talking!" She opened her eyes, and when she spied Rhonwen's shocked expression, she warily lowered her hands. "Just go away," she ordered. "Go back to wherever you came from and leave us alone."

Rhonwen could not help but admire the child's bravery. Although her motives were misguided, she was at least willing to fight for what she thought was hers. Then again, Isolde was half-Welsh. Prior to marrying Randulf FitzHugh, her mother, Josselyn, had been as brave a woman as there had ever been. And although Isolde's father was English, even Rhonwen would not call him a coward. The girl came by her courage honestly. It was only her girlish affection for her undeserving uncle that was tripping her up.

Then again, misguided affections were too often the weakness of brave woman. Josselyn had fallen that way, and Rhonwen had very nearly done the same. How could a mere child be expected to do any better?

In spite of the animosity in Isolde's face, Rhonwen smiled kindly at her. " 'Tis not I you need fear when it comes to your uncle, Isolde. No doubt there are any number of willing women who will draw his fickle eye. Do you mean to warn every one of them away?"

"You think because I am a child that I am helpless. Well, I am not!"

"I would be the last person to ever think you helpless." Rhonwen's own childhood experiences were testament to that. "Still, 'tis not safe for you out here. Get you home before any evil can befall."

Isolde glared at her. "*You* go home. I am entitled to be here, for these are Rosecliffe lands."

Rhonwen's fists tightened. English brat! These were Welsh lands. Welsh lands.

She stared at Isolde as realization struck her. She'd never have a better chance to take one of Josselyn's children hostage that this. To strike a blow for Cymru.

Though she had decided upon Gwendolyn, could she afford to waste this unforeseen opportunity?

She glanced around, filled suddenly with mixed emotions. *Just do it*, her Welsh heritage demanded. *Take the girl and ransom her for the castle.*

But what if she is harmed? her nurturing side countered. *I could never forgive myself if she was harmed in any way.*

Then a whistle sounded, the call of a hunting kite. But Rhonwen knew it was not a kite. She knew also that the decision whether or not to capture Isolde had just been stolen from her.

Reluctantly she responded to Rhys's signal with a whistle of her own, and in a moment he and two others appeared on silent feet from out of a stand of willows.

Isolde gasped and tried at once to dart away. But Fenton caught her, and though the child fought gamely, he was too strong. Rhonwen hurried up to them. "Give her to me," she demanded. "You're frightening her."

"She ought to be frightened," Rhys remarked, sauntering up and grinning wolfishly. "But tell me, Rhonwen. What curious game have we captured today?" His eyes lit briefly upon

Isolde, then turned back to Rhonwen. " 'Tis the eldest. Isolde. I had not expected success so swiftly."

"Truth be told, you did not expect success at all," Rhonwen muttered, clasping Isolde to her. "Be still," she added to the child. "We mean you no harm."

"Why do you say that?" Rhys asked her.

"I hate you!" Isolde screamed.

"I'm sure you do." Rhonwen responded to Isolde first. To Rhys she said, "If you trusted me to succeed, you would not be lurking in the forest spying upon me."

Rhys shrugged. "I prefer to term it 'lending you my support.' Here. Give the brat to me."

"No!" Isolde shrieked, clinging now to Rhonwen, from whom she'd been struggling to escape.

"I can manage her," Rhonwen told him.

Fenton, who'd been silent up to now, chuckled. "Bad enough a woman telling you what to do. Are you now to jump for the both of 'em?"

Rhys swore. "Give her to me, Rhonwen." So saying, he pulled Isolde out of Rhonwen's embrace. Then, grasping her by the shoulders, he scrutinized her face. "Outwardly she favors her mother. But inside . . . you're purely an English wench at heart, aren't you? Aren't you?" he repeated giving the child a hard shake.

Tears spilled over Isolde's face and Rhonwen's heart ached for her. She grabbed Rhys's shoulder. "You're frightening her."

"Good. She ought to be frightened of me. For if she misbehaves, she'll have me to answer to. Do you understand?" he said, staring coldly at Isolde.

Gone was Isolde's bravado. She was a little child who'd stumbled into the clutches of her father's enemy. Tears rolled down her cheeks, but she managed to nod an answer to him.

Mollified, Rhys relaxed his hold. "All right, then. Here." He thrust her at Fenton. "Keep a close watch on her while I speak privately with Rhonwen."

But Rhonwen did not want to speak privately with Rhys. Her emotions were too disarrayed, her loyalties too unsure.

Added to that, she did not like the suddenly possessive look in his eyes. "We can speak another time, Rhys. 'Tis more important that I reassure the poor girl that she is safe. I doubt any of you is equal to the task."

For a long moment he stared down at her, and she knew she was but delaying the inevitable. She'd made a terrible mistake kissing him that one time. He seemed bent on repeating the act, and pursuing it further still. She needed time to figure a way to deal with his newfound lust for her, and Isolde's plight seemed her best way to achieve it.

"We can speak later," she repeated. "Now is not the time."

He shrugged and gestured with his head. "Go to her, then. Meanwhile, I'll post men to watch for riders from the castle. Soon enough they will realize she has gone missing. It will be my pleasure to watch the search for her, and see when they discover my message."

The message was written in Welsh. It was already dark when one of the searchers found it pinned to a tree by a Welsh arrow. Though Jasper spoke Welsh fluently, reading the language was more difficult. He did not want to misinterpret anything, so he reluctantly showed it to the worried Josselyn.

She read it in silence, but when she looked up at Jasper, the color had drained from her face. "He wants the castle in trade for her life." In her hand the single sheet of coarse parchment trembled. "Isolde for Rosecliffe. We must send word to Rand." Her voice only wavered a very little when she added, "Do you think he truly would go so far as to kill her?"

Jasper clenched his jaw. "I don't know. I don't think so. But he forgets that two can play at this game. There are Welsh hostages to be had."

A shudder ripped through Josselyn. "But no hostage you take will have a personal kinship to him," Josselyn countered. "For he has no one. Besides, if you take Welsh hostages, it will only strengthen his position with the people who presently remain neutral, and he would welcome that." Then her composure broke. "Oh, Rhys. Rhys! How could he do this to her, to my little Isolde, whom he once so admired?'' She dropped the parchment onto the floor and, with her head bowed and her face in her hands, she began silently to weep.

Jasper had never felt so helpless, nor so outraged. God curse the man who would stoop so low as to use a child as a weapon in his battles!

The messenger shifted anxiously from one foot to the other. In the hearth the logs popped and creaked, but all else in the hall was deathly still. Two maids huddled in one corner. A manservant held one of the hounds by its collar. Gavin and Gwendolyn had been sent to the nursery with their maid. Everyone who was not actively involved in the search for Isolde was huddled somewhere else, praying for the young girl's safe return.

But it would take more than prayer, Jasper knew. He hadn't believed for a moment that the child had simply wandered off. Seeing his suspicions confirmed, however, did not make him feel better. Worse, he suspected that more Welsh loyalists than Rhys ap Owain were involved.

And first among his suspects was the beautiful, but devious, Rhonwen ap Tomas.

The night was long. The sky rumbled low, unhappy threats, and lightning flashed its warnings. But the rain was slight, and by dawn's gray light the countryside looked no different than any other morning. Green and muddy. Chilly and damp.

Only it was different. Isolde was gone, held captive by that damnable Welsh outlaw.

Jasper had sent a rider south to inform Rand. He didn't like to think of his brother's reaction to the dire news. Rand had left Jasper with the simple task: Keep his family and lands safe. And what had happened? Jasper had let himself be distracted by a woman who'd already tried once to kill him.

He tightened his fist until it shook. Damnation but he was a fool! When Rhonwen had appeared at Rosecliffe, he'd thought his gallant gesture of releasing her that first time had altered her attitude toward him. Like a fool, he'd panted after the beguiling she-devil, and in so doing had allowed his innocent niece to be captured by his most ardent enemy.

God help the pair of them if they harmed even one hair on Isolde's head!

His horse stamped restlessly, while Jasper's gaze scanned the village constantly. He'd not slept, nor had any of the men with him. A search of the woods from Rosecliffe to Carreg Du had revealed nothing. The villagers were equally taciturn. Even Nesta, who loved Josselyn's children dearly, could tell him little. Rhonwen had lingered behind, near the very tree where the message was found. That was all the woman knew, she swore through her tears.

Though Jasper knew he should not, he felt betrayed. Rhonwen had been so sweet and yielding when he'd kissed her, so passionate and yet at the same time innocent. What an idiot he'd been! She'd taken him in completely, and fool that he was, his sudden obsession with her had ruined him for any other woman.

What a deceiving bitch she had turned out to be! But he should have known. He should have known.

He stared at his right hand, at the place where his severed finger had been. Rhonwen might have saved his hand ten years ago—and maybe even his life. But she'd done it for her own purposes, not to spare him any suffering. Since then she'd tried to kill him, stolen his horse, and then stolen his niece from beneath his very nose. Whatever debt he might once have owed the Welsh bitch was long past paid. The only thing he owed her now was vengeance—and that, by God, she would have from him.

That she would have.

He stared up at the flinty hills that rose beyond Carreg Du. He remembered a place, a clearing, a ravine carved out by a spring-fed creek. That whelp Rhys and his rebel band had a hidden camp somewhere in the wildwood, one they moved from time to time. Why could it not be in the same place the treacherous boy's father had once used?

He wheeled his horse abruptly and within a few minutes his new plan was in place. A large noisy group—almost half the search party—set off through the woods by horse. They whistled and called back and forth to one another, and sent their mounts crashing through the fern and bracken.

Jasper led the other half of his men into the forest also, but they swiftly abandoned their horses and silently, on foot, made their way toward the ravine Jasper recalled.

The wind was in their faces, damp with the scent of the deep woods. For an hour they toiled on, spread wide as they pressed forward. Then another hour.

Suddenly Jasper stopped. A new scent caught his attention. Fire. A fire somewhere ahead.

He signaled to Uric and the message was relayed up and down the line. Their pace slowed. Their weapons slithered out from their sheaths. As the men crept forward, Jasper's flesh prickled in anticipation. His knuckles turned white, he gripped his sword so violently.

Twelve years he'd trained for war, but he'd had few opportunities to use that training, save on the practice field. But today . . . today would see the fruition of his labors.

The sound of a voice focused his thoughts and he and the others froze. Jasper proceeded forward alone. A Welshman said, "Come, now, man. How much longer till it's done?"

"Eat it raw if you like," came the muttered response.

Jasper edged behind a stone jutting up from the hillside. A rotted stump provided further cover. When he peered warily past them, he saw a handful of men standing around a fire where something boiled in a pot. The clearing was barren of undergrowth; it had obviously been their camp for some time. A lean-to shelter looked empty and for a moment he feared he had the wrong group of men. Then he spied a flash of yellow fabric and a small foot projecting from the lean-to.

Isolde. It could be no other. The foot drew back, out of sight, but Jasper had seen enough. A rage like nothing he'd previously known rushed over him. Isolde was not his child, but she was of his blood and under his protection

His eyes shifted back to the men near the fire. Seven of them. Was there another guarding Isolde? Then a figure burst into the clearing and he tensed. Rhonwen!

Fast behind her was a man, young and yet fierce. It could be none other than Rhys ap Owain himself.

The man caught up to Rhonwen only because she skidded to a halt when the men at the fire all turned toward her. Their grins and winks made it clear what had been going on. So did the way Rhys snatched her hand.

Damn her! Damn the bitch, Jasper silently swore. That she was Rhys ap Owain's woman did not surprise him. He'd suspected that from the moment Isolde disappeared. But his rage at seeing them together, at watching the man finger a lock of her hair, then grin when she batted his hand away—that stunned him. He wanted to murder the lanky bastard.

"Say," one of the men at the fire called, "how long d'ye think those fools will thrash about in the woods around Carreg Du?"

Rhys watched Rhonwen walk away before he turned to answer. "Until the fool that leads them is taken to task by his brother."

Jasper marshaled his fury and leaned forward to study the Welsh outlaw. He'd killed his father; it seemed inevitable he must kill the son as well. He was but a half-grown youth, Jasper realized, for ten years ago he'd been but a lad of six or so. Jasper understood why the boy hated him, but that changed nothing. He'd taken Isolde. He would pay with his life.

Jasper gathered himself for the attack. His heart pounded; every muscle tensed. Behind him he sensed his men's readiness to charge. Then Rhys ap Owain sauntered over to the other, older men. "Randulf FitzHugh will skewer his sot of a brother for this," he said. "And then I will skewer Randulf FitzHugh—"

The rest was lost in Jasper's battle cry. As one the Englishmen rushed the Welsh, screaming murder as they brandished their swords.

The Welsh reacted instantly. Within seconds metal clanged on metal. Welsh curses echoed English ones.

Jasper slashed with his sword, felling one hapless fellow, then attacking another. But all the while his eyes focused on

Rhys ap Owain, who fought two attackers. Skewer him, would he? The truth of that would be learned soon enough.

For his part, the young Welsh rebel fought gamely. He dispatched one of the foot soldiers and held off one of the knights like a man well trained in warfare. But the English were better armed and had the element of surprise with them. One by one the Welshmen went down. Step by step the survivors fell back, until only Rhys fought, and he surrounded by Englishmen.

At a signal Jasper's men dropped back so that Jasper faced his enemy alone. Jasper lifted his sword to the ready, breathing hard from his exertion. Rhys labored for breath as well. Blood streaked down his cheek from a glancing blow. Jasper also had been wounded, pricked in his left thigh. But he felt no pain, only the need to fight on.

So this was the bloodlust Rand spoke of. It overcame fear and pain, and once roused, it was a vicious beast to tame. Still, Jasper had learned the rules of knighthood well, and honor demanded that he draw the line at murder. To attack this solitary Welshman while his men surrounded him would be murder.

"Throw down your sword," he ordered. When the narrow-eyed youth did not respond, he repeated the order in Welsh.

"Fuck you," the boy said, first in his language, then, insolently, in English. Jasper's men crowded in on him, ready to slay the cocky young rebel, but Jasper stayed them.

"Fetch Isolde," he told the nearest man. "And bring the woman too." That drew a wary look from Rhys. He glanced toward the lean-to and Jasper laughed. But there was no real mirth in it.

" 'Twas a fool's plan, to think you could drive us out of Rosecliffe Castle. Now, instead of you holding Isolde, I hold you—and Rhonwen."

Their eyes met and held, and for a moment the boy's expression was so fierce Jasper was certain he would attack. He hoped he would attack, for Jasper was not ready to sheathe his sword. He needed to fight—especially to fight this man.

He raised his sword, taunting the youth. "Did she tell you

how willing I was—and how willing she was?''

"You bastard—''

Then an urgent cry interrupted them. ''She's not here. The girl's gone—and so is the woman!''

Eight

Rhonwen had no choice but to be ruthless.

She dragged Isolde away at the first rush of the English soldiers. Though she had no time to search for Jasper among them, she knew he was there. So she hauled Isolde out of the lean-to, prodded her up onto one of the few horses they had, then clambered up behind her and sent the horse plunging into the forest.

She knew little about riding, nor had she much experience taking hostages. But she rose to the occasion. She bullied both Isolde and the horse, and not until they were completely lost and night had settled over them like a cold, black blanket did she at all relent.

By then she was exhausted, as was the drooping girl and the laboring horse. In the shelter of a mammoth fir tree she slid off the weary animal, then helped Isolde down. It was a measure of the child's exhaustion that she did not fight her. But once on the ground, the girl turned away and curled into a ball of misery.

Rhonwen stared around her, feeling just as miserable as Isolde. What was she to do now? Their headlong flight had kept her going, but now panic threatened to overwhelm her. What had happened back there? Had Rhys and the others escaped? Had they even survived?

Had Jasper?

She bowed her head and buried her face in her hands. Dear God, was the whole world coming to an end around her? Nothing that had happened in the past several days made any sense. *She* didn't make any sense. Was she a murderer? A spy? A child thief? All that and more could be said of her now. To make matters worse, she no longer seemed to fit anyplace. Not in her mother's household. Not in one of her own. Even her friends would turn against her now. Nesta. Josselyn.

She cringed to think of Josselyn's terror since Isolde had disappeared. And it was all on account of her.

And if Rhys was dead . . . or Jasper . . .

"Oh, God," she prayed. "Oh, God, please, not that."

God did not answer her. But Isolde did, and in her thin child's voice, the accusation of God seemed to resound. "I hate you. I *hate* you!"

Tears welled in Rhonwen's eyes and she could not stop them. She did not begrudge the child her anger. Indeed, in that moment, in that dark corner of the wildwood, she hated herself. She raised her head and wiped the tears away and tried to think. She could not resolve all her worries or any of Isolde's fears, not tonight. They were lost and hungry, and soon they would be cold. Shelter first; food second.

As for what had happened back there . . . tomorrow she would try to find out.

Squaring her shoulders, she looked at Isolde. "I know you hate me. Nevertheless, you have to trust that I will protect you."

"Protect me? Protect me? 'Tis you who are most likely to kill me!"

"I will not!"

"Then why did you make me your hostage?"

Why indeed? Rhonwen sighed and pressed her lips tightly together. "That was never my aim. I will return you to your home—as soon as I determine how to get there."

Isolde stared at her suspiciously. "To my home? To Rosecliffe?"

"Yes, Isolde. To Rosecliffe Castle." But only after she determined what had happened back there—and whether or not any of her countrymen had been captured. If that was the case, perhaps she could barter Isolde for their freedom.

And if Rhys and his men were all dead?

Rhonwen wrapped her arms around herself and shuddered at the suddenly oppressive cold. If they were dead—if Jasper FitzHugh had killed them all—it would fall to her to avenge their deaths. Though she could not do so through Isolde or any other child, she could strike back at Jasper. Beguiling he might be. Handsome. Charming. Virile. But he was an Englishman first and her enemy forever.

She would never make the mistake of forgetting that again.

Newlin brought the news to Rosecliffe Castle.

At dawn the squat bard sat on the stone ledge where the moat bridge rested when the gate was lowered. The bridge guard spied him and sent word to Jasper. Somehow Josselyn heard of it also, for she reached the gate tower at the same time Jasper did.

"Lower the bridge," she ordered. When the man looked to Jasper for approval, she turned also to him. "Tell him, Jasper. Tell him to lower the gate. Newlin knows something."

No doubt he did. But Jasper was not certain he wanted Josselyn to hear that news.

After their victory, they'd searched for Isolde and Rhonwen, but to no avail. She'd melted into the deep forest like a wild creature, taking Isolde with her. They could not have gone far, he knew. But like the hunted creatures they were, they'd gone to ground. He'd been torn between tearing the forest apart and transporting his prisoners back to Rosecliffe. Had two of the Welshmen and one of his own men-at-arms not been so badly wounded, he would have stayed. But they'd desperately needed the village healer's aid. Though he knew better now than to trust Rhonwen, he reassured himself that she would not harm Isolde. Indeed, so long as he held Rhys ap Owain, Rhonwen was not likely to stray far.

Still, he'd dreaded returning to Rosecliffe and to Josselyn without Isolde safe under his protection.

Josselyn had been waiting, and though distraught, she'd accepted the news with surprising stoicism. She'd arranged for bandages and salves, and worked alongside the healer, even stitching up two of the men herself.

It had been very late before any of them had stumbled into their beds. But even then Jasper had lain awake a long while worrying about Isolde, raging at Rhonwen, and berating himself for letting her escape. It had taken three glasses of wine to deaden his brain. Now, however, just three hours later, he was back at the gate tower, clenching his teeth against the piercing grate of the lowering bridge, and dreading what news the elusive Newlin carried to them.

Josselyn started across the bridge before it was fully seated. Despite his pounding head, Jasper forced himself to keep up with her. At least Newlin's expression was not grim.

"Do you bring us word from that deceiving bitch?" he asked before Josselyn could.

Newlin shrugged. "To some she appears deceptive. To some she appears a bitch. But to others, she appears loyal and brave."

"Is Isolde safe? Does Rhonwen have her?" Josselyn asked, wringing her hands in anxiety.

"Put an end to your fears," Newlin said, fixing both of his wandering eyes on Josselyn. "Your daughter is safe. No one means to harm her." Then his eyes once again wandered independent of one another and he turned to Jasper. "She wishes to bargain with you. Her prisoner for yours. What will be your answer?"

Both relief and satisfaction surged through Jasper. He'd been right about Rhonwen. Then he reminded himself that this was the first time he'd been right about her, and his enthusiasm faded. "A trade?" he said. "Why should we agree to—"

"We agree," Josselyn interrupted him.

"Perhaps we agree," Jasper countered. When she turned to contradict him, he took her by the shoulders. "We will trade for Isolde and get her back. But this is a complicated matter. Rhonwen has one hostage, but we have five."

He looked at Newlin. "I'll make the trade. Four Welsh hostages for Isolde. But Rhys ap Owain is not part of the deal. He remains in Rosecliffe's gaol.''

If it were possible to decipher the expression on Newlin's twisted face, Jasper would have guessed he was surprised, maybe even impressed. ''Isolde for four Welsh rebels. I will relay your offer to Rhonwen.'' He turned to leave, but Josselyn caught his sleeve.

''Is Isolde all right? Is she hurt?''

He patted her hand. ''She is a brave little soul, much like her mother at that age. She is doing well.''

''Tell her I love her.'' Josselyn squeezed his arm tighter. ''You'll tell her, won't you?''

''I will.'' Then he left, trundling down the road with his curious sideways gait.

In less than an hour he had returned. This time he awaited them at the *domen*, near the edge of the wildwood. ''Is she agreed?'' Jasper asked, scanning the woods beyond them. Newlin had not been gone long. That meant Rhonwen and Isolde were nearby.

''She has not agreed,'' Newlin announced.

''What?'' Jasper's gaze jerked back to the tiny bard. The dregs of his headache rose again to torment him.

''I feared this,'' Josselyn murmured. '' 'Tis Rhys she most wants freed, Jasper. They are very close.''

Very close. His hands knotted into fists. ''He will remain my prisoner.''

''And what of Isolde? What of my daughter—your niece?'' Josselyn cried. ''If Rand were here he would release the devil himself in order to gain his daughter's freedom.''

Jasper stifled a curse beneath his breath. It was true. Rhys ap Owain was not nearly so valuable as Isolde. He should never have implied otherwise. He stared at Newlin, who swayed back and forth, ever so slightly. The bard remained silent, waiting while Jasper's mind raced. There had to be another way. He could stall for a bit, and meanwhile send his best trackers back into the woods to search.

''She is not here,'' Newlin said, as if in response to Jasper's thoughts. "She has hidden herself far from Rosecliffe and Carreg Du."

Jasper crossed his arms. "You were not gone an hour. She cannot be so far."

The bard's smile was sweet and simple. His words were less so. "Not all the truths in this world are immediately obvious. Some truths require faith to discern."

"Am I to make sense of such maunderings?"

Josselyn caught him by the arm. "Newlin has knowledge that others of us do not possess or understand. But he never lies. I believe him when he says Isolde is not nearby. You should believe him too."

"He knows where she is. He could tell us."

" 'Tis far more complex than that, Jasper. You want this country to be English, but it is not. It is Welsh. I am Welsh. Our ways are not so easy to understand."

His eyes narrowed. In that she was right. The Welsh were a mystical lot, superstitious and strange. But they were brave and loyal also, a trait he realized he could trade upon.

"Very well," he said. "If she wants Rhys freed, I will do it. But it will cost Rhonwen her own freedom. Isolde for the four. Rhonwen for Rhys ap Owain."

Why he did it, he could not say. As he stalked the wall walk two hours later he berated himself for a fool.

Newlin had smiled. In approval? Jasper didn't know.

Josselyn had been ecstatic and grateful. No doubt she paced her solar this very minute in happy anticipation of her daughter's imminent return.

But Jasper was not happy. Would Rhonwen agree? And did he want her to? He wasn't certain about his feelings in the matter. Though he did not want to release Rhys, he had to get Isolde back. He also wanted to get hold of the devious Rhonwen. He wasn't sure, however, what he would do with her. And how long would he keep her?

Long enough to assuage this ungodly desire she roused in him, he swore. Long enough to teach her the consequences of her deceitful ways.

He fought the rise of inappropriate desire, angry at the

power she yet held over him. He would make Rhonwen his prisoner—and his mistress. Meanwhile, her presence would deter Rhys ap Owain from attacking the people of Rosecliffe.

But Jasper would taunt the Welsh rebel with the conquest of his woman, he vowed, staring blindly past the crenellations to the town and forest beyond. He would make certain Rhys learned of it when Rhonwen warmed his bed, and he would draw the rash young man out—and capture him once more.

He struck his leather-gloved fist against the chiseled edge of the stone cap piece. He would have Rhonwen, and he would recapture Rhys. Then he would quit this damnable land once and for all.

Meanwhile, it was past time for him to have a little chat with Rhys ap Owain.

Rhonwen rode with Isolde before her. Newlin had declined to ride with them. Still, at the end of the three-hour journey, down rocky trails and through shadowy forests, Rhonwen knew he would be waiting for them at Carreg Du. She didn't wonder how he did it. Some things were not for ordinary folk to comprehend. Better for her to ponder the consequences of what she'd agreed to—that is, assuming Jasper FitzHugh meant to abide by their agreement.

What if it was a trick?

She frowned. Isolde's head dropped, then fell back against Rhonwen's shoulder. Rhonwen shifted so that the child rested more comfortably in her arms. The fact was, whether or not Jasper meant to deceive her, she must return Isolde to her family. They were wrong to have taken the girl hostage. Now she must pay the price for her error in judgment.

But what would that price be?

The horse picked its way along the forest trail. It seemed to know where it was going, and Rhonwen was happy to give it its head. The wildwood was solemn. The clouds prevented the fog from burning away, and the damp earth seemed to suck all sound into itself.

In an hour she would be there. In an hour she would face Jasper across the meadow. Rhys and Fenton and the others would be there too. They, however, would walk to freedom, as would Isolde. She alone would be walking into captivity.

What would her captor do with her?

She was afraid, and yet a part of her—a tiny part of her—knew an unexpected anticipation.

Anticipation!

She shook her head at such a perverse thought. Jasper had every right to despise her, he had every right to punish her for the things she'd done. Whether he would or not remained to be seen. In either event, she would find out soon enough.

Rhys ap Owain marched across the field, the last of the line of prisoners. Like the other Welshmen, he was ebullient. One and all, they considered this trade—their freedom for Fitz-Hugh's daughter—a victory.

They would not think so for long, Jasper swore as he rode alongside them.

He had not told Rhys that Rhonwen must pay the price for his freedom. The youth had been so cocky when Jasper interviewed him, it had grated on Jasper's already raw nerves. Had he ever been that obnoxiously sure of himself? Perhaps. In his own case, Rand had doused the flames of his overweening pride. There was nothing so effective as an older brother who thought his younger sibling an inept fool.

Since no one else seemed likely to perform that role for Rhys, Jasper was more than satisfied to do so.

"Anxious to regain your freedom?" he said conversationally.

The youth shot him a smug look. "There's not an English gaol that can long hold me."

"Mayhap a Welsh one can do it."

The boy snorted. "You're a fool if you think my people would cast me in gaol. I fight for them and they love me for it. Especially Rhonwen," he added with a sly, superior grin.

"Especially Rhonwen," Jasper echoed, tamping down an unwonted spurt of jealousy. "You are fortunate to have the affection of so brave and loyal a woman." He took great pleasure in watching the boy's confident expression turn suspicious.

"If you think by your admiring words to cast doubt on her loyalty, it will not work. I am no fool to be manipulated so."

"Perhaps not by me. But there is no man living who has not been made a fool of by a woman. I caution you, lad, not to think yourself immune."

"Damn you to hell—and your advice with it!" Rhys snarled. "And don't call me lad. I'm a man and have been since the day you killed my father."

"Ah, yes. Your father," Jasper drawled, his temper roused now. "The brave Owain. I recall that day very well. He was holding a blade to a Welshwoman's throat when my arrow felled him. To Josselyn's throat. Considering his craven behavior, it comes as no surprise that his son would seek to hurt Josselyn's innocent daughter. You are both brave enough to attack women and children," he taunted. "How you fare against men is another matter—as is evidenced by your stay in Rosecliffe's gaol."

"But we go free, don't we? Don't we?" Rhys goaded right back.

Jasper studied him through narrowed eyes. "Yes. You go free. But, as always, the cost must be borne by a woman. Ah, here they are now."

He kicked his horse forward, as much to distance himself from the irritating Welsh rebel as to get a better look at Rhonwen. Did she have some sort of trick planned?

He'd brought sufficient men to stymie any such plot, and he'd secretly positioned more men in the forest to intercept anyone who might attempt to foil the exchange of hostages. He did not want her plotting any more deviousness. He wanted her to concede that he had bested her.

But another, more primitive part of him hoped she would try to renege on the deal. For if she broke faith with him, he would be justified in doing the same. He would secure Isolde's freedom, then he would recapture the rebels and cast them back into the dungeon. And he would have Rhonwen too.

He halted his horse and signaled his men to hold the captives back. Rhonwen stood alone on the far side of the burial vault. Newlin sat on the flat top stone of the *domen*, rocking back and forth in the faint motion familiar to him. But Isolde was nowhere to be seen.

"Where is she?" Jasper demanded. "I have brought my captives. Where is Isolde?"

"Here." The muffled call came from within the *domen* and Isolde burst out grinning. She ran unrestrained toward Jasper and in an instant he scooped her up before him.

"Are you all right?"

"Yes. Though I am hungry, and I would like to change into clean clothes." She sat across his lap and threw her arms around his neck. "I hate her," she muttered, glaring at Rhonwen. "I hope you cast her down in the dungeon and never let her out."

"I kept my word," Rhonwen called. "Will you keep yours?"

Jasper met her hostile gaze. She was dressed in her green cloak and most of her body was hidden. But he could envision what he could not see. She was slender yet womanly. She appeared vulnerable and frail, yet he knew she had a will of iron. She hated him, yet she returned his kisses with passion.

Did she respond that way to Rhys?

Probably so, and more, he decided, clenching his jaw rhythmically. With a gesture he signaled his men to release the prisoners. The four Welshmen scurried forward, two of them carrying one of their injured comrades in a crude litter between them, while the fourth one limped ahead.

"What is this?" Rhys shouted, struggling against the two stout guards who held him back. "He is betraying his word! You see, Rhonwen? You see!"

Jasper kept his eyes on Rhonwen and he saw the accusing look in her eyes. "You didn't tell him?" she asked.

"I concede that pleasure to you, Rhonwen. 'Tis your sacrifice, and he sets such a great store by the affection you feel for him."

Slowly she came around the *domen*. She paused to speak to the wounded man on the litter, to assure herself that his wounds would not prove fatal. Then, taking a breath as if it might give her strength, she marched over to Rhys.

Disentangling himself from his niece's embrace, Jasper slid over the horse's rump, leaving Isolde in the saddle. Ignoring the girl's objections, he caught Rhonwen by the arm before she reached Rhys. "You won't mind if I watch his face when you tell him the cost of his freedom?"

"*Asyn ffiaidd!*" she swore. But though the words were angry, in her eyes he thought he saw a flash of pain. She abruptly turned from him to face Rhys.

"You are set free. You can go. But I must stay," she said to him in Welsh.

"No! No, Rhonwen! How could you agree to such a thing?" Rhys struggled against the men who held him. "How can you choose him?"

"I'm not choosing him! It was the only way I could secure your freedom."

Jasper flinched at her words and his hand tightened on her arm.

"I was afraid for you in that English gaol," she told the stunned Rhys.

"What of your safety? You know what he has planned for you—" Once again Rhys fought fruitlessly for his freedom.

"I will not be harmed. If nothing else, Josselyn will see to it."

"Josselyn." He spit on the ground. "She is a traitor to her people! She would not hesitate to betray you."

"My mother is not a traitor!" Isolde screamed from her perch on Jasper's horse. "You're a horrible man and I hate you!"

"Enough!" Jasper roared. He hauled Rhonwen backward and grabbed his destrier's reins.

"You can't take her! No!" Rhys twisted and kicked but to no avail.

Jasper signaled one of his men to take Isolde up before him. Then he lifted up a struggling Rhonwen and mounted behind her. "Be grateful, boy," he growled at Rhys. "Were it not for her, your head would no longer be attached to your shoulders.''

''Yours will not long be attached!'' Rhys threatened.

In the midst of all the confusion and angry shouting, Newlin finally reacted. His rocking ceased and he stood up on the *domen*. His tattered cloak fluttered around him, rising and falling, though there was no discernible wind.

Isolde gasped. Rhonwen froze in Jasper's lap, and even Rhys ceased his struggling. The tiny bard seemed to grow and expand, and though Jasper knew it was but a trick of their imagination, he was nonetheless impressed.

Then the bard spoke, his words slow and somber. '' 'Tis oft said that man is born to struggle—for his first breath, for every bite of bread, to protect his family. To protect his land. God gifts us with eyes to see and ears to hear, lips to speak. A mind to reason. To use those gifts wisely is to honor the Creator.''

He spread his arms and let his unfocused gaze sweep over all of them. ''Go forth and be wise. Be wiser than you have been heretofore.''

Then he sat down and became again the squat little man they knew.

With a last hard look at Rhys, Jasper wheeled Helios about and took off for Rosecliffe. He'd be wise, all right. He'd not let his emotions interfere again in his dealings with Rhonwen. And the next time he had that damned Welsh rebel in his clutches, he would not let the hothead off so easily.

Rhonwen too vowed to search for wisdom, for she knew the coming days would be a trial for her. The man who held her so impersonally was the same man who had forced her to confront passions she'd not known she possessed. To keep those passions under control . . . she feared that would take a strength and a wisdom she'd never before needed.

Riding behind them, her eyes burning with angry tears, young Isolde kept her gaze on Jasper. How she hated that woman in his arms. But she must do as Newlin said. She must be wiser than she had been, wise enough to drive Rhonwen out of Jasper's life forever.

Of them all, only Rhys ignored the old bard's words. Wisdom was not what he needed to bring down the English. Finely honed blades of steel, and sufficient men to wield them—that was what he needed. Horses enough and shields enough and armor enough.

The English soldiers released him, then mounted their horses and thundered away. But he stood in the clearing, the *domen* behind him, the castle village beyond the fields to the right and, in the distance, Rosecliffe Castle looming over all.

The time would come when he would bring them down, all of them. Or else he would die trying.

Book Two

Would God that it were so
As I coude wishe betwixt us two!

—anonymous medieval verse

Nine

The mad gallop back to Rosecliffe was blessedly short. But for Rhonwen it was unbearable all the same. What was to become of her? What would Jasper do with her when they reached the castle?

The gate tower looked far more forbidding today. The moat was wider; the gate impenetrable. As they thundered across the bridge, the clatter of the horses' hooves gave way to cheers. It seemed as if everyone in both the village and the castle crowded the bailey to welcome Isolde home.

The little girl fell into her mother's arms weeping, and the cheers grew. Jasper dismounted to receive Josselyn's heartfelt thanks, and the people shouted until they were hoarse. Only when he turned to face his prisoner did silence fall. But it was not a true silence. An uneasy muttering rippled through the throng as they all glared at her.

"Bitch . . ." someone yelled.

"Whore . . ." another snarled.

Rhonwen sat the horse as straight and unbowed as she could. But inside she cringed at every insult. She did not blame them for their ill will, and that made it even more painful. She met Josselyn's eyes, and saw disappointment in them. For a moment she thought her old friend meant to approach her. But Isolde held her back, and Jasper blocked her way.

"I need to question her," Jasper told Josselyn. "Take Isolde inside. I'll join you in the hall before too long." Then he turned his attention on Rhonwen.

Everyone watched him approach her. Rhonwen watched too, afraid in a way she hardly understood. He had demanded her in exchange for Rhys's freedom. He'd wanted her in his grasp and, like a fool, she'd complied. It was because she feared for Rhys, she told herself. Jasper would punish Rhys in ways he would not punish her.

But she was afraid for herself now, though not entirely of physical punishment. Nor did she fear imprisonment, though God knew she should. To be locked up, away from her beloved wildwood, to never see the sun or feel the wind . . . She should be terrified.

No, it was an entirely different sort of fear that gripped her now. For she had the awful feeling that this man had the power to rip her heart to shreds.

It made no sense. She should be able to master her foolish reactions to him. But she seemed unable to, and she knew with a sinking certainty that he sensed that weakness in her. And that he meant to use it to his advantage. She feared also that she knew just what that advantage would be.

He did not speak to her, but grasped her by the waist and effortlessly lifted her down. Without thinking she braced her hands against his shoulders. When her feet touched the ground they stood, just for a moment, face-to-face. In differing circumstances it might have been a lovers' embrace. But when he caught her by the wrist and hauled her behind him toward the slate-roofed barracks that illusion vanished. The crowd parted, then closed again as they passed, and the muttering grew more threatening.

". . . to harm a child!"

"Heartless . . ."

"The spawn of Satan."

Then something struck her in the back, something flung with angry strength, and she stumbled forward. Jasper turned, frowning, and started to yank her upright. Then he must have realized what had happened, and his fury turned on those who crowded in on them.

"She is my prisoner and I alone will decide her fate. Harm her without my approval and you will suffer the same punishment in return, only more so. Do I make myself clear in this?"

The throng fell back but Rhonwen was not much reassured, for the expression on Jasper's face was fierce, and his grip on her wrist unrelenting. He alone reserved the right to punish her.

Even Josselyn could not help her now, not that she would want to.

Rhonwen scrambled to her feet and scurried to keep up with him, dreading with every step the fate that awaited her.

The garrison lay quiet and empty, save for the horses stabled on the lower level. Jasper slammed the steel-strapped door and bolted it, then dragged her up the stairs to the men-at-arms' quarters. Down the row of pallets he strode, dragging her behind him until he reached another heavy door. He pushed her inside, then followed her in and bolted that door as well.

Light fell thought one window, illuminating a simple room with a bed, a chest, and garments hanging from hooks on the wall. His private quarters, she realized.

She must have gasped, for he looked up sharply from the lamp he lit. "My quarters," he confirmed. "Get used to them." Then he lowered the rare glass lamp front, and as the pale glow warmed the room, he bolted the shutter too.

She was alone with him, with no hope for escape and no one to intercede on her behalf. Rhonwen swallowed hard, beating back the rise of panic. She must not succumb to fear, she told herself. She must be brave in the face of her enemy, as brave as so many of her countrymen had been. To lose her life—or anything else—was no more than a thousand Cymry had done. But to lose her dignity . . . that would be the true tragedy.

So she squared her shoulders and lifted her chin, and met his contemptuous glare without flinching. "What is to be my punishment?"

"Your punishment?" He gave a bitter laugh. "An apt punishment would be to turn you over to that mob out there. They want your blood, you know.''

''But you have something else in mind. Something worse. So tell me what it is.''

He didn't answer. Instead he unfastened his girdle and hung it and his sheathed sword on one of the wall pegs. But his gray eyes, dark and opaque, remained fixed on hers. The message they sent was unmistakable: He would have her, here. Now. There would be no gallant gesture this time, nor was there a little child to awaken and prevent him finishing what they'd begun twice before.

A shiver ran down her spine and settled in the depths of her stomach, where it writhed in heated agitation.

She was appalled by what he intended, and yet a part of her was mesmerized. She hated him, and yet felt the perverse edge of anticipation. Like a mountain hare caught in the fixed, unblinking stare of the lynx, she knew her fate and the futility of flight.

Only when he drew his tunic over his head and broke the contact of their eyes was she able to look away. She crossed her arms, holding her fears inside. ''So you will rape me. That is to be my punishment?''

''I do not intend to rape you.''

Rhonwen's eyes jerked back up to his. But he forestalled her words. ''I do not intend to punish you, Rhonwen. Your loyalty to your people is understandable, and on one level, at least, commendable. Rather than punish you, I have decided to reward myself and thereby punish the outlaw who commands your loyalty.''

At her look of confusion he laughed once more. ''I want no more from you than what you give to Rhys ap Owain. I have spared your lover his life, Rhonwen. You should be grateful. So, show me your gratitude.'' He took one slow, confident step toward her, then another. ''Show me how very grateful you are.''

Rhonwen stared at him, unable to comprehend. She understood well enough what he wanted of her. She just did not comprehend why. The silence of the small chamber beat like a drum in her head. *Show me your gratitude. Show me. Show me.*

She shook her head and hugged herself tighter. "Call it what you like. But if you mean to rape me, then do as you will and have done with it."

"I take no pleasure in rape."

"Then we are at an impasse, for I will not—" She broke off, shaking her head vehemently. "I will not agree."

His eyes glittered with dark amusement. "My pleasure will be in proving you wrong. Twice now you have protested your disinterest, and twice now you have succumbed to the heat that burns between us. This time will be no different. You have a passionate nature. Your young lover has tasted that passion. Now I would do the same."

"Ryhs is not my lover!"

It was clear he did not believe her, for he laughed. "'Tis pointless to lie, and anyway, he has boasted otherwise."

"What?" Stunned by that remark, she watched as he shrugged out of his linen chainse. The air was cool and his bare skin should have prickled with the chill. But the warmth of his flesh was plain. Hard muscles, taut skin, and the whorl of dark hair on his chest started a fire in her own belly.

"You but delay the inevitable, Rhonwen. I traded him for you. Now I would have my reward. Let me see you."

She didn't realize she had backed up until she hit the door. He did not advance on her. But then, he did not need to. There was no place for her to hide and no one for her to run to. He could afford to be patient, she realized.

So do as he asks, a part of her urged. Do it and get it over with.

But Rhonwen could not be so practical as that, so unemotional about the use of her body for a man's pleasure. She raised her hand as if to ward him away. "I have not been Rhys's lover. Nor will I be yours."

"He says otherwise. He says you are his woman."

"I am my own woman!" she cried. "No one else's."

Surprise flickered in his eyes, but it was swiftly replaced by skepticism. "When first I spied you along the river, you deliberately shed your clothes to entice me."

"I did not shed them."

"You started to."

"I thought I was alone. I . . . I meant only to bathe myself in the river."

"You meant to lure me out so that you could shoot me. That's hardly the behavior of an innocent." He crossed his arms over his chest. "Enough of this foolishness, woman. Remove your clothes so that I can see what I have purchased."

Without weighing her actions, Rhonwen snatched up a pottery vessel sitting on a shelf on the wall. "You have purchased nothing!" she shouted. The she threw the vessel at him, spun about, and yanked at the bolt.

She managed to get the door open. But with one hand he slammed it shut. Then he jerked her around and she found herself trapped. The door behind her, his powerful male torso in front of her, and his thickly muscled arms framing her. She shoved at his chest, then drew back when her hands met with bare skin. Warm bare skin. She flattened against the door and met his mocking gaze.

"I despise you," she muttered between clenched teeth.

"I desire you," he answered, slowly pressing nearer.

He was so close they nearly touched. Then she took a breath and they did touch. Her breasts grazed his chest, then pulled back. He pressed nearer still and her nipples, now stiffened, were agitated further by the feel of his chest through her thin chemise and plain kirtle.

"I despise you," she whispered again. She turned away from the triumph she saw in his eyes.

"You desire me," he corrected. One of his knees slid between her legs at the same time he shifted his chest from side to side. The friction was exquisite. Her nipples tightened into highly sensitive nubs, and the knot in her stomach began to writhe. Was this desire, this dark magic he worked on her body? With hardly a touch he struck sparks inside her. How did he manage it? More importantly, was he aware how easily he achieved his aim?

She willed herself not to reveal it to him. "Shall you rape me against the door, then?" she hissed, keeping her face averted from his.

He nuzzled her hair. "No." The word was hot in her ear. His knee shoved higher, abrading her inner thighs and making her insides quiver. "But I might make love to you against it."

"Call it what you will." She could barely get the words out.

"I shall." His weight came fully against her. Then his hands moved down to cup her derriere and he lifted her up so that her feet left the floor and she straddled his leg.

She gasped and caught his arms for balance. How had she come to so dire a circumstance as this? The intimacy of their position was overwhelming. She was wholly in his power and though she knew there was much more involved in the mating process, she could not imagine anything more intimate. His face was but inches from hers. She felt the heated touch of his breath and the hot touch of his eyes. He pressed his hips against hers and her legs opened to deepen the contact. Everywhere they touched—breasts and hips and thighs—was on fire.

Then he bent nearer, seeking her mouth.

For one rational moment she avoided his kiss. She twisted her head away from his and pushed against his shoulder. "Don't do this," she pleaded. "It will accomplish nothing."

His teeth caught her earlobe, then began a devastating trail of bites and kisses down her neck to her shoulder, then over to her throat. She could feel herself dissolving, melting, becoming his to do with as he pleased.

"If nothing else, it will douse this fire that rages between us. Once we have exhausted ourselves together, mayhap we can get on with finding a way to peace between our people."

"No." She was panting now and pressing as hard against him as he did against her. "This will make matters worse . . ."

The remainder of her words were lost in their kiss. It was a hard kiss, savage and hungry, very nearly brutal. He devoured her mouth, demanding entrance, demanding submission. She was pinned to the door, her arms and legs wrapped

around him, her body open and welcoming. And it was that
welcome, that intense longing for a closeness with him, that
saved her from feeling completely out of control.

She wanted him. He could not force her if she wanted this
as fiercely as did he. And she did. She welcomed the onslaught
of desire—the physical need and the emotional hunger—and
she welcomed him.

His braies held his arousal in check, but when he thrust his
thickened manhood against her damp center, she groaned and
bucked against him. Then he pushed her skirts aside and one
of his hands found the bare skin of her thigh.

Their mouths clung in an endless kiss, one kiss after another, while his hand moved between them, up her thigh, until
he found the place between her legs that ached most. His
thumb brushed the damp curls and she gasped. But she could
not close her legs and he would not end the kiss.

"Let me ease that fire." He murmured the words against
her lips. "It must burn out completely if you are ever to find
peace."

Again he brushed the curls, and caught her moans with his
mouth. Again and again, but each time the touch was stronger
and more determined.

Rhonwen thought she would die from the exquisite torture.
Then his thumb pressed deeper, right up into her, and she
erupted.

"That's right. That's right," he murmured over and over,
never ceasing the little rhythmic thrusts. And all the while she
gasped and bucked and squeezed her legs around him.

Would it never end? Would she burn to cinders like the
Welsh maiden of legend, consumed in the dragon's fire? She
knew the childhood tale. Now she knew a woman's reality.

Only when she was limp and collapsed around him did he
cease the wondrous movements of his hand. For a moment he
rested heavily against her. She heard his labored breathing and
for the first time considered his desire. Was he sated?

Was she?

She did not know, but in a moment she found out. As if
her weight were inconsequential, he lifted her off his thigh

and in a moment sat down on the bed, with her still in his arms. Though her mind still spun from what had just happened, she was nonetheless aware that she sat on his painfully rigid manhood. He was not finished. Not yet, she realized.

Without words, he swiftly removed her kirtle and chemise. Then he laid her back on the bed, peeled off his boots, hose, and braies, and in a moment stood naked and proud before her.

Rhonwen stared. She couldn't help it. She'd never before seen a naked man—at least not a young, virile one. She'd certainly never seen one fully aroused.

Sudden awareness of her own nakedness made her shy. She rolled to her side, but he stopped her. "You are mine now. Mine to look at. Mine to touch. Mine to make love to."

As if to prove his claim, he covered her body with his, letting his weight come fully upon her. It was a strange feeling, and yet it felt natural and right. He was so much taller than she and yet they somehow complemented one another. He was hard where she was soft, coarse with hair where she was smooth. He braced himself on his elbows and stared down into her eyes. "I will make you forget him."

Forget who? Then she remembered. He thought Rhys was her lover. Pain unaccountably stabbed at her heart, pain and sorrow. Was that what this was about? He must possess what he thought his enemy possessed?

Unwilling to be a pawn in their struggle, she shoved at him, nearly toppling him over. "Get off me."

But he easily overpowered her, trapping her wrists and pressing her down into the moss mattress. "We're not finished here."

"I'm finished," she swore, staring up at him.

He grinned. "If you think you are finished, your previous lover must have been a selfish bastard, or else inept. No, Rhonwen. There's much more to come, starting with this."

He slid down her body and, despite her renewed attempts to buck him off, in a moment he was nuzzling her breasts. When his lips tugged at one nipple, she twisted away. But that brought her other nipple into harm's path and he took full advantage. He licked her nipples, then blew across the wet surface. He kissed spirals around her breasts, torturing her into wanting him to satisfy the aching peaks. He made her pant for him, to press her belly up in blind longing. He made her submit once more.

"Sweet Rhonwen," he whispered, as short of breath as she. "God, but I want to devour you."

And she wanted him to. Was she mad to feel so? She feared she was. "Do it." She breathed the words. "Do it."

At once he pulled one nipple fully into his mouth, biting and tugging until she thought she would again erupt. She writhed beneath him and of their own volition her legs looped around his waist. Like a wanton, she pressed desperately up against him.

He responded with a groan and slid up her body. She felt the prod of his manhood. It should have terrified her, but passion had long ago burned away her fear. She needed him in her. She knew that, if she knew nothing else. So she lifted her hips and he heeded her request. He positioned himself and, with a low growl of satisfaction, sheathed himself fully inside her.

She gasped and jerked.

He cursed and froze.

"God's blood! You're a virgin?" he asked in a cracked, disbelieving voice. "An untried maiden?"

Like cold water, she was rudely doused with reality. They were pinned together, his manhood buried deep inside her, but the thrill of desire had vanished. Though her voice trembled, Rhonwen refused to let him see her sudden pain. "I *was* an untried maiden," she muttered. "I'm not so any longer."

Ten

Jasper made the best of it. He was in bed with a beautiful woman, a passionate lover. That she'd been a virgin was a shock. But she was a virgin no longer. He could not undo what had just occurred between them.

But though his flagging desire revived quickly enough as, with little effort, did hers, there remained a pall over their joining. He kissed her and worked hard to rebuild her passion, and only when she returned his kisses did he begin to move within her.

He went slowly this time, easing in and out until she rose to meet his thrusts. Her little cries of pleasure and discovery urged him on. Her hands clutched his shoulders, she writhed in passion, and he felt the coming explosion.

But the blind madness that had gripped him was no more. At the last moment he pulled out, not willing to risk getting her with child. She was his hostage, he reminded himself. She could never be more than that.

Still, as he lay beside her in his bed, catching his breath, feeling the prickle of his skin cooling in the evening air, he felt a hollowness foreign to him. This was when he should tuck her close. A laugh, a tickle, then he would pull the coverlet over them both and fall into sated, untroubled sleep.

That's how it had been with all the women in his past. But he was unable to behave thus with Rhonwen.

"God's bones," he muttered. He flung himself off the bed and, by the light of the single lantern, cleaned himself. Then he donned his braies and hose, and his wrinkled chainse.

He heard her shift upon the bed. She was awake. What was he to do with her now? He'd thought to exhaust his frustrations upon her, but if anything, he was more frustrated than ever.

Damn her for being the most troublesome wench he'd ever known. How could she have been a virgin?

He turned to her, frowning. "This changes nothing."

She was sitting up with the coverlet pulled up to her chin. Her cheeks were flushed, her lips reddened from his kisses, and her inky black hair spilled, wild and silken, over her shoulders.

She was the very image of a woman rising from her lover's bed—save for the wary expression in her eyes.

"I did not think it had," she answered in a low voice. "What happens now?"

Jasper ran one hand through his hair. Bedamned, but he did not know. He bent to draw his boots on, muttering, "Wait here. I've matters to oversee."

Then he snatched up his tunic, girdle, and sword, and quit the room. He bolted the door from the outside this time, then paused, staring at the plain boards.

A hundred women he'd lain with. A hundred women, maybe more. Some experienced—some whores. A few virgins, but all of them willing. As *she* had been willing, he reminded himself. Yet he felt neither sated nor content. He wanted her again—only not like this.

But what other way was there to have her?

He struck the door with his fist, rattling it on its iron hinges. Then he stalked away.

Inside the locked room, Rhonwen jerked at the sound, then cringed when she heard Jasper's retreating footsteps. She'd been miserable already, but the finality of his departure broke through the last of her resolve. One tear leaked out, then another, then two more, until she gave up the fight and her tears flowed in earnest.

She had done it. She'd succumbed to the passions of the body and now, just as the priests had warned, she was paying for her sins. She rolled over, burying her face in the luxurious down-filled pillow, and sobbed. She'd never been so miserable in her entire life. She felt as if she'd given away a part of herself, the most valuable part of herself, and now had nothing to show for it.

But as she lay there, wallowing in her misery, she feared it was not her lost virginity she mourned. That part had not been so bad. In truth, that part had been wonderful. But why had he withdrawn at the end? Why had he withheld his seed from her?

The answer was as painful as it was obvious. She might have been innocent of a man's touch, but she knew how babes were made—and how they were prevented. He'd withdrawn from her because he did not want to get a child of his upon her. She was nothing to him but a casual tumble. A moment of pleasure. He did this all the time.

But she didn't.

She'd given him her virginity, but more importantly—more pitifully—somewhere along the way she'd given him entrance to her heart. How she could be so foolish she did not know. She'd hardly known him long enough to feel any emotion for him. Added to that, he was English and her mortal enemy.

But sadly, reason had no part in her emotions. When he'd pulled out of her it had felt like the cruelest sort of rejection. He'd rolled away from her, eager to be gone from her side. Like a meal, he'd sated his hunger upon her, then forgotten her. Now he was off tending castle business and she had no place in his mind whatsoever.

She pulled the covers over her head, then curled into a ball, feeling a twinge in muscles unaccustomed to her recent erotic activities. What was she to do now? How was she ever to face him—or anyone at Rosecliffe? Rhys and the others were certain to learn of her shame also.

A fresh wave of misery burst over her. They would think her a traitor. She *was* a traitor.

For a long while she lay there in the bed that smelled of him—of them. Her sobs subsided to hiccups, and then to slow, unhappy breaths. She had to pull herself together, to gather what little was left of her pride. Eventually Jasper would return to his quarters. He would either demand the further use of her body or be done with her and send her to the dungeon.

As she sat up in his bed, she hoped it would be the latter. She could suffer imprisonment. She could bear the misery of confinement, and feel a certain pride in enduring it. But if he pleasured her again . . .

The pure joy to be had in his arms, then the terrible letdown of rejection—That was what she could not bear. That would be the cruelest punishment of all.

That was what she feared more than anything.

Jasper came late to the dinner table. From cook to page to serving wench, one and all congratulated him on the safe return of young Isolde. He accepted their accolades reluctantly, though he made the appropriate responses. But with every slap on the back and every bow and curtsy of respect, he felt more and more an impostor.

What had he done to deserve a hero's praise? He'd allowed Rhonwen to escape the castle with Isolde. Then, although he'd found Rhys and captured him, he'd relinquished the outlaw to get Rhonwen back. Any fool could have done that. He should have held firm. He should have kept Rhys in the dungeon and hunted Rhonwen down, and returned Isolde to her mother's arms.

To make matters worse, now that he had Rhonwen he was caught, like a madman, between wanting her and hating her. He vented his anger at Rhys by holding her captive, and vented his anger at her by forcing his attentions on her. When she'd accepted him willingly in her arms he'd felt justified in seducing her. But when she'd proven to be a virgin, his anger had risen to new heights. He'd seduced an untried maiden! How in God's name could *she* be a virgin?

Yet he could not ignore his intense relief to find she'd not been Rhys's lover. He'd kill the man for having boasted that she was!

Meanwhile, what was he to do about her?

When Isolde spied him entering the hall, she scurried to his side. She'd bathed and washed her hair and donned a fresh gown. Considering her ordeal, she did not look much the worse for wear. She grabbed his hand and tugged him toward the high table. "Sit with me, Uncle Jasper. I would do you honor, for you have saved my life this day."

As he made his way behind her across the hall, Josselyn signaled one of the pages to bring him a trencher and wine. Then she pulled out the lord's chair and bade him sit. "Rand would want it," she said.

Jasper grunted and sat, with Isolde on one side and Josselyn on the other. Gavin intercepted the page and delivered Jasper's food himself, while little Gwen carried an ewer of wine to him.

"I am in your debt," the boy solemnly pronounced. "You have saved a member of my family and—"

"She's my family too," Jasper interrupted. "You owe me no debt."

" 'Tis I who owes the debt," Isolde said, leaning against his shoulder.

"Me too," Gwendolyn piped up as she precariously set the ewer on the table. Jasper grabbed it before it could topple over.

" 'Twas nothing, I say. Nothing." He snatched up the pewter goblet Isolde filled and drained it in one long pull. When he lowered it and wiped his mouth, Josselyn was studying him with a curious gaze. He knew that look, and knew it meant trouble.

God's bones, would this hideous day never end?

When Josselyn said, "Leave us now, children," he knew he could not escape. "I would converse awhile with your uncle. In private," she added when Isolde began to protest.

The trio went off grudgingly, while Josselyn waved away any servants who thought to approach. Only when they were completely alone did she lean forward.

"Eat," she urged him. "Eat, Jasper, for I know you have built up a mighty appetite this day. Or mayhap," she added in a knowing tone, "you have assuaged one portion of that appetite already."

He glanced sharply at her, then looked away, uneasy. Any desire he had for food disappeared. As for his other hunger . . . He gritted his teeth. "Be plain with your queries and I will answer them plainly, though I do not owe you any explanations."

"No? You bring in a woman—my friend—as your captive, then drag her away to your private quarters." She paused. "I do not condone rape, Jasper."

"I did not rape her," he bit out. "Besides, why should you care about the well-being of the woman who kidnapped your own daughter?"

"Because I am not certain she did kidnap her."

"What? Oh, come, now, Josselyn. She had Isolde—"

"She had her, yes. But she did not kidnap her. I questioned Isolde closely, and she revealed that she was the one to follow Rhonwen. She left the castle through the postern gate without telling anyone. She followed Rhonwen, and when Rhys appeared, it was he and his men who took her captive."

"But Rhonwen is a part of his band of outlaws."

Josselyn pursed her lips. "To be a Welsh loyalist is not the same as being an outlaw."

"Damnation! Do you truly mean to excuse her role in this?"

"No. No, I do not excuse it, but I do understand it. And I am grateful that it was a woman who stayed with Isolde."

He reached for the ewer and refilled his wine cup, then drank. He did not want to hear any of this—or believe it. Frowning, he said, "Why would Isolde follow Rhonwen? It makes no sense. She must have somehow lured the child to her."

Josselyn shrugged. "Isolde was evasive on that point, but I have my suspicions. But that is neither here nor there. The point is, I will not have Rhonwen mistreated. I will not allow you to force her—"

"I did not force her," he swore. "And if you believed I would do such a thing, why did you not intercede sooner on her behalf?"

Josselyn smiled at him, as if he'd revealed some secret to her. "I did not believe my intercession necessary."

"Then why do you harangue me now?"

"Because you appear here without Rhonwen," she snapped right back. "Why have you not brought her to dinner? Is it your plan to starve her as punishment for her crimes?"

Jasper stared at the grilled haddock and gravy heaped on the trencher of white bread set before him. "Send her food, then," he muttered.

"To your quarters? Humph," she snorted. "And confirm to everyone that she is your leman now? I will not. Tell me, Jasper. What shall you do when your men-at-arms emulate your behavior with the women they encounter—especially Welshwomen who do not appreciate the English presence on Welsh lands? Shall you punish your men or applaud them when they force their unwanted attentions on—"

"I did not force her!" He jerked to his feet, bumping the table and toppling the ewer. The wine spilled, spreading a blood-red stain over the table linen. In the ensuing silence, the wine dripped to the stone floor in slow, audible splats.

Josselyn stared up at him, neither afraid nor enraged by his temper. "I will grant that you have not. But I am not convinced others will make the distinction. There is only one way to undo the damage you have wrought," she added.

"The damage I have wrought?" He ran his hands through his hair, almost as frustrated by Josselyn as he was by Rhonwen. But he controlled his temper, for a part of him knew she was right. If he appeared unable to restrain himself with women, the men under his command could not be expected to do any better.

"God's bones!" he swore. "What is it you want of me, woman? Say it now—all of it—so that I may eat my dinner in peace."

She gave him a faint, unperturbed smile. "Bring her to me. She shall be a guest at Rosecliffe and—"

"A guest? Are you mad?"

"And you shall treat her with every courtesy," she continued. "You will treat her as well as you would a fine English lady come to visit us from London town."

"To what end would I act such a farce?" he demanded belligerently.

"So that others will learn by your example and do the same. So that any hint of your impropriety with her is disproved." She paused and stared at him. "She was untried, wasn't she?"

He clenched his teeth until his jaw ached. Then he sat down with a weary sigh. Though it galled him to admit the truth, he could not lie. "She was."

She nodded. "Let us hope you did not get her with child—unless, of course, you intend to set this shameful deed to rights."

He did not honor that ridiculous remark with a response. Was the woman mad? She must be, to think he might wed so untrustworthy a wench, one who had lied to him, deceived him, and tried to kill him. And whether or not Josselyn held her at fault, the fact remained that she had participated in the kidnapping of Isolde.

Besides, if Rhonwen had cared about her innocence, she could have spoken up. He would never have gone so far had he known. He would have stopped.

At least he wanted to believe he would have stopped.

But none of that mattered now. What was done could not be undone. "I took precautions," he muttered. "Since you insist, I will bring her to you. But have you considered that she will seek escape at every turn? Have you thought about the continuing threat she presents to your children?"

Josselyn waved one hand dismissively. "I trust you to prevent her causing any further trouble."

"What—"

"Between the two of us," she continued blithely along, "we shall turn my headstrong young friend into a lady fit to grace any hall in the land, Welsh or Norman."

"The hell you say. I will not play lady-in-waiting, especially to a wench that—"

"You will do it, Jasper. You have created this disaster and now you must see it through." She stood, more imperious in her simple garb of kersey and linen than any highborn lady in silks and gold braid. "Now fetch her here and let us make the best of these circumstances."

Jasper stood, this time toppling his chair backward with a crash. Several servants looked up in alarm. But Josselyn only shooed him with her fingers. "Go fetch her. Go."

There seemed no choice but to do as she asked. But as Jasper strode across the bailey he fumed—raged—with every step. God curse the day he'd ever laid eyes on Rhonwen ap Tomas. She'd caused him nothing but trouble with her interference, and there seemed no end in sight to it.

Her interference saved you once, a voice rose, accusing, in his head. He flexed the fingers of his right hand and stared at the place where his little finger should be. But for a little girl's interference ten years ago, he'd be missing far more than one finger.

He ran his hand though his hair once more, and felt his anger ease. He would try it Josselyn's way. He would prevent Rhonwen's escape while his brother's wife tried to tame their captive's wildness. And he would treat her with the deference he knew should be accorded all women.

But he would be damned before he'd ever again trust the devious wench. And he'd be damned before he touched her again either.

He was damned the moment he unbarred the door.

He didn't touch her. He managed somehow to restrain himself from that foolhardy mistake. But it was hard when he spied her, perched forlornly on the windowsill, peering between the cracks of the shutter.

She didn't look at him. She stayed as she was, her arms wrapped around her bent legs, her chin resting on her knees. But she stiffened a little, and color rose in her cheeks, warm and telling. She was afraid, uncertain, and embarrassed to face him.

And he, curse his miserable soul, wanted nothing but to gather her up, lay her down, and make her smile again.

Blood rushed to his loins and he felt the rise of desire. Was he a fool or a madman to want her so?

Or was God punishing him for the many sins of his past—for too many sins with too many women?

Anger with himself made him curt. "Come with me. Now!" he barked when she did not leap immediately to his order.

Slowly she unfurled her arms. Stiffly she unfolded her legs. She slid from the high sill but remained with her back to the wall. "Where are you taking me?" she asked, still not meeting his eyes.

"You'll know soon enough," he muttered. "Come along."

"Please, Jasper." She raised her eyes to his, eyes round with uncertainty, sorrow, and resignation. "I know you have every right to your anger. But I implore you, do not make of me a whore."

Sudden shame swept through him. Were a man to treat a woman of his family thus, he would kill him. But Rhonwen had no one to defend her—no one but Rhys, he reminded himself. But even the Welshman had betrayed her, for he'd claimed to be her lover and, in so doing, had tarnished her reputation.

Still, none of those details were proof against the entreaty in her face. Though he steeled himself not to care for her feelings, he did not entirely succeed.

"Josselyn has another punishment in mind for you. One that you will not find so repugnant." The relief that flooded her face stung his pride. He was unable to prevent adding, "Though you did not seem to find the first few hours of your captivity here repugnant."

At once color stained her cheeks and he saw her swallow. The skin on her throat was so smooth and sweet. It would be warm against his lips—

He jerked his eyes away from her and scowled. "Come along. My meal has been interrupted long enough."

Rhonwen did as Jasper commanded. She crossed to the door, then, under his harsh gaze, proceeded past him. But with every step she was conscious of the huge change in their relationship. She was his hostage now, subject to his whim, and earlier it had been his whim to take possession of her body. But in so doing—in seeking her pleasure first, in not forcing her in fear, but in seducing her with passion—he'd captured much more than merely her body.

She caught a sob before it could escape and she hurried through the barracks ahead of him. He desired her—or he had. But he hated her too. Were he to realize how she felt about him . . .

She quashed the rise of emotions that should never be. Enemies could not love one another.

Then she halted in her tracks, stopped by that insane thought. Love was not what she felt for this man. Passion, perhaps, and to an unexpected degree, respect. But that was not the same as love.

Was it?

"Come along." His hand wrapped around her arm, propelling her on. But once she stumbled forward again, he released his hold. Did he find her that distasteful now, so much so that he could hardly bear to touch her?

They crossed the bailey, him herding her forward, much like a dog with a sheep. With every step Rhonwen became more depressed. He'd had what he wanted of her and though he'd been considerate of her feelings then, he made it plain now that he was done with her. He was turning her over to Josselyn, and clearly he could not wait to be rid of her.

She halted before the tall twin doors of the great hall. Just a few days ago she'd entered this same hall a welcome guest, but a secret enemy. Now she returned unwelcome, recognized as an enemy of Rosecliffe.

Then she'd hoped not to see Jasper. Now . . . now she didn't know what she hoped for. But she knew what she dreaded.

Suddenly panicked, she turned to Jasper. "Does Josselyn hate me? Does she?" she begged to know.

"I don't know," he answered after a moment. He looked away, above her head to the door at her back. "I don't know what Josselyn feels. Were it my brother who summoned you . . . Just be grateful he is not here."

Their eyes met and held, and he leaned forward. Or perhaps

it was she who swayed toward him. In any event, Rhonwen's heart began to race. But then the door opened behind her and, with an abrupt nudge, he steered her into the hall.

Josselyn observed the two of them enter with an avid curiosity. Rhonwen obviously worked hard to control her features, but there was a stricken look in her eyes and a shakiness about her that had not been there before. Was it fear of her punishment at Josselyn's hands, or did it have more to do with her feelings about Jasper?

As for Jasper, what did he feel for Rhonwen? His handsome face wore a forbidding expression Josselyn had seldom seen on him, though it looked somehow familiar. She hid a smile when she realized why. In the beginning, Rand had often worn such a look when dealing with *her*. He'd desired her and hated her and yet had loved her all along. Though he'd not revealed that fact until after they were wed.

Could it be that their own Jasper, lusted after by women wherever he went, had finally found a woman able to touch his remote heart?

Josselyn studied them both as they halted before her. Hard, unrelenting man. Stubborn yet vulnerable woman. She almost smiled at the thought of the struggles they faced in finding love together. But smiling would not do. Not at this particular moment.

She drummed her fingers on the arm of her chair. "Well, Rhonwen," she began. "I had not thought to see you back at Rosecliffe Castle under such circumstances—"

"What is she doing in here?" a shrill voice cried.

They all looked up to see Isolde staring down from the open balcony above them.

"She does not belong here with good, civilized people. Cast her into the dungeon, Sir Jasper." She clutched the rail, glaring down at her foe. "She tried to hurt our family. If you love us you will cast her down into the dungeon and never, ever let her out again!"

Eleven

How Rhonwen wanted to flee. But of course she could not. She was Jasper's captive. His prisoner. She had no choice but to stand there in the grand hall, silent as Isolde heaped insults upon her. Josselyn tried to still the child, but that only increased Rhonwen's misery. When the little girl hurried down the stairs, then flung herself weeping into her uncle's arms, Rhonwen wanted to die, to shrivel away to nothingness and slink shamefully from the suddenly cold chamber.

To be despised by a child was truly as low as a person could sink, she realized. That Isolde was totally justified in her contempt was bitter enough. To be defended by Josselyn, who by rights should also despise her, made it crueler still.

Jasper held the sobbing Isolde as Josselyn sought to console the child. "Listen to me, Isolde. The dungeon is not always the answer. 'Tis important that the punishment befit the crime."

"To betray your liege is the act of a traitor. And . . . and traitors are always hung," Isolde declared through her tears.

"Now, who told you that?"

"Gavin did. He . . . he said traitors are not to be tolerated."

"It's far more complicated than that, dear." Josselyn smoothed a lock of hair back from her daughter's damp cheek. "First of all, your father is not her liege."

"But he is! How can you say he is not? These are English lands now, and Papa is lord here."

"It is not that simple. We've discussed this matter before. And anyway, that's not all that this is about, is it?"

Isolde swallowed a sob and sent her mother a guilty look. But when she glanced over at Rhonwen, obstinate dislike took the place of guilt. "She's not a nice person. She made me go with those awful men! I don't understand why you are taking her side!"

"I'm not taking her side," Josselyn explained with admirable patience, more patience than Rhonwen possessed. She could no longer keep silent.

"Then why *don't* you throw me in the dungeon?" she snapped. "I'm not denying my guilt."

Josselyn folded her arms and stared sternly at Rhonwen. "Believe me when I say I am sorely tempted. But in the dungeon your unwarranted hatred of the English would only fester and grow. And you would become a martyr in the eyes of those who share your feelings."

Rhonwen shook her head, bewildered. Jasper would not free her; Josselyn would not cast her into the dungeon. What did they mean to do with her?

She crossed her arms, mimicking Josselyn's pose. "If I am not to be imprisoned, then what? I will not be your servant, if that is what you plan. I will not scrub your floors nor scrape your pots."

"Watch your tongue," Jasper ordered, grabbing her shoulder in warning. "There is no shame in honest work. You'll do whatever you're told."

"And what will you tell me to do?" she asked, her voice bitter, her heart breaking.

He didn't answer and Rhonwen wasn't certain she wanted to hear it if he did. Would he avoid her or bed her? Two extremes with no middle ground, she feared.

He still had an arm around Isolde's shoulder and the child stared up at him adoringly. He'll break your heart, Rhonwen wanted to warn her. He's your uncle, and anyway, he's too old for you.

But Isolde's heart would never listen to the likes of her. Isolde's heart would have to mend in its own way—as would her own, Rhonwen dismally thought.

" 'Tis I who have decided your fate," Josselyn announced, drawing everyone's attention again. "And I have decided to mold you into a proper lady."

Rhonwen gaped at her. That made no sense at all. "A proper lady? An English lady, I suppose," she added, sneering.

"But Mama! That's not fair!"

"Ah, but I think it is. It's the best punishment of all for our Rhonwen of the wildwood. To make someone see the error of their ways is always the best punishment. And you shall help me."

"Not I," Isolde vowed.

"Jasper has agreed to help."

Both Rhonwen and Isolde turned to stare at him. He, however was glaring at Josselyn. But he didn't contradict her, and Rhonwen took some satisfaction in seeing him bow to someone else's bidding for a change. Josselyn had been ten years wed to an Englishman, and in many ways she seemed more English than Welsh. But under that polished exterior of fine cloth and impeccable grooming beat the heart of a strong-willed Welshwoman, it seemed, the same woman she'd been ten years ago: brave and determined.

That did not mean, however, that Rhonwen wanted to become like her. "You will never make me into a spineless English bitch," she said, being deliberately coarse.

"You will do exactly as Josselyn tells you," Jasper ordered, his voice cold and menacing.

For no reason that she could discern, tears pricked Rhonwen's eyes. She refused to look at him, but inside, what little confidence she had left deserted her. Jasper would wed an English lady someday. Someone with a gentle demeanor and cultured manners, with silken gowns and golden baubles. No wonder he disdained her, with her plainspoken ways and pauper's garb. No wonder he could hardly bear to look at her now. She possessed only one thing of interest to him—and he'd had that. There was nothing left.

She swallowed her pain, bottling it up where no one but she could ever find it. "If you wish to play this game, so be it," she said to Josselyn, shrugging.

" 'Tis no game, Rhonwen. But only time will convince you of that. Very well. Let us eat."

"But Mama—" Isolde protested.

"Enough, Isolde. If you cannot behave properly in the company of your elders, you may take your meal in the nursery with your sister."

The sullen child made no response to that, and with a nod, Josselyn led them all to the table.

To her surprise, Rhonwen was seated at the high table between Josselyn and Jasper. Isolde sat on Jasper's opposite side. A maid came around with damp cloths for their hands. Then red wine was poured and the platters of food presented to them before being circulated among the other tables. It was no particular feast day, so the food was ordinary fare. But it was well prepared and there were copious amounts of it. Jasper piled his trencher high with roasted capon, stewed vegetables, and steamed oysters, then ate with vigor. So did Isolde.

But though Rhonwen's stomach growled with hunger, food held no appeal. Perhaps it was the stares directed her way from the other plank tables arrayed below the salt: hostile ones, curious ones. Leering ones. Let them think what they wanted of her. She didn't care, she reassured herself.

It was more likely, however, that her distress was caused by Jasper's proximity. It only increased her agitation to see how unaffected he was. He was enjoying his meal as if nothing whatsoever had passed between them.

Of course he was enjoying it, Rhonwen fumed. He felt none of the devastation she felt. He'd lost nothing, not his honor nor his home—nor his heart. She stared morosely at her food. How was she ever to return to her former life?

It was a foolish question, given that she didn't even know how she was to eat without her knife.

Josselyn sensed her dilemma. "When you have proven

yourself trustworthy, I will restore your knife to you. Until then, you must make do with a spoon.''

"Like a baby," Isolde sneered.

Rhonwen shot the girl a sharp look. A grown woman should not feel animosity toward a child, especially not toward a child who had every reason to behave as she was doing. But Rhonwen could not help it. Isolde's animosity was not due solely to the kidnapping. The child wanted her uncle all to herself. She sensed his interest in Rhonwen, and therein lay the problem. In fact, the entire kidnapping would not have occurred if Isolde had not been so jealous of Rhonwen.

But Jasper's interest in Rhonwen was only carnal—if indeed, that interest existed any longer. Rhonwen knew an innocent little girl could not be expected to understand such things.

Yet knowing that did not entirely help. There was still a perverse part of Rhonwen that wanted to defeat Isolde in this foolish struggle the child had created between them. It was only to prove a point, she told herself. It wasn't because she truly wanted to win Jasper for herself. She could never succeed at that, nor did she wish to. But Isolde would learn a valuable lesson—two valuable lessons. First, that Jasper FitzHugh was not worth wasting her emotions on. And second, to pick her battles—and her enemies—more carefully.

Slowly Rhonwen straightened in her chair. That was advice she too should heed. Perhaps she could not win in a battle with Jasper. But it was Josselyn who controlled her fate now, and that changed everything.

Rhonwen's mind spun. Josselyn wanted to change her into a lady.

She pushed her tangled hair behind her shoulders, cringing to think how shabby she must appear to Josselyn, and even to Isolde. But that was all right, she told herself. If Josselyn wanted to turn her into a lady, then so be it. Rhonwen would let her do it. And in the process she would learn everything she could about the English and their castle, and their curious ways. She would study and listen and learn.

But Josselyn was mistaken if she thought Rhonwen would

be seduced by their fine clothes and haughty ways. She pressed a hand to her heart. She was Welsh and she would ever remain true to her people. And to herself.

She glanced sidelong at her countrywoman, someone she'd much admired and tried long ago to emulate. She would affect that role again, only this time she knew better than to idolize Josselyn. She might practice how to hold her utensils as Josselyn did. She might emulate how to sit and stand and smile in the serene way that Josselyn did. She might even learn to be gracious and how to direct a castle full of servants.

But she would not forget how to fight, and eventually she would escape and help Rhys defeat the English who meant to subjugate them all.

Feeling better for having some sort of plan, she began to eat. The food was good and, to her surprise, she ate everything put before her. She was not surprised, however, to feel Josselyn's gaze upon her.

"You see," Josselyn said. " 'Tis not so bad to be among us."

Rhonwen looked at her, then away. "I will endure it."

"Yes. I imagine you will."

Josselyn raised her right hand in a faint gesture and at once a manservant appeared with a tray of sweets. The aroma was intoxicating. But when the man present the selection to Rhonwen, something obstinate prevented her from partaking of the stewed pears and fried sweet dough. It was one thing to eat the food given her. She had to eat to live. But to share in the dessert?

No, she did not want to enjoy her meal among her English enemies *that* much.

She stood as if to leave the table, and was promptly yanked back into her seat. "You're not going anywhere," Jasper snapped.

"Not even to the garderobe?" she snapped right back.

"Not alone."

"Now, Jasper," Josselyn put in. "In order for Rhonwen to become a lady, she must be treated like a lady. None of this yanking and ordering about."

"God's bones!" he exclaimed. "She's a prisoner, and an uncooperative one, at that!"

Everyone in the hall had stopped to watch the goings-on, but Josselyn didn't seem to care. "She doesn't seem particularly uncooperative to me."

"Just wait," he warned her. "She's not the sweet little girl you remember. She's a—" He broke off, his jaw clenching an agitated rhythm.

"She is the same person she always was," Josselyn stated with unruffled calm. Then she covered Rhonwen's hand with her own and squeezed it, and Rhonwen felt unaccountably as if Josselyn were squeezing her heart.

She didn't want to like Josselyn again. She didn't want to respect her or be beholden to her. So she snatched her hand away. "I'm not the girl you remember," she swore. "Nor the woman you would make me out to be," she said to Jasper.

Again she stood. "I need a moment of privacy."

After a short conversation with Josselyn, Jasper accompanied her, much to her chagrin. He waited outside the garderobe, not meeting her gaze when she came out. "Come along," he ordered.

"Now what?" she muttered.

He didn't answer but led her to the kitchen. There a young boy ferried pots of heated water from the hearth to a huge wooden tub. Josselyn entered with an armful of toweling.

"Ah, there you are. A proper bath and fresh clothing shall start you off well. Afterwards you may join me in my solar."

"I'll leave the pair of you to your task," Jasper said, and turned to depart.

"But Jasper," Josselyn asked, "what if she tries to escape?"

Jasper scowled. "She won't."

"I might," Rhonwen countered, just to be contrary.

"You won't," he growled.

She shrugged and simply smiled.

"You'd better stay," Josselyn told him, arranging the soaps and towels on a chair next to the tub.

A prickle of alarm skittered down Rhonwen's back. Stay? In the kitchen? While she bathed?'

The same thought must have occurred to him, for his scowl turned slowly into a smile. He crossed his arms and leaned against the doorframe. "All right, then. I'll stay."

Rhonwen looked aghast at Josselyn. "You cannot mean for him to stay here. Not while I'm bathing!"

Josselyn pointed to a pair of hooks on the ceiling. "A curtain will protect your privacy."

"Why can't he wait outside?"

"There are two doors," Jasper answered smugly. "And too many knives and other implements you might use as weapons. In this Josselyn is right. So, as she suggested, I'll just sit here."

He straddled a chair opposite the hearth, still grinning. "Get on with it, Rhonwen. I've other uses for my time than to nursemaid you."

" 'Tis not I who wishes your presence! Send someone else to guard me. Anyone would be more welcome than you—"

"Enough!" Josselyn cried, clapping her hands sharply. "You two are worse than a pair of bickering children. Even Gavin and Isolde are not this quarrelsome." She yanked the curtain closed between Rhonwen and Jasper. "Now give me your soiled clothes and get into that tub while the water is yet warm."

Rhonwen glared mutinously at her. She would do no such thing! Then she hesitated. Though she wanted to oppose Josselyn, to do so would contradict her newly conceived plan to go along with this ridiculous punishment. She hated to acquiesce, with Jasper lurking on the other side of a thin length of canvas. But the truth was, the bathtub looked awfully inviting. Certainly it would be a more pleasant bath than the chilly ones she usually took in the river.

So, taking a slow, calming breath, she willed her anger away. It was for the best, she told herself. And at least she couldn't see Jasper's smirking expression.

But there was no smirk on Jasper's face as he watched Rhonwen disrobe. Josselyn added two logs to the fire so that

Rhonwen would not grow chilled. The leaping flames added another benefit, however, one only Jasper could appreciate. Though the plain canvas hid the exasperating Rhonwen from clear view, her silhouette was plainly displayed.

He watched, round-eyed, as she lifted the hem of her kirtle and pulled it over her head.

He saw her loosen the bit of ribbon that held her hair back and gaped in fascination as she finger-combed the luxuriant tangles.

He leaned forward, rapt with the scene being played before him. He could not see her save in shadow. Yet somehow the lack of detail in the shadow fired his imagination. He could almost feel those silky tangles and see their rich color in the firelight.

A hesitant rap on the opposite door broke Jasper's reverie. "Mother?" came Gavin's voice. "Isolde is sick. I think you should come."

"Sick? How so?"

"She has vomited. Ugh," he added. "You'd better hurry."

"All right."

In silhouette Jasper saw her look up at Rhonwen. "I'll be back shortly. Everything you need is here."

"Yes, but what of . . ." Rhonwen gestured with one hand. To him, Jasper realized.

His fingers tightened around the chair back. They would be alone.

"He will not come inside the curtain," Josselyn said in a tone he knew was meant for his ears. "Do not fear, I will be back before you complete your ablutions. Go on, while the water is yet warm."

She stepped from behind the curtain and gave Jasper a stern look. "I believe you know your duty." Then, not waiting for his response, she departed.

Jasper's attention returned at once to the curtain and Rhonwen's shadowy form. She stood very still, her hair cascading around her, her chemise not entirely hiding the feminine shape beneath it.

He had to bite his tongue to prevent himself from urging

her to take it off. The flames leaped and twisted, and against the canvas her silhouette seemed to sway. Then he heard her sigh and slowly she pulled her chemise up.

He knew he would never forget the sight. He'd had her in his bed already. He'd kissed and touched every portion of her smooth, delicious flesh. But the sight of her standing there in shadow, her arms raised over her head, her legs long, her waist slender—her breasts full and outthrust—made him groan. He shifted painfully on the wooden chair, and she froze, her arms still tangled in the thin chemise. The suggestion of her nakedness was just as erotic as the reality of it.

Then her arms came out of the chemise, and her hair tumbled down.

He could just imagine her, staring at the curtain, wondering what he was doing. She probably held her arms across her naked chest, he speculated. He couldn't be certain because of the silhouette of her heavy hair. But that only shifted his focus lower, to the apex of her shapely legs. The fire danced behind her, igniting new fires in him.

If he didn't do something to cool his ardor, he feared he would embarrass himself!

"Get in the tub," he muttered, pressing the heel of one hand against his aching groin. As if that would help him!

She shrank back even nearer the fire, for her silhouette grew longer. In his fevered state he could believe that she was approaching him. But she wasn't, and even if she were, he could not risk anything here, where Josselyn or anyone else might barge in.

"Get in the damned tub! Else I will come and put you in it myself!"

"*Asyn,*" she swore. She leaned over the tub, testing the water, he assumed. But in reality, she presented him with a mouthwatering profile. Her derriere was high and firm. Her calves curving, her ankles narrow. And when she pushed her hair behind her back, her breasts showed, round with noticeable peaks.

He lurched out of the chair, sending it crashing to the floor. He must have her again or explode!

With a shriek of alarm, however, Rhonwen leaped into the tub. A splash. The slosh of water.

When he yanked back the curtain, she was chin deep in water, with rose petals floating around her face and her hair spread out like a rich cape of black velvet behind her.

"Get out of here," she ordered. "Get out or I'll scream."

Though it was madness, he could not help taunting her. "Why scream, Rhonwen, when you know I can make you moan?"

Two spots colored her cheeks. She shook her head and the water rippled about her. But it still hid her from view. "Josselyn will return any minute. How will you explain this . . . this vile behavior?"

It was vile behavior. Jasper knew it as well as she. But something had taken hold of him and he seemed unable to conquer it.

That he was a man of strong passions was no secret. That he enjoyed women and knew how to give them an equivalent enjoyment was a point of pride. But this lack of control, this urgent need to possess her against any precept of logic, honor, or self-preservation, was madness. Desire was a raging beast within him and it took all his strength to rein it in.

"Josselyn, of all people, understands about passion," he said, justifying his behavior. "Though she will leap to your defense for propriety's sake, she will not judge me harshly for my desire."

The spots in her cheeks grew brighter and she looked away. "I . . . I have done nothing to encourage your . . . desire."

"No?" He drew a long breath. "With every move you make—"

He broke off, stunned by what he'd begun to say, stunned by the truth inherent in those words, and the power that knowledge of his weakness would give her.

He stepped back, his hands knotting into fists. "It will not work this time," he muttered in a hoarse voice, though more for his benefit than hers. "You will not seduce me from my duty. Whether wench or lady, you will remain my hostage. And despite your intrigues and his, I will recapture Rhys ap

Owain. Sooner or later, I will have him back in Rosecliffe's dungeon.''

She looked up at him and the pain in her eyes was evident. What was the hold Rhys had over her? It was driving him mad.

"What will be the benefit of capturing him?" she asked in small voice. "Will you imprison him forever? Or execute him? Will his head on a pike bring my people to their knees?"

She swallowed, then straightened a little so that her neck and shoulders were no longer hidden. She sat up further still, revealing the upper swells of her breasts and drawing his hot gaze. "What is it you want of me, Jasper? You desire me. You hate me. You desire me again. You intend to destroy Rhys and everything of my people. Where will it end? How can I end it?"

Jasper could not give her an answer. Desire was a thing worlds apart from logic. Hatred and desire, even more so. At his prolonged silence she bowed her head.

"You want the use of my body, without consequence, without guilt. But there is consequence. And there will always be guilt."

Then without warning she pushed to her feet.

The water sheeted off her, leaving her hair clinging in long tangled webs to her lovely body. Her skin was flushed with the heat of the water, pink and smooth and gleaming in the firelight. Jasper gaped at the sight, unable to move a muscle. He wanted nothing more than to touch her. To taste her. To possess her.

"Do you want me?" she asked, as if she read his mind. When he still did not respond, she took a shaky breath. Her breasts quivered with the movement. Her nipples peaked.

And the pain in his groin nearly killed him.

She held out a hand to him. "If I thought I could buy peace between us in this way, I would. Is it possible? Will you leave Rhys and the others alone?"

Jasper closed his eyes and, miraculously, his brain began again to function, though feebly. He shook his head. "Sit down, Rhonwen. Sit down and think. Will Rhys end his rebellion because you are in my bed? Even were I to cry pax, he would not. If anything, your presence here urges him on."

"And that is why you keep me your captive, isn't it? You use me as bait to lure him into a trap."

He heard the resignation in her voice, then the slosh of the water when she sat. But still he kept his eyes averted.

"Rhys ap Owain will never forget that I killed his father. No matter that I saved Josselyn in the process, he sees me as a murderer. Rand took his father's woman and I took his father's life."

He clenched his teeth and finally looked up at her. "Owain was a dangerous man, a murderous thug who was not above brutalizing women and anyone else weaker than himself. Everyone knows that, even you Welsh. 'Tis only twisted loyalty that prevents you from admitting it. But I understand Rhys's loyalty. He is the son. He must avenge the wrong done his family and so he will never relent until he wreaks havoc on my family. Only I will not let him succeed."

The room was silent save for the hiss of the flames. Rhonwen did not reply, nor did he want her to. There was no solution to their dilemma. They were enemies who desired one another. It was as simple and complicated as that.

In a moment of clarity he knew that taking her again to his bed would not change things. Nor would setting her free. The die was cast. Their tangled destinies would work themselves out with pain enough to go around for all.

Without a word Jasper turned on his heel and quit the overheated kitchen, leaving the door standing wide as he departed. He hurt as he strode away, physically hurt—and not just the pain of urgent desire unfulfilled. His chest hurt, as if something inside had been wrenched out.

In the past he'd always known how to kill pain. When women did not work, wine always did. But no amount of wine could kill this pain, and anyway, he didn't want wine. He wanted Rhonwen.

Twelve

Rhonwen sat in a patch of sunlight in Josselyn's well-appointed solar, scowling at the strip of flurt silk in her lap. She could sew a kirtle or a hood as well as the next woman. She could patch hose and repair a hem. Serviceable goods she understood. But stitching a chain of leaves and flowers merely to ornament an already extravagant girdle? It was a waste of time—and much more difficult than she would have expected.

She looked up. Perched in a window quite as far from Rhonwen as she could get was Isolde. Three days and the child had not once looked at her, save with bitterness. Meanwhile, she worked on her own strip of the same silk with a zeal Rhonwen suspected came from competitiveness. She meant to prove herself better than Rhonwen at decorative needlework, and Rhonwen had no doubt she would.

Perhaps then the child's hostility would ease. Rhonwen certainly hoped so.

"I have knotted the thread again," Rhonwen announced. "Hopelessly, this time," she added, gesturing to Josselyn with the pitiful girdle. Sure enough, Isolde sent a smug look in her mother's direction.

For her part, Josselyn sighed. "You're not putting your complete effort into this, are you, Rhonwen? But that's no matter. Rip it all out and begin again. Eventually you shall get it right.''

''Begin again! But this is the third time and the work is so tedious—''

''Pardon, milady,'' the maid Enid slipped into the solar. ''There is a messenger come from milord Rand.''

At once Josselyn laid aside her sewing. ''Send for Jasper. Meanwhile, I'll speak to the man in the hall. Then go you to the kitchen and fetch food and ale for him.''

''Yes, ma'am,'' the girl said, then disappeared.

For a moment Josselyn simply sat there unmoving, and Rhonwen wondered at her calm. Then Josselyn's head bowed and her lips moved silently. In prayer?

Of course, Rhonwen realized, and she felt a sudden kinship with her old friend. Josselyn prayed for her husband's safety just as Rhonwen prayed for Rhys's.

But there was a world of difference between those two sets of prayers. For Josselyn truly loved Rand. It became more and more obvious to Rhonwen with every day she spent at Rosecliffe Castle. What Rhonwen felt for Rhys was love too, but the love for a friend or even a brother. She wished she could love him in the full way a woman loved a man. But that love was reserved for another.

But not for Jasper, she told herself. Her love was not reserved for Jasper but for another man, one she'd yet to find.

One she feared never to find.

But that was neither here nor there. At the moment there was a messenger come from Randulf FitzHugh, and Josselyn's immediate response was to pray. That she should fear for her husband's safety while he was in the company of his own countrymen piqued Rhonwen's curiosity much more than did the intricacies of embroidery. She too lay her work aside, and rose.

''Are you all right?'' she asked, touching Josselyn's shoulder.

Josselyn startled but immediately recovered. ''Quite all right. Why do you ask?''

Rhonwen shrugged. ''You looked worried.''

She turned to go, but Josselyn caught her hand. She stared earnestly up at Rhonwen. "I miss Rand when he is gone. I worry about him always, and I cannot be completely at ease until I have him safe in my arms again." She smiled, and in her face the truth fairly shone. "I love him. He is the center of my life." Then she stood and placed one hand over her stomach. "And I have news of my own I would share with him."

She left the room, a serene woman made even more beautiful by the love she shared with her husband and children. Rhonwen stared after her, forgetting about her initial animosity. What must it be like to love so intensely, to love with your entire being—and be loved that way in return?

That was assuming, of course, that the Englishman Fitz-Hugh did love his Welsh wife.

But honesty bade Rhonwen to admit what everyone knew. Randulf FitzHugh doted on Josselyn. Were it not for that fact, the people around Rosecliffe Castle would be more discontented by the English presence in their midst. From Afon Bryn south to Radnor Forest, Welsh leaders forever plotted ways to throw off the yoke of English oppression. But in Carreg Du and the lands between the River Geffen and the sea, it was harder to generate that sort of discontent. Rhys had often raged at the complacency in their narrow portion of Wales. The apathy. He called it fear, but Rhonwen wondered if it was something else. It was almost as if the love between Josselyn and Rand had cast a softer light upon this part of Wales they ruled.

The soft slap of shoe leather on the stone floor put Rhonwen's reverie to an end. Josselyn and Rand might have found peace together, and cast it over their lands, but within their family they'd sired an irksome brat. Whenever her mother was out of sight, Isolde made certain to taunt or insult or otherwise annoy Rhonwen.

As the girl crossed to her now, Rhonwen braced herself and smiled. "Ah, Isolde. Perhaps you can advise me on this." She held out the hopelessly knotted embroidery. "I try, but as you see, I do not succeed. And it comes so naturally to you."

Instead of softening under the compliment, which was partly

sincere, Isolde's piquant features wrinkled in suspicion. "You will never possess a fine hand with the needle because you do not value the skill. You may fool my mother when you pretend to try, but you do not fool me. You will never be a fine lady," she finished smugly.

"Really? And why is that? Because I am Welsh? Your mother is Welsh, and you are half-Welsh, or do you forget?" She studied the truculent child. "You know, Isolde, I knew your mother long before she met your father, long before she became the 'fine lady' she is now. You yourself were born a Welsh baby in a simple Welsh cottage."

"I was not!"

"Oh, but you were—" Rhonwen broke off. Did Isolde not know the circumstances of her own birth? Did she not know her mother had wed another man before she was born and had passed Rand's child off as a Welsh child? Staring at the girl's petulant face, Rhonwen was sorely tempted to tell her the truth of it. How Rand had not known she was his child. How her supposed father's death and Owain's mad rages had nearly resulted in her death, and her mother's.

Owain's mad rages.

Yes, Rhonwen thought. He had been mad, and perhaps Rhys had inherited a certain amount of the madness from his father. But that was a matter separate from the one at hand. If Isolde believed herself born into Rosecliffe Castle with her father in attendance, it was not Rhonwen's place to reveal the truth. But it was an accusation she could wield over Josselyn. She was getting exceedingly weary of being the most powerless person in the castle.

"You are right, Isolde," she said with a bland expression firmly in place. "You are the pampered firstborn of a handsome father and a beautiful mother. Your life is one of ease and you deserve every luxury that you have been given. By comparison, I am baseborn and undeserving. Truth be told, you should not be forced to endure my lowly presence. So I will leave you now. I will leave you to bask in your own bright glory while I slink back into my misery."

She gave the child an arch smile then, and strode away,

humming under her breath. She knew she should not stoop to quibbling with a child, but Isolde's determined dislike had begun to wear on her.

But it was the message from the lord of Rosecliffe that interested her now. On silent feet she made her way down the stone stairs, then halted when she heard Josselyn's voice.

". . . but for how long?"

A man cleared his throat, and when Josselyn peeped past the curving stone wall, she saw the nervous fellow, worrying the Phrygian cap clutched in his hands. "Not above a fortnight, milady. He says to make you this oath. He will be home within a fortnight of this very day."

"A fortnight." Josselyn turned away and her hand flitted momentarily to her stomach. From where she stood Rhonwen could see the disappointment in her face, and though she didn't want to be affected, her heart went out to Josselyn. She'd meant to eavesdrop, but instead she again started down the stairs.

"I hope the news is good," she said, announcing her presence.

Josselyn looked up just as Gavin came bounding in. "Is there word from Father? Is he started home?"

Isolde brushed past Rhonwen and descended the stairs, as graceful and dainty as any princess of legend. "We should give a feast for Father upon his return," she suggested. " 'Tis near to his nameday. What say you, Mother? A feast for Father."

"Ho, there's an idea. A feast for Father," Gavin echoed.

Josselyn put an arm around the pair and in each of them Rhonwen saw their mother's likeness—and their father's. Isolde had her mother's face, but for the eyes. Gavin had her mouth and jaw. Children of Wales and England, and beloved of both parents. What sort of future did the land of their birth hold for them and their younger sister?

Rhonwen stared at them, at the loving family they were, and felt like an interloper. She debated retreat, but Josselyn caught her eye. "Come down, Rhonwen. Come down—and walk like a lady. Head high, shoulders back."

Head high. Shoulders back. Measured tread. Rhonwen hesitated, recalling Josselyn's earlier instructions. Even before she'd become mistress of Rosecliffe Castle, Josselyn had possessed the bearing of the highborn. But then, she'd been the daughter of a Welsh leader. Like her mother, that same serenity came naturally to Isolde. But Rhonwen vowed to master it as well.

Just then one of the tall oak doors swung open and Jasper entered. His riding cape flared out behind him as he crossed the hall with his long-legged stride. "What news does Rand send?" He looked from the messenger to Josselyn. "Does he fare well?"

Rhonwen froze on the stairs, unable to tear her eyes away from Jasper. What was it about the man? she bemoaned. He walked into the room and immediately sucked every thought out of her head. There were other men as handsome, as manly and strong. Other men were as confident and arrogant. But he was the only man who made her heart trip over itself. That she hadn't seen him in two days made her reaction even more pronounced.

As she watched from the stairs, Isolde sidled up to him and he absently stroked his niece's hair. Rhonwyn watched the movement of his hand, like one mesmerized. Then she registered the smug smile Isolde sent her, and she reacted instinctively.

Head high. Shoulders back. She moved down the stairs, one measured tread at a time, as if she owned the castle.

As if she owned Rosecliffe and all of northern Wales.

It was gratifying to see Jasper's hand still when he spied her. It was thrilling to see appreciation and desire heat in his eyes.

It was mortifying to trip over the too-long hem of the elegant gown Josselyn had given her, and totally humiliating to stumble down the last three steps and land painfully on her hands and knees.

"Are you all right?" Josselyn cried, hurrying to her side.

"Yes," Rhonwen muttered, ignoring the hand Jasper extended to help her up. She climbed to her feet and he backed away.

The only one smiling was Isolde.

Jasper frowned and turned back to Josselyn. "What word have you from Rand?"

Josselyn sat down, as did they all. "He left LaMonthe's stronghold yesterday, thank God. He proceeds now to Oaken Hill." She looked at her two older children, who flanked their uncle. "LaMonthe offered to foster Gavin but, of course, Rand declined. He hopes to reach an agreement with Lord Edgar. Then there is the matter of Isolde's betrothal."

"I do not wish to become betrothed," Isolde announced. She leaned against Jasper.

"He will not match her with one of Lord Edgar's sons," Jasper said. "Not if Gavin fosters there. I know Rand and he will want to gain separate alliances for Rosecliffe through his children."

"But I don't want to be betrothed!" Isolde exclaimed.

"Don't fret, dear. I will do what I can to delay," Josselyn reassured her daughter.

" 'Tis only a betrothal," Jasper said. "Just a contract. She's hardly of an age to wed."

"I'm not a child!" Isolde cried.

"This is Wales," Rhonwen interrupted. "No woman can be forced to wed against her will, even by her father."

At her unexpected words, Jasper twisted his head and sent her an exasperated look. Isolde stared at her too, shocked and a little suspicious. Then the girl turned hopefully to her mother. "Mama, is it—"

"I am well aware of our Welsh customs," Josselyn interrupted, staring at Rhonwen. "But I am mindful of my husband's customs as well."

"So you will wed me to someone I hate?" Isolde's chin trembled with emotion. "I won't do it. I'll run away!"

Josselyn turned to Isolde and caught her daughter by the arms. "Listen to me, child. He may betroth you against my wishes and yours. But you will never be wed to a man you do not want. Never," she vowed.

Jasper shot an aggravated look at Rhonwen. "You should not meddle in matters that do not pertain to you."

Rhonwen planted her fists on her hips. "We women must support one another."

"Even Englishwomen?" he mocked.

"She is half-Welsh. And anyway, we women have suffered at the whims of our menfolk for longer than the Welsh have struggled against the English."

Josselyn looked up. "You are sorely outnumbered here, Jasper. Best you wait for your brother to bolster your position."

He looped his arm across Gavin's shoulder. "Soon enough Gavin will also be a man of this family."

"A man who also is half-Welsh," Rhonwen threw in.

Josselyn raised a hand to forestall Jasper's reply. "There is no need to debate this matter now. Upon his return I will take it up with Rand. Meanwhile," she said, turning back to Isolde, "you are not to fret over this. Do you understand what I say?"

Isolde swallowed hard, then nodded, her face solemn. Then her round eyes sought Rhonwen, and for once there was no animosity in her expression. Rhonwen shrugged and smiled, and to her great satisfaction, received a hesitant smile in return.

It was a beginning.

"Now," Josselyn said, "you two children run along. Your uncle and I have matters to discuss." When they complied, she turned her attention to Rhonwen. "I believe you have your needlework to occupy you," she said.

" 'Tis pointless. I will never master it," Rhonwen replied.

"Perhaps you can practice coming down the stairs," Jasper muttered.

Rhonwen stalked away, furious—and hurt. Hateful churl! she fumed, stomping up the stairs. Arrogant ass! He was all the crude and evil habits of men rolled into one obnoxious package. Rude. Selfish. Mean.

Worst of all, he thought her sorely lacking as a woman.

In the empty solar she stared glumly at her abandoned needlework, at the hopelessly knotted mess she'd made of it. It was true. She couldn't stitch, at least not the fine work proper Englishwomen did. Nor could she manage her too-long skirt.

Her manners were coarse, her education slight, and she was wont to curse at the first provocation. No wonder he disdained her. No wonder he mocked her and did not see her as worthy of serious attention. He'd had the one thing he wanted of her, and though he might want her in that way again, it was not enough. She needed him to want the whole of her. Only he did not.

She felt the hated sting of tears and with the heel of one hand dashed them away. Why should it matter what he thought of her? He was nothing to her. Less than nothing.

But no matter how she tried to convince herself of that, she could not. Something in her, something perverse in the deepest part of her, wanted him to admire her. And for a moment he had. As she'd descended the stairs in the lovely mauve gown with its snug-fitting waist, his eyes had glowed with admiration.

No, she amended. They'd glowed with lust. It was not the same thing.

She snatched up her pitiful handiwork and climbed into the window seat, intent on flinging the symbol of her failure out into the moat. Let the ducks use it to line their nests. It was good for little else.

She opened the rare window glass and stared out past the castle walls where the masons yet labored, beyond them to the rooftops of thatch and slate in the growing town, and farther, to the brown fields and green forests, and dark rising hills. She sucked in great draughts of the crisp air and suddenly felt overwhelmed by sorrow.

She wanted to go home.

But where, precisely, was home?

The tangle of threads in her hand was no more a muddle than her life. To remain Jasper's captive was eventually to fall prey to his lust for her—and hers for him.

She let out a sad, ironic laugh. Even in his lust she could find no real compliment. For his main purpose in keeping her was not for lust, but to lure Rhys into his trap. He'd had to let Rhys go to ensure Isolde's safety. But he would not let Rhonwen go until he had Rhys back.

To complicate the situation even further, should Rhys some- how manage to elude Jasper and set her free, then *he* would expect an appropriate gratitude from her.

Rhonwen stared at the embroidery, then slowly began to pluck at it, following the tiny knots to their source and pains- takingly unraveling what she'd done. What if she escaped on her own? She would then be beholden to no one. But where would she go? Back to her mother and her stepfather's house- hold? There was nothing for her there.

And therein lay the true source of her dilemma—and Isolde's dilemma, and that of every other woman. She had no way to live on her own. Under her parents' roof, or her hus- band's, or the Church's—those were the meager choices women had.

Or remain a captive in another man's household, she thought.

She lowered the embroidery to her lap. There must be an- other way, a life and livelihood she was overlooking.

At that moment Enid reentered the solar. She made a slow circuit of the chamber, putting an armful of clean linen into a chest, replacing candle stubs from the fresh supply of candles in her pocket, and checking the water pitcher used for ablu- tions. She did not at first notice Rhonwen as she performed her tasks, humming under her breath. When Rhonwen shifted, however, the stout Englishwoman gasped, then frowned.

"What are ye doin' in here alone? Does milady know?"

"Lady Josselyn sent me here, not that it's any concern of yours. Go about your business," Rhonwen replied crossly.

The woman harrumphed, then did as she was told. But Rhonwen watched her and considered the maid's situation. She had a roof over her head, food enough to sustain her, and a very few silver pennies paid to her every quarterday. In truth, that was more than any wife or daughter received. Perhaps taking service was the alternative she sought, if only until something better presented itself.

Jasper did not like the way Josselyn studied him. "May I see Rand's missive?" he asked. She handed it to him without speaking, then watched him the whole while he read it.

"Rand plays a dangerous game with LaMonthe," he muttered.

"What do you mean by that?"

Jasper grimaced. He hadn't meant to alarm her. "Just that I do not trust LaMonthe to do what he says."

She frowned. "Nor do I. But would he go so far as to profess support for Matilda and then betray her?"

"The man is more like to pledge allegiance to both Stephen and Matilda, then watch and see which of them can benefit him most." He thought for a moment. "LaMonthe does not concern himself with matters of the English kingdom. 'Tis his own kingdom here in Wales that he seeks to strengthen. To ally himself with us or any of the other Marcher lords allows him to probe our weaknesses. Do not forget. He is rumored to have hastened the death of his wife's father. And his brother-in-law, sent by him on an errand to Chester, was killed in a tavern brawl."

"And the lands under LaMonthe's control increased." Josselyn's fingers wove nervously together. "Does Rand hide anything from me, Jasper? I implore you to tell me if he does, for I cannot be a true helpmate to him if I do not fully share his burdens."

Jasper covered her hands with his. "He keeps no secrets from you, Josselyn. But if you would help him, then do not fight him in the matter of fostering Gavin and finding a husband for Isolde." She stiffened, but he held her firmly. "He seeks only to ensure their future, and that of Rosecliffe."

"Is that what you do as well? Is that why you hold Rhonwen captive?"

He released her hands. " 'Tis Rhys I want. 'Tis he I will eventually hold in Rosecliffe's dungeon."

"To keep Rosecliffe safe."

"What other reason is there?"

She shrugged. "I don't know. I only wish . . . I wish there were a way to peace between you and Rhys."

Jasper ran a hand through his hair and sighed. "I killed his father, Josselyn. I pulled the bow and released the arrow and he will never let that go. That it was to save you matters nothing to him."

"Yes, I know. But I cannot help believing that in time he could come to see it differently. That he could come to see the benefit of the Welsh and English living together in peace. Together we are stronger than we are apart. Rand and I are better together than we ever were singly. Certainly Carreg Du is a better place to live since Rosecliffe Castle and the village outside have grown up."

"Rhys is too hotheaded to care about that."

"But he does care about Rhonwen."

It was Jasper's turn to stiffen. "I am well aware of that, and I plan to use that knowledge to defeat him."

"I wonder . . ." she said, after a moment. "I wonder whether that is, in fact, *why* you wish to defeat him. To prove to her which one of you is the better man."

"She has nothing to do with this," he muttered.

"Indeed? I think she has everything to do with it, going back ten years, even, to the day she saved your life."

"Rhonwen saved my hand, not my life. And even that was only to protect you. She did not care about my life then or since. She has boasted as much to me. Do you forget that she tried to kill me? That she kidnapped your own daughter?"

Josselyn folded her arms. "I forget nothing. Not her bravery as a child, nor Rhys's."

"They are no longer children, Josselyn. The game they play now is a dangerous one, as is the game you play."

"I play no games. What do you mean?"

He stared at her innocent-looking face. "Why do you shape Rhonwen into an English lady?"

She met his suspicious stare without blinking. "So that when she returns to Rhys she can have a civilizing effect on him."

Quick anger made him sharp. "She will never return to him," he vowed.

Her brows arched and she smiled knowingly. "So. You plan to keep her for yourself?"

"I plan to release her once I have Rhys ap Owain. Do not

make her presence here into something more than it is.''

''Very well,'' she said, waving one hand dismissively. ''Do as you will and I will do the same. But beware, dear brother, that you do not get caught in your own trap.''

She departed then, and Jasper watched her leave the hall. But her words would not so easily go, for Jasper feared they were prophetic. Already he felt ensnared by the wild and beautiful hostage he kept. When he'd seen her today, descending the stairs, radiant in that close-fitting violet-colored gown, he'd been struck dumb. With the air of a queen and the breathtaking beauty of an angel, she'd leveled all his defenses and roused all his desires.

Thank God she'd stumbled, else there was no telling how he would have embarrassed himself.

But he could not rely on that sort of intervention to strengthen him in the future. Eventually she would master the full skirts of English garb. Eventually her wild Welsh spirit would be cloaked in English manners and reserve.

But he knew already what passions lurked in her heart. Disguising them would only sharpen his need to reveal them again.

God help him when she figured that out!

Thirteen

Rhys ap Owain sat his horse in the middle of a rough meadow, midway between Afon Bryn and the River Geffen. His compatriots lined the north edge of the field, where the coarse grasses met the encroaching forest. Across the sloping meadow to the south, an indistinct line of English men-at-arms moved out of the shadowy tree line, then halted.

The time had come, Rhys thought. If this was a trick LaMonthe planned, to lure the thin ranks of Welsh rebels out, then slaughter them, the signal would come momentarily. His hands tightened on the leather reins as unaccustomed panic burned up from his stomach and into his throat. His horse snorted and tossed its head nervously, and Rhys fought the urge to bolt for the safety of the wildwood.

He was too young to die. He had too much yet left undone. He had Rhonwen to set free.

A rider broke from the trees. Rhys squinted to see, but the sun was in his eyes. LaMonthe had planned that, he realized. Just a small disadvantage to the Welsh, but a telling one. Still, the man rode at an easy canter, and when he pulled his horse to a halt five paces distant, wariness displaced Rhys's earlier panic. This might not be a trick after all. Still, the English lord wanted something. Since Rhys did not usually roam the lands LaMonthe controlled, the man had to be an emissary from

FitzHugh, no matter that his messenger had sworn he was not.

LaMonthe studied him impassively. "Is it true you are but ten and six?" He spoke in Welsh.

"My age is like to my rage," Rhys sneered. "As old as these hills."

A faint smile thinned the man's lips. LaMonthe was pale of skin and pale of eye. A bloodless English bastard whom Rhys would as soon skewer as look at. But he'd arranged this meeting for a reason, and Rhys was curious enough to be patient.

"You are said to be brave beyond your years."

"You speak like an old man. 'Tis my youth that *makes* me brave," Rhys countered disdainfully. "Old men fear the approach of death, and so they cower before their hearths, hoping to fend it off. But young men fear only the miserable lives proscribed for them. And so we are brave and daring and not cowed by the enemy who would keep us in our misery." He met LaMonthe's unblinking gaze with a frigid one. "If you come to parlay for FitzHugh, then give him this answer." He spit on the ground between them. "He is a coward who hides behind a woman. Well, I will make a woman of him!"

LaMonthe lifted a hand. "Hold. Hold!" he said, chuckling.

"You laugh at my solemn vow?" Rhys's hand whipped to the hilt of his sword, but LaMonthe was not alarmed.

"Listen to me, boy," he growled. "Listen and learn and do not disappoint my faith in you."

Rhys glared at him. "I do not covet your faith in me."

"But you do covet the lands FitzHugh has wrested from your people."

When Rhys did not respond to that, the man smiled again, a smug stretch of narrow lips over uneven teeth. The feral grimace of a beast of prey. But Rhys understood at once that this beast meant to prey on his own kind. LaMonthe had not come to aid FitzHugh's cause. He'd come to undermine it.

Rhys schooled his features so as not to reveal his contempt for such a man. If LaMonthe's betrayal could benefit Rhys— and Rhonwen—what care had he for the man's morality? "I want FitzHugh ousted. In that you are right. But what interest have you in that?"

"I too would have him ousted." LaMonthe was silent a moment. "There are ways we might join forces to better achieve our common goal."

"My goal is to oust him, but not so that another Englishman might take his place."

"Aid me in this and Rosecliffe Castle will be yours."

Rhys stared at him suspiciously. "Why do you seek his defeat, if not to claim his fortress and his lands?"

"My motives are my own," LaMonthe snapped.

"And I do not trust them," Rhys bit back at him. "I will not fight your battles for you, only to have you cut me and my men down."

They stared across the short distance between them. Rhys's horse tossed its head. In the distance the cry of a hunting falcon pierced the strained silence. Then LaMonthe shrugged.

"FitzHugh is the one man who can sway—or bully—the other lords of the Marches. With him gone they will bend to my will."

Rhys snorted. "Is that knowledge meant to reassure me that you will leave Rosecliffe in my hands? For I tell you, it does not."

"Do you want Rosecliffe Castle or not, boy? Once Fitz-Hugh is gone, it will be yours—yours to hold and defend like any other lord defends his demesne. But the man who controls Rosecliffe will not easily be removed from power. The place is a fortress and impenetrable. It must be undermined from within. 'Tis Randulf FitzHugh's death I want, not his castle."

"Randulf FitzHugh?" Rhys blurted out.

LaMonthe cocked his head to one side. "Yes, Randulf FitzHugh, Lord of Rosecliffe. Who do you think I—Aha! Now I understand. 'Tis not Rand who provokes your ire, but his brother. Jasper."

Rhys did not bother to lie. "Our enemies are not strictly the same, but it appears our goals are."

"Good," LaMonthe said. "Good. I want Randulf FitzHugh gone. You want Jasper gone. But the fact remains: The castle must be undermined from within."

From within. Yes, Rhys knew that. Then, once overrun by

Welshmen, no Englishman could retake Rosecliffe, not even LaMonthe. But the only person inside Rosecliffe who was loyal to his cause was Rhonwen, and he was loath to risk her safety. Still, the very thought of her in Jasper FitzHugh's clutches drove any thought of caution from his mind.

"Rand is absent the castle."

"And en route to Oaken Hill," LaMonthe supplied.

"Can you prolong his absence?"

LaMonthe pursed his lips. "I can."

Rhys swept the meadow with his eyes, thinking. Considering. "I have someone in the castle. A prisoner."

"What good is that?"

Rhys allowed a small smile. It was painful to remember Rhonwen's beauty and her bravery, knowing Jasper FitzHugh held her completely at his mercy. But he would free her, he vowed, and then that beauty would be his.

They would rule Rosecliffe Castle together, and people it with fine Welsh babes. He met LaMonthe's skeptical gaze.

"She is more than a prisoner," he vowed. "She is a beautiful prisoner and Jasper is infatuated with her."

LaMonthe's feral grin showed again. "And she is loyal to you?"

"Aye," Rhys swore, convincing himself it was so. "She is completely loyal to me."

"Velvet must always be brushed," Josselyn explained, handing the forest-green gown to Rhonwen. "Water can ruin the lay of the pile."

"Let me try," Rhonwen said. Holding the clothes brush as she'd seen the maid do, she attacked the dried mud on the hem of the luxurious garment.

"That's very good. Very good," Josselyn murmured as the silk pile slowly raised back to its former plushness.

Rhonwen smiled down at the soft fabric in her lap. For the past three days she'd applied herself to the lessons of household and manners. Three days that had pleased the bemused Josselyn and filled some of the emptiness inside Rhonwen. She did it not to satisfy Josselyn, however, nor even to fill her restless hours. Nor did she do it to aid Rhys's cause by deluding her captors into relaxing their guard. She did it for herself, for her future, which heretofore had seemed so bleak. She was learning a skill, one she could sell to a wealthy family, and she wouldn't care if they were English or Welsh.

She bent over the velvet, brushing the dried stain, first in one direction, then in the other. Once she was free of Rosecliffe, she would depart these hills of her childhood. She considered her choices every night as she lay in the small chamber given her—the small locked chamber—and she'd come to a hard conclusion. Once she was freed she must somehow make her way to Llangollen or Betws-y-coed or some other fair-sized town, and take service in a household there.

She paused a moment and sighed. She would be alone and far removed from the world she knew. Then again, there was no reason for her to stay here. Certainly there was no husband for her to build a home with, nor was there likely to be.

"Rhonwen?" Josselyn laid a hand on her shoulder. "Is aught amiss with you?"

Rhonwen started, then returned earnestly to her task. "My mind wandered a moment. That is all. Here. Is this well cleaned?"

Josselyn spread the lustrous velvet smooth. " 'Tis very well, indeed. Just as your efforts at spinning, at scenting the candles, and at mixing herbs for the rushes have been very well performed. I confess to a curiosity, however. Your resistance to my efforts has vanished of late."

"And you wonder why."

"I do."

Rhonwen stood and shook out the gown, then began carefully to roll it up as Josselyn taught her, sprinkling dried lavender inside the garment and smoothing out the folds as she went. There was no reason not to be honest. Josselyn might have some advice on how she might go about finding a suitable position.

"I have decided to take work in a rich man's household. That is," she added with a snort, "I will do so whenever Jasper sees fit to set me free. So long as I remain at Rosecliffe it seems the wisest course for me to learn everything I can.''

Josselyn nodded. "I see. 'Tis a wise plan. But what of Jasper? And of Rhys?"

Rhonwen frowned. "They are two men bent on destroying one another. I cannot prevent what will surely occur. Nor do I wish to witness it," she added in a lower tone.

Josselyn was quiet a moment, then waved the two maids in the solar away. Only when the oak door closed with a quiet thud did she speak. "Jasper vows that he will not let you go until he has recaptured Rhys. You cannot avoid witnessing their clash."

Rhonwen threw her hands up in dismay. "Do you *want* them to meet in battle, Josselyn? Do you *want* one of them to kill the other?"

"Of course not. But they are both stubborn. They hate one another—and they both want you."

Rhonwen turned away and walked to the tall, narrow window, wrapping her arms around herself. "Well, I do not want either of them."

"I see."

"I mean what I say. I do not want either of them. They are bent on vengeance and each of them sees me only as a tool he might use against the other."

"Surely you do not believe that. I know Jasper sees you as more than a tool for his vengeance."

"He does not! He behaves as if I do not exist! He'd rather me banished to the dungeon than be given the freedom of the keep as you insisted. He hates me," she finished, in a voice that came precariously close to trembling.

Josselyn chuckled knowingly. "Jasper is well aware of your existence. Trust me in this. If he behaves otherwise, I assure you it is not because he hates you."

But that was no consolation. Rhonwen bent her head, letting her hair swing forward to cover her hot cheeks. "You think that because he . . . because he lusts after me that he does not hate me. But you are wrong. He wants me only because of Rhys. And he hates me all the more because he wants me!"

At that Josselyn began to laugh in earnest. Rhonwen whirled

around. "Is my unhappy existence such an amusement to you? I assure you, I do not think it so!"

"Not amusing, no," Josselyn said, managing to repress her laughter but not her smile. "You but suffer the terrible pangs of love—"

"I do not!"

"—as does he."

"He does not!"

But Josselyn was not listening. She went on. "Love is much like birthing a babe. It takes time to grow, and comes to fruition only amidst much pain."

"Women are known to die in the process," Rhonwen snapped. She hoisted herself up into the window well and stared gloomily across the valley.

"Is that it?" Josselyn asked, her voice soft and kind. "Do you feel as if you will die from the love stoppered inside your heart?"

Rhonwen shook her head. She could not answer with words, for words could not make sense of the knot of emotions she felt. "I do not love him," she finally whispered. "I only endure my captivity and prepare for the day when I may leave here."

"As you say," Josselyn replied after a moment. "I applaud your efforts to improve yourself, and so will help you any way I can. When the time comes for you to go, I will write you a letter of introduction to aid you in your search for a position in a good household."

Rhonwen looked over at her. She hadn't thought of that, and despite their angry exchange, she gave Josselyn a small, grateful smile. "Thank you. But I beg you," she added, "do not reveal my intentions to him."

"To Jasper?"

Rhonwen nodded. "So long as I am his hostage he controls my fate. But when I am freed, my life will be my own. He need not know my plans, for they do not concern him."

"What if he makes them his concern?"

Rhonwen met her friend's teasing gaze with a solemn mien. "He will not. You would play at matchmaker, Josselyn, but

it is a foolhardy game, with only pain to come of it. I fear
they will fight to the death, these two. Whatever the results of
their struggle, I will be left to mourn one of them—and despise the other.''

Jasper spent three days away from the castle. Daily he visited
the Welsh village Carreg Du, sweeping the fields and woods
with his men, searching for any sign of Welsh rebels in the
area. When he found none, relief was nearly as strong as disappointment.

He wanted the cocky Rhys. He wanted him in Rosecliffe's
gaol as an example to rebels not satisfied with the peace and
prosperity Rosecliffe Castle had brought to this portion of
Wales. He wanted Rhonwen to see that the boy was not only
a liar, but a failure as well. He wanted her to see that failure,
and he wanted to drive out any affection she might still harbor
for the boy.

When he caught Rhys, though, he would have no choice
but to set Rhonwen free. He'd have no reason to hold her, and
anyway, Josselyn would never condone it. So he acknowledged the reason for his relief, but at the same time berated
himself for it. What purpose did keeping her at Rosecliffe
achieve if he avoided being anywhere near her?

As he rode now up the road to Rosecliffe, he studied the
castle with a dispassionate eye. It was a fine fortress, well
sited, with stout, impregnable walls. It was a credit to England,
but more especially, a credit to Rand, who continued to add
towers and fortifications to it. And like the handsome castle,
the lands surrounding were a credit to Rand's foresight and
perseverance.

But would Rand have succeeded half so well had he not
wed a Welsh maiden?

How much of the peace and prosperity of Rosecliffe was
due to the contentment Josselyn and Rand shared?

Fool! he chastised himself. It was more than merely contentment those two shared. Their love was real, apparent in
every look, in every touch. Even when they fought. They had
passion, but they also had love.

Could he have that with any woman?

Could he have it with Rhonwen?

He shoved his cowl back from his sweaty hair and leaned forward. His weary animal responded at once, laboring up the hill, then thundering across the timber bridge.

Damnation, but that woman was driving him mad! He threw himself down from the horse, tossed the reins to a waiting page, and strode angrily toward the keep.

He would not be kept out of his own home. He would not be denied the release necessary to any normal man. She was his prisoner and he wanted her—and Josselyn be damned!

Firm in his purpose, he slammed into the great hall, then stopped short. Young Gwendolyn sat in a tub before the hearth, howling as if she were being tortured. Rhonwen scrubbed the unhappy child's hair. But Rhonwen hadn't been able to control the soap. It had seeped into Gwen's eyes, and the child was inconsolable.

"Just rinse," Josselyn told Rhonwen. "She's clean enough. Just rinse her hair and her eyes."

"I'm not gettin' into that tub," Gavin vowed from his position near the door to the pantler's closet. "I had a bath not a week ago. And I'm not even dirty!"

"You smell like a whole litter of swine," his mother countered. "You are next."

"But Mama!" he implored. Then he spied Jasper and immediately bolted his way. "Uncle. Tell her! 'Tis embarrassing to be bathed like a child, in plain view of everyone. I'm nearly a man!"

"You're only seven years old," Josselyn said, planting her hands on her hips.

But Jasper was not interested in the war of wills between Josselyn and her son. It was Rhonwen he'd come for, and Rhonwen his eyes sought. She'd finished dousing Gwen and the child's wails had subsided to childish sniffles.

"Am I finished yet?"

"Yes, sweetling, you are," Rhonwen said, averting her startled gaze from Jasper's searching one. "Here, stand up and I'll wrap this length of toweling around you."

"I'm cold," the child complained, standing up in the tub. "Hurry."

"You see!" Gavin interrupted. "You see? I'm not standing up naked in front of a lot of women."

But Josselyn would have none of his argument. While Rhonwen lifted Gwen from the tub, then efficiently rubbed her down, Josselyn crossed to Gavin and Jasper. "Remove your clothes and get in that tub this very minute, else I will have Rhonwen perform the task for you."

"But Mama!" he cried, ducking behind Jasper.

"Would that I could take his place," Jasper muttered. Just the thought of Rhonwen stripping his clothes from his skin, then bathing him with warm, soapy hands pushed any other thought from his brain. He could feel the rush of blood to his loins, and he had to fight to keep his voice calm. "I'm dirty and tired, and in need of the ministrations of a competent housewife."

"Indeed?" Josselyn said, her brows arching with interest. "Heretofore you've taken your baths elsewhere. But if you're willing . . ." She glanced back at Rhonwen. "Perhaps it would be a good lesson for both Rhonwen and Gavin. Yes," she decided, grinning. "Gavin, fetch another bucket of hot water. You will see now how a man behaves at his bath. And Rhonwen, you will learn the proper way to bathe a male guest, a task you are certain to find useful in the future."

"Hold on," Jasper said, realizing the bath his imagination had conjured was not the bath Josselyn intended him to have. "I did not expect an audience."

"Such modesty," she teased. "But if you wish it, we will position the screens. Come, now, Jasper. You are not known for your modesty. You need a bath and Rhonwen needs to learn how to bathe a man."

He scowled, first at Josselyn, then at Rhonwen. He'd spoken unwisely and now he was torn. "Why does she have to learn that?"

"So she may—" Josselyn broke off when Rhonwen gasped. Some silent communication passed between the two women before Josselyn continued. "It is a part of the educa-

tion of every young woman in a proper household. I told you
I meant to make her into a lady and that your assistance might
be required. Well, your assistance is required now, and anyway, 'twas your own suggestion. If you're concerned she will
not do a good job, I assure you, she's been most adept at every
other task I've set her. I'm confident she can learn to scrub
you down in a manner to your liking.''

Jasper stared at Josselyn. She was a witch, a devious witch
who obviously enjoyed torturing people, for she'd done this
to him before. The first time it had been Rhonwen bathing and
him suffering agonies knowing she was so near. This time
their roles were reversed.

He was not certain which situation was worse.

Now, though he wanted to renege on his hasty offer, he
could not find his voice. Josselyn's careful choice of words
had made certain of that. To have Rhonwen scrub him down
in a manner to his liking was a lure far too powerful to ignore.

His jaw worked back and forth as he glared at Josselyn. But
she deflected his ill humor with a smug grin. She clapped her
hands at Gavin, sending him about his task. Then she turned
to Rhonwen.

''Here. I will dress Gwendolyn and finish drying her hair.
You set out fresh towels and soaps as I instructed before.''
She took Gwen from Rhonwen, who stared at the older
woman, slack-jawed.

''As for you, Jasper,'' she continued, ''come over here. Do
not remove your sword or cowl or any other of your garb.
Rhonwen must learn all those tasks. It may take a little longer
this first time. But be patient. You will be rewarded with a
bath I'm certain you will never forget.''

Fourteen

Rhonwen gripped the length of thick, bleached toweling so tightly her fingers hurt. Why was Josselyn behaving so? Why was Jasper allowing it?'

But she could guess the answer to that. She'd taunted him at her bath in the kitchen that time, boldly displaying herself and offering him the use of her body if he would just abandon his battle with Rhys. It had been a foolish gesture, she now knew. But it seemed he meant to make her pay for it.

She watched as Gavin dumped another bucket of hot water into the tub. He was obviously relieved that the water was for Jasper, and not himself. "Come along," the boy said, looking at her. "We have to move the screens into place."

Together they positioned the wood and tapestry screens to shield the tub from whomever might enter the spacious hall. Then, with the water hot and the myriad bathing accoutrements in place, Rhonwen had no further reason for delay. Yet still she hesitated.

Gavin perched on a stool next to the massive hearth, poking idly at the coals, oblivious to the byplay between the adults. Josselyn sat near him on an upholstered bench, holding Gwen in her lap as she dried the child's fine dark curls. After setting everything in motion, the woman had become suspiciously unconcerned.

Rhonwen took a slow, steadying breath. She could manage this. With everyone so close at hand, there was nothing to fear. Nothing untoward could pass between Jasper and her. Not that Jasper appeared at the moment even remotely so inclined. If anything, the harsh set of his mouth indicated quite the opposite.

Unfortunately that only deepened Rhonwen's despair. What did the man want of her? No matter what she did, she seemed never able to please him. She was either too reticent or too forward. Too difficult or too obliging.

She clenched her teeth and faced Jasper. "Come over here, then. Let us begin."

"Now, now," Josselyn interrupted in mild reproval. "A better approach is to invite your honored guest to partake of the bath. Never demand his cooperation. Request it."

Rhonwen pursed her lips in irritation, then forced a false note of civility into her voice. "Your bath is prepared, milord. Might I assist you with your clothing?"

"Much better," Josselyn murmured. She began to comb Gwendolyn's hair.

After an awkward silence, Jasper responded in a grudging voice. "Thank you." He moved nearer the softly steaming tub and halted, and another silence ensued.

"Start with his weapons first," Josselyn instructed. "And progress layer by layer. The last garment should be his small cloth." At Rhonwen's look of consternation, she added, "You should turn your back and allow him to remove it himself. Once he is in the water, you can then begin his bath."

It proved not too difficult to remove his sword. The ornately designed buckle that fastened it around his lean hips was well sprung, and it released easily. She laid the heavy weapon and finely tooled belt aside, but then she was confronted with his cowl of chain mail. She stood face-to-face with him, lifting her arms to his shoulders, until he obliging bent forward.

Her heart pounded a fierce rhythm. This was so like an amorous embrace. But his frown made it clear it was not am-

orous for him. He would not even meet her eyes. So she
tugged the mail cowl over his head and, with shaky hands,
laid it aside. His cape was no easier, for it was pinned at his
throat and she had to stand unbearably near him to unfasten
the intricate brooch that held it closed.

Would this torture never cease?

But it had only just begun, and with every successive garment, her torture increased. His tunic was next, heavy and
warm with the heat of his body. He stood rigid, his eyes shuttered, his expression pained. He saved her asking his aid, however, and it was fortunate, for she was certain she had no voice
to speak. He held out his arms, then bent at the waist so she
could tug his tunic over his head.

If his tunic was warm, his chainse was even more so, and
it was damp from his exertions of the day. Worse, as she
loosened the ties at his wrists, she smelled the familiar scent
of him, of horses and leather and sweat. Of virility.

As she reached for the hem of the loose linen garment, the
trembling in her hands transmitted to her entire body. Dear
God, she was not sure she could view his naked torso and
function, all at the same time.

"No, no. His boots and hose next." Josselyn's instructions
came none too soon.

Rhonwen gasped in relief, then ducked her head to hide her
flaming cheeks. "Sit down," she croaked out.

"If you please," Josselyn prompted.

"If you please," she managed to echo.

He sat on a three-legged stool beside the tub, then looked
up, and for a moment their eyes met. For that moment, so
fleeting she might have imagined it, she saw past the guard
he'd erected to a desire that seethed perilously near eruption.
She saw it, and though he blinked and it was hidden once
more, she knew she had not imagined it. He hated her, but he
also desired her—and he did not want anyone to see that unhappy duality. Least of all her.

She knelt down and focused her attention on his heavy
leather knee boots, while her pulse thundered in her ears. He
felt much as she did, and like her, he struggled mightily to

bury the inappropriate desire that burned inside him. Were it not for Josselyn's determined interference, they might both manage this awkwardness far easier. Still, there was no use denying that desire existed for both of them. That could not be blamed solely on Josselyn.

Rhonwen forced herself to a calm she did not truly feel, then took hold of the first boot.

"Perhaps I should do this part," Jasper said.

"No," Josselyn replied from her seat by the fire. "Let her do it. Let her learn how to wait upon a nobleman."

"Why should she learn such a thing?" Jasper demanded to know. "How likely is she to wait upon any noblemen in the future?" He lurched up from the stool and stepped past Rhonwen.

For her part Rhonwen bowed her head and drew in great draughts of air. She'd been given a reprieve.

But not by Josselyn.

"Think, Jasper. What does the future hold for a woman with no wealth or property to commend her? Rhonwen has no father to look after her, and so she must be grateful if any man offers for her. What if none offers for her? Without a husband her choices are limited. She can try to find a place in the Church and hope one of the holy orders will take a penniless woman, or else seek employment in a noble household."

She ignored Rhonwen's dismayed gasp at that revelation. "At least she recognizes her need for employment," Josselyn continued. "Her confinement at Rosecliffe allows her to learn skills she otherwise might never gain. Since none of us has the ability to foresee what future awaits her, it behooves her to learn whatever she can while she is here."

The older woman's eyes glinted stubbornly. "You need a bath. She needs to learn how to bathe a man. So sit down and let her do it."

Rhonwen's eyes darted back and forth between the iron-willed Josselyn and the furious Jasper. Surely Jasper would win this battle, for Josselyn could hardly force him to bathe if he did not wish it.

They glared at one another in silence until Josselyn muttered a Welsh curse under her breath. "Very well, then. Perhaps someone else will be willing. Gavin, send for Sir Louis."

The boy had been watching the confrontation between his uncle and his mother with considerable interest. But at Josselyn's order he jumped up. "Yes, Mother," he said, heading past the screen for the door.

"Hold!" Jasper muttered. "Hold on, Gavin."

Josselyn crossed her arms and arched her brows. " 'Tis you or Sir Louis. Make your decision before the water chills." To Rhonwen she added, "Sir Louis is master of the stables."

"You mean he is a randy old goat," Jasper growled.

"I'm sure I know nothing about that," Josselyn replied with a smug smile.

"Bloody hell!" Jasper swore.

"Do not speak so in front of my children," Josselyn admonished him, clamping her hands over Gwendolyn's ears. She glanced at her son, who'd already edged nearer the door. "You are dismissed, Gavin. 'Tis plain you'll learn little from your uncle's behavior this day. But take your sister with you. Bring her to the nursery."

Gavin hurried to the door, clearly grateful to put distance between himself and any hint of a bath. Once the children were gone Josselyn fixed Jasper and Rhonwen with her narrowed gaze. "Get on with it now."

Rhonwen waited, gnawing her lower lip, and finally Jasper sat down and she approached him once more. She took his boot in her hands and tugged it free, then removed the other as well. Efficient movements, she instructed herself. Like washing clothes and churning butter. Perform this task as you would any other.

Easy to say; harder to do. Impossible, when she began to roll his stockings down. His calves were strongly muscled. His ankles hard and bony. His feet, humble appendages though they ought to be, fascinated her. Large, well shaped.

She jerked the finely woven hose off his last foot and flung it at the growing pile of his soiled garments. Oh, but she must be mad! That was the only explanation for such a perverse reaction to the man's feet. His feet, for pity's sake! She had to complete this bath of his before she truly lost her mind.

She snatched up the hem of his chainse and when he obligingly lifted his arms, she tugged the supple garment over his head. She kept her eyes determinedly cast down, but she knew he was naked, save for his hips and legs. "Stand up. If you please," she added, none too graciously. Would this never end?

He stood and she took a deep breath. She raised her eyes, intending only to locate the ties for his braies. Unfortunately, what she saw was a broad, muscled chest and lean, rippling stomach. A dark, curling patch of hair shadowed his chest, then arrowed down the center of his stomach toward the ties— and toward a suspicious bulge beneath the bunched wool of his braies.

Rhonwen's eyes jerked up to his—a huge mistake. For after that, there was nothing left of efficiency in her actions. She reached for the ties with hands that shook and fingers that fumbled. When she somehow managed to release the knot, she pulled the tie too hard and it slid completely free of its casing. As she stood there, holding the limp strip of cord, the braies sagged, then slid down over his hips.

She looked away, but not soon enough. She heard Josselyn behind her, rearranging the logs on the hearth. But beside the waiting tub there was no sound save, perhaps, the collapse of Rhonwen's willpower.

She turned away as Josselyn had said she should. She heard the harsh escape of his breath, then his soft curse as he removed the straining small cloth. The water splashed as he stepped into the tub, and sloshed over the sides when he sat. But still she could not turn around.

She stared instead at the uneven distribution of rushes strewn across the floor, and tried to recall Josselyn's instruction for the proportions of dried straw to aromatic herbs. She spied the small iron pot of simmering herbs and recited the favored ingredients: cedar bark and dried rose petals and mint. But her desperate efforts at distraction were for naught. One thought only dominated her mind: Jasper sat naked behind her.

"Go on," Josselyn urged. "There is no room for modesty, for you must work quickly, especially in cold weather when the water loses its warmth so swiftly."

Slowly Rhonwen turned. Her fate had been decided, she realized, and struggling against it was fruitless. She was fated to desire her enemy, no matter that she was but a tool in his plans to subjugate her people. That he was similarly fated and fought his desire for her was bitter comfort. The truth remained that she was here, in his power, though thankfully under the watchful eyes of Josselyn. And right now, in order to escape his overpowering nearness, she must first bathe him.

She reached for a cloth and the square of soap, steeling herself. "Shall I begin with your hair, milord, or with your . . . your person?"

Jasper's jaw ached from clenching it so hard. But that pain was nothing to the pain of repressed desire. And he must now endure her hands on his bare skin? Her small, soapy hands on his slick, overheated flesh?

He slid under the water, ducking his head, wishing he did not ever have to surface.

When he came up she repeated the question more haltingly. "Your hair or your—"

"My hair," he snapped. "Do my hair first."

Across the room Josselyn looked up at his words, a smile curving her lips. Damn her for an interfering witch, he silently swore. If she thought to escape his wrath she was sore mistaken.

Then Rhonwen touched his head and his anger at his brother's scheming wife vanished. Rhonwen had lathered her hands and now, with a tentative touch, she began to wash his hair.

Her fingers were slender but they were strong, and Jasper had to remind himself to breathe. The water steamed and lapped at the sides of the tub, the soap smelled of chamomile, and her fingers stroked every portion of his scalp. He subsided against the back of the tub and she knelt down just behind him.

"You needn't be so easy with him," Josselyn instructed. "Scrub harder. He will inform you if you're too rough."

The pressure of her fingers increased. Her short nails scraped his scalp. Her movements yanked at his hair.

"Sorry," she muttered after a particularly sharp tug.

"It's all right," he answered hoarsely. Pain was good, for it distracted him from how obscenely delicious this felt. "Don't forget my ears," he added, immediately cursing himself for a madman. When her soapy fingers rubbed his temples, then slid behind his ears, he groaned. He'd been bathed before and enjoyed it well. But he'd never feared to die from the pure pleasure of it.

"Duck your head," she said, her voice soft and breathy. He did, then nearly choked on a huge gulp of water when her hands followed him down, threading through his hair to rinse it.

He lurched up, sputtering and shaking water from his eyes. "Jesus God," he swore.

There was a muffled laugh from Josselyn, and Jasper glared at her, murder in his eyes. But she only grinned and stood. "I think you've got the idea, Rhonwen, so I'll leave you now to finish the task. When you are done here, seek me out in my solar." Then she swept from the room as if she were not in the least worried that he might have more than bathing on his mind.

What was she up to? Jasper wondered. The curtains swished behind her and a gust of outside air raised goosebumps on his flesh. But it did nothing to cool his desire for the woman left behind.

He glanced over his shoulder at Rhonwen. She knelt as she had before, following Josselyn's exit with worried eyes. Then she looked back at him, and he admitted to himself that she had every reason to worry. He was hard and frustrated, and his bath had just begun.

And there was only one way this could end.

"Finish your task," he ordered her, cursing himself for a

perverse fool. "Bathe my body." Then he faced forward again and waited.

He did not have to wait long. She leaned nearer him. Though he could not see her movement, he sensed it. She dipped the cloth in the bathwater and soaped it with little slurping sounds. Then she began to lather his shoulders.

Her touch was exquisite. The warm water, the rough cloth, her smooth fingers. She scrubbed his back and neck, massaging the tense muscles there. Then she reached past his shoulders to wash his chest. It was strangely anonymous and erotic, two disembodied hands ministering to him. But it was also exquisitely personal. Only Rhonwen had the ability to rouse him so completely.

He caught her wrists and pulled so that her breast collided with his soapy back. "Wash lower," he muttered, hardly able to speak. He slid her hands down his chest, forcing her to shift position. He felt her palms open against his stomach, and the slide of her full breasts up toward his shoulders as she bent over him. Curling tendrils worked their way loose from her bound hair and tickled his ear. The slender strength of her body stoked the fire in him further still.

"Lower," he ordered in a pained voice.

Against his shoulders he felt every breath she took. He held each of her wrists in his grip and forced her hands in slow circles on his stomach. He wanted to let go, to allow her to take over the movement, to feel her instigate an erotic exploration of his body. But he was afraid to release her, afraid she would pull away.

"Why do you do this?" she murmured, her breath caressing his ear.

His hold on her wrists tightened. "Because I must." Then he twisted sideways, drawing her around the tub so they were face-to-face. Her cheeks were flushed with desire. Her eyes were bright with it. "I want you," he pressed her. "And you want me."

"And Josselyn obviously approves," she threw in bitterly. "How fortunate that we are all in accord. But her goals are not the same as your goals, are they? Are they?"

"What she wants is not important. Josselyn is not a part of this."

"She thinks she can force us to wed, Jasper. She throws us together like this so we will . . . so we will . . ."

"Make love?"

She looked away. "What other reason could there be? She's training me in the ways of an English lady. If she catches us in a compromising position, she will force you—"

"She cannot force me to do anything. Nor can Rand."

It was the wrong thing to say, an exceedingly stupid thing to say, and he could have kicked himself for it. But once said, Jasper could not take the words back. Rhonwen recoiled as if from a blow, and when she jerked her hands from his, he let her go.

"Ah, damn. I'm sorry, Rhonwen."

"No. No, there is no need to apologize for the truth. You do not want me for a bride, and I do not want you for a husband." She stood, crossing her arms across the wet front of her kirtle.

She did not want him for a husband. That came as no surprise, and yet the words still stung. "Who do you want for a husband?

"Why should I want a husband at all?"

"Rhys?" he persisted. "He wants you."

"My future is none of your concern. Why do you torment me so?" She let out a frustrated breath and shook her head. "We would the both of us be better served working to thwart Josselyn than allowing her to torture us this way."

She stood there, hurt and unhappy, stricken and yet beautiful in a way that defied description. There were other women as fair of face, as feminine in form. But Rhonwen was more than that. Everything she'd said was true. He should not allow Josselyn's machinations to trap him. And yet he could not stop himself.

"Are you tortured, Rhonwen? Are you as tortured by desire as am I?"

She closed her eyes and a shudder wracked her slender body. "Please, Jasper. Enough of this."

"But I need more. More of you."

"More of me?" She shook her head. "What you want is a whore. A mistress. A leman, or whatever you English term it. But I cannot be that for you. I will not."

Jasper grasped the sides of the tub, ready to lunge at her, to take her in his arms and prove the lie on her lips. She could be his again. She wanted to be.

"Don't!" She gestured with both of her hands as she backed toward the door. "Don't, Jasper, not unless it can mean more than a few greedy moments of pleasure." Then she darted for the door, slamming it behind her, and he was left alone.

He surged to his feet, furious. Frustrated.

From her place in the pantler's closet, Josselyn's eyes widened at the sight. No wonder both Englishwomen and Welsh alike tripped over one another in their efforts to be with her handsome brother-in-law. Naked and fully aroused, he was a splendid sight indeed, and she was not above taking a good, long look. The light from the two torcheres glinted wetly on his wide chest, flat stomach, and lean hips. His legs were strongly muscled, as were his arms and shoulders. But the muscle that intrigued her most was the one that strained upward between his legs. Were it not that she loved her husband so, she might stare a little while longer at it.

But loyalty made Josselyn look away. She turned from the split in the heavy curtains and reminded herself of her purpose. Jasper and Rhonwen were both stubborn. Then again, ten years ago she and Rhys had been equally stubborn. It had taken physical passion to break through the barriers to the love in their hearts, and she was sure it would work as well for these two.

She heard the splash of water as he sat down in the tub, and grinned when she heard him curse. Time to return to his side and gloat, she decided, peeking into the room once more. Then he groaned. His head fell back against the tub and her eyes widened in realization.

Yes, he was frustrated, all right. But though he sought to relieve his frustration himself, she suspected that relief would be temporary. She smiled and turned away. He needed his privacy for a while longer. But as she made her way to her solar, she thought of her own virile husband and how much she missed him.

How *very* much she missed him.

Fifteen

A pair of riders approached the town gate at dusk. They were promptly escorted to the castle and granted an audience with Josselyn. Jasper stood attendance beside her in the hall, as did several of his men. Though Josselyn received them graciously, offering food and drink and every hospitality for the night, Jasper sensed her tension.

These were Simon LaMonthe's men.

"Lord Simon bids me convey his sincere respects to you, Lady Josselyn," the burlier of the pair stated, bowing awkwardly.

"How kind of him," she murmured. "I believe you said you carry a message from him?"

"The message is for Lord Randulf," the man said. "But in his stead . . ." He trailed off and his muddy brown eyes veered from her to Jasper, then back again.

Josselyn held out her hand. "I believe Jasper and I are sufficiently in agreement that we can share this information. Unless, of course, it has to do with another woman."

Jasper managed to stifle his shock at such a remark, but the two messengers nearly choked in surprise. They glanced at once another, and the younger of the pair actually blushed.

"Come, come!" Josselyn exclaimed. "I do but jest. Here."

She extended her hand imperiously. "Give me the missive you bear and sit you down to sup."

The first man unfolded a grimy roll of parchment from around his girdle and gave it to her. Then he and his cohort took their seats and set to their meal with gusto. But Burly watched Josselyn as she read, and then Jasper when he received the missive in turn.

It was nothing. A frivolous bit of information regarding a Lord Claridge whose household would be suitable for fostering Gavin. Jasper read it twice, searching for some hidden meaning. But he found none. Still, Simon LaMonthe was no fool. Nor was he of a generous or helpful nature. There was another reason behind this message; Jasper was convinced of it. But what?

"I believe my husband has made arrangements elsewhere for our son's education," Josselyn said to the pair stuffing their faces with victuals. "But I will send my thanks to Lord Simon for his consideration."

"Rand is due back on the morrow, or the day afterwards," Jasper lied. If this pair sought to probe Rosecliffe's weaknesses, Jasper meant to convince them there were none. But what would be the purpose for such probing? LaMonthe could not be fool enough to consider attacking Rosecliffe.

He tossed the parchment onto the table, but he did not sit. Something was afoot, though he knew not what. But he would find out.

Josselyn gestured to one of the pages, who promptly pulled a flute from his belt. Another page fetched a drum to keep rhythm, and soon a merry tune filled the hall. Meanwhile, Josselyn sent Jasper a speaking look.

They were of the same mind, he realized. She too sensed that all was not as it appeared. But they would not ferret out the truth if they behaved suspiciously.

So the evening ritual resumed. A few men gambled with dice. Servants scrubbed the tables down and stacked them to the side. Water heated on the remnants of the fire, to be used for washing dishes and bodies. The dogs fed on the scraps while a courting lad and the object of his affection mouthed the words of the sentimental song the piper piped.

Were it not that Josselyn's children were sequestered above-stairs, it could have been any other night. But it was not any other night. While the two strangers hoisted mugfuls of Rose-cliffe's ale, Jasper assigned a page to their needs.

"Keep your eyes open and your ears attuned," he told the eager lad. "Then come to me once they are abed. There will be an extra coin in your pocket come quarterday," he added.

"Yes, milord. You may count on me."

As Jasper settled himself in a chair and covertly watched the lad refill the men's mugs, Josselyn approached him. "I shall go abovestairs to bid the children good night. Is there anything else I ought to do?"

"Have them sleep with you. And bolt your door. I'll post guards at the bottom of the stairs."

She gave him a smile. "I know you will keep us safe. But what of Rhonwen? Shall she remain in the tower room?"

Jasper looked away from her frankly curious face. He did not want to think about Rhonwen.

No. That was not true. He had not seen her since his dis-astrous bath earlier, but she'd been a constant distraction to his thoughts. "The tower room—or the dungeon," he mut-tered.

She chuckled. "The tower room or the dungeon. And wherever she is, so do you also wish to be."

He scowled at her. "Leave it alone, Josselyn."

"Very well," she answered. "Do it your own way, if you must."

"I've not required your advice with women in the past. I do not need it now."

She bent down and kissed his cheek. "And as a result, you are a very happy man. Am I right?" Then, not waiting for his reply, she glided regally from the hall.

LaMonthe's men watched her go, then shared a look. At once the skin on the back of Jasper's neck prickled. Something was most assuredly afoot. Not even a week had passed since Rand had left LaMonthe's stronghold and already LaMonthe plotted mischief.

Jasper sent a page to fetch Gilles, a squire with a fearless manner and a particular talent for riding fast through the night.

Before the squire arrived, however, Rhonwen appeared in the stairwell. She still wore the blue kirtle she'd had on earlier, but the loose apron that had covered it was gone. The snug lacing of the soft fabric complemented her feminine shape well, and though she was covered neck to wrists to toes, his imagination saw more. It didn't help matters that her hair had been unplaited, as if she'd been preparing for bed.

What would it be like to watch her let her hair down every night? he wondered. His heart began to race and he downed the contents of his mug in one gulp. What would it be like to close the door to his chamber each night and lie down beside her? He straightened in his chair and when her eyes met his, he pushed to his feet. Was she coming to him? Desire rose like a beast in him, desire and an intense longing he'd never before experienced. She *was* coming to him.

Rhonwen scanned the room, then fixed her gaze on Jasper. Thanks be that he was fully garbed. But the way he was staring at her . . .

Heated color immediately stained her cheeks, and she had to swallow to moisten her dry throat. Just march up to him and deliver Josselyn's message. How hard can that be? she admonished herself.

Excruciatingly hard, as it turned out. But she forced herself to it anyway, only marginally aware of the two strange men whose eyes followed her progress across the hall. "Josselyn bids me tell you that I will stay tonight in her chamber."

He looked down at her from his superior height without responding.

"She wishes me to bring up hot water. And chamomile leaves. 'Tis for Gavin. The boy . . . the boy suffers from an ache in his belly," she continued, aware she was beginning to babble. But it was hard to remain coherent when he was devouring her with his eyes. "Isolde is . . . um . . . beginning to complain as well."

"I warned them not to taste those green berries," he muttered. Then his eyes shifted to focus beyond her and his expression changed. "Come, I'll escort you to the kitchen."

"Oh, no," she protested, shaking her head. "You and I alone? No. 'Tis precisely what Josselyn wants. But we both know 'twould be unwise. I need no escort."

His eyes returned to her. In a lower voice he said, "You need an escort for the same reason you are sleeping in Josselyn's bedchamber."

"LaMonthe's men?" She dismissed that notion with a wave of her hand. "They can have no interest in a Welshwoman—a captive held against her will," she added tartly.

"None beyond the obvious," Jasper muttered. His gaze moved over her, leaving no doubt as to his meaning.

Was he jealous? Rhonwen found it ludicrous, and yet it seemed to be true. She smiled archly. "I am well able to decide whose interest I desire and whose I do not." Then she started for the door.

A squire entered as she departed and he held the door open for her with a gallant gesture. A streak of pure devilment seemed to control her, for on impulse she said, "Would you be so kind as to escort me to the kitchen?"

A pleased grin lit his face. But before replying he glanced warily at Jasper, who she knew had come up behind her. It galled her to no end that he must seek Jasper's permission, but finally he bobbed his head. "Yes, miss. It would be my great pleasure to accompany you."

It did not take long to fetch the dried chamomile, so Rhonwen was hardly better composed when she returned to the hall. Jasper watched her with hooded eyes as she entered, his face dark and brooding. The squire joined Jasper while she crossed to the hearth to fetch hot water for the children's soothing tea. Only when she moved toward the stairs again did she notice LaMonthe's men.

There were Englishmen, and then there were Englishmen, she decided. Like Welshmen, some were basically decent, while others . . . She shuddered. Others should never have been foisted upon the land. She knew instinctively that the older of LaMonthe's two men belonged in the latter category.

She held her head at a haughty angle as she passed near them on her way to the stairs.

"Say, miss. Miss," the older one called to her.

She paused warily on the first step. "Yes?"

He'd stood, and now he approached her. "Your friend, Rhys, sends his regards," he said in a low, knowing voice.

"What?"

Across the room Jasper had pushed to his feet. Whatever the message this man carried, Rhonwen knew it was not meant for Jasper's ears. So she forced a smile to her face and relaxed her tense posture. "What are you talking about?"

" 'Twill not be long 'ere you are set free. On the dark of the moon, leave the postern gate unlocked."

Rhonwen could hardly credit what she heard. Could it be true? Then she spied Jasper's determined approach and she averted her eyes. "You flatter me, sir," she said in carrying tones. "But I am not free to come and go. Even now duty bids me return to Lady Josselyn. Good evening to you."

Then she fled, away from the grinning oaf—away from the glowering Jasper. As she hurried up the curving stairs, however, she could not flee the terrible dilemma that had just been thrust upon her.

Rhys meant to rescue her from Rosecliffe. She could hardly credit it.

And Simon LaMonthe meant to aid him.

But for their plan to succeed she must play a crucial role. She must let Rhys and his men—and his traitorous English allies—into the heart of Rosecliffe Castle.

She paused on the landing outside Josselyn's apartments, breathing hard and trying to think. How had Rhys come to ally himself with Simon LaMonthe, of all people?

Then again, was he truly allied with these men, or were they lying to her, using her loyalty to Rhys to gain access to Rosecliffe for their own devious reasons?

She leaned dejectedly against the rough wall, pressed her head back against the cool stone surface, and stared at the high, shadowy ceiling rafters. Sweet Mary, what was she to do? How was she to determine the truth?

And even if it was a message from Rhys and no trick at all, could she unlock the postern gate and let her countrymen in, knowing the violence that was bound to ensue? Knowing that Rhys meant to confront Jasper? A fight between them would be to the finish. One of them would surely die.

The door creaked open and Isolde stuck her face out. "Come along, Rhonwen. The water will cool and Gavin is whining like a baby."

He *is* a baby, Rhonwen thought as tears of frustration stung the backs of her eyes. You are all babies and undeserving of the misery awaiting you. She pushed off the wall and entered the solar, then busied herself preparing the tea. Isolde and Gwen settled into their mother's high bed. Gavin sipped his tea, then lay down upon a pallet on the floor.

As for Rhonwen, she folded two woven wool blankets into a makeshift pallet in the corner opposite Josselyn's bed. Then she removed her shoes and unlaced her gown. But she didn't remove the garment and she didn't lie down. Instead she stared into the flickering remains of the small fire in the hearth.

"Are you all right?" Josselyn asked from her seat beside Gavin. "Does something trouble you, Rhonwen?"

For a moment Rhonwen almost confided in her. Almost. But what could Josselyn do? Josselyn was bound to fight anyone who threatened her family and home. So Rhonwen turned away from her. "No," she answered, unable to tell Josselyn the truth. "No. I but say my prayers."

Only the prayers would not come. What was she to pray for? Rhys's success or his failure? Should she be grateful for the alliance he'd made, or should she dread it? She lay down fully clothed and sick with worry. And since she did not know what else to do, she prayed for divine guidance.

What she needed, however, was divine interference, for no matter what she did, she feared there would be the devil to pay.

During the long restless night, two things became clear to Rhonwen. She could not in good conscience let Rhys and LaMonthe into Rosecliffe Castle. Too many innocent lives would be lost in the battle that would surely erupt. Nor could she ignore the risk to their own lives which they were willing to take on her behalf. She knew how badly Rhys wanted Rose-cliffe, but she could not be a part of his plot. She simply could not.

In the light of a gray and watery dawn, she came to the only solution possible. She must escape.

The dark of the moon would occur in three days. Prior to then she must be gone from Rosecliffe.

She rose from her pallet, folded up the blankets, and put them in a trunk, then wearily scrubbed her hands across her face. The best she could do was to disappear, for with her gone, Rhys would have no need to confront Jasper—at least not immediately. She knew she only pushed back the day of their reckoning. But at least she would not feel guilt over the outcome of their battle.

And if she fled far enough from these hills, perhaps she might never hear which one of them killed the other.

She looked over at the high bed draped with green damask, and found Josselyn watching her. "You had a restless night, Rhonwen. I heard you twisting and muttering in your sleep."

"You forget that I am a hostage, not a guest. Would you sleep easy in your enemies' stronghold?"

"If you mean an English stronghold, well, I do so every night," Josselyn said with a little smile.

" 'Tis not the same. Rand is not your enemy."

"Nor is he yours. Nor is Jasper."

Rhonwen did not want to speak to her about Jasper. Josselyn was too eager to pair them, too certain that it would solve everything. What Josselyn did not understand was that Jasper's feelings for Rhonwen did not mirror Rand's feelings for his wife.

"I am held here against my will, Josselyn. How can he not be my enemy?" She left then, and Josselyn did not try to stop her. Downstairs, the capacious hall was coming to life. A maid stoked the fire in the huge hearth. One bleary-eyed page staggered in with an armful of additional wood. Two other servants pulled the tables away from the walls.

LaMonthe's two men were not there, much to her relief. She did not want to be forced to give them an answer. Let them think what they would. Let them inform their lord that they had delivered their message. She would escape before the night in question.

But how?

One of the maids slanted her a suspicious look. "Does milady know you're about?"

Rhonwen stared coldly at her. "Yes. I slept in her chambers," she answered tartly. " 'Twas she who has sent me after water for her morning ablutions."

"But I filled that ewer last night," the woman protested.

"Gavin was ill during the night. We used it for him. Now she needs more," Rhonwen finished. Then she turned and walked away from the maid, as if she had free run of the castle. It was only partially a lie, and fortunately, the maid did not stop her.

Outside, the bailey was quiet. Two men stood in the stable opening, talking. A cock flew up to a windowsill, stretching and ruffling his feathers, then crowed his morning best.

She'd better hurry.

Taking a circuitous route to the well, she carefully scanned the base of the high inner walls of the castle. The stables and barracks took up the greater portion of one side of the yard, and the great hall, the keep, and the chapel took up the other. Flanking the gatehouse were storerooms on one side and a holding pen for cattle on the other.

On the far wall, perched nearest the edge of the cliff, was the kitchen. A pair of timber lean-to sheds, and a smokehouse clustered around it, and it was there Rhonwen focused her search.

Thunder rolled heavy across the sky, and she wished she'd brought her mantle. No hint of spring showed this ugly morning. Cold and damp settled over the land, and settled deep into her heart. She must find that gate!

The castle walls were solid stone, tall and impenetrable. She paused near the kitchen, searching for a break in the surface, but she saw none. When the kitchen door screeched open she ducked behind a trio of empty ale barrels. The last thing she needed was to be hailed by the cook. She squeezed backward behind the temporary barrier—and made a startling discovery.

The kitchen did not fully abut the outer wall. A narrow passage, partially hidden by the kitchen and the barrels stacked before it, led behind the kitchen.

Holding her breath, she put down the bucket and made her way down the passage until she encountered a heavy iron door embedded in the outer wall.

This must be it, the postern gate that led to the outside and the narrow walkway that descended the cliffs to the sea!

She inched her way back to the barrels and peeked out. No one was looking for her. She turned back to the gate and reached for the ring handle. With a slight scrape of metal on metal, it turned.

Rhonwen was so stunned she fell back and toppled a neatly propped trio of fishing nets. Alarmed that she would be heard, she hastily righted them, then held her breath, listening. Her heart pounded as she examined the narrow space behind the kitchen. Fishing poles, baskets, nets. A pair of long oars and several iron-tipped fishermen's spears. This must be a frequently used passageway for those heading down to the sea, she realized. And if it was not presently locked, it must be because someone had already used it this morning.

Holding her breath, she turned the ring handle once more, and when the lock clicked, she pulled the door open. Another passageway with a low ceiling, and lined with ropes and corks and several unlit lanterns, led right through the width of the wall to a second door. In addition to a sturdy iron lock, this door also boasted a heavy crossbar. But the bar now leaned against the wall, so, taking a chance, she opened that door as well—but only a narrow crack.

A blast of pungent sea air proclaimed her success, and Rhonwen drew in a great draught of the freedom it promised. Freedom. Could it really be this easy?

Then she heard voices and, looking up, spied two guards on the wall walk. No escape today—at least not during the light of day. But would the doors remain unlocked from the inside at night? She peeked out again and saw the path that angled down the face of the sheer cliff, to the narrow beach below. From their strategic perch the watchmen could see anyone who used the path. Only under the cover of darkness could a person depart or enter without detection.

Lightning flashed far out across the sea, and after several seconds thunder echoed. If the clouds held, it would not matter about the light of the waning moon. And if it rained, even better.

She pulled the stout door closed and rested against its damp, grainy surface. So it was resolved. She would leave tonight and put this trial behind her. And once shed of this place she would never return, not to Rosecliffe, nor to Carreg Du, nor to the rebel camp on the way to Afon Bryn. There was nothing for her here—nothing that she could have, anyway, and too much of what she did not want.

Somehow she would send word to Rhys that he need not attempt a rescue of her. Then she would strike out for the west to discover a new life for herself.

She pushed off the door and, taking up the bucket she'd left in the first passageway, cautiously made her way back into the bailey. But as she drew water from the well and made her way back to the keep, she was gripped by a loneliness more profound that she'd ever felt before. She'd long felt alone in the world, but of late, it seemed, her life had been crowded with people. Rhys and his determined men. Josselyn and her darling children. And Jasper.

She looked around, searching for him without success. Her heart grew heavier still. But she was not giving him up, she told herself. For he had never been hers to possess. She was just removing herself from harm's way.

Even the simplest beast of the forest knew the wisdom of doing that.

Sixteen

"Who were those men?" Isolde asked. She sat on a short three-legged stool opposite Rhonwen, holding her hands out as Rhonwen wound freshly spun yarn into a convenient skein.

Rhonwen glanced at the girl, then back at her task. Ever since Rhonwen had defended Isolde's right as a Welshwoman to select her own husband, the girl's attitude toward her had undergone a remarkable change. "Why do you direct that question to me? Why not ask your mother? She knows more about them than I."

"She doesn't like to tell me anything that might make me worry."

"Why should anything they say worry you?"

Isolde dropped her hands and the yarn skein into her lap, forcing Rhonwen to look at her. "I'm not a child. I know there is trouble in the land. King Stephen. Matilda. The old king's grandson." She sighed. "I know that whomever Gavin fosters with and whomever I wed are important to Father. Important to Rosecliffe and to England. Peace in England will keep peace in Wales. That's what Father says." Then, realizing she spoke to a Welsh loyalist, she added, "I am half-Welsh, you know."

"Yes. I know. Pick up your hands so we may finish this

today," Rhonwen instructed. "Your mother should have the dye bath prepared by now."

"But what of those men? What message did they bring?"

What message indeed? Not one Rhonwen could reveal—nor one she could ignore. "That is difficult to say. Their liege lord knows your father is away from Rosecliffe. Perhaps they brought a message from him?"

Isolde sent her a disgusted look. "If that were true, why would Jasper have posted guards at the stairwell last night? I saw him when they left. He was sore relieved to be rid of them. Everyone was."

Rhonwen studied the child's serious face. "You are quite the clever one, aren't you? All right, then. I'll tell you my suspicions. Everyone—Welsh and English alike—knows that Simon LaMonthe is not a man to be trusted. He is cruel and greedy. No doubt Jasper and your mother know it too. If LaMonthe sent men here, it was for his benefit and no one else's."

Isolde's eyes grew round. "To spy upon us?"

"Mayhap. But you need not fear, Isolde. Jasper would never allow any harm to befall you or anyone at Rosecliffe."

The child smiled at that. "He is so wonderful. He's brave and handsome and funny too."

Rhonwen concentrated on winding the thin-spun yarn around the little girl's outstretched arms. Yes, he was all those things, and too appealing for her own good. She didn't need Isolde to tell her that.

"I know you love him," Isolde stated.

Rhonwen dropped the spindle and it skittered across the floor, unwinding yarn as it went. "What a ludicrous idea!" she exclaimed as she bent to fetch the spindle.

"It's all right. I'm not angry anymore. I know I cannot marry my own uncle. The Church will not allow it."

"I think . . . I think you are confusing your feelings for him with mine," Rhonwen countered. But the girl's remarks had unsettled her. "You love him, but I . . . I merely think him . . . He is my captor," she finished angrily. "He is my captor and this is my prison."

She faced the girl once more, holding the spindle while the strand of yarn stretched between them. "I am trying to make the best of the time I must spend here, Isolde. That is all. He cannot keep me forever, though. Eventually I will be free to leave."

She wound the last of the wool yarn around Isolde's arms. "There. Take this skein and all the others down to your mother. I'll put the spindle away and straighten up the chamber."

Isolde stood, frowning down at the neat coil of yarn in her hand. "I don't understand you, Rhonwen. You ought to be happy that Jasper admires you so."

Rhonwen had no answer for that—at least none that was fitting for a child. "You are too young to understand such things."

"I am not!"

Rhonwen abandoned the solar before Isolde could mount any further argument. What could a mere child know of such grown-up matters?

She knows you love Jasper. She's wise enough to recognize that.

"Bendigedig!" she muttered. Just wonderful. If she could not escape tonight, she would surely go mad!

It seemed, however, that she was to be pushed to madness even sooner than that, for as she stormed down the stairs, Jasper met her coming up.

They both halted, facing one another in a curve on the steps, and her heart began perversely to trip over itself. He wore a gray tunic over a bleached white shirt, and the combination intensified the gray of his eyes. He stood there, two steps below her, putting their faces on a level, and stared moodily at her.

He looked weary, as if he had not slept well, and though she'd slept poorly herself, her first instinct was to offer him comfort. She wisely bit back the words, however, before they surfaced.

"If you seek Isolde, she is—"

"I do not seek Isolde."

Tension crackled between them, sharp as a dagger, cutting to the heart of her. She looked away, down at the spindle she'd forgotten she yet held. "Oh. I must put this away."

But when she turned to retreat up the stairs, he followed her. "I would speak a moment with you, Rhonwen."

Speak with her? The very idea terrified her. She increased her pace. Isolde was not far; she would be the buffer Rhonwen needed between Jasper and herself.

At the landing, however, he caught her wrist, staying her progress. "Rhonwen. Wait."

She snatched her hand from his and faced him, trembling with emotion. "Begone from here, Jasper. I do not wish to be alone with you."

"Why?"

"Why? Because . . . because . . ." She swallowed hard and sought a plausible reason, anything but the truth. In the end it was a partial truth she revealed. "You have a way of banishing a woman's good sense. You know it is so, for you pride yourself on it. If I am to retain my sense, then it follows that I must keep my distance from you."

Where was Isolde?

"You have a way of banishing my good sense as well." He took a step closer. "But it is when you are absent that I become an utter fool." Another step. "When you are near to me . . . that is when all my senses peak. My sense of touch—I need to touch the silk of your hair, the satin of your skin."

Rhonwen's eyes widened in shock.

"My sense of smell," he continued. "You smell of flowers and the forest. Of woman."

Her heart's pace tripled. Her chest hurt, it pounded with such violent emotion.

"My sense of taste." He stepped closer still. "I want to taste you again."

Rhonwen backed away, shaking her head. "No. No. You must not . . . must not say such things to me."

"Why? It is but the truth." He closed the distance between them.

"Because . . . because it is not talk you truly want." She

came up hard against a door. "You want more than merely to talk."

Their eyes held, his dark and compelling, and hers . . . She did not want to think about the truth her eyes must reveal to him. He was so close that, though they did not touch, she fancied she could feel the imprint of his body upon hers. The heat of him pressed in on her and she was helpless in his thrall. She was surrendering. She could feel it.

He braced his weight on the door, trapping her within the span of his arms, and slowly let out a sigh. "No, you are wrong in that. Though I want more than talk from you, Rhonwen, this time . . . this time I will restrict myself only to talk."

To talk? He had not come to seduce her? If he was being truthful, then she was a bigger fool than she'd thought. Even when he wished only to talk, she succumbed to desire. Her face flamed in humiliation. What would she do if he truly set out to seduce her?

"What is it you wish to talk about?" she managed to ask.

He pushed back from her, then looked away. A hint of color rose in his cheeks and Rhonwen stared. Was he blushing? What could this possibly be about?

He cleared his throat and her curiosity grew. When he spoke, however, he made no sense. "I know from Josselyn that your father is not living. Have you some other man—an uncle or stepfather—who takes responsibility for your well-being? And do not say Rhys. For he is not a part of this."

She was completely bewildered. "I have a stepfather. But he is nothing to me. I cede him no responsibility for myself."

"What of your mother, then?"

"What is this about, Jasper?" Then she gasped. "Surely you do not think to ransom me?"

"Damnation!" He ran both hands through his hair so that it stood out in rumpled spikes. " 'Tis not ransom I have in mind, but marriage! Marriage," he repeated, his tone lower, meeting her eyes this time. "Who am I to make my request to, Rhonwen? Who?"

Rhonwen had no answer to give him. The question was too unlikely, too illogical to have an answer. Instead, in a thin voice she asked, "Who is it you would have me wed?"

He stared at her as if she were mad. "Why, me, of course."
Then he frowned. "Think long and hard on this before you
turn me down, woman. You could be content at Rosecliffe.
Josselyn is happy to have you here, and I—"

He broke off and folded his arms across his chest. "I will
make a good husband—as good a husband as you will make
a wife."

There was no compliment in that statement, but Rhonwen
was not slighted. She was too stunned by this unexpected offer. "Why?" she asked. "Why would you wish to wed with
me?"

His eyes moved over her, a delicious stroke that made her
insides quiver. "We are well suited, I think."

It was her turn to blush. "In one way, perhaps."

"Perhaps?" He gave her a cocky, one-sided grin. "Perhaps?"

"Perhaps," she stated, frowning. "But in every other way—
no. A marriage between us makes no sense." It was gratifying,
though, but Rhonwen would not let him know that. She
crossed her arms, mirroring his stance. "You have another
motive for this. Is it to spite Rhys?"

His grin disappeared. "He is not your lover, though he
claimed otherwise. I have thought long on this, Rhonwen. If
you and he are not lovers, it is because you have rebuffed him.
There is nothing between you, not on your part, anyway. So,
no, my offer has nothing to do with him. It is for me."

Rhonwen had never been so confused. She'd expected seduction. Instead she'd been completely undone by pretty
words and an offer of marriage. He wanted to make her his
wife!

For a few blessed moments she let herself envision such a
unlikely future with him. Waking up beside him each day,
happy, knowing she belonged somewhere. Dining alongside
him. Sharing secret looks, secret smiles, that only they understood.

Sharing his bed.

A heated flush stole over her as she imagined them closing

the door against the world every night and turning to one another.

And then there would be children. Even now there could be a child. She was not certain when her monthly courses were next due—

"You've not said nay, Rhonwen. Does that mean you will accept my offer?"

Rhonwen blinked, and that fast the rosy picture in her mind turned to the murky color of her reality. The dark of the moon would bring an attack on Rosecliffe Castle. Were she to accept Jasper's offer, she would have to reveal the plot to him. But could she betray Rhys that way?

She knew she could not.

Her crossed arms slid down to her waist and she hugged her terrible knowledge to herself. She could not meet his eyes.

"I . . . I thank you for the . . . for the offer you make. I am mindful of the honor in your proposal and . . . and I do not decline it easily. But . . . but decline it I must."

When he did not respond, she hesitantly peered up at him. His expression was hard to decipher. He appeared neither angry nor hurt, but rather bemused.

"You do not love Rhys. I will not believe that. So why do you turn me down?"

"Because . . . because a marriage between you and me is destined to fail. We are too different."

"In the same manner that Rand and Josselyn are different? Their marriage has succeeded, as you term it. They are well pleased with one another. Surely you see how content she is."

"But they love one another!" she burst out. "They have more than desire between them."

"We have—" He broke off, frowning. "Do you want declarations of love from me? Is that it?"

"No! No," she gasped. Dear God, would this agony never cease?

Only if she convinced him she was serious.

She realized what she must do and sucked in a hard breath. "I do not love you. That is the problem. I do not love you any more than I love Rhys," she vowed, and stared at him as if that were not the biggest falsehood of her life.

This time his expression was easier to read. His jaw tensed, his lips thinned, and the warm light in his eyes turned to a hard glitter.

"So you see," she continued on recklessly, needing to end this before she broke down completely, "you will not be able to avoid making a decision about your hostage by marrying her. Will you free me now, or will you keep me locked up here forever? Which will it be, Jasper?"

Her heart thudded in her chest as she met his ferocious glare. She'd not meant to goad him quite so far, but once begun, her own frustration had not let her stop. This was not fair, none of it. She loved the wrong man; he wanted her for all the wrong reasons; and Rhys demanded her aid in an attack that was all wrong.

And now Jasper looked at her with such contempt she wanted to die. "Perhaps you are right. Perhaps you are wiser than I. Marrying you to gain freer access to the delights of your body is an extreme gesture, especially when we both know you can be had without benefit of a clergyman's blessing."

"No!" She darted to the side, but his arm stopped her. His other arm blocked the other side. Again they were face-to-face, too close. But this time her emotions were far too near the surface. With just a little push they might burst free, boil over, and burn the two of them with their heat.

And it was clear he meant to push.

In desperation her hand slid along the door, and when she found the latch she lifted it. Under their weight the door at once swung inward. A muffled cry, a thud, and it stopped midway.

"Ouch! Oh, you're squashing me!" a youthful voice cried. Isolde!

"What in hell?" Jasper exclaimed.

Thankful for the reprieve, Rhonwen took advantage of the confusion and ducked below Jasper's arm. Behind the door Isolde lay in a crumpled heap.

"What happened?" Rhonwen asked, helping her up and avoiding Jasper at all costs.

"She was eavesdropping, that's what happened," Jasper bit out. "Do I have the right of it, Isolde?"

The little girl crowded against Rhonwen and would not meet his gaze. "I was in here first. Then you stopped outside the door."

"And so you put your ear to the lock to hear better still."

"Leave her alone, Jasper. This is not her fault."

His expression was thunderous. He looked as like to strangle Isolde as to strangle Rhonwen, for his hands flexed then clenched, flexed and clenched.

"Go away, Jasper," Rhonwen said, more quietly. "These are the women's quarters. You have no business here."

One last time their gazes met and held. She could still change her answer to him. She sensed that. But there were too many reasons not to, reasons he did not need to know.

"No," he said at last. "I have no business here any longer."

When he was gone, when even the echo of his steps had faded away, Isolde looked up at Rhonwen. "I'm sorry," she whispered. "I should not have kept my presence unknown."

"You have nothing to apologize for." Rhonwen squeezed the girl's shoulders, then released her. "It was for the best. Truly, it was." She stared blindly around the solar, shaking inside, searching inanely for the spindle she'd again dropped.

"But . . . but I don't understand," Isolde said. "You and he . . . I'm not a child anymore. I know what he wanted to do."

"He didn't mean anything by it," Rhonwen assured the girl. "He and I, well, we seem to bring out the worst in one another."

"But why won't you marry him? I heard him ask you, Rhonwen. Why did you say no?"

Rhonwen stared down at the girl, battling the urge to weep. How could she explain to Isolde what she could not explain to Jasper, nor even to herself?

"Is Jasper wrong about that awful man, that outlaw?" the younger girl continued. "Is it Rhys ap Owain you love? I know he's the reason you helped to kidnap me. Mother says you would never have let anyone harm me. But him—that Rhys—he looked at me so mean! But then Jasper caught him and you let yourself be taken prisoner so that Rhys could get away.'' She stared up at Rhonwen, her face a study in childish confusion, and dejection. ''You do love him, don't you?''

''Yes. I love him, Isolde.'' Rhonwen knelt down and took the child's hands in hers. ''But it is the love of a sister for a brother. I love him the way you love Gavin. Rhys is not truly my brother, but . . . but I feel like he is. And I feel responsible for him.''

''But he's not a nice person.''

''Oh, but he can be. He can. It's just that . . .'' Rhonwen bit her lip. ''He has reasons for hating Jasper and everyone who is English.''

''But if you don't love him like someone you could marry, why don't you love Jasper? Why don't you marry him?''

Rhonwen smiled sadly. ''I thought you wanted to marry him.''

The girl sighed. ''I told you, I can't marry him. He's my uncle. But if I could, I would.'' Then, not diverted, she added, ''I don't understand why you won't.''

''It's very complicated,'' Rhonwen answered, standing up. ''Too complicated to explain. But one day, when he is married to someone else, you will see that I was right.''

I was right, she repeated to herself again and again as they resumed their daily tasks. She was right to turn him down, and right to escape Rosecliffe Castle.

But no matter how many times she repeated it, the thought of leaving Jasper forever, the thought of him someday wed to another, felt horribly wrong.

Painfully wrong.

Unbearably wrong.

Seventeen

The routine of the castle was no different that night than any other. From the chapel, vespers rang across the valley calling the shepherds and their woolly charges down from the fields. The day workers—the weavers and laundresses, the masons and carpenters—made their way in pairs and small groups across the moat bridge and down the hard-packed road into Rosecliffe village.

In the bailey Gavin and a group of small boys chased the fowl into their pens. Then the boys moved into the hall to pull the tables out and line up the benches for the supper. The kitchen workers hastened to prepare the final meal of the day so they could seek their rest.

Then the kitchen bell rang as dusk crept across the budding spring green, and as one, the people of the castle came together for their evening meal. It was the end of the day, a time to eat and drink and relax. A time for entertainments and song, and easing into the night.

But for Rhonwen it was anything but easy. As the day had dragged by, her nerves had wound tighter, The afternoon had seemed to stretch out endlessly. Surely the bell ringer had forgotten his chores. Surely the sun had stalled in the sky. She had worried one nail, biting it to the quick, then moved on to another.

This was the night she must make her escape. She could not delay. She must make certain the postern gate remained unlocked, save for the inner crossbar. That she could remove herself. If the key were put to the lock, however, she would be trapped.

So she kept a careful watch on the comings and goings at the kitchen and the gate it sheltered behind it. But at the same time she also cast a wary eye about for Jasper.

Had he left the castle after their confrontation?

Following their disastrous meeting in the stair hall, she'd been too distraught to realize that his whereabouts could determine the success—or failure—of her plan. At the time she'd been beset alternately by regret then resolve, by sorrow and then resignation. By the time she'd reined in her runaway emotions and realized the importance of his whereabouts, it had been too late. She might have asked around and discovered his location, but she hesitated to do that. She'd been only marginally accepted among the castlefolk. Though Josselyn and Isolde did not hold the kidnapping against her, there were others who still viewed her with suspicion. And everyone knew of Jasper's interest in her.

No, she did not need to draw attention to herself by asking for Jasper.

So she sat at a window in Josselyn's solar, craning her neck to see the comings and goings in the bailey, and praying for darkness so she could make good her escape.

When Gwendolyn skipped into the chamber, her heart lurched. Guilt feelings, she realized, smoothing the linen embroidery panel in her hands.

"Aren't you coming down to sup with us?" the little girl asked. She opened a cupboard and rummaged through her belongings, then turned with a comb in her hands. "Mama said proper young ladies do not appear before company with tangled hair. Will you help me?" She held the comb out to Rhonwen. "Then we can go down together."

Rhonwen did not want to go belowstairs at all, for she was not certain she could maintain the pretense of everything being normal. Everything was *not* normal. But to remain absent was to rouse attention, and that she must not do. Besides, it was impossible to ignore the entreaty in Gwendolyn's plump baby face.

"All right, sweetheart. Climb up into my lap and we'll comb out your lovely curls."

With a flash of dimples Gwen did just that. They sat together in the window well, Gwen's warm weight a comfort to Rhonwen. As she worked the fine bone comb through the child's hair, slowly untangling the knots from the ends up to the roots, she inhaled deeply. Soap, dogs, and a trace of mint. How wonderful were children.

Suddenly she missed Davit and Cordula, though her brother and sister were very nearly grown. In a matter of hours she would be missing Josselyn's three children also. Gwen and her trusting innocence. Gavin and his derring-do. And Isolde, willing to hand her beloved uncle over to Rhonwen's safe-keeping.

On impulse she kissed the top of Gwendolyn's head. At once the girl turned and gave her a hug. "I'm glad you came to live with us. Gavin says that one day you'll leave and go back to the wildwood. But I think you should stay here."

"You do?"

"Yes. 'Cause . . .'cause you never told me the rest of the story. You know, the one about the Welsh princess and the unhappy dragon."

The story she'd told Gwen when she and Jasper had tucked the child in bed. It seemed months had passed, though in reality it had only been two weeks or so. "Was the dragon unhappy?" she asked, combing Gwen's hair once more.

"Oh, yes. He was very unhappy. I could tell. An' only the princess could make him happy again. Right?"

"Right." In fairy tales a princess could make a dragon happy, and allow him to become a man once more. But real life was far more ordinary, and far more complex. Rhonwen set the comb aside and began to braid the top portion of the child's hair. "We must hurry, else our supper will be cold."

So Rhonwen descended to the hall hand-in-hand with the little girl, who was innocent of the conflicts that worried her elders. In the hall's massive hearth the fire leaped and danced. A half-dozen torcheres and small lanterns scattered about seemed to impart a special warmth to the chamber this evening.

Rhonwen gazed around her with a new awareness of the tall pale walls. As with the rest of Rosecliffe Castle, the hall was not completed. A half-finished fresco adorned one wall, with fresh plaster and paint expanding its boundaries daily. She would not see the fresco complete, she realized. She would not see St. Aiden and St. Francis meet on a field of flowers, as was planned, for this would be her last visit to this place. She would never return to Rosecliffe and its great hall, she decided, even should Rhys someday succeed in his quest to bring the castle under Welsh control. It would be too hard for her to return. She already had too many memories of Rosecliffe. Good. Awful. Confused.

"Come on, Rhonwen. You can sit next to me," Gwen said, dragging her out of her somber thoughts and toward the high table. Isolde and Gavin already sat there, while Josselyn conferred with two of the maids near the hearth. Jasper was nowhere to be seen.

That was good.

That was devastating.

Rhonwen frowned and rubbed a spot on her temple that had begun to throb. It occurred to her suddenly that Isolde might have revealed to her mother what she'd overheard today between Jasper and Rhonwen.

As she took her seat, Rhonwen peered sidelong at Josselyn, hoping the girl had somehow kept silent. When Josselyn turned from her task, unfortunately, it took but that one look for Rhonwen to know the truth. Isolde had confided in Josselyn. And now Josselyn was certain to pester Rhonwen about it endlessly.

Why couldn't Josselyn see that though her unlikely alliance with an Englishman had succeeded, such an alliance between Jasper and Rhonwen was not meant to be? It simply was not meant to be.

As Josselyn approached the table, Rhonwen steeled herself.

To her surprise, Josselyn only nodded and asked, "Would you have gravy? The parsnips are good. They are Oto's specialty. Come, have more."

They were good, but even so, Rhonwen's appetite remained unaffected. Her stomach was a twisted knot and she did little more than play with her food. They were an hour at the meal, and they spoke primarily of recipes and spices and matters dear to women's hearts. The cloth merchant from Chester was expected the next market day. The butcher's wife was so big with child that Josselyn feared twins.

With every passing minute, however, Rhonwen's anxiety increased. Then Gavin said, "Shouldn't Jasper be back from the beach by now?"

At the mention of his name, Rhonwen jerked, dropping her spoon, then toppling her wine goblet over. There was not much wine in it, and Josselyn righted the pewter vessel at once. But as she dabbed at the wine stain she said, "Good Lord, but the pair of you will have all the table linens stained red before you patch up your differences."

Rhonwen lurched to her feet, her temper flaring completely out of proportion to Josselyn's remark. "Just let it be, Josselyn. Can you not just let it be?"

The older woman looked up at her. "What, the stain? 'Tis better to rinse out wine before it can dry and set the color."

"Not the stain!" Rhonwen clenched her hands so tightly she trembled. " 'Tis not the stain I speak of, and well you know it."

Josselyn's expression was kind; the children's faces showed concern. Gwendolyn touched her arm tentatively. "It's all right," she whispered in her sweet, lisping little-girl voice. "Mama never stays angry if you say you are sorry." The child leaned closer and her warm weight was both a balm and a torture. "Just say you're sorry. Then everything will be all right."

"I'm sorry," Rhonwen whispered after a moment, although her apology was not for the spilled wine. But then, Josselyn clearly knew that, for her eyes were filled with more kindness than Rhonwen deserved. "I'm sorry," she repeated. "I think I'd better go. Will you excuse me?"

"Of course," Josselyn answered. "But Rhonwen—"

Rhonwen could not bear to hear any more. She could not bear to be among a people who would forgive her many crimes against them even as she hid new secrets from them. How could she help anyone hurt the people of Rosecliffe Castle?

She disentangled Gwen's hands from hers and, with a brief nod, left. But with every step she grieved. She could not even bid them farewell. She would not be able to explain her abrupt departure, or thank them for their many kindnesses to her.

In the bailey she halted, staring wildly about, too distraught to decide where to go or what to do. It was dark; she should leave now. But she couldn't. Not yet.

Perhaps she could leave a message for Josselyn to find. A letter.

She filched a sheet of parchment from the seneschal's office as well as ink and a quill pen. Her letters were not so neat as his, and she had no sand to blot them. But it was legible and, though brief, she hoped it conveyed the depths of her feelings.

I am gone to seek my fortune. You have my thanks for your many kindnesses, Josselyn, when I have done nothing to deserve them. I cannot betray you and your family, but neither can I betray Rhys and my people. So I must remove myself from Rosecliffe and Carreg Du and the many conflicts here. I pray you will convey my regards to Isolde, Gavin, and Gwendolyn . . .

Rhonwen stared at the scrawled message. Then, unable to resist, she dipped the quill once more into the ink pot.

. . . and to Jasper, she added. Then she signed it, laid the pen down, and left the parchment there on the desk, where, come the morn, someone was sure to find it.

Back in the bailey she refused to dwell on Josselyn's reaction to the news of her escape—or Jasper's. She must protect herself. That was all she could do, and to do that, she must flee Rosecliffe before Rhys mounted his attack.

Around her, shadows loomed in the gathering dark. A brick cart sat idle beside one of the stairs that led to the wall walk. A mason's scaffold dangled over her head, empty and swaying from its ropes as the wind rattled along the walls. Everyday objects, yet this night they were ominous. Sinister, even. They were the tools used to make the stones of Wales grow into the thick walls and mighty towers of Rosecliffe, just as the old song foretold. Would the noon turn black and the winter turn warm, as was also foretold?

She paused and stared around her, suddenly cold. The one was as like to happen as the other when the whole world was coming to an end. And indeed, Rhonwen was so filled with sorrow she felt as if her whole world were coming undone. To run from such catastrophe was very likely foolishness. But she could not stay.

Across the bailey a guard shifted, his silhouette on the wall walk clear against the western sky. She ought to wait a while longer. But she simply could not. Her nerves were over-wrought and she feared she would go mad. So, keeping to the shadows, she headed toward the kitchen and the dark alcove behind it that led to freedom.

"... if he asks me."

"Ah, Gert. Surely he will," a woman answered the first speaker.

Rhonwen halted just outside the kitchen, pressing a shaking hand to her chest. It was only two maids finishing their evening chores, cleaning the kitchen in preparation for the morning's tasks.

"You know how these men are," the woman named Gert continued. "One bit of quim is much like another—or so they believe. But I'm a patient girl ..."

Rhonwen did not want to hear any more of their depressing words. Yes. To most men, one woman was the same as another. Certainly Jasper was a prime example of that, with all the women he was said to have conquered. He'd made her seem special, though. She'd been his captive and no one would have stayed him from anything he wished to do to her. Yet he'd nonetheless made her feel as if she were the only woman that mattered to him.

She shook her head. It was just a talent he had and no doubt that was the reason for his enormous appeal with women. He made every woman feel exciting and adored, and unique above all others.

But how many of those other women had he asked to wed with him?

That stopped Rhonwen in her tracks. She stood just beyond the kitchen door, next to the barrels and the deeply shadowed crevice that hid the postern gate. He'd asked her to marry him, and she knew with sudden clarity that he'd put that question to no other woman before her. If he had, he would have long ago been wed. No woman of Rosecliffe or Carreg Du would have turned down so magnificent and high-placed a man. None of them was that foolish.

She alone claimed that title: fool among women.

She pressed her aching brow against one of the empty barrels. The wooden staves were rough and cool. Was she making a terrible mistake? Should she marry him?

But what of Rhys and his plan to attack the castle? What of his unholy alliance with Simon LaMonthe? She could not abandon Rhys.

Perhaps, however, she could reason with him.

She discarded that idea as soon as it occurred. Rhys was far beyond reasoning when it pertained to the English presence in Wales—especially to Rosecliffe and either of the two Fitz-Hugh brothers. There was no way for her to have Jasper or to appease Rhys. She had no choice but to leave them to their battling and carve out a new life for herself in some other place, far from either of them.

Resolved, she took a shaky breath, then froze when she heard a new voice. Jasper's voice. "Have you any scraps left here to feed a hungry man?"

Rhonwen stifled her gasp and shrank back against the barrel. He'd found her!

But though his silhouette loomed tall and familiar just beyond her reach, he must not have seen her in the deep shadows. For it was not to her he spoke, but to the maids inside the kitchen.

"Oh, Sir Jasper. La, but you give us a start, milord!"

"We've plenty to give you, milord. Anything you'd like."

He entered the kitchen but Rhonwen did not stir from her place against the barrels. She hardly dared to breathe. He hadn't seen her.

No doubt he'd been too distracted by the clear offer in the voice of that Gert woman. Anything you like! Was he already after another taste of "quim," as they termed it?

"A hunk of yellow cheese will do, and a crust of bread." Jasper seemed to answer her silent question.

"Such plain fare. I'd happily fetch you a trencher of meat and gravy from the hall, milord."

"No."

When he said no more, Rhonwen strained forward. Why would he not go to the hall or send a maid to fetch food for him? Because she might be there? Did he so despise the sight of her—or fear it?

A rush of desire overwhelmed her, a longing so intense it stole the breath from her chest. One last time, it pleaded with her. One last time go to him. Share that ultimate intimacy with him. Leave him at least with the knowledge that you care for him in a way you have cared for no one else before, and never will again. At the least you can then take with you memories of the closeness of that final joining—and perhaps the enduring proof of it.

She pressed a hand to her belly, aghast at her own thoughts. Could she be that bold? Could she take such a chance?

The better question was, could she go on if she did not do it?

A knife came down on the heavy wooden table. Someone moved a bench. "Will you remain alone in the kitchen, my lord?" Gert again, with the same seduction in her voice.

"I've rounds to make."

Rhonwen heard the rattle of keys. Of course! He would be the one to lock the postern gate. Had he already locked it?

Slowly she backed around the barrel. She had to know if escape was possible.

It was. Feeling the way down the pitch-dark passage, she found the door barred with a heavy iron rod—but the lock was not fastened. She could still leave.

She should do so now.

But Jasper was so near . . .

Her hands rested, one on the bar, the other on the ring latch. But her face turned back to stare wistfully down the passageway. She could see absolutely nothing in the darkness. But in her mind's eye she saw so much. Jasper, handsome of face, virile and strong. Would he lay her down if she came to him? She thought he would. She wanted him to.

"*Ffwl*," she cursed her own perversity.

But wasn't she entitled to some measure of joy in her life? Even if it was only a brief hour in his arms, couldn't she at least take that much with her? It was the most she would ever have of joy.

She started down the passageway, and as she came into the alley she spied the two women departing the kitchen. It was a sign, she told herself. She was right to do this.

The women left. Jasper stood in the doorway and bade them a good night. Then he returned to his plain meal. This was her moment. She could flee and put him forever from her mind—or at least try to. Or she could go to him of her free will this time.

And if he turned her away? After all, she'd declined his honorable offer of marriage. He would be justified in scorning her advances now.

She crept nearer the kitchen door. If he spurned her, then she would do as he had done to her. She would use every device, every talent, every bit of her imagination and allure to fire his ardor. She would kiss his resisting lips and caress his resisting body.

In short, she would seduce him.

Eighteen

Jasper stared into the empty well of his pewter cup. Gert had been willing. She'd made that perfectly clear. Surely under her eager ministrations he would have been distracted from his miserable thoughts. At least for an hour or so. Then he would probably have fallen asleep—another several hours of blessed oblivion.

But the morning would eventually come and with it the inability to avoid the bitter truth. Rhonwen would not have him.

No. He could not stomach the thought of lying with Gert tonight. Nor any other night.

Nor with any other woman. Save one.

He exhaled, a long, heavy sigh. Bad enough he wanted her. Bad enough she'd turned down his offer of marriage.

His offer had surprised her—as it had surprised him. He had not planned it, but once the words had come out, he'd felt a huge relief. All things considered, a marriage between them was the most practical solution to their situation. But she had turned him down and now, it seemed, she'd ruined him for any other woman.

How in God's name could that be?

He sprawled back in the heavy chair, let his head fall against the headrest, and stared blankly at the ceiling. The oak beams had long ago gone from golden to a smoky black, and even though nothing turned upon the spit, the place was forever scented of roasted meats.

He'd been at Rosecliffe too long, he decided. This kitchen had been new, the walls still oozing sap, when he'd arrived. It was new no longer.

He raised his head and reached for the corner of bread. But he had no appetite to eat. He put the bread down. He would have to face Rhonwen. He could not avoid her forever. And he would have to decide what to do with her. Holding her at Rosecliffe made less sense with every passing day. Holding a hostage as a guarantee to peace only worked so long as the captor was willing to punish the hostage for the transgressions of her comrades. If he could not bring himself to punish her, however . . .

The door hinges creaked.

"Go away," he ordered, not even looking up. He did not want company, especially if it was Gert.

"Jasper?"

His head jerked up. But he remained seated. He maintained an outward calm. Inside, however, all his senses had come alive. As if in a headlong rush into battle, his entire being came quiveringly alert. Tensed. Expectant.

Fearful.

The blood roared in his ears, but he only reached for his mug and lifted it to his lips. His hand did not shake, he noticed with strange detachment. Amazing. He would not credit such control to his legs, though. So he remained in the chair.

"Jasper," she said again in a voice that was soft and breathy.

"What?"

He heard the quick inhalation of her breath. She was as jittery as he and that gave him a small comfort. It allowed him also to shield himself with anger.

"What do you want, Rhonwen? For I warn you, there's little I wish to hear from you."

Rhonwen looked at Jasper's back, so stiff and unrelenting. She'd hurt him cruelly and he hated her for it. She fell back a step, before halting her retreat. "I'm sorry," she whispered. "I'm sorry things cannot be different between us."

He set his cup down and she moved to pick up the ewer at the end of the table. She filled his cup again, then found another and filled it for herself. Should she sit beside him? Across from him?

Maybe she should just leave. Maybe this was simply a wretched idea.

She was poised to run when he slowly turned his head toward her. His face was impassive.

He hated her!

Then she met his eyes and saw the sharp glint of pain. It was brief. It could have been but the accidental flicker of the single lantern in his eyes. But she thought it was more, and if it was . . .

"I could not end this day without seeing you once more," she said. She put the unwanted wine cup down and tentatively moved nearer him.

His gaze followed her. "Why?"

She wanted to be honest. She needed to be. But there was only so much of the truth she could reveal. "I . . . I have been thinking about . . . the offer you made me." That was true enough. She could think of little else.

His eyes narrowed. "Have you come here to change your answer?"

The word *yes* rose in her throat. Emotions like floodwaters battered her resolve. She swallowed hard. "I have come here to see how strong is this bond we share."

He was silent a long while before he spoke. "It is strong," he said, his voice husky, his gaze fixed with hers.

His right hand lay on the table, tanned and square-palmed, missing the little finger. Who could have predicted on that awful day so long ago that they would come to this? She placed her hand over his, her heart pounding with both fear and a desperate longing. Then his hand turned, and their fingers wove together, and she knew he loved her as she loved him.

"It is strong," he repeated.

Rhonwen lifted their clasped hands, too consumed with the power of her feelings to speak. She kissed his knuckles one by one. His fingers tightened around hers, almost to the point of pain.

Then he groaned and pulled her into his lap, and the dam gave way.

Like a flood it broke over them, every repressed emotion, every secret longing. Every burning desire. The past was washed away and the future did not yet exist. Only the present mattered.

"Rhonwen. Rhonwen . . ." He murmured her name over and over between a rain of kisses. She lay in his arms, her own arms tight about his neck as she rose into the kiss. He would be hers this night and she would not think beyond that fact. He wanted to marry her; she wished to marry him. That they could not do so was pushed into the background. This was as perfect a moment as she would ever have and she refused to waste it.

He rose to his feet, sweeping her up in his arms. The chair crashed backward. They ignored it. He kicked the door open and when he strode across the dark bailey, carrying her high against his chest with her skirts streaming behind them and her hair fanning loose across his shoulder, the rest of the world faded away. She saw no one but him. She heard nothing but the heavy thudding of his heart and the determined tread of his boots on the gravel yard.

He took the back stairs two at a time, and when they reached his private chamber—when he closed the door with his heel and just stood there, holding her close in the dark—she felt like she'd arrived at last in heaven.

"I dared not hope—" he began, then broke off and buried his face in her hair.

Tears stung Rhonwen's eyes. She was lying to him. With every kiss and every caress she was lying. He thought she'd changed her mind. He did not know that this was her good-bye.

Before she could confess her cruelty, she kissed him. She caught his face in her hands and kissed him. His lips were hers to devour. His mouth was hers to explore. He was hers. Just hers!

But her hungry seduction worked like a goad upon him, for he swiftly overpowered her aggression with his own. He laid her down upon his bed and himself over her. His weight pressed onto her, into her, marking her as his.

"You are mine," she whispered between the erotic play of their lips and tongues.

"And you are mine." One of his hands tangled in her hair, the other swept slowly down her side. Slowly. "You are mine," he repeated, and gradually eased his entire weight onto her. It was a hard, hot, wholly erotic movement. A claiming. He could do with her whatever he wished, and she would not object.

But she would do the same to him, and to prove it, she clutched at his tunic. As he slid down along the length of her, she drew the soft wool garment over his shoulders and head.

He unfastened her girdle with his teeth.

She slid one hand down his back, inside his chainse, so that her fingers explored his bare skin.

He raised her kirtle up, and her chemise as well, and let his palm glide up her leg. His fingers traced the curve of her ankle, the swell of her calf, the smooth indentation behind her knee.

With a bit of cooperative wriggling he pushed the garments up past her hips. She pulled his chainse off.

"We've got this all wrong," he murmured, kissing her navel, then pressing the side of his face against her belly. His jaw was scratchy with the day's growth of his beard, but it felt wonderful to her.

"All wrong?"

"Your lower half is naked." He rubbed his jaw against her and she clenched her hands around his shoulders.

She laughed when she understood. "And your upper half is naked. There's a remedy for that," she added, growing serious once more.

"There are several remedies," he replied. Then he slid down farther, trailing kisses past her belly to her thighs. She trembled with anticipation.

"Jasper," she begged, though for what, precisely, she could not say. No matter which portion of her body played recipient to his magic, the whole of her was thrilled.

But what of thrilling him?

"Let me kiss you that way," she said, reaching down to cup his face. "Let me give pleasure to you, Jasper. I want to."

He looked up from his task and his eyes burned with the fever of the moment. "Soon enough, Rhonwen. Soon enough." As he spoke, one of his fingers began to tease her. With her own dewiness he moistened his fingertip and began with the easiest of movements to caress her.

She sucked in a breath at the exquisite pleasure of it, then could not breathe at all as he increased the pressure. Their gazes were locked, and between them no emotion could be hidden. In his eyes she saw desire, and possession, and love. And hers . . . surely he saw how she loved him. But did he see that she meant to leave?

She closed her eyes and, as if it were a signal, he turned his attention wholly to her pleasure. With his clever lips he burned away her guilt. With his strong, yet gentle hands, he branded her flesh with his touch. And when her panting turned to helpless cries of capitulation, he urged her on. He cupped her derriere and she raised her hips in supplication.

She wanted to give him her whole self, everything she was or ever could be. But there was no way to tell him, no words to explain. She needed to be a part of him.

Oh, God. Give me a child of this man, she pleaded silently as the heat began to rise in her belly. Hotter, faster, harder. Please, God.

". . . Please, God . . ."

Then it burst and she cried out in an agony of exquisite pleasure. "Jasper. . . . Jasper . . ."

He covered her at once.

"I'm here, Rhonwen. Here . . ."

Before the tremors could end, he slid inside her. Her kirtle was gone. His braies had disappeared. They were naked and joined, and she wrapped herself, arms and legs and soul, around him.

Please, God, her silent chant began again, echoing the rhythm of their joining. A child, please, God. His child.

He brought her to the peak again, and kept her there until she was sure she must die from the intensity. Then he plunged groaning into her, and their union was complete.

Complete . . .

In the aftermath they lay tangled together, connected in every way they could be. Their bodies. Their wills. Their hearts. It was a moment of perfection, a moment Rhonwen knew she would treasure all the days of her life. Should she die tomorrow or live to see her children's children's children, it did not matter, for she was complete. Jasper had made her so.

But she was not dead yet, and when he rolled to his side, taking her with him, she forced her sated body to move. He was relaxing into near sleep. She could feel it. But he was naked and warm and damp, and she had a compelling need to explore his body. So she faced him and in the dark room began to touch him. She could barely see him, but she could learn the contours of him, the textures, with her fingers and her lips.

The heavy muscles of his arms were smooth. The relaxed muscles of his chest were, nevertheless, hard. His nipples, flat and small, were intriguing, and he groaned when she teased them. One of his arms circled her, pulling her against him.

"What are you up to?" he asked in a husky voice.

"Be still and you will see," she answered, then deliberately shifted her hips against his. She felt the instant response of his manhood.

What a wondrous organ it was. From small and peaceful to huge and aggressive, it could change in seconds. Then, sated, it subsided, only to rouse again at the suggestive thrust of her hips.

Her hand slid down his chest, playing in the damp curls, gliding across the ridged stomach, then finding curls again below it. She hesitated only a moment. She must go easy with him, as he'd gone easy with her. At first.

A brush of her knuckles. The tickling stroke of her fingertips. When he thrust convulsively against her hand, she knew he was fully revived.

"Come over me, Rhonwen." He rolled to his back and dragged her on top of him.

Though she was more than willing, she was not yet done with her exploration. She sat up, straddling him and liking the way it felt. "I want to see you."

He shifted and reached for a flint and steel beside the bed. With just a few strokes he lit a candle. The tiny flame made a soft golden pool of light near his shoulder, illuminating one side of his face, one side of his body. He was light and shadows, golden and ebony.

He was wicked and yet wonderful. He tortured her and yet brought her to utter joy. He was hers—but he could never be hers.

Suddenly her exploration took on a new urgency. This night would not last forever, yet for her it must. She sat across his hips, conscious of his fully aroused manhood pressing between her wide-spread legs. She was also aware of his eyes drinking in her nakedness.

Though her first instinct was to shyly cover herself, she fought it down. She'd come to seduce him and so she would.

She shook her head, letting her hair fall freely about her, then slowly leaned forward, cocooning them in the dark curtain. She kissed his mouth, thrusting her tongue deep, discovering what he liked best, slow and sinuous, fast and urgent. When he caught her shoulders, she pushed his hands away.

"Let me, Jasper. You must just lie here and let me please you."

"You please me—"

"But I'm not finished. I've barely begun. . . ."

This time instead of her fingers, she explored him with her lips and tongue. She tasted his throat, and caught his nipples between his teeth. She nipped the skin of his belly and circled the indentation of his navel.

Then she moved lower and made a small, experimental stroke along his raging erection.

"God's blood," he groaned. "You're killing me."

She did it again, but slower. This time he thrust upward, nearly oversetting her.

"Enough," he grated out. Then he dragged her up the sizzling length of him so that she straddled him on all fours. "I cannot wait."

"Why not—"

He caught her hips and guided her down over him. This time they both groaned. His hands fastened about her waist, holding her impaled upon him, and she knew she would have it no other way.

"Rhonwen," he whispered.

"Oh, Jasper . . ."

She began to move and he kept pace. Slowly, or as slow as she could stand. Then faster as the fire flared out of control.

How could this be happening again, so soon? But it was, and she leaped gladly into the flames. Hotter, faster. Harder, higher. When it came she cried out and collapsed. But he kept on until she had melted over him, burned to cinders, consumed by the fire. Then he spilled his precious seed into her, holding her so tight she could not breathe, and gasping her name over and over.

"Rhonwen. . . . Rhonwen . . ."

Book Three

All other love is like the moone
That wexth and waneth.

—*anonymous medieval verse*

Nineteen

Jasper . . . Jasper . . .

His name plagued Rhonwen with every step that led her away from him. The candle had guttered as he slept, and when it did, she knew the time had come. Already a hint of the false dawn edged the castle walls.

She stood in the quiet bailey now, beating down her doubts. She'd had more than she should ever have hoped for, a magical night in the arms of the man she loved. She must content herself with that.

But still her fingers crept to her belly. Please let it be so, she prayed. Despite the obstacles a fatherless child would present for her, she wanted to carry Jasper's babe, to bear it and care for it and flood it with all the love she would never be allowed to give him.

A cat yowled in the dark, startling her. Another answered. A dog barked lazy admonition to the cats, and Rhonwen forced herself to be practical. It was time to leave Rosecliffe Castle.

She peered carefully around the bailey, then, keeping to the shadows, made her way to the kitchen. Jasper had never made it to the postern gate. Unless someone else had a second key, only the bar would be up. No one from outside could enter, but anyone could depart. Even a hostage, like her.

She felt her way down the kitchen alley and into the cavernlike passageway. She raised the bar, wincing at the shriek of metal on metal. In the resounding silence that followed, she listened for some indication of alarm.

Nothing. Only the hard hammering of her heart.

She turned the ring latch. It was well oiled, but the heavy metal hinges creaked as she opened the door, then again as she closed it. But she'd made it outside. She flattened against the wall, holding her breath as she listened for the guards to raise a hue and cry.

Again, nothing.

A quick glance around revealed no one, only a few sparse shrubs and the pale pathway leading down the sheer face of the cliff. Below her the sea was nearly invisible. Only the rare reflection of starlight signaled from its moving surface.

Below her the surf crashed on the narrow beach. The wind pressed her into the north-facing wall. It was cold, as it should be. The winter yet wrestled for hold of the spring. But it was more than the wind and the sea and the remnants of winter that chilled her. She was cold and she would never be warm again. The fire that had heated her, that had burned her to the core, was no longer hers to enjoy. She left it behind as she fled into the cold unknown.

But she would never forget how it felt to be warm.

She picked her way down the path, careful in the dark, for one slip could send her hurtling to the rocky beach so far below. Grasping saplings and shrubs, she slowly descended. The sounds of the sea grew stronger. The wind was damp, heavy with the scent of salt and fish and oyster shells.

To the west a thin crescent of moon showed. To the east the first sheen of the sun's ascent tinged the horizon. She must hurry.

The wind carried a man's voice to her and she froze.

"... cold as a witch's ..."

Someone mumbled an answer and she chanced a look behind her. From below, Rosecliffe Castle was a forbidding sight. Its half-built crenellations were a jagged black slash across a nearly black sky.

Could Rhys truly mean to storm this fortress? Rhonwen shook her head. Could he not see how impossible a feat that was?

That's why he asked for your aid.

He'd asked for her aid and her answer was to flee.

She turned away, sick at the thought of how she'd betrayed him. Rhys. Jasper. Josselyn. On and on, the list grew of those she'd let down. Isolde. Gwen and Gavin. Nesta. Her own mother.

She swiped at a tear before it could fall. There was no other way, she told herself. She must escape while she could. Glancing up again, she could not see the guards who'd spoken, and she prayed they could not see her. She must hurry.

The cliff path proved even more arduous in the dark than she'd anticipated. But eventually she reached the beach. Three boats lay on their sides. Was there a guard? If so, she did not see him.

Staying near the cliff, she angled west to where the hills dropped down in sharp, rocky clefts. A tree clung here, a shrub scrabbled for sustenance there. The tide had begun to come in, and she had to wade part of the way in the ice-cold surf. But she trudged onward, fixed on her goal.

Her feet and legs grew numb. Her hands were scraped and sore. Finally she reached the little inlet she sought, and slogged out of the unforgiving sea. She sat down on a grassy bank, trembling with the cold and her exhaustion, trying to catch her breath, trying to think.

She had no food and her clothes were drenched. She needed to find a protected spot where she could dry her kirtle and stockings and rest for a while. She should press on, she knew. But she was so weary, and so cold.

By the time the sun raised above the horizon, she had moved inland and found a protected crevice near a rivulet that fed into the River Geffen. She filled the shallow cave with leaves and was preparing to remove her wet clothes when a voice hailed her.

"Rhonwen?"

She whirled, her heart in her throat, and grabbed a rock for a weapon. But it was not Jasper who came forward, nor any man-of-war. On silent feet the tiny bard Newlin appeared, dipping and swaying as he walked. His beribboned cloak drifted like wings around him. He smiled as he approached, and extended a bag out to her.

Normally he frightened her. She did not like things she could not understand. But today he was a welcome sight, neither friend nor foe. She had none of the former and too many of the latter, so his noncommittal presence came almost as a relief.

He stopped before her, still holding out the bag.

"Am I to take that?" she asked.

"You are hungry. I have food enough to share."

"How did you—" She wrapped her arms around her waist and glanced warily about. "Are you alone?"

He smiled, and though his wrinkles belied it, his expression held the sweetness of an innocent child's. "I am with you," he answered. "Take this. There is bread and cheese and dried fish. Also, ten raisins."

She took the old canvas bag, blinking back sudden tears. "Thank you. Thank you."

As she ate he watched, not speaking but only swaying a very little. " 'Twill be a day to remember," he said when she returned the empty bag to him. "A day that will be recounted whenever people gather together of a long night."

"Because I have escaped the English?" she asked, doubtfully. Then a new horror occurred to her and her heart stopped. "Is there to be a battle? Is this the day Jasper and Rhys cross swords? Please, Lord Newlin, do not let it be so."

"I am no one's lord," he answered in his simple way. One of his wandering eyes fixed on her face, then drifted away. The other one caught and remained. "This world of ours is vast. It expands far beyond the tiny circles of our lives."

Rhonwen struggled to follow the direction of his thoughts. Was there some mysterious meaning in his reply? Beyond the one occasion when he'd carried messages to Rosecliffe and helped her return Isolde, she'd had few reasons to converse with Newlin. She had no experience deciphering the ancient bard's words. But he was wise above all others in these hills. If he knew something of what was to come, she must try to understand.

She hugged her arms closer around her. "What is going to happen today? Please, you must help me."

"Help you to escape? You succeed already in that quest."

"No. No. Help me . . ." She shook her head. "I don't want them hurt. Either of them."

"You speak of the young lord—"

"Jasper FitzHugh."

"—and your friend—"

"Rhys ap Owain. Yes, and—" She broke off when both of his strange eyes focused on her at the same time.

" 'Tis not an easy thing, to love your enemy."

"I don't—" But she could not bring herself to finish the lie. Besides, it was clear he knew the truth. Indeed, she felt a certain relief knowing she need not hide her true feelings from him.

He smiled again, another sweet smile that neither gloated nor mocked. Then he raised one arm, the shriveled one, and swept it softly through the air. "Listen. Look around you."

Wrinkling her brow, Rhonwen did as he asked. A rabbit darted past him. A trio of wrens dove through the clearing, then disappeared into a stand of fir trees. A fox yipped from just beyond them; another answered from very nearby.

Then a doe sprang from a thicket, her tail raised in alarm. She and the tiny fawn that trailed her were gone in an instant.

That was odd. Even in her agitation, Rhonwen recognized that much. Concentrating now, she looked around her and knew at once that something was not right in the forest. The animals were too bold. The air was heavy with portent. Even the trees seemed to toss their branches and budding leaves, though there was little enough wind.

Her eyes glanced heavenward, but the clouds were of the wrong sort to presage a storm. Then she shivered with a new fear. The animals behaved oddly, and the trees . . . Her eyes widened in alarm. The priests often spoke of the second coming, of the end of the world, when sinners were cast down into hell while the repentant rose up to heaven.

"Is it the end of the world?"

He did not smile and her heart sank.

"Some will say yes. The end of the world as they know it. But not in the way you fear."

"But . . . the end of the world is . . . the end of the world."

Newlin had turned his twisted face up to the heavens and began the same slight swayings he'd noticed before. "When stones shall grow and trees shall no'. When noon comes black as beetle's back . . ."

Rhonwen gasped, relieved and yet horrified. She knew the rest of the chant. Every Welsh child did. *When winter's heat shall snow defeat. We'll see them, all, ere Cymru falls.*

"Is this the day?" she pressed him. "The day Cymru falls to England?" When he did not answer, she grabbed him by the shoulders. "Jasper is going to defeat Rhys, isn't he? Today. He's going to defeat him—and kill him! Is that what you see? Is it?"

"I do not have the talent to foretell the future, Rhonwen."

"You do! You already have. So tell me the rest!"

"I read the signs. The trees, the birds. The doe and her fawn. But people . . ." He shrugged his one good shoulder and stared at her with eyes so filled with compassion she could not bear it. She released him and backed away.

"People," he continued, "are free to decide, to pick one course and follow it to its end, or change their direction and choose another path. I cannot foresee what Jasper FitzHugh will decide, nor Rhys ap Owain. Nor Rhonwen ap Tomas."

A willow sapling gnashed its tender branches. An ancient hawthorn shivered and sighed above them. Despair settled heavily upon Rhonwen. Despair and desolation.

"What should I do?" she whispered. But she knew. "Where is Rhys? Do you know that much? Can you tell me?"

"He comes for you."

She sighed heavily. "He thinks that on the dark of the moon I will open the castle's postern gate to him."

"But you cannot." He said no more than that, but Rhonwen knew he understood her motives. He might not be able to predict how people would behave, but he had an uncanny ability to know what they already had done, and why.

"I could not help him in that way," she admitted.

"So he will find the gate barred to him." Again Newlin shrugged. "He will be forced to abandon his plan."

"But what if Jasper comes out to meet him?" She swept her hand around them, at the expectant forest and its fearful creatures. "You said yourself that it is the end of the world."

"As you know it. But not necessarily in the way that you fear."

She pressed her fingers to her temples. She was dizzy trying to make sense of this. Her weariness was forgotten. Her cold but a memory. If she stayed here, doing nothing, she would surely go mad.

"Where is he? Where is Rhys? At the least you must tell me that."

"He comes to Rosecliffe Castle along the coast path."

"Then I must intercept him," she said, less to him than to herself. "I must stop him before he can be the author of his own demise."

She left without bidding Newlin farewell. Her mission was too vital to delay. She had to turn Rhys back. It was the only way to save him.

What if he refused to turn back from a fight? she fretted as she scrambled up a rugged slope. What if he accused her of being a traitor to their cause, of protecting the English from the wrath of the Welsh people they sought to rule?

She paused, winded by her climb. If she could not change his mind with her words, then she would resort to Newlin's. She did not understand the chant or what part it played in the terrible possibilities this day held, but she would tell Rhys and if he was not frightened, his men would be. Without his men he could not hope to attack the English fortress.

But what of his English ally? What of Simon LaMonthe?

Rhonwen had no answer for that. No solution. First she must find Rhys. After that . . . after that she would do every-

thing in her power to turn him away from Rosecliffe. Some
how she would stop him. Somehow.

Half a day later, Rhonwen leaned stiff-armed against a lime
tree, fighting for breath and for calm. She must not panic!

But it was hard to remain calm when the sun was past its
zenith. She'd not come upon Rhys. Had she gone wrong?

She caught her breath, listening. The wind had risen, though
the sky remained bright. Only thin, hazy clouds obscured the
sun. There were no signs of an impending storm. Yet every
thing felt somehow askew. She knew it, as did the small crea
tures of the forest.

Perhaps Rhys sensed it as well. Perhaps he'd called off this
mad plan. She hoped it was so, but she did not believe it. So
she listened and after a moment she heard it, the boom of the
surf against the rocky shore. She'd not gone wrong. If Rhys
came along the coast, she must meet with him soon.

She pressed a hand to her aching side. She was no longer
hungry; that pain was long gone. But she was tired. Her feet
ached. Her hands were scraped and the stitch in her side was
a recurring aggravation. But she must go on. So she took a
deep breath and started forward.

It was then she heard it. A twig snapped.

She halted; her heart pounded with a new urgency. Was it
Rhys or one of his men?

Something hit her shoulder and she whirled around. A peb
ble ricocheted to the ground and her eyes darted wildly about.
It must be him, tossing small rocks at her. Teasing her as he'd
always done.

"Rhys?" she called. "Come out. Don't tease me, for I have
come a long way to find you. Rhys? Rhys!"

Something moved to her left and she jerked to see. When
there was nothing there, she jerked around again—

And came face-to-face with Jasper.

Twenty

Jasper tossed the remaining pebbles at Rhonwen's feet. She had expected Rhys. That came as no surprise. Who else could she have been running to?

Yet the undeniable proof of her betrayal still caught him unaware. Like a low blow in a camp brawl, it nearly doubled him over. He sucked in a painful breath.

"You were expecting Rhys," he said, relieved at the even tenor of his voice. "I'm afraid, Rhonwen, that you are destined ever to be disappointed by that one."

She backed away, but her eyes remained fixed warily upon him. Her color was high, he noted. Her plait had begun to unravel and shredded bits of leaves and twigs clung to the dark tangle. The hem of her gown was muddy and torn, and her shawl was tied in a lump around her hips. All in all, she was ragged and disheveled, more an earthy wood nymph than the fine lady Josselyn would make of her. But to Jasper's eyes she was beautiful. Beautiful but treacherous, and never again to be trusted

She'd betrayed him in the worst way a woman could, and she'd played him for a fool. But he would never be fooled by her again.

He advanced on her, reining in any sign of either fury or pain. This time she would pay for her duplicity. "Did you truly think you could escape Rosecliffe Castle so easily?'' he taunted. ''Tumble me once or twice and you could befuddle me sufficiently for you to escape through the postern gate?''

He laughed derisively, but he knew the truth. Her plan had worked. She'd come to him so sweetly, so willingly, with words of love upon her lips. And he'd believed every word. He'd been a fool to offer her marriage, and an even bigger fool to believe she'd changed her mind. But then, he'd been a colossal fool from the first moment he'd laid eyes on her.

Even when he'd awakened to find her gone he'd been unable to admit the truth. He'd torn the castle apart searching for her. Then he'd found the postern gate unbarred, and he'd finally been doused with the cold reality of what she'd done.

''You were a sweet mouthful,'' he continued. ''But I've tasted innumerable women. You were just one more among them.''

He hurt her with that lie. He meant to do it and when she gasped and raised one hand to her throat, he knew he'd succeeded. It didn't ease his pain, though. If anything, it increased it. But he brutally ignored his own aching heart and pressed on.

''He's not here, Rhonwen. It should be plain by now that Rhys is not going to rescue you. And I'm not going to let you go.''

''Why?'' Her voice was thin and shaky. He could barely hear her in the chaos of the rising wind. ''If I mean so little to you, why will you not just let me go?''

Then, like a startled doe, she turned and fled.

Though caught unprepared, Jasper was swift in his pursuit. She was small and fleet of foot, despite her weariness. But he was stronger and he was driven by the devil, it seemed. He caught her shoulder, but she twisted away. Around an oak, then skidding down a hill, she lengthened her lead. But he hurtled a felled tree trunk that she had to climb over. He was gaining on her. Then he launched himself at her and caught her around the waist.

With a shrill cry followed by a grunt, she went down, though he managed to cushion her fall. But that did not end their battle. When he shifted his position, she swung at him, catching the side of his head with her fist. But Jasper was impervious to her blows. With a jerk he rolled over and she was suddenly trapped beneath him.

Just as suddenly she ceased her struggles.

They lay in a newly green bed of ferns, locked in an intimate embrace, made obscene by all the wrong emotions. Fear and rage were all wrong. Jasper knew it and yet could do nothing to change them. She was afraid of him and he wanted to strangle her.

He drove his fingers into her hair, locking her head in place. His breath came in hard gasps. Her chest heaved and fell in an equally violent pattern.

He wanted her. God, but he wanted her! He would have married her, had she agreed. But now—

"Let me go, Jasper. Please," she begged him quietly. "The world is coming to an end. Newlin said so. Please, just let me go."

"The world is coming to an end?" He snorted derisively. " 'Tis only a storm. We've weathered worse."

"No, no!" Tears started in her eyes, but he would not let her look away. He wanted to see her pain. He needed to.

"Something terrible is going to happen," she whispered. "Please, just listen to me."

"What? What is going to happen?"

"I don't know, not exactly."

"That's because it's already happened. I've got you back and your precious Rhys can't—or won't—do anything about it."

He glared at her and saw tears slip down her cheeks and disappear into her hair. A smudge on one of her cheeks showed the clean trail of two of those tears.

"Son-of-a-bitch," he muttered, then rolled off her. He yanked her to her feet and swore again. Then he started up the hill, dragging her behind him.

They'd nearly reached the crest of the hill where he'd first found her, and he'd nearly gotten his anger under control when Helios whickered. At once Jasper stilled. He pushed Rhonwen down, and simultaneously wrapped a hand around her mouth as he drew out his sword.

"Keep quiet," he hissed in her ear. "Keep quiet and I might not put this blade through your beloved Rhys's black heart." She nodded, but that only deepened his rage. Damn her for loving Rhys ap Owain!

He crept forward, not daring to let go of her. She moved alongside him, but she clutched at his tunic with one hand and wrapped her other hand around the wrist of his hand that muzzled her. He could almost believe she clung to him, for there was no longer any resistance in her.

But there was no time for that sort of speculation. He strained to hear, but Helios was silent. Nothing else was, however. The trees groaned and birds called out in agitation. Nightcatchers and ravens and kestrels. A rabbit bolted practically from beneath his feet.

What in God's name was going on? The day was bright, yet in every other way a storm seemed to threaten.

"Jasper," Rhonwen managed to say, though his fingers muffled her. "Jasper."

"Shh." He forced her to kneel behind a boulder near the crest of the hill. Someone was nearby. Several someones. Though Jasper had parted ways with his men an hour before, he was not certain it was them. He craned his neck to see.

"Save yourself," Rhonwen whispered.

The hairs on the back of Jasper's neck prickled and he spared another glance down at her. Why would she say that? Did she know something he did not?

Had he, in his rage, hunted her into Rhys's lair—into a trap? Then an even worse thought blindsided him. Had she lured him into that trap?

Had that been her role at Rosecliffe all along?

His right hand tightened around her mouth, the left on the hilt of his sword. If his world was to end this day, he would take his share of Welshmen into the hereafter with him.

". . . can't be far . . ." a Welsh voice carried above the increasing winds.

"Fan out. Find him," another answered.

So, it was as he suspected. Jasper steeled himself against any hint of fear and glanced about, searching for the best position from which to make his stand. The undergrowth was still thin and the forest bright. To run would not get them far. But even as he studied the slope of the hill, the sunlight began to fail. Sunshine and shadows evened out to gray.

He peered back over the hill and saw a small band of men. One of them held Helios's bridle. Rhys ap Owain!

His options were now clear. Stand and fight—and probably die, for he was not likely to defeat so many. Or run and hopefully elude them. He looked down at Rhonwen. There was little time.

"Come with me." He released her, allowing her to run or cry out or whatever she wanted to do. It was madness to trust her, but then, he'd been a madman from the first day he'd spied her beside the river. "Come with me, Rhonwen, while there is still time."

She stared at him as if unable to comprehend what he asked of her. "I . . . I cannot."

"You can."

". . . to the river. You two, come with me . . ." The voice drew nearer. Rhys's voice.

Jasper flexed the wrist of his sword hand. If he did not leave now, he'd have to fight Rhys. Though he'd been prepared to do that all along—indeed, he welcomed the chance to meet his foe in battle—suddenly he did not want Rhonwen to witness that confrontation.

"Go, Jasper!" She pointed down the hill toward the river. "Go, please. While you still can!"

But Jasper did not want to go, not without her. The wind blew her hair back and molded her moss-green gown against her slender body. Had ever a woman pleased him so—or tortured him more?

He stepped forward to catch her hand and somehow convince her. But an enraged cry halted him.

"FitzHugh! Touch her and you will die!"

"No!" Rhonwen gasped.

"Get away from him, Rhonwen," the Welsh rebel ordered triumphantly.

"Please, Rhys. Don't do this. He—"

"Do as he says," Jasper interrupted her. He held his sword up and pointed the razor-sharp blade at his nemesis. "Go on Rhonwen. Get away from here."

"Jasper. Rhys." She pleaded first with one and then th other. But Jasper circled away from her, and with a gestur from Rhys, two of his men caught her arms and dragged he away. "No! Don't do this! Don't kill him!"

Who did she mean? Jasper wondered as he took his oppo nent's measure. Whose life did she hope to spare?

A tree branch creaked above him, then cracked and crashe down between him and Rhys. He jumped back, as did hi adversary. Perhaps the storm would come to his aid, Jaspe hoped. He glanced up to gauge the storm, but he saw no cloud to speak of, only a fitful haze. A strange foreboding ran dow his spine, and despite the men who surrounded him, h searched the heavens.

What he saw chilled him to the core. "God's bones!"

Rhys glanced up, then stared wide-eyed at the sky. He to cursed, though in Welsh. One by one the other men crane their necks, then fell back in horror, pointing up at the sk and blubbering in fear.

Jasper was dumbfounded by the vision in the sky. Then h recalled Rhonwen's remark. Newlin had foretold the end o the world. Could it be true?

Around them the light began to falter. It was midday. Th sun hung high in the sky. But it was disappearing before thei very eyes. "God save us," Jasper muttered. "God save u all." Bit by bit the sun was eroding, disappearing, and with the heat and light it afforded. The very light of the world.

" 'Tis as was foretold," one of the cowering men shouted *"When noon comes black as beetle's back!"* The man turne and bolted. Another of his comrades followed suit. Helio whinnied and reared, then tore away from the terrified fellov holding him.

Was it the end of the world? Jasper wondered. Then h

searched for Rhonwen. If it was the end of the world, running would save no one. Better to die alongside the woman he loved than to die alone.

Ignoring Rhys and the increasing dark, he darted toward Rhonwen. Cursing, Rhys came after him. But Rhonwen eluded Jasper. "Get away. Get away!" she screamed at him. Then she ran into Rhys's arms.

Jasper hesitated, staring at her, stunned. Rhys hugged her a moment, then tried to set her aside. But she clung to him, preventing his pursuit, and finally Jasper reacted. Taking advantage of the dark and the confusion, and Rhonwen's interference, he flew down the hill, in the same direction Helios had gone.

He ran, dodging and twisting, through brush and whipping branches, through darkness and wind. But every pounding step drove home the bitter truth. She'd chosen Rhys.

She'd chosen Rhys every time she was presented a choice. He paused behind a rocky outcropping, winded, and dropped to one knee, fighting for breath. How many times must he be faced with the truth before he would recognize it? How many times?

He glanced around, straining to hear any sounds of pursuit. The wind had eased somewhat, but it was nearly as dark as night. Then his eyes fixed on a movement. A rabbit crouched beneath a nightshade, not two paces distance from him. Too frightened to run—or too wise. Jasper peered up at the sky, searching for the sun above the strangely shadowed forest.

It was gone. It was gone, and only a faint halo burned into the heavens marked where it once had been.

He made a sign of the cross. He'd prepared himself to die by the sword, but to witness the end of the world?

Then, as he squinted, the edge of the sun reappeared. He blinked and shielded his eyes with one hand. What was happening? Was the sun coming back?

He did not waste time judging the answer. If the sun was gone, all was lost anyway. But if it was coming back, he must act quickly. He pushed to his feet and the rabbit dashed away.

Heartened, he continued on, more careful now of his direction and the trail he left.

Slowly light crept back into the forest, and when he spied fresh hoofprints in a muddy patch, his hopes rose further. He found Helios cropping new clover near the riverbank, and once assured the destrier had suffered no injury, he mounted the beast.

In the sky the sun was halfway restored, and though Jasper was not superstitious, he shuddered with profound relief. For some reason God had seen fit to save him from certain death. He'd spared his life, and yet at the same time, had destroyed it. Jasper would survive this day, it seemed. But would he survive the endless empty days to come? The ache in his heart proclaimed the truth: He loved Rhonwen. But she did not love him.

Sunk in his own misery, he turned Helios and kicked the animal into motion. Best to cross the river and make his way north to Rosecliffe along the far bank. He'd lost this round to Rhys, but he knew they were bound to meet again.

And next time he would not charge unprepared into the fray, blinded by rage or love—or the torturous mix of both those emotions.

He crossed the river where it was wide and the banks strewn with gravel. The water was shallow enough that Helios never lost his footing. Jasper glanced periodically up at the sky where the sun had bloomed almost to its full circumference again. It was as if something had blocked its light, then moved on.

The moon? he wondered, staring at the dark orb now visible beside the sun. They had not collided at all, it seemed, but had briefly overlapped.

He should take a lesson from the heavens, he told himself, urging Helios up the riverbank. He and Rhonwen had been drawn into one another's paths, and for a while it had seemed that they had collided. But they had merely overlapped. Now, like the sun and the moon, they would go their opposite directions.

But no matter that he tried to characterize it otherwise, Jasper could not escape one fact. Going a direction opposite Rhonwen's was ripping his heart in two.

"God curse me for a fool," he muttered.

The words had barely left his mouth when a phalanx of riders burst from the trees. Helios reared in surprise and in a trifling Jasper was surrounded by hooded knights. English knights, with their swords drawn and their intentions clear.

He whipped out his own sword and held it in a defensive position. "What is the meaning of this?" he demanded to know, bringing Helios under control.

The circle of riders parted and a man rode forward. When he pushed back his mail cowl and gave a feral grin, Jasper's blood ran cold.

Simon LaMonthe. And if his triumphant expression was any indication, he'd not come to save Jasper from the Welshmen who pursued him.

Twenty-One

Rhonwen rode before Rhys. She'd wanted to walk. She'd wanted to escape his presence. But he'd not afforded her that luxury, and now, when her heart was breaking, she must pretend to be grateful that he had saved her.

She hunched forward, trying to control her shaky emotions. Why couldn't she be happy? This was what she'd wanted, to get away from Jasper and to avoid a fight between him and Rhys. But her mind kept returning to Jasper. Had he escaped? Would he make his way safely back to Rosecliffe Castle?

Would he come after her again?

Did she want him to? Oh, but she was perverse. How could she even think such a thing?

Rhys guided the horse down a hill, following a faint deer trail. "That was not a sign," he muttered, more to himself than to her. "That darkness meant nothing. Only a superstitious fool would believe it did."

"There are more than a few superstitious fools residing in these hills," Rhonwen responded.

When noon comes black as beetle's back echoed in both their minds. Well, that day had come.

The children's song which had been so comforting was now coming true before their astounded eyes. Stones that grew. A midday shadowed by darkness. All that remained was for winter to burn as hot as summer. Could such a thing truly occur?

She was beginning to believe it could.

Rhys kicked the horse to a faster pace. He was in a ferocious mood, and she knew why. He'd had Jasper in his grasp—at least for a few minutes. He'd had the man who'd killed his father. But Jasper had escaped.

"I want to know what you learned during your days in the English fortress," he said in a terse voice. "LaMonthe's men said you had much freedom there, the run of the hall and the bailey. They said also that they delivered their message to you. But you left Rosecliffe before the dark of the moon. Why? Why didn't you do as you were ordered?"

"I am not yours to order about. I am not one of your men—"

"You are Cymry! If you love your land and your people, then you must give your all in its defense."

He pulled up the horse in a muddy clearing and slid over the animal's rump. Then, scowling, he caught her by the waist and rudely dragged her down. His grip on her arms was harsh; his expression was furious. "But for your cowardice, we would take that fortress tomorrow night!"

"I am not yours to command!" She tore out of his hold and faced him with her fists knotted. "Nor am I a coward. You men know only one sort of courage, only one form of bravery. You throw yourselves at one another, you impale yourselves upon each other's weapons, and you bleed your lives out onto these lands."

She pressed her knotted fists passionately to her chest. "But we women, we are the ones who watch that blood seep into the earth. As children we see our fathers die, and our mothers weep and then carry on. As women we lose our brothers and husbands—and friends—to the gruesome lure of war. Always war! Then we grow old and we lose our sons as well."

Her chest heaved with the force of her emotions, but her anger burned itself out. She lifted her arms, then let them fall in a gesture of hopelessness. "Will it never end, Rhys? Will it never end?"

"Yes. Yes, it will end." He caught her again by the arms

but he was earnest now, and his hands were gentler. "When we drive our enemies away from our lands, then it will end."

Rhonwen was silent for a minute, just looking up at him. He'd been waging this war of his so long, it was easy to forget how young he was. Only six-and-ten, yet he'd shouldered the responsibilities of a man his entire life. Had he ever played like other children played? Had he ever cavorted across a meadow, or laughed purely for joy?

She cupped his cheek with one hand and felt the faint fuzz that promised a man's beard someday soon. He was unbearably young and, for all his experiences, still unaware of life's possibilities. She, meanwhile, felt old and so world-weary. "Oh, Rhys," she murmured.

He covered her hand with his, then turned his face and pressed a fervent kiss to her palm. "To know he held you was a torture. Sweet Rhonwen—"

He broke off when she curled her fingers against her palm.

"No. Don't." She backed away from him, shaking her head regretfully. "Please don't do that, Rhys. It can never be like that between you and me."

The longing in his eyes froze and became an accusation. "Why? Why do you spurn me?"

His men had ridden into the clearing behind them, and now they sat their horses in silence. Rhys did not seem to care that they heard all. "Is it that FitzHugh?" He stared at her as if she were someone he didn't know. "It is, isn't it? You gave yourself to him." He shook his head in disbelief. "You gave yourself to him." Then his debelief turned to fury. "My God, you've become his whore!"

He stalked her and she fell back. His men watched their interplay. Only Fenton interfered. He cut his horse between them, then slid down to face Rhys. He was shorter and older, but he faced Rhys fearlessly.

"Think, lad. She mightn't have been willing. The man most likely forced her." He spat on the ground. "She wouldn't be the first woman as has suffered that way at the hands of our enemies."

Rhys looked past Fenton to where Rhonwen stood and she

saw the question in his eyes. "Is that what happened?" he asked. "Is it?"

A fit of trembling seized her. She clasped her arms across her chest. "You want to know what happened. You all do. I wonder, though, which answer would satisfy you more." Her trembling increased and her teeth began to chatter. "Would you rather that he raped me, Rhys? Would you rather that he used his greater strength to hold me down and force me, no matter how much I might have struggled and fought?"

Her tortured gaze swept the silent circle of men. "Would it make all of you feel better if I said he violated my body and stole my innocence? Is that the answer you would prefer to hear?" she finished in a stricken voice, facing Rhys once more.

His face had turned ashen at her words, but nonetheless, it did not deter him from his goal. "Is that what he did?"

"Do you want that to be my answer?"

"No," he swore. "How can you think it?"

"So you'd rather that I had gone to him willing."

She stared at him until he could not avoid answering her. "No." This time his voice was a hoarse whisper.

She gave a bitter laugh. "Those are the only two choices. Which one do you prefer?"

"What I want is for none of this to have happened," he hissed. "But I cannot have that."

"No. You cannot. So tell me. Which answer do you prefer?"

He shook his head, and she saw the misery in his eyes. "I have never wanted you to be hurt."

She pressed her lips together. "When men fight, women are always hurt."

"But there is no other way."

Rhonwen sighed and looked away from him. Tears stung her eyes, but she did not let them fall. "I know," she whispered, staring around the bleak clearing. "I know."

One of the horses whinnied. At once the audience of men-at-arms went rigid. Swords slithered from their sheaths as the ragged Welshmen jerked their attention to the encircling forest. Forgotten in the sudden tension, Rhonwen darted for the dubious shelter of the gnarled trunk of an ancient yew tree.

Rhys had flung himself onto his horse. He glanced momentarily at her, then kicked the animal into the center of his milling men. At the same moment, a trio of horses burst into the clearing.

They were English!

Rhonwen pressed her hands to her mouth in horror. The battle she'd tried to avoid had found her.

But although the Welsh warriors did not relax their grip on swords and battle-axes, neither did they raise those weapons to attack. Then Rhys spurred forward to greet the English leader and Rhonwen understood. This was Simon LaMonthe and his men, Rhys's English allies. Behind the three riders, another, larger group emerged, and their jubilance was plain.

Rhonwen leaned forward to better hear their parlay, but the milling horses muffled their words. Then Rhys looked back at her. So did LaMonthe.

Rhys's face was troubled—both anger and triumph seemed to war for dominance. LaMonthe's feral features were easier to read. He was elated. It put her in mind of a vulture's smugness. Something had happened, and she sensed immediately that she would not like it.

LaMonthe signaled to someone, and a knot of horses moved forward. But Rhonwen stared at Rhys, stared at him until he averted his eyes. Only then, with dread hovering over her, did she look at the riders who moved to the center of the clearing.

Jasper sat in the midst of them. Jasper, riding Helios, with his cowl pushed down and his hands tied behind his back.

"No!" She did not realize she'd rushed forward until Rhys cut his horse in front of her.

"Stay back," he ordered in a low, threatening voice.

"What are you going to do to him? Rhys!"

"Hold your tongue," he hissed, trying to herd her back from the knot of mounted riders.

But LaMonthe had noted her concern and he edged his animal toward them. "What is this?" he asked as his eyes raked her with an unpleasant thoroughness. Too late Rhonwen realized that Rhys was not only trying to keep her from Jasper. He also wanted to protect her from LaMonthe. Instinctively she leaned against Rhys's booted leg as LaMonthe circled them both.

"She is my woman," Rhys said. "And I don't share." His horse made a nervous circle too, but Rhonwen stayed close. Only when the two men ceased their deadly measuring dance did she risk a glance over at Jasper. What she saw caused her blood to run cold. Though he sat his great destrier unbowed, it was clear he'd been beaten. Blood crusted his brow. One of his eyes had swelled shut, and the front of his tunic was torn and caked with mud. But he met her gaze, and she could not look away.

I love you. I love you! She did not say the words, but with every fiber of her body she sent the message to him. *I love you and I am so sorry I have brought you to this.*

"She is your woman?" LaMonthe chuckled. "From what I have heard, she is naught but a whore for the English. Well, I am English. And I am sore in need of a woman of her talents. Victory does that to a man," he added with a chilling smile in her direction.

Rhys ripped his sword from its sheath. "She is not the issue here."

LaMonthe did not flinch. "No?" His brows raised. "It seems to me she has managed to position herself in the midst of everything. Kidnapping FitzHugh's brat. Exchanging the girl for your men—and herself for you. And now, in our moment of triumph, she once more appears."

"You go too far, LaMonthe," Rhys growled. "She has led FitzHugh straight into our clutches. What else would you have her do?"

The man smiled, then rubbed his crotch, an obscene gesture that made Rhonwen gag. He leered at her, ignoring Rhys entirely. "She could fuck me—a goodwill gesture, you understand."

Rhonwen shrank back against Rhys's leg. At the same moment Jasper cursed out loud and his horse abruptly reared, drawing everyone's attention. Rhonwen gasped. She was certain Jasper would fall and be trampled. But even with his hands bound, he managed to retain his seat. In the pandemonium of milling horses, Rhys leaned down and hissed, "Go." Then he gestured and shouted, "Fenton! Take her!"

Rhonwen ran as Rhys ordered, toward the other Welshman. When she reached the shelter of Fenton's protection, she looked back to see two men yanking at Helios's head, while two others dragged Jasper down from the horse. But amid all the stamping horses and shouting men, she lost sight of him and that increased her fear tenfold.

"Jasper. Jasper," she whispered, horrified by what she'd led him into. She'd tried to keep him away from Rhys and his awful ally. But instead, she'd drawn him into this hell! Abandoning Fenton, she darted toward the men who surrounded Jasper.

"Rhonwen, no!"

But she ignored Rhys's cry. Yanking and scratching, she fought her way into the group of men-at-arms who struggled to control Jasper. Then a man raised his arm to strike Jasper.

"No!" she screamed as the heavy hilt of the sword swung down. It caught Jasper on the side of his head and drove him to his knees.

"Hold!" LaMonthe snarled dismounting and pushing himself into the middle of the throng.

At the same time Rhys caught up to her and flinging himself down from his horse, trapped her in his arms.

"Damn you," he muttered in her ear, holding her so tight she could scarcely breathe. "Damn you for being a traitorous bitch!"

"Well, well." LaMonthe strolled up to Jasper. "This grows more entertaining by the minute."

His men and Rhys's drew back to form a circle, all of them plainly eager for the bloodletting they anticipated. Jasper's blood, Rhonwen knew with increasing desperation.

LaMonthe looked sidelong at Rhonwen and Rhys, a nasty speculative stare. With a wave of his long-fingered hand he signaled them to join him before the kneeling Jasper.

Against her back Rhonwen felt every breath Rhys took. She

felt also his tension and his seething anger. Would he make her watch Jasper die? Had she provoked him that far?

To her utter shock, he held her closer.

"She is not a part of this. Two of my men will escort her to Afon Bryn."

"She stays," LaMonthe countered. He smiled as if to soften the curt order, but his pale eyes were dangerously cold.

Rhonwen did not understand. Rhys hated her for betraying him and his cause. But still he would protect her from La-Monthe?

"She stays," LaMonthe continued, "until we have dealt with FitzHugh. I find it more satisfying to deal with one little problem at a time."

It was not going to end well between Rhys and LaMonthe. Rhonwen recognized that at once, as, she sensed, did Rhys. His hands tightened on her shoulders and he whispered, "I want you to be safe, Rhonwen. Trust me and do exactly as I tell you."

She gave a brief nod. When Rhys shoved her to one side, toward Fenton, she went. "Let us be done with this," Rhys said. "Randulf FitzHugh has not yet returned to Rosecliffe Castle, and his brother is in our hands. I will kill this one and then take the castle as planned. You have only to intercept Rand when he returns to Rosecliffe. He will be caught between us." He spat on the ground between them. "Then our pact will be done."

"So it will," LaMonthe answered.

It was plain, however, that the end of their unholy pact would make them the bitterest of enemies. The death of Jasper or Rand or any number of people, English or Welsh, would not change anything, Rhonwen saw. War and its attendant miseries would remain like a plague forever upon the land. Today's darkness and the prediction it fulfilled had changed nothing. The world was the same as ever—as unhappy as ever.

Without thinking she edged nearer Jasper, gazing at him with a breaking heart. He was watching LaMonthe intently. Did he think the man a more dangerous enemy than Rhys? Then again, traitors usually were.

And Rhys thought *she* was a traitor.

Then Jasper looked up at her, his eyes dark and turbulent and she wondered if he too thought she was a traitor.

"Let us begin," LaMonthe said, jerking Rhonwen's attention back to him. He drew out his sword. The cold slither o steel on hide sent a frisson of renewed fear up her spine.

"He is mine to kill," Rhys snapped, glaring at LaMonthe "You can have his brother, but this one is mine."

"Do you seek revenge for your father," Jasper asked in calm, clear voice, "or is it for Rhonwen?"

A muscle jumped in Rhys's jaw. "It should make no difference to you. Dead is dead."

"Think of it as my final request. If you think to claim Rhonwen, the answer to my question must eventually be made. She will want to know."

Rhys hesitated. His face creased into a furious frown, bu when he looked at Rhonwen she saw doubt in his eyes. Hi youth was against him, she realized. Two older, seasoned warriors, both LaMonthe and Jasper knew how to play on hi volatile emotions.

But what did Jasper think to accomplish?

She glanced wildly about, searching for someone to intercede, some way to stop this. Some way to help Jasper escape

"You get no final request," Rhys snarled.

"Be careful," Jasper said, smiling at him confidently. "I you want her, you will not gain her by slitting the throat o an unarmed man."

Again Rhys hesitated, and Rhonwen felt a glimmer of hope

But LaMonthe interrupted. "Enough of this. If you have not the stomach to slay an unarmed man, I do."

It happened so fast Rhonwen had no time to think. In three strides LaMonthe crossed to where Jasper was held still on hi knees between two burly Englishman. LaMonthe lifted hi blade and she threw herself at him, grabbing his arm.

"Rhonwen! No!" Jasper cried.

"Damn you!" LaMonthe screamed, trying to shake her off He twisted his wrist and she fell forward. But she scramble to her feet just as he thrust at the struggling Jasper.

She felt a searing pain in her side.

She heard someone call her name.

Then the sky grew gray, as it had before. Gray, and then black.

Twenty-Two

Jasper jerked against one captor, then the other, then backward as they both tightened their hold. They stumbled into one another as he jumped to his feet. But his hands were bound and he could not stop LaMonthe's thrust.

"No. No! Rhonwen!" he screamed. But it was too late. Rhonwen jerked, then went horribly limp, more like one of Gwen's cloth babies than a living woman.

"Rhonwen!" This time it was Rhys who cried her name. The anguished youth somehow caught her before LaMonthe had fully withdrawn his weapon from her side. But as Rhys bent over her, cradling her in his arms, LaMonthe raised his weapon once more.

Blood was smeared on the blade—Rhonwen's blood—and Jasper let out a bellow of pure rage. Before LaMonthe could fell the unsuspecting Rhys, Jasper plowed into the black-hearted Englishman. They went down in a screaming, cursing heap.

Jasper had no hope of surviving. But he could save Rhonwen. If he saved Rhys, he would save Rhonwen, and maybe give Rhys the time to fight back and kill LaMonthe. Rhys was at least justified in his venom toward Jasper. But LaMonthe was a traitor to his country and to all his countrymen.

"Behind you!" he screamed when the other Englishmen

jumped into the fray. Rhys heard and ducked, then elbowed his attacker and split his face open with the butt end of his sword.

The battle erupted into a full-scale war. Slashing and cursing. Screams of pain. Grunts of deadly effort.

LaMonthe scrabbled backward, trying to untangle himself. But Jasper tripped him with one foot, then kicked at the man's sword hand. If LaMonthe recovered, Jasper was a dead man. "Free me!" he screamed at Rhys, even as he stomped LaMonthe's fist. "Free me!"

He risked a fast look at Rhys, and for a second their eyes locked. For less than a second. But in the fraction of a moment, their eyes conveyed a wealth of emotions. Jasper had just saved Rhys's life, and the boy knew it. Hesitating only to lay Rhonwen down, Rhys flicked the tip of his sword and sliced through Jasper's bindings.

Though Jasper had no weapon, in close quarters it was not as great a disadvantage. Before LaMonthe could scramble upright, Jasper tackled him, clutching his wrist with one hand and his throat with the other.

Around him the battle raged. His nostrils flared at the sharp stink of blood and the potent stench of fear. But for himself he felt no fear, only the overwhelming need to kill the man beneath him.

LaMonthe tried to throw him off. He tried to roll him over. But Jasper was consumed by bloodlust. Rand had spoken of the red haze of fury that overtook a man in the midst of battle. But though Jasper had felt its pull when he'd attacked Rhys's camp to save Isolde, this time was different. This time it consumed him. This time it turned him into a madman. LaMonthe fought like a demon, but Jasper foiled his every move.

When the man fumbled for his dagger, Jasper wrenched it from his hands. But LaMonthe was stronger than he looked, and fought for his very life. He brought one knee up hard. Jasper turned aside barely in time. Taking advantage, La-Monthe sliced wildly at him with his sword.

The razor-sharp blade whizzed past Jasper's ear. But LaMonthe was off balance and trying to rise to his feet. Jasper slashed once with the dagger and sliced open the man's thigh. Then another thrust, forward and up, and he felt La-Monthe sag.

LaMonthe gasped something unintelligible that ended in a gurgle of blood and vomit. But Jasper had no time for revulsion or triumph. He shoved the man backward, then swung around, taking a quick survey of the battle. Several bodies littered the ground. Three battles were ongoing, though the Englishmen began to retreat when they saw their leader fall.

Then he spied Rhonwen with Rhys hovering over her, and he couldn't move at all. He stared, still on his knees, with LaMonthe's blood dripping from the raised dagger onto his hand.

She could not be dead. God have mercy, Rhonwen could not be dead!

But she was so pale. Her outstretched hand was milk-white. Her face, always so animated, now held the pallor of death.

Somehow he scrambled through the mud and gore to her side. But when he tried to press his fingers to the place where her pulse beat, Rhys snarled, "Don't touch her! Don't you come anywhere near her!"

The Welshman spread his arms over her, as if to protect her, and Jasper saw the anguish in his face. He put the dagger down and caught Rhys by the wrist. "She saved me. I have to try to save her."

"No—"

"Yes, damn you! Do you *want* her to die? If you can't have her, would you rather see her dead?"

Rhys's youth had never been so evident as now. Stricken, he stared at Jasper, the man he'd hated more than half his life and had vowed to kill when he was but a lad of seven. He looked up at Jasper now, desperate for some reason to hope. "Can you save her? Can you?"

"I don't know," Jasper answered honestly. He felt along her throat, holding his breath, praying as he'd never prayed before. Then he felt her life's pulse, weak and slow, but beating with some semblance of regularity.

"She's alive," he muttered. But how long would she remain that way?

Around them the battle had ground to a halt. Two men lay dead. Six others lay strewn about, groaning and suffering from various wounds. But Jasper focused solely on Rhonwen, as did Rhys.

Jasper found the wound, a hideous gash just below her ribs. It was deep, but clean, and he pressed the ends of the gaping wound together. "I need something to bind her side."

In short order Rhys handed him the crossbanding of one of the fallen Englishmen. Together they managed, Rhys carefully lifting her as Jasper wrapped the cloth around her waist and chest.

Once she moaned, and Jasper's hands stilled.

"Rhonwen?" Rhys's voice cracked with emotion. "Rhonwen, do you hear me? We've got you now, safe from harm. And we'll take care of you. You're going to be all right." He looked up at Jasper, pale beneath his tan. "She will be, won't she?"

Jasper set his lips in a tense line and finished his task. "If we can get her into a warm bed, then clean this wound and pack it properly—and nurse her carefully—then yes. I think she will recover." He could not bear to imagine any other outcome. Most especially he could not imagine her dying because she'd bravely tried to save him.

He stood up. There was no time to spare. They were less than a league from the road, and from there Rosecliffe was not even an hour. When he looked around for Helios, however, he was met by suspicious stares and black frowns. The Welshmen had bandaged their wounded as best they could. Someone had gathered the horses. But they were all waiting for orders from Rhys. If Jasper had not been so worried about Rhonwen, he would have been impressed that a youth could so easily command men years his elder.

He looked back at Rhys. "Tell them we have to take her to Rosecliffe Castle," he demanded in a low, urgent voice.

"To Rosecliffe Castle?" Rhys glanced up at him, then stood. Where he'd looked to Jasper for help just moment be-

fore, he stared at him now accusingly. "This foul day's work
is all your doing and yet you think I will give Rhonwen back
into your keeping, especially now, when she is weak and
barely alive?" His hand moved to the hilt of his sword, a
threatening gesture that Jasper did not underestimate.

Jasper spread his arms wide. He had no weapon. The dagger
lay in the mud beside Rhonwen. "We have defeated a com
mon enemy." He gestured to LaMonthe, who lay as he'd
fallen. "We have a common goal to save Rhonwen's life. Can
we not put our differences aside, at least until she is safe?"

"She goes to Afon Bryn."

"That's twice as far as Rosecliffe."

Rhonwen moaned and Rhys's gaze went to her. Jasper knelt
beside her again. Her heartbeat had not worsened, but had not
improved. He pressed a hand to her brow. Her skin was un
naturally cold. At the moment he would almost welcome a
fever.

He looked up at Rhys. "She needs to be bathed and changed
into clean, dry clothing. She needs a medicinal bath for her
wound, and a healing tea to give her strength. Every minute
we delay works against her."

"She will heal better among her own people."

"If she lives to get to them. Use your head, man! Do you
hate me more than you love her? Is it more important to thwart
me than it is to save her life?"

Rhys swallowed hard and in the boy's face Jasper saw life
long hatred war with loyalty for one of his own.

"I want her to live," Jasper continued urgently. He knelt
beside her and began carefully to pick her up.

"Don't touch her!" Rhys slid his sword out and waved it
threateningly at Jasper. "Leave her there. Leave her!"

But Jasper could not comply with the boy's demand. As he
cradled Rhonwen in his arms, her very lifelessness urged him
on. She seemed so light. She was a small woman, but as he
rose to his feet, her weight seemed inconsequential. He
breathed deep, seeking the fragrance of her, the essence, and
without thinking, he pressed a kiss to her brow.

"*Lofrudd!*" Rhys roared. "Murderer! I will kill you fo

every insult you have done her!'' He advanced until the point of his sword was a scant inch from Jasper's throat. "Take her from him," he ordered his men. "Take her so I can kill him now."

When none of his men moved forward, his rage increased. "Fenton. Take her! Then one of you, give him your sword."

A horse whinnied in the terrible silence. Helios. Another answered. One of the Welsh ponies. Jasper's hold on Rhonwen tightened. She was dying in his arms!

Then two of Rhys's men stumbled aside and Newlin appeared. His pace was unhurried, dipping and swaying with every crippled step. But his wayward eyes were focused together—focused on Rhonwen.

"She lives," he murmured.

"You see?" Rhys said. "Newlin says she will live."

At his words the odd bard's gaze turned slowly to him. "She lives—now. I cannot foretell the future, not of people who possess a free will. She lives. But for how long I cannot say. That depends on you."

"Let the man take her," Fenton pleaded with Rhys. "The English castle is closer and Lady Josselyn will mind her better than—"

"Enough!" Rhys cried. But Jasper saw the sword waver in the boy's hand. Was it doubt, or merely exhaustion?

Then Rhys abruptly shook his head and slid the sword back into its sheath. "We will accompany you. You will give us assurances of safe passage." His eyes flashed with hatred, but his words were those of a wise leader. "Newlin will accompany us to bear witness to your honesty—or its lack."

"Agreed." Jasper started for Helios but Rhys blocked his path. He held out his arms.

"I will carry her."

"There is no need. I have her," Jasper said.

A muscle ticked in the youth's jaw. "She is Welsh, and she has been struck down by English treachery. 'Tis Welsh comfort she needs. Welsh strength."

"But it was my life she saved!" Jasper countered. To let her go was something he could not do.

"You quibble like children," Newlin snapped. "Mount your animal, Rhys. Now give her into his keeping," he ordered Jasper.

Rhonwen sighed, a soft flutter of shallow breath. Was it her last? Jasper's heart quickened in panic. But her breathing resumed and at last he lifted her reluctantly to Rhys. She needed help that they could not give her in this godforsaken place.

Once she was settled in Rhys's arms, Jasper stepped back, bereft as he'd never been. Let her live, he prayed. I can endure anything else if You will just let her live.

Newlin moved up beside him, an oddly comforting presence in the unforgiving Welsh forest. "Go now, all of you. I will prepare the way."

Jasper complied, without questioning him. Any doubts he had about the ancient bard vanished beneath his need to believe in Newlin's powers. To get Rhonwen to Rosecliffe alive was the task that consumed him.

As Rhys cantered away, Jasper ran for Helios and threw himself astride. Then, with Jasper fixed on the same goal as his enemy, they all rode for Rosecliffe.

Twenty-Three

Rhonwen felt light. Lighter than the air. She floated along, buffeted by a difficult wind, blown up into the rugged hills, then down into the damp valleys. The forest brimmed with life, green and vibrant, then, without warning, turned gray and barren. The sky brightened and the sun heated her skin. Then the sun faded and a terrible twilight consumed the land.

She whimpered, searching for the light and the verdant spring hills she loved. But the wind had her and would not let her go. Faces came and went, looming huge, then dwindling away. But one face lurked just beyond the lines of her sight. A familiar face, old and reassuring.

Newlin floated on the wind, impervious to is buffeting, and, encouraged, she tried to reach him.

Help me. Help me, she pleaded, and he reached out in response. But she couldn't quite reach him. She couldn't quite reach him. . . .

Thunder shook her partially awake and she looked up into a brilliant light. Heaven? She passed just as quickly into shadows, beneath a towering gate. Heaven's gates? she again wondered. If that was so, she should find peace. But Newlin wouldn't let her. . . .

"She tried to speak," Rhys told Jasper when they halted inside the bailey at Rosecliffe Castle. "She begged for help."

The boy was visibly distraught, and that shook Jasper's hard fought calm.

They'd ridden as hard as they could, under the circum stances. Now, inside Rosecliffe's heavily fortified walls, the young Welsh rebel's eyes darted swiftly about. His few men had followed their leader beneath the massive steel-strapped gate. They bunched around him now, a ragtag band, pitifully outnumbered.

To take them captive would be an easy task. But impris oning Rhys was the last thing on Jasper's mind. He stared at the woman so limp in Rhys's arms, so small and pale, and all he could think of was Rhonwen.

Rhonwen.

He flung himself down from Helios and threw the reins to a startled lad. As the castle folk ceased their labors and drew near, he barked orders.

"Call my lady Josselyn. Prepare a sickbed. Send for the village healer." He stopped beside the still-mounted Rhys, and his heart pounded with fear. But he took a steadying breath. "Hand her down to me."

"She begged for help," Rhys repeated in a stricken voice. "Her eyes opened, but I don't think she knew me," he added in less than a whisper.

"Give her to me," Jasper repeated.

Rhys's expression hardened when he looked down at Jasper. "It is a measure of my love for her that I have brought her here. I want her to live. I need her to live—" He broke off and took a harsh breath. "But if she does not live . . . 'tis you I will hold at fault."

Jasper met his menacing stare without flinching. "If Rhon wen dies I will hold myself responsible," he swore, though his even voice belied the intensity of his emotions. "Give her to me. You have the freedom to stay or leave. No one here will harm you or prevent your free passage."

Slowly Rhys lowered Rhonwen's limp form. He did not want to release her to Jasper. That was plain. Jasper looked down at the woman in his arms and fought down a crushing wave of panic. She was so pale.

Around them people whispered, for they'd recognized Rhonwen—and Rhys. Two serving women led the way as Jasper strode toward the keep. As he mounted the steps two at a time, Josselyn rushed out.

"Jasper! Dear God, but we were so worried." Then she spied Rhonwen and she blanched. "Is she—"

"She is alive. But barely."

"The healer is on his way, milady." One of the maids pointed at a man hurrying toward them. "The old one, Newlin, awaits you in the hall."

Newlin! Rightly or wrongly, Jasper took heart from the bard's presence.

Josselyn paused, looking back toward the gate. "Could it be? But no. Is that Rhys?"

"It is. Some of his men are hurt. Could you see to them?"

Rhys watched as Jasper disappeared into the stout stone keep. Though consumed with doubt, he still clung to hope. She must live. She must!

A woman watched him from across the yard. Josselyn. He'd seen her but briefly when Jasper had held him captive. Now he studied her closer.

She'd changed little since she'd wed the Englishman. She was three times a mother—and no doubt despised him for taking her firstborn hostage. When she descended the steps and made her way toward him, he braced himself for her scorn. It was no matter to him what she thought. He'd long held her in contempt for taking an Englishman to her bed.

She stopped directly in front of him. The horse he rode stamped and tossed its head, and Rhys had to force himself to relax his tight grip on the leather reins.

"Rhys." She nodded her head in greeting.

He nodded in response. "You will attend Rhonwen? You will oversee every aspect of her recovery?" His voice was harsher than he'd intended.

"I will. What of you and your men? Jasper tells me there are wounded—"

"We can tend our own."

She sighed, then placed her fists on her hips and cocked her head. "As you wish. I will tell the cook to bring ale and victuals."

"We will not stay."

"There is nothing to fear—" she began.

"And nothing here that I fear," he snapped. "Nothing save Rhonwen's injuries."

"Then stay. Stay and rest and sup with us."

She looked up at him without rancor. Her garb was the simple fitted tunic and kirtle of a Welshwoman. But the tunic was made of a pale blue caddis, a finer weave than was common, with ornate cording at the wrist and back. Still, her head was uncovered and her long braids were familiar.

She'd looked much the same when she'd arrived in Afon Bryn so many years ago. So long ago it was, but he remembered. His own father had wanted her. He understood that now. But his grandfather had been the one to wed her. Meanwhile, it had been Randulf FitzHugh's child she'd borne.

Despite his distrust of her back then, he'd been a motherless little boy and so had been inextricably drawn to her. To her warmth and her beauty. To the mothering qualities she'd wanted to shower upon him.

Now, almost ten years later, he could feel her working those same wiles upon him. A part of him wanted to accept her invitation, to let her minister to him and to his sore and weary men. How many women had ever sought to give him comfort beyond the brief use of their bodies? None since his mother, and he remembered very little of her.

Then he reminded himself that Josselyn was his enemy and not to be trusted. But his stomach growled, and his everpresent hunger raised a clamor. "We have a need for food," he muttered. Why should he not sate himself on English stores? Why not take whatever he could from them? They'd taken enough from him.

"Very well." She gestured to a wide stone building abutting the fortified keep. At just that moment three children burst through the doors of the keep. A boy, followed by two girls, one of whom Rhys recognized.

She recognized him too, for she skidded to a halt, then

dragged her younger sister back toward the shelter of the doors. "Mama, Mama! Look out! 'Tis him—Rhys ap Owain. The outlaw!"

The boy hesitated only a moment, then dashed toward his mother as if to protect her.

Josselyn turned to her children. " 'Tis all right, Isolde. He has brought Rhonwen back to us. She's hurt."

The girl glared at him. Though she was a slight little thing and delicate in her features, her lowered brows and down-turned mouth made no secret of her hatred of him. "Did he do it?" she cried in an accusing voice. "Is he the one that hurt her?"

Rhys stiffened. Though he allowed that she was entitled to her distrust of him, he was not inclined to suffer the invective of a child. Drawing on his reins, he backed his mount away from Josselyn. "Send word of Rhonwen's condition to your aunt in Carreg Du," he snarled at her. "Most especially I will want to know when she is strong enough to return home."

"Wait, Rhys. Don't leave!" she begged.

But he ignored her plea. He whirled his horse so sharply that it reared in alarm. But the sturdy beast swiftly regained its footing and, with little urging, it scattered the crowd and thundered across the bridge and into the harsh emptiness of the Welsh countryside. He drove the animal to the limits of its endurance and his men strung out in a line behind him.

But Rhys could not outrun his memories of the past. Nor his fear of the future.

Jasper hovered outside the door, straining for any sound from the chamber where Rhonwen lay. But there was none. No sound pierced the muffled silence of the thick stone walls and the heavy paneled door.

He exhaled harshly, then scrubbed his hands across his face. He was filthy and exhausted, and splattered with blood—both his own and that of others. Lowering his hands, he stared at them. Were any of the dark rust-colored bloodstains that creased his knuckles from Rhonwen?

He shuddered and felt an unaccustomed ache in his chest,

as if his entire body were caving in on itself, disappearing int
the hole where his heart used to be. He pressed one fist to h
chest. God in heaven. Did he love her?

The pain in his chest grew worse. He could hardly breath
for it. He leaned stiff-armed against the wall, afraid he migl
collapse.

He loved her.

He loved her, and in his selfish need to possess her, he'
nearly caused her death. She might yet die.

He squeezed his eyes shut, horrified by his own selfishnes
He'd had to have her, and so he'd pursued her long past th
time when he should have simply accepted that she did no
want him. And now, because of his stubbornness and his over
weening pride, she lay near death.

It didn't help that he'd slain LaMonthe. It didn't matter tha
he'd bullied Rhys into bringing her here. If she died . . .

He cringed, unable to contemplate such a thing. He couldn
let himself think about the possibility of her dying. She migl
yet live. The healer had a well-known talent, and Jossely
would do everything she could. And if his prayers meant any
thing at all, she might yet live.

And if she did . . . if she did, he must let her go. He mu
give her back the life she wanted. Even if Rhys were not he
lover, he was someone she did love. She'd been running bac
to Rhys when Jasper had caught her.

He stared blindly at the cold gray wall, seeing instead th
coldness of his life and the gray sameness of his future. Empty
No love. No joy.

No Rhonwen.

When the door hinge creaked, he jerked in alarm. Isold
slipped out, then closed the heavy door behind her. Her youn
face was pale and worried, but she spoke with a maturity he'
not previously seen in her.

"Mama says if you will clean yourself you may come in
see Rhonwen when she and Romney are finished."

"How is she?" His voice was a hoarse croak.

Isolde frowned. "She is weak. Romney wanted to bleed he
but Mama said no. She'd already lost enough blood. So the

cleaned her wound and stitched it closed." Her face puckered in a grimace. "It was a dreadful cut in her side, Jasper. I could see her entrails." She stared solemnly at him. "I never saw anyone get stitched before."

Jasper swallowed hard and fought down a wave of nausea. He couldn't bear this! "Will she live?" He caught Isolde by the shoulders and crouched down so that they were face-to-face. "Will she live?"

Tears started in the child's eyes. "I hope she will. I . . ." Her voice caught on a sob and she looked away. "This is all my fault, isn't it?"

"Your fault?" With a finger beneath her chin he tilted her face up to his. "Isolde, why would you think this is your fault?"

"Because . . . because I followed her and got caught, and then you followed her and caught Rhys, and then she . . . she traded us for him and . . . and he hated you and you had her and then . . . and then she got away and you followed her and . . and then she got stabbed!" She began to cry, huge sobs that shook her slender little frame.

"No, sweetheart." He hugged her close and rubbed her back. "No, Isolde. This is not your doing. None of it."

"But . . ." She shuddered with the force of her misery. "But I wanted her to die. In the beginning . . . I prayed to God that she would die. But I changed my mind, only now . . . now she really might die."

"Listen to me, love. You had nothing to do with what happened to Rhonwen. Nothing." He held her, murmuring reassurances as the storm of her tears slowly wore itself out. When she was finally only hiccuping into his damp shoulder, he held her slightly away from him. "Better?"

She shrugged, averting her unhappy face. "You should never pray for someone to die," she said in a small voice.

"Probably not. But I doubt God is impressed by such prayers. Why did you want her to die?"

Her lower lip trembled. "First . . . first I just wanted her to go away because . . . because I knew you liked her."

"And then?" he prompted when she hesitated.

"Then when she and Rhys made me into a hostage, I . . . prayed to God that they would both die. And all their men too."

Jasper smiled at her and wiped her wet cheek with his thumb. "That was a normal reaction, love. Anyone would have felt the same way. But you're not the one at fault."

I am.

The girl rubbed her eyes with the backs of her fists. "It' that man. That Simon LaMonthe. That's who Mama says is really to blame."

Jasper nodded. "It was his sword that struck her down though it was meant for me. She saved my life," he added in a whisper.

"She did? Oh." The little girl stared at him with round serious eyes. Then she wound her arms around his neck an gave him a fierce kiss on the cheek. "Rhonwen must love yo very, very much."

Unsettled, Jasper untangled her arms and stood. If only i were true. "Rhonwen would have done the same for Rhys o your mother or anyone she cared for. That's the sort of woma she is. Brave. Loyal."

They stood there in silence for a long moment. Then Isold took him by the hand. "Come along. I'll help you wash your self so that you may go in to see her."

Jasper followed her, letting her mother him and test the rol she would one day play in a household of her own. He re moved his filthy tunic and chainse, and bathed his face an hands and arms. He donned the fresh garments she fetched fo him, and combed his damp hair down. Then again, hand i hand, they returned to the second-floor chamber where Rhon wen lay.

At the door Isolde gave him an encouraging smile. "I'll g in first."

She went in, leaving him alone, and without the task o reassuring her, he fell quick prey to his own fears. What i Rhonwen did not recover? How could he live with the los and the guilt? And if she lived, how could he bear to let he go? His stomach knotted until he felt like retching.

Then the door opened with its telltale creak and Josselyn beckoned him in. He hesitated, watching as Romney gathered up his instruments and powders and vials of dark liquids. The healer left with a silent shrug, and with a gesture from her mother, so did Isolde. Then it was only him and Josselyn and the still figure lying in the high bed.

"She is resting easily, Jasper. Her breathing is not too labored. Her heartbeat is not too weak." She placed a hand on his elbow and urged him to enter farther into the dimly lit room. "I believe she will recover if she does not contract a fever. Your bindings around the wound kept it clean and closed. Come. Sit with her while I go refresh myself."

"You're leaving?" He couldn't hide the panic in his voice.

"I'll be back directly."

"What if she . . . I don't know. What if she needs you?"

"All she needs now is reassurance. Just give her that, Jasper." She steered him nearer the bed. "Talk to her. 'Tis hard to know for certain, but perhaps she'll hear you and respond." Then she was gone and he was alone with Rhonwen, though in a manner he'd never considered.

He stared at her, searching for some sign of recovery. Color in her cheeks. A smile on her lips. A sparkle in her eyes. But there was nothing. Her face was pale, and her lowered lids but a smudge of bruised color. She was the lovely wood nymph that had turned his head, but the spirit that had captured his heart was not there. He touched her hand, so cool and limp. In desperation he smoothed his trembling palm over her brow.

"Rhonwen. Come back to me, love. Don't abandon me now." Then he bowed his head and kissed her, touching his lips tenderly to hers.

He expected her mouth to be cool—as cool as she appeared—but it was not. Her lips were warm and full, and as he lingered over her, they moved, as if in response.

He jerked away. Hopeful. Chagrined. Though she mumbled something unintelligible, her eyes remained closed. He, meanwhile, felt an undeniable rush of desire at her small, innocent reaction.

''Damn you for a selfish bastard,'' he cursed himself out loud.

Her brow wrinkled slightly at his words, and he could have damned himself again. Then he recalled what Josselyn had instructed. Talk to her.

''Rhonwen?'' he cautiously began. ''Rhonwen, if you hear me, then I beg you to believe me. I need you to get better.'' He clasped her two hands between his, marveling at their delicacy. Yet they were strong hands too. With God's help they would be strong again.

''Rhonwen, we are all of us waiting for you to awaken. LaMonthe has been dealt with. You need never fear him again. And Rhys. He and I have buried our differences. We share the same goal now: We want you to recover and . . . and share in our joint victory.''

Her lips moved and Jasper's heart soared. She made no sound, though, and he swallowed the piercing disappointment. But he would not let her down. Not this time.

He'd let her down before, but if he had to sit vigil all night, he would. If he had to hold her hand and exhort her—if he had to pray until there were no prayers left to wring from his soul—he would do it.

He would not let this most precious of women go without the fight of his life.

Twenty-Four

Rhys kept his own vigil. He'd climbed an ancient oak at the edge of the forest and perched in a fork that allowed him a view of the English castle. Now, as darkness crept on cat feet over the land, wrapping the world in a shroud of lavender dusk, he nursed a nearly empty wineskin and stared morosely at the crenellated fortress.

Did she live?

He closed his eyes and leaned his head back against the rough bark. How could he have abandoned her there? She was alone among their enemies. But she didn't see them as enemies. Not like she used to. Jasper FitzHugh had turned her head, just as his brother had turned Josselyn's.

A wave of self-pity washed over him, threatening to unman him. One by one he'd been abandoned by his own people, beginning with his mother.

And your father.

He scowled and, lifting the wineskin, drained the last bitter dregs. His father had died for his people. For his family and his son. And the brothers FitzHugh were to blame.

He crushed the leather wineskin in his fist, wishing it was Jasper FitzHugh's neck. For a short while, in his concern for Rhonwen, he'd forgotten how much he despised the man.

If she died he'd have even greater cause to slay the unholy bastard.

And if she lived?

He stared blindly at the darkening sky. If she lived it changed nothing. She would never have been hurt had Jasper FitzHugh—scoundrel that he was—not hounded her to death.

No, whether Rhonwen lived or died, he owed FitzHugh nothing, except the sharp edge of his blade and the bitter taste of revenge.

Rand pressed on, eager to be home. Eager to see the light of welcome in Josselyn's warm eyes. It had been a long, strange day. He and Osborn had been hard-pressed to calm the men during the fearsome dark at midday. Thank God it had not lasted long enough for a full panic to set in. Afterward there had been little talk—but many a silent prayer, he suspected.

They'd pushed themselves and their weary animals harder than ever, and now, with night closing in, they were but a league distant from their home. The next rise would give them a glimpse of the pennants and walls that marked the fortress he yet improved upon. With the threat of a war between Matilda and Stephen looming over the kingdom, it behooved him to increase the masons' pace.

He was sunk in thoughts of the town wall and strategies to increase its defenses, when the forward rider halted and stood in his stirrups. At once the entire column of men reined in. Swords slithered from sheaths and the familiar forest turned ominous.

"A horse, fully rigged," Osborn relayed the news to him.

"English or Welsh?"

"The saddle is Welsh; the bridle English. As for the animal, he's finely bred. Probably English—but perhaps stolen."

"And the rider?" Rand asked.

Osborn shrugged. "Nowhere to be seen."

Rand stared through the forest and the rapidly waning light. A man led the horse toward him while three other searched the undergrowth. A riderless horse, and so near to Rosecliffe Castle. He'd received Jasper's two messages—first that Isolde had been taken by Rhys ap Owain, then that she'd been safely recovered. Had some further mishap occurred since?

"Probably due to that strange darkness earlier today," Osborne muttered. "Mayhap the rider panicked and the beast threw him."

"Mayhap."

Then an owl hooted and Rand glanced up—and spied a booted foot dangling from the branch of an oak tree.

He nudged Osborn and pointed. In short order the men stealthily circled the tree. Three archers drew a bead on the body barely discernible above the foot. Then a nimble young man-at-arms scaled the sturdy tree.

The man in the tree was either asleep or dead, but Rand meant to take no chances. At his signal the climber gave a quick yank on the foot and the fellow toppled from his perch.

His startled cry proved he was alive, as did his quick grab for a slender branch, breaking his fall. That left the fellow in an even worse predicament, however, for he dangled now in plain view of all. One of Rand's men lit a torch and held it up to illuminate the fellow.

He was big and young, and more than a little drunk, Rand surmised. He was also Welsh, and though a sensible man would be terrified by his situation, the brawny lad's eyes blazed with anger, and hatred.

Rand urged his mount to a position just before the swaying fellow. "Well, well. We weren't even hunting, and yet what game we've bagged. Who are you?"

The lad shot him a contemptuous look as he adjusted his handhold. "I'm a loyal son of these hills, which is more than can be said of you," he spat in Welsh.

One of Rand's men translated the words for those who were not fluent in the language, and a grim muttering arose. Rand stilled it with a single gesture. He was but a beardless youth, he showed no fear, and he understood English. At once Rand knew.

"Rhys ap Owain." He chuckled. "You've grown, lad. But I see you still maintain a penchant for climbing trees."

With a deft leap, Rhys landed nimbly on the ground. "And

I still have a hatred for Englishmen,'' he snarled. He drew his sword out, then also his dagger, and faced the circle of Englishmen. ''You'll have to kill me, for I'll not go any other way.''

''Take him,'' Rand ordered without blinking. ''But don't kill him.''

It was violent but brief. Two swordsmen engaged him in battle, while a third man found a heavy oak branch. One well-aimed blow to the head and the lad went down.

Rand did not linger over the troublesome youth. ''Tie him on his own horse,'' he told Osborn. ''And cast him in the dungeon. As for me, I'm in need of my wife's comfort. It's been a hell of a day.''

The morning mass was attended by everyone in the castle save Jasper, Rhonwen, and Rhys. The latter nursed an aching head in the dungeon, while Jasper nursed an aching heart in Rhonwen's sickroom.

There was much to pray for, and both pleas and thanks rose in the castle's small chapel dedicated to St. Valentine. Josselyn thanked God for Rand's safe return and prayed he would be merciful to Rhys. Rand thanked God for protecting his family and prayed for an hour or two alone with his wife.

Isolde thanked God for bringing her beloved father home and prayed he would leave that awful Rhys locked in the dungeon until he rotted. Gavin prayed his foster household would include other boys his own age.

They all prayed for the recovery of those injured in the previous day's melee, most especially for Rhonwen. But none prayed so fervently as Jasper. When Rand and Josselyn sought him out after the mass he was haggard and red-eyed, his clothes rumpled and his hair standing out around his face.

''You see?'' Josselyn grasped Rand's arm and whispered in his ear. '' 'Tis as I said.''

Rand frowned as if he could not credit such a change in his carefree brother. ''How fares the patient?''

''Rhonwen,'' Jasper said in raspy tones. ''Her name is

Rhonwen. There is no change," he added, his shoulders slumping.

"Maybe we should let Rhys visit her," Josselyn mused out loud.

"He is here?" Jasper asked.

"I caught him last night, asleep in a tree, just beyond Newlin's *domen*," Rand explained. "Josselyn has informed me of all that has passed—LaMonthe's treason, the battle, and Rhonwen's injury. However, Rhys does not answer my question about his role with LaMonthe."

"He conspired with LaMonthe to take Rosecliffe." Jasper looked down at Rhonwen's pale visage. "Two days ago a pair of LaMonthe's men delivered a message here to you. But it was nothing, just an excuse to gain entrance to the castle. I suspect the true purpose of their visit was to pass a message to Rhonwen."

He raised tortured eyes to his brother. "But yesterday Rhys called her a traitor. I don't know if it was due to her defense of me then, or if there was more to it. I think . . ." He paused and his hand ran lightly along her arm, lying beneath the stitched-together marten skins that kept her warm. "I think that perhaps . . . perhaps she could not bring herself to conspire with him and LaMonthe. I think she ran away instead."

"And you followed her," his brother said.

In the silence that followed, it was Josselyn who spoke. "He did. Tell him why, Jasper."

Jasper's face was desperate. He thrust his hands through his unruly hair, standing it on end in uneven spikes. "I could not let her go."

"And why is that?" she pressed him.

"Because . . . because . . ."

Rand circled Josselyn's shoulders with one arm. "Enough, Josselyn. 'Tis plain enough for a fool to see." He shook his head, scowling. "It must be a curse visited upon the Fitz-Hughs. We may love no woman save she who is our avowed enemy."

"Such a curse," Josselyn chided him. She kissed him on the cheek. Then she returned her gaze to Jasper and grew serious once more. "Tell her your true feelings, Jasper. Tell her. Mayhap that will bring her out of this heavy sleep that holds her in its grip."

Jasper stared at her, doubt etched in his eyes. "What if it is Rhys she loves?"

Rand looked down at his wife too, and Josselyn pursed her lips. "I do not believe it is so. She cares for him, but in a different way. Perhaps you should speak with him."

Jasper shook his head. "He despises us too much to be honest. He will say whatever he believes will cause the greatest amount of pain, and gain him the greatest advantage."

They could not argue with that, and after soliciting Jasper's promise to eat something, they left. Alone with Rhonwen, Jasper once again scrubbed his hands across his face. He was so weary. His eyes burned; his hands trembled. Yet he was afraid to sleep, afraid her fragile life force would slip away if he did not remain diligent. But he was so tired.

On impulse he lay beside her, curving his arms around her as if he might ward off any evil, most especially the angel of death. She stirred and shifted in his arms, and he held his breath.

"Rhonwen?" The curls at her temple moved with his breath. "Wake up, Rhonwen. Please wake up. We . . . I need you. I . . . I love you, sweetheart." His voice broke. "Please Rhonwen. I love you."

Rhonwen was so cold, and yet she felt the hard warmth beside her. It was so quiet, and yet she heard the soft words of entreaty and felt the sweet breath of life in her ear. She shifted, then moaned at the slicing pain of that brief movement. What was it?

In the fog that held her down, she saw Rhys's face, so angry. And then the blade, sharp and deadly, aimed at Jasper's heart. *'No. No, Rhys!'* she screamed.

Jasper's face went white at Rhonwen's faint moan. Rhys. She had called for Rhys, not for him.

But at least she spoke, he consoled himself. She spoke and that in itself seemed like a miracle. She called for Rhys, and he would make sure her call was answered. "All right, Rhonwen. Rhys will soon be with you. I'll see to it.''

His heart ached, though, and he could not stop himself from
holding her a little tighter. But she flinched away from his
touch. ''No,'' she moaned again. ''No.''

Jasper never cried, not since his mother had died when he
was a lad. But tears stung his eyes as he eased from the bed.
For too long he'd been a thickheaded fool, unable to accept
the truth. He must accept it now, though. He took a deep
breath and then another. He must accept the fact that Rhonwen
was not meant to be his. She'd saved his life—once as a child,
and then again now. But that did not mean she loved him.

He owed her his life, though, and he would do whatever he
must to preserve hers.

As he stared down at her, her eyes opened. They closed
again, without really focusing on anything. But a faint frown
marked her brow and once again she shifted.

On impulse he bent down and kissed her brow. He should
have stopped at that. But he could not. He kissed one cheek,
and then the other as well. Then he paused over her lips.

One last time. One last kiss to wish her well, and to always
remember how sweet it might have been had she loved him
as he loved her.

He lowered his lips to hers and kissed her. Like a friend
might kiss a friend, he told himself. But her lips moved under
his and though it was madness, he could not prevent himself
from pressing a little more. Her mouth was warm and supple.
And welcoming. She sighed and parted her lips, and he could
not pull away.

He bent over her stiff-armed, wanting her so fiercely he
hurt. But he held back, all except for his mouth. He fitted his
lips to hers and tasted her with his tongue, and wanted to take
her up in his arms.

Rhonwen. Rhonwen!

His mind pleaded with her to love him. To be his.

Then she sighed and he pulled away, and their last kiss was
done. He backed away from the bed, stricken. It would have
been less painful had she allowed LaMonthe's sword to pierce
his heart.

He had his emotions under control by the time he reached the main hall. To the servant who had started up to the sick room with a pewter tray of bread and pot cheese, he said, "Bring another tray like this and an ewer of wine." He didn't pause, however, but strode to the narrow stairs that led to the lower levels. Halfway down he encountered a guard. "Is Rhys ap Owain held here?" he barked.

The man snapped to attention. "He is that, Sir Jasper. Lord Rand says he is to—"

"Release him."

"What?" The man stared at him in amazement. But Jasper continued down the stairs until he encountered the forged steel gate that prevented escape. The lock required no key, but the elaborate design prevented an inmate from freeing himself.

Rhys lay on a pallet, his back to the door. But at Jasper's noisy approach, he sprang to his feet. His fist knotted and his posture tensed as he glared suspiciously at Jasper.

"But milord," the guard protested when he caught up with Jasper. "Lord Rand will have my hide if I release this man. So will Sir Osborn. This one here, he's a dangerous thug, he is."

"I know that better than anyone," Jasper answered the man. His eyes held with Rhys's. "But Rhonwen is calling for him."

Jasper saw the wariness in his nemesis's expression turn to concern. "She calls for me?" Then he frowned. "Is this some sort of trick?"

Jasper threw up the latch that held the crossbar in place. " 'Tis no trick. She hovers yet near death, but she speaks your name." He flung the crossbar aside, then jerked the barred gate open. "I want her to live. Did she call for the devil himself, I would seek him out."

"Huh," the man-at-arms snorted. "That 'un's verily the devil himself." He held his sword at the ready, the tip pointed at Rhys's chest. But Jasper did not bother with a weapon. He strode into Rhys's prison cell and gestured for him to proceed.

Rhys was wary, though, and he did not immediately react. He stared at his lifelong enemy, not an arm's length away. "Feeling guilty?"

Jasper met the boy's belligerent stare. "Yes."

It was obviously not the response the young Welshman expected, and the bald honesty of it left him speechless. Jasper pressed his advantage. "I want her to live. If you feel the same way, then come. There is no time to waste." He grabbed Rhys's elbow and propelled him toward the door.

But the boy shrugged off his hold. "I do this for her sake," he snarled. "Hers, not yours." Then he spit on the ground between them. "You and your kind despoil our fair land. You wreak havoc with your greed. You rape our women and kill our men—"

"Rhonwen was never raped," Jasper swore. His teeth gritted in fury. "And you yet live."

"But for how long?" the boy sneered.

In the furious silence, Jasper's words came as both a threat and a reassurance. "So long as she wills it," he answered.

The man-at-arms followed wide-eyed as the two avowed enemies made their way up the narrow stairwell to the hall. He stood in the low-ceilinged doorway and watched as they crossed the hall together. Everyone else in the hall ceased their work and did the same.

Jasper marched Rhys across the rush-strewn floor to the broad stairs that led to the upper chambers of the keep. Jasper carried no weapon, and from steward to kitchen drudge to lowly page, everyone gasped at the recklessness of his behavior.

Only one among them dared counter the obvious intentions of the grim-faced Jasper. Isolde saw the hated Rhys who'd held her hostage, and her anger flared with righteous fire. She grabbed the nearest page and gave him a hard pinch.

"Fetch my father," she ordered. "Now!"

The boy dashed away at once while she watched Jasper and Rhys disappear up the stairs. Then she grabbed a fire poker and, though her heart hammered with fear, she hurried across the hall to follow them.

Twenty-Five

Rhonwen was no longer floating. She'd drifted down and seemed now to rest in some sort of bed. Not a hard pallet of reeds and sheepskins, nor a raised shelf alongside a rough wall. This was a well-stuffed mattress atop greased ropes and lifted high above the cold drafts along the floor.

It was a wonderful bed, warm and secure. Were it not, however, for the warm coverlet tucked so securely around her, she might easily have floated away again. Even now the temptation was great.

But the soft coverlet held her down and if she strained she could hear voices, voices she recognized. Then a hand curved around hers and, without realizing it, she smiled. Jasper was still here.

She'd dreamed he'd stayed with her, anchoring her down, preventing her from drifting, and so, it seemed, he had. She struggled now to open her eyes and finally see him.

"... Rhonwen? Can you hear me?"

His fingertips smoothed her brow, urging her to wake up. With an effort she opened her eyes, only it was not Jasper' face she saw.

"Rhys ..." She barely managed to croak. How could this be? She wanted Jasper, not Rhys. Jasper. Dismayed, she let her heavy eyelids close.

"Yes, Rhonwen, it's Rhys. I'm here." His hand tightened on hers. "Come, love. Open your eyes for me again. Come back to me, Rhonwen," he pleaded. But she was too tired, and too disappointed.

"Try again," another voice said. "Don't give up on her now."

Rhonwen frowned and struggled to sort out the muffled words.

"She's hurt too grievous," Rhys retorted. "To save your unworthy life she has forsaken her own!"

"Keep trying, damn you! Don't give up on her."

Rhonwen's eyes struggled open again, easier this time. Was that Jasper she heard? But it was Rhys's face that filled her line of vision. He bent over her, his brow furrowed, his black eyes anxious.

"Rhonwen. I'm here. I'm here and you are in good hands if you will just not give up." One of his hands stroked her cheek.

She blinked. It was so bright. But slowly the room came into focus. High-beamed ceilings. Carefully fitted stone walls. The bed that cocooned her had deep green damask bedcurtains pulled back to admit the sunshine that streamed through a deep-set window.

It seemed so familiar, and yet she wasn't sure. She tilted her head in the other direction. It hurt to move, but she forced herself. It all looked familiar. Then she gasped—and grimaced at the immediate pain in her side. She was at Rosecliffe Castle. She lay in Josselyn's very own bed.

But Rhys was with her, not Jasper, and that made no sense at all. Her heart began to race in panic.

Sensing her distress, Rhys shifted nervously from one foot to the other. "Don't worry. You're going to be all right. You're going to be all right." He glanced across the bed and his worried expression turned angry. "The blame for her misery lies fully at your door!"

"Damnation, will you lower your voice? You're supposed to be helping her."

Rhonwen tossed her head back and forth. Jasper again.

Where was he? She heard him but could not see him. And she needed to see him.

"Jasper," she whispered.

Her feeble call enraged Rhys. "You're the one upsetting her," he accused Jasper. "Every time you speak she becomes more distraught."

"No," she whimpered. "No." But her voice was too weak to overcome Rhys's rage. Then the door swung open with a sharp crack, and another voice raised high in anger.

"Get away from her. Get away!" a child cried.

Isolde. With her shrill words everything began to come back to Rhonwen. There had been a terrible battle. But Jasper had survived. Rhys had wanted to kill him, but he'd hesitated. So someone else . . . LaMonthe! She trembled to remember. Simon LaMonthe had assumed the task of killing Jasper. He'd lunged at Jasper . . . She frowned. After that she remembered nothing.

"I'll kill you," Isolde cried, breaking into Rhonwen's gruesome memories.

"Get out of here, Isolde." That was Jasper again.

Rhys pulled his hands away and turned toward the girl. "Begone from here, brat," he snarled. Then another voice added to the confusion. An older man's voice, deep and commanding.

She could not follow their argument, not and force herself up onto her elbows too. Once partially upright, however, she took in the entire scene, like watching the mummers' play at Yuletide. Rhys had his back to her with his arms widespread as if to protect her from the others. Beyond him in the doorway stood a newcomer. When Josselyn came up behind him and caught him by the arm, Rhonwen realized it was Rand.

Then off to the side she spied Jasper, and her eyes stopped there. He had caught Isolde in an embrace and as Rhonwen watched, he removed a steel poker from her angry grip. It was plain the child had intended to attack Rhys with it.

"I hate him!" Isolde cried, still struggling against her uncle. "He'll hurt her. He hurts everyone! I wish . . . I wish he was dead!" she shrieked.

"Isolde, no." Josselyn took her daughter from Jasper.

Rand's hand moved threateningly to the dagger at his hip. "Why is he not in the dungeon?" Rand thundered at Jasper, though he glared at Rhys.

"No!" Rhonwen cried, though it came out as a weak gasp. "No. Don't hurt him."

It was Jasper who heard her. And Jasper who held his brother back.

"Rhonwen," he said, his expression one of shock and, perhaps, gratitude. At once the others focused on her and the weight of their scrutiny was enough to make her collapse on the pillows again.

"Rhonwen!" Isolde broke free of her mother's grasp and rushed to the side of the bed opposite Rhys. Josselyn hurried forward too. Rhys turned to her, but he kept a wary eye on Rand and Jasper.

"You must not try to sit up," Josselyn ordered. But her stern words were softened by the relieved smile on her face. "You were gravely wounded, but your body has blessedly begun to mend. And now you are awakened." Tears glistened in her eyes when she raised them to Rhys. "Thank you for drawing her back to the land of the living."

Rhys looked momentarily nonplussed. Then his face returned to its habitual scowl. "I do not want your thanks. Only hers. Unless your thanks include the return of my freedom."

Josselyn glanced pointedly at Rand. But his expression remained obstinant. "To have one Welsh rebel save the life of another Welsh rebel hardly warrants an Englishman's reward," he stated.

"But Rand—"

His raised hand stopped her. "We will discuss this matter later. You, come." He signaled to Rhys. "The sickroom is the domain of women."

"Rhonwen needs me to stay," Rhys countered. He looked to her for confirmation. But Rhonwen had turned her face away. Through half-closed eyes she stared at Jasper, hoping he would say something to her.

Needing him to say something to her.

But although Jasper's eyes were fixed upon her, he kept silent. He looked haggard and drawn, as if he'd just come from battle. How long had she been here? What had happened? Did he blame everything on her?

Then she recalled the black sky of midday and it was all too much. The end of the world, Newlin had said. The end of the world as she knew it.

She closed her eyes, but she could not prevent two tears from escaping. Her brief life at Rosecliffe was over.

"Mama, he's making her cry. Papa," Isolde implored, "send him away."

Rand glared at Rhys. "Will you go peacefully, or will I be forced to drag you out?" His voice was as cold and unyielding as steel.

"He is here at my request," Jasper spoke up at last. Rhonwen opened her eyes to see Jasper's gaze fixed on his brother. "He came to her aid and has roused her with his presence. I would have him treated with respect, if for that reason only."

"Spare me your respect," Rhys sneered.

"No . . . no more," Rhonwen muttered. The pain in her side throbbed fiercely. But it was nothing to the pain in her heart. Nothing had changed. She was still caught between loyalty to Rhys and love for Jasper. Only now she did not even have control of her body. The tears began in earnest and she could not stop them.

"You will settle this argument elsewhere," Josselyn demanded.

She circled the bed and, grabbing Rhys by the hand, began to drag him toward the door. He planted his heels and looked at Rhonwen. But she shook her head. "Go. Just go," she said in a voice that cracked.

He shook off Josselyn's hold, but after a long glowering moment, he acquiesced. Rand's dagger stayed in its sheath. Jasper shouldered between his brother and Rhys, and with angry strides, the three men left. When the door closed behind them, Josselyn leaned back against it with a relieved sigh. Then, spying Rhonwen's tear-streaked face, she hurried to her side, a determined smile on her face.

"Men can be more than tiresome. Did they not occasionally exhibit some paltry example of their usefulness, we women could be well rid of them." She ruffled Isolde's hair, then pressed a hand to Rhonwen's brow. "But since they are now and again of some use, I suppose we must suffer their foul tempers and unreasonable stubbornness. Dry your tears, Rhonwen. They will settle their differences without us. You need only to work at regaining your strength. You gave us a terrible scare," she added in a voice that suddenly trembled.

With gentle hands she pulled back the bed linens and began carefully to probe the dressing on Rhonwen's side. "Now let us see how you fare," she said, returning to her efficient manner. "Isolde, fetch the lamp nearer."

No one visited Rhonwen for three days, save the women of the castle. Even Romney, the healer, left the ministering to Josselyn, who had an able assistant in Isolde. But neither Jasper nor Rhys came to see her. And when Rhonwen inquired about them, she was told only that Rhys was well treated and Jasper was out hunting.

"Papa brought back a pair of breeding falcons with him," Isolde told her as she rummaged through one of her mother's cupboards. "The falcon master will only be here a fortnight, so Papa and Jasper must learn all they can of falconry."

The girl paused and stared out the widow to the bright spring day. "You should see how fine the two birds are, Rhonwen. Their eyes are so brilliant and they stare at you as if they understand your every word. Gavin is mad for them," she added, resuming her search. "Oh, here it is." She held up a pale green kirtle, simple in design yet made of the softest kersey wool. "You will look lovely in this one."

Rhonwen could not rise to the girl's level of enthusiasm. She was to dine in the hall today, her first venture from the sickroom. Isolde had helped her wash her hair, then combed it until it was dry. It lay now, clean and sweet-smelling, shiny and loose across her shoulders.

But to what purpose? Why take such care with her appearance when the one person she wanted to impress cared so little he would not even climb the stairs to see her?

Not that she should want to impress him. But the truth was impossible to deny. She wanted to see appreciation in Jasper's eyes when she descended the stairs, just like before. But this time she would take care not to tumble down the last two steps like a fool. Except that he probably did not appreciate her charms anymore—not now that he'd had a sufficient taste of them. Not since she'd proven herself to be a traitor.

She steeled herself against any show of despair. "I will wear my own garments. They are clean, and you mended both the kirtle and my mantle. I saw you do it."

Isolde laid the apple-green gown in Rhonwen's lap. "Feel how soft it is, how nicely made."

"It's too long for me," Rhonwen countered, pushing it aside. She threw off the coverlet and, with a grimace, swung her legs around. Her side hurt nearly as much today as it had on the first day she'd revived. But she was stronger now, and better able to bear it.

"You're not supposed to get out of bed without someone to assist you."

"Then assist me," Rhonwen retorted. At Isolde's look of consternation, she sighed. "Forgive me, Isolde. I am an ungrateful wretch, I know. But this idleness chafes me so. And I worry about . . ."

When she hesitated Isolde prompted her. "You worry about whom?" Her mouth curved in a coy smile. "Jasper?"

Rhonwen set her jaw. Isolde had become unrelenting on the subject of Jasper, rhapsodizing about how Jasper had carried Rhonwen away from the battleground. In the child's mind, that made Rhonwen and Jasper lovers of epic proportions. Rhonwen knew better, for if she'd not lured Jasper to follow her, neither of them would have been in any danger. But as often as Rhonwen tried to correct the story, Isolde simply would not let it go. Several of the chambermaids seemed equally smitten—more the fools, they.

"Why should I worry about Jasper?" She pushed to her

feet, stifling a groan, and held on to the bedpost for support. " 'Tis Rhys's well-being that troubles me."

As always, mention of the man held in Rosecliffe's dungeon brought a scowl to Isolde's face. "Well, you've no need to worry on his account," she muttered. "He should have long ago been hung. Any other outlaw of such foul reputation and unrepentant nature would have been."

Rhonwen's grip on the bedpost tightened. Her knuckles were white with fear, for she knew Isolde spoke the truth. "What do they plan to do with him?"

Isolde shrugged as if she did not know. But she avoided Rhonwen's eyes. The girl knew more than she was admitting; Rhonwen was certain of it, and she meant to ferret out the truth. "You should know, Isolde, that Rhys is not nearly so cruel as you would make him out to be. He is, in fact, a most kindhearted lad—"

"He is a hateful thug!" Isolde cried. Angry spots of color heated her face. "He has a black heart, a foul temper, and . . . and no manners at all!"

"That's not so."

"It is! It is! But he will change his evil ways when Friar Guilliame takes charge of him—" She broke off with a gasp, then turned guiltily back to the cupboard. "If you insist on wearing your old kirtle, Mother will—"

"Who is Friar Guilliame? Who is he?" Rhonwen repeated when Isolde did not answer right away.

"I wasn't supposed to tell you that," the girl muttered. "I'm not even s'posed to know of it."

"Who is this Friar Guilliame?"

Isolde raised a mutinous face to Rhonwen. "My father knows him. He is seneschal of a castle in Northumbria."

"A friar, seneschal?" Then realization struck and Rhonwen's unsteady legs nearly gave way. "Northumbria? Rhys is being sent away to a castle in Northumbria? But why?"

"I don't know. And I don't care," Isolde retorted. But her antagonism dissolved in the face of Rhonwen's distress. She pushed a stool toward Rhonwen's. "Sit down. Please, before you fall and injure yourself anew."

"Northumbria," Rhonwen repeated as the enormity of Rhys's punishment pressed in on her. "But . . . but that's in England."

"Northern England, very nearly to Scotland. Father has a map of all the isles of Britain. I know where Northumbria is and London town and Eire. Here, sit," she added, pressing Rhonwen down onto the stool.

They were both silent. Rhonwen clutched her hands together on her knees, consumed with guilt that she'd brought her dearest friend to such an end. She looked up at Isolde, her face pale with fear for him. "What will they do to him there? What will the Friar do to punish him?"

Isolde shrugged. "I don't know. I didn't hear that part."

"Was this Jasper's doing?"

Isolde pushed out her lower lip. "You should not be angry with Jasper, Rhonwen. 'Tis not his fault, but Rhys's. He brought this on himself."

"Where is Jasper?"

"I told you. With Papa, working with the new falcons."

Fear for Rhys lent Rhonwen strength. Resolute, she rose to her feet. "Give me the kirtle," she said, indicating the pretty green gown. If she was to argue on Rhys's behalf, she needed every advantage at her disposal.

Twenty-Six

Gavin helped Rhonwen make her slow way down the stairs. Isolde brought her a carved cherrywood cane. Josselyn watched, but did not question her beyond a simple inquiry regarding her health. But Rhonwen suspected Josselyn knew her purpose.

The guard at the entrance to the dungeon turned her away with a curt admonition. "No visitors allowed. These are me orders."

Had she the strength, Josselyn would have tried to force herself past him. But she knew she was too weak. So despite her flagging energy, she made her way back across the hall and outside, through the bailey to the gatehouse.

Isolde and Gavin trailed in her wake, as did young Gwen. Beneath the shade of the overarching gatehouse she stopped and, bracing herself with one hand, she leaned heavily against the cool stone walls. After a moment, Gavin rolled a small wooden barrel over to her, then set it upright so she could sit upon it. Grateful, she sat, clutching the curved end of the cane and supporting herself on it.

She was much weaker than she'd thought. At the moment, she doubted she could even return to the hall under her own power. But she had no intention of returning, not until she'd confronted Jasper.

The brilliance of the late morning sun gave way to a cloudy afternoon. The men did not return for the midday meal. But still Rhonwen waited. Eventually they would return and she would be there when they did. Jasper would evade her no longer.

Isolde fussed over her like a mother hen. She brought her a mug of goat's milk and some raisins and two kinds of cheeses wrapped in a clean cloth. But after a while when her every attempt at conversation petered out, the girl drifted away.

Around Rhonwen the daily hum of castle life resumed, unaffected by either her personal trauma or Rhys's. A pair of masons fitted the second row of stone for the crenellation along the western curtain wall. A team of apprentices heaved the roughly shaped blocks onto the rope lift and, through din of sheer muscle, raised it inch by inch up to the wall walk and the older masons.

The dairy maid herded the cows and goats in one by one for their evening milking. The laundress collected her dried linens before the threatening rains could ruin her handiwork.

A sullen young man made his way, muttering, to the trap door for the cess pit, accompanied by a jovial guard. Someone had to periodically clean the collection of refuse at the base of the garderobes. The task was often given as a punishment to slackers, for the foul nature of the work generally guaranteed no further such transgressions on the part of the unlucky person.

Rhonwen's gaze made a slow circuit of the bailey, seeing it in a way she'd not done before. Rosecliffe Castle was a self-sufficient place, an abode made pleasant by the continued coordination of its residents' activities. Carreg Du had been marginally as efficient while Josselyn's uncle had lived. But after his death and with no clear-cut leader to maintain order, it had become more like Afon Bryn, a rough place to live with factions constantly at odds with one another.

The truth struck her, unwelcome and yet also undeniable. Rosecliffe Castle was a good place to live and work.

That didn't mean the English king's determination to rule

Wales was right. Nor did it mean that every English lord would bring the same settled sort of peace to the lands he ruled. But in the case of Rosecliffe Castle, the truth was evident wherever she looked. Save for Rhys's rebellious presence, this part of Wales was peaceful and prosperous, for both its Welsh citizens and its British ones.

Why was that?

She heard a woman call to a child, Josselyn scolding the rambunctious Gavin. She spoke in Welsh, and he responded the same way.

It was the intermarriage of the lord and lady which made such a success of Rosecliffe, Rhonwen realized. A melding of two cultures and a care for the feelings of both. She smiled, warmed by the hope that understanding roused in her. If only Rhys could see it that way.

But it was more than merely the marriage of Welsh and English, she realized. Marriage alone would not have sufficed. Love was the secret to the peace that permeated this place. Josselyn loved Rand, and he loved her equally well. They loved, and they prospered.

Her smile faded. Had she been too hasty when she'd turned down Jasper's offer of marriage? If she had accepted, could she have avoided all this heartbreak?

She rubbed the cane handle in agitation. The answer was no.

She and Jasper were not Josselyn and Rand. For Jasper did not love her like Rand loved Josselyn. Though Rhonwen loved him, he did not return that emotion. It always came back to that.

The shadows in the bailey grew long while Rhonwen sat, mired in her unhappy thoughts. Then one of the watchmen in the gatehouse shouted to a guard across the way, rousing her. The hunting party approached.

She pushed heavily to her feet. She would not confront Jasper as an invalid. He would not avoid her by worrying over her health.

The gate was open; the bridge was down. She saw them approach, a loose line of riders breaking from the town's main

road and climbing the long hill toward the castle. Rand and
Jasper rode at the head of the party, side by side, tall and
strong. Though different in so many ways, their physical sim
ilarity was obvious. Yet only one of them pulled her heart
strings; only one of them aroused all her senses.

She sucked in a harsh breath and straightened to her ful'
height. Her side ached. She wished she did not need the cane
But none of that was as important as saving Rhys from life in
an English gaol. Though Rhys had earned the enmity of the
English, he nonetheless did not deserve that. Life was so pre
cious. She saw that now. She only hoped she could find the
words to sway Jasper.

The horses' hooves raised a thunder on the timber bridge
Rand's brows lifted when he spied her, and his gaze angled
toward Jasper.

Jasper's expression was harder to decipher.

The two of them halted before her while the other men rode
past. The falconer paused and took Rand's bird from his arm
then rode on. When the dust settled and quiet again reigned
Rand addressed her.

"I am pleased you heal from your wounds, Mistress Rhon
wen."

She stared up at him without pretense. "I will ever be in
your debt, yours and Josselyn's, for tending me so well."

" 'Tis I who owe you a debt. Not once, but twice have you
kept my brother safe. You have my thanks and my aid, insofa
as I may give it."

She smiled faintly, understanding why he qualified his offer
"Rest assured, Lord Rand, that I will never again conspire
against you or any of your family. They have become very
dear to me," she added in a huskier tone.

He nodded, then again glanced sidelong at his brother
"Was there some matter you wish to discuss with me? Or is
it an audience with Jasper you seek?"

Inside, Rhonwen began to tremble. She clutched the cane
tighter before allowing her eyes to seek out Jasper's stern fea
tures. "If you can spare his presence, I would speak with
Jasper awhile."

"As you wish." Rand gave her a courtly nod, then wheeled his animal past her.

Then it was only Rhonwen and Jasper—and the two nosy watchmen on the gate tower, and the maidservant lingering deliberately at the well, and the curious laborers beside the scaffolding.

Jasper saw them too, and his leather saddle creaked when he restlessly shifted his weight. He pushed his cowl down while his horse, Helios, tossed its head, eager for the stables and the meal waiting there. "Perhaps you would prefer some other place." With a gesture of his hand he indicated the hall.

"No. Not there. Perhaps . . . perhaps we could walk."

His eyes ran over her assessingly. Skeptically. "You hardly appear able to walk ten steps. What moved you to seek me out here? You are too ill—"

"You have stayed away three days! What else was I to do?"

He glanced up at the guards, who looked down at them with undisguised interest. Then he frowned at her. "We'll ride."

He edged his horse next to her, then leaned down to lift her up. When she stiffened, bracing for the pain such an action would incur, he misunderstood. "Damnation, Rhonwen. What is it you want of me?"

She stepped back, grimacing at the ache that sharp movement caused. When she pressed a hand against her bandaged side, he blanched.

"Curse me for an idiot," he muttered, swinging down from the animal. "Forgive me my short temper," he said when he faced her. He released the reins and, given his freedom, Helios ambled toward the stables.

" 'Tis nothing," she said. She looked past him, toward the bridge and the moat and the town beyond it. She'd waited the whole day long to see him. Now she did not know what to say.

"Would you like to sit?"

She nodded.

From somewhere behind them a door shut with a thud and he heard Isolde's voice, determinedly nonchalant. "Come,

Gwen. If we hurry, we can find the spotted kitten before it becomes too dark to see.''

Rhonwen fought back the absurd urge to laugh. Did everyone at Rosecliffe wish to eavesdrop? The same door thudded again, only this time it was Josselyn who spoke. ''Girls. Come back inside at once.''

''But Mama. I only want to help Gwen.''

''Look,'' Gwen interrupted. ''There they are. Rhonwen! Uncle Jasper!''

''Perhaps this is not a good time,'' Jasper said. ''Besides, I am filthy from my labors.''

''No,'' Rhonwen insisted. ''I would have this out between us now.'' Before I break down in tears, she added to herself.

''If we must.'' He bit the words out tersely. He looked around. ''Out there. We'll have privacy alongside the moat.''

''Very well.'' She started forward, determined to make the short walk. But with every step Rhonwen felt her energy failing. She made it to the bridge, relying heavily on the cane. She made it half the way across, though each step came slower and slower. Jasper kept pace with her, but finally his patience broke.

''I will carry you.''

''No!'' She could not bear that level of physical closeness with him.

''You will not make it otherwise. Come, Rhonwen. I will be gentle with you. Just tell me where to put my hands.''

''No,'' she repeated. But she could feel her legs beginning to buckle. With a frustrated noise she relented. ''Oh, all right.''

He caught her just in time. He slid one arm around her back. The other he placed carefully behind her knees. ''This will be the hardest part,'' he murmured, his mouth very near her ear. Then he lifted her up.

She let out a gasp. But after only a moment, the sharpest edge of the pain eased.

''Better?''

She nodded.

''Can you put your arms around my neck?''

She managed that with only a slight grimace of pain. After that it was not physical pain that affected her.

He strode across the bridge, holding her high against his chest. But what he meant only as a kindly gesture, she felt as an embrace. She knew better. But in the several minutes he held her, with dusk turning the sky from lavender to deep purple, she had no defense against her deepest feelings for him.

Would it be so bad to marry a man who did not love her? Surely it could not be worse than pining for him the remainder of her days.

Though it was unwise, she let her head rest against his shoulder. She breathed deeply, reveling in the smell of horses and leather and honest male sweat, and let herself relax into the strength of his embrace.

Her long wait and endless worrying vanished in the few minutes of unparalleled joy she found in his arms. She wished it would never end. But when he turned from the road and moved through the tangle of rose vines that lent their name to the cliffs, she forced herself to remember her purpose.

"This is far enough," she murmured self-consciously.

"A little farther. There's a soft, grassy patch where you will be more comfortable."

"I'm not so fragile as you fear, Jasper."

She felt him stiffen. Just a slight thing, but she sensed it just the same. "So it seems. But then, I've made a habit of misjudging you, haven't I?"

He set her down in a thick bed of new grass with a boulder at her back half-overgrown with the wild rose vines. She tucked her skirt around her legs and tried to compose herself. What did he mean by a habit of misjudging her?

Then she looked up at him, with his legs splayed and his arms folded across his chest, and her resolve faltered. He looked unreachable like that. Stern and implacable.

"Well?" he prompted her. "What is it you wish to say to me?"

Rhonwen frowned in frustration. "I cannot speak to you when you glower down at me like some angry god on high."

Even in the increasing darkness, with only a rising moon to illuminate him, she saw his jaw flex. "Very well," he muttered. He unfolded his arms and lowered himself to one knee, leaning his elbows on the other one. But he still looked uncomfortable and ready to flee.

How he must hate her for betraying him so!

She closed her eyes, fighting to control her wayward emotions. If she lingered much longer with Jasper, she would surely come undone.

She cleared her throat, but Jasper spoke first. "It occurs to me that I have been remiss in my behavior to you. I should long ago have thanked you for saving my life."

She raised a startled face to him. "Saving your life? 'Twas you who saved my life. You bound my wound and carried me to Rosecliffe."

He leaned toward her, his expression earnest. "You took the blade meant for me, Rhonwen. LaMonthe would have killed me but for you. Don't you remember?"

Rhonwen digested that shocking bit of news. She remembered Jasper forced to his knees by two burly guards. She remembered Rhys hesitating when LaMonthe exhorted him to slay the helpless Jasper. Then LaMonthe had lunged forward. But beyond that she remembered nothing. She shook her head. "I don't remember. How did you get free from your bindings?"

Jasper told the entire story, and she listened, wide-eyed, to his tale of Rhys's horror at LaMonthe's deed, of Rhys freeing him and how the two enemies had combined to fight off a third enemy.

When Jasper was done with his tale, the two of them sat a long minute in silence. Then he said, "So you see, you have saved me yet again. Ten years ago it was my hand you saved, and mayhap my life as well. Now I most assuredly owe you my life."

She made a wry face. "You forget that just a few weeks ago I tried to put an arrow through your heart."

"So you did," he answered in an ironic voice. "But the debt I owed you canceled your misguided attempt at assassi-

ation. Now you have saved me again, and I find myself once
more in your debt.''

Then pay your debt with an offer of marriage, she wanted
to shout at him. *Renew the offer you made for my hand and
let me agree this time. Then will any debt you owe me be
finally paid.*

But what of Rhys? another voice persisted.

With shoulders slumping she said, ''We have both of us
survived a difficult time. Ten years ago 'twas Owain, a Welshman, that mistreated and betrayed his own people. This time
it was LaMonthe, an Englishman. But . . . but we are alive and
. . and . . .'' She looked down at her lap, at her fingers twisted
together in agitation. He was an honorable man; he paid his
debts. She had but to ask.

She took a breath and raised her eyes back to his. ''Will
you explain to me why Rhys is held in Rosecliffe's dungeon?
If he freed you to fight LaMonthe, then he saved your life
more so than did I.''

His face closed at the mere mention of Rhys's name. Even
his frown vanished, to be replaced by a hard blankness she
could not decipher. Behind the shuttered darkness of his eyes
she saw only a tense watchfulness. ''Speak plainly what it is
you want of me, Rhonwen. Do not leave me to guess at your
thoughts. I have not proven to be adept at that,'' he grimly
added.

She pressed her lips together and her fingers twisted to the
point of pain. Must they ever be at odds with one another?
''Please,'' she began, then halted when her voice trembled
with emotions better forever buried. ''If you are honest in your
profession of debt to me, then . . . then I beg you to free Rhys
from his confinement.''

A muscle ticked in his jaw. Otherwise he remained as still
as a stone carving. ''He is my brother's prisoner, not mine.
Better that you plead your case with Rand.''

''But it is you Rhys aided. With your own words you admit
. Intercede for him, Jasper.'' She leaned forward and, without
thinking, reached out a hand to him.

He recoiled as if she had threatened him with a weapon.

Jerking to his feet, he began to pace. "I have already done as you ask. I pleaded my case before Rand but he will not free the boy. You forget that Rhys's crimes are many. He has long harried our English people and also your Welsh folk who seek to live at peace with us. Those crimes are petty, though, in the face of his recent activities. He stole Isolde—a mere child—from the safety of her family. Had we not foiled him, who knows what he might have done to her—"

"He would never have hurt her!"

"So long as you were there to prevent it," he countered. "Isolde has made that clear. But he has never paid for that crime. Then he conspired with LaMonthe to overthrow Rose-cliffe Castle."

"He never put that plan into effect."

"Again, because you spoiled it."

At her surprised look, he gave a short laugh. "You wonder how I know that. You forget that he is but a boy and his emotions are easily manipulated. By baiting him I have learned enough to deduce the truth. You left Rosecliffe before he could enact his scheme." He had paused in his pacing. Now he faced her. "Why did you did that? Why?"

Rhonwen closed her eyes in dejection and turned her face away. "Only a man would ask such a question. I did not wish to see blood spilled, neither Welsh nor English. I could not lend my assistance to Rhys, knowing the ugly battle that must surely ensue."

"So you left."

"I left."

"And I followed you."

She looked back at him. "Yes. You did. Why?"

He'd begun to thaw, but he froze at her question. She saw his face grow hard once more, and his lips curled in derision. "Why? Surely you can answer that question yourself. I desire you still. 'Tis no more than that."

'Tis no more than that. How deeply those casual words struck her. How cruelly. And yet, somehow something in his

manner did not ring true. Rhonwen was afraid to risk her fragile emotions, and yet she was more afraid to go on not knowing the truth.

She braced herself and met his mocking stare. "You can still have that."

His fierce frown did not encourage her. "You are hardly up to such energetic activity."

"I will be soon enough."

Again the muscle jumped in his jaw. His eyes glittered with angry emotion. "So you will whore for him? To free Rhys you will play the whore with me. Again."

She could not bear the accusation in his voice. "I never whored for him. Ever."

"So you say. But what was that last night between us? You searched me out deliberately, to ensure I did not lock the postern gate."

"I came to you for my own sake."

"Oho. I see the difference clearly. You whored to ensure your escape."

"I came to you for my own sake," she repeated, rising painfully to her feet. "For my own ... my own ..." She could not go on.

"For your own pleasure?" He nodded his head and laughed, but without any real mirth. "At least you leave my pride intact. So you came to me for your own pleasure. I am comforted. That is one crime, at least, that cannot be laid at your lover's door."

"He is not my lover! You of all people must know that!"

"Perhaps he has not had the love of your body. But damn you, Rhonwen, 'tis clear enough he has the love of your heart! Everything you've done, even your presence here now, has been for him."

They faced one another in the chill darkness, and his words seemed to echo in the night.

"Is that what has you so enraged?" she asked in a low voice. "That he might have the love of my heart?"

She heard his harsh breathing, but nothing else.

"Jasper, will you not answer me? Do I have the right of it?"

"Yes," he snapped. "But that signifies nothing." He swept the air with one hand. "Enough of this. You've made your offer to me, but to no end. Rand will not free Rhys and I will not encourage him any further to do so. There is nothing more to be said on that subject. Come," he added, his voice gentling. "You are exhausted. I will carry you back to your chamber."

He took three steps toward her, then halted an arm's-length away. They faced one another in the night, two enemies, yet they had been lovers. Rhonwen had never felt so hopeless. Once they returned to the castle, she was certain he would avoid her completely. She was not ready to face that possibility, however. So, ignoring the hurt in her heart, and ignoring his ability to hurt her further still, she said, "You have lain with many women."

He drew back, his face wary. "That is not your concern."

"I know. I am only trying to understand."

"What is there for you to understand?"

"Your rage that Rhys might possess my heart." When his wariness increased she pressed on. "Has it been your wish to possess the heart of every woman you have laid with?"

After a long silence he answered, "No."

Unaccountably her heart leaped. "Then why . . . I mean . . . why should it matter . . ."

When she halted, he continued, "Why should it matter with you? Why should it drive me to madness to think you love him?" he laughed, a bitter, derisive sound. "Why do you think that is, Rhonwen?"

She stepped nearer to him. The moonlight made him a creature of pale shadows and darker ones. Cold and remote. Yet tortured, and perhaps on account of her. "Tell me," she whispered. She raised a hand to his chest and rested it lightly upon the coarse wool of his tunic. "Tell me why it matters to you."

His eyes burned down into hers. She saw fury and misery and something else she had only hoped for. One of his hands closed over hers. "I was foolish enough to think . . ." He hesitated, and she held her breath. "To think you would make me a suitable wife."

She let out a disappointed breath, but she was too close to back away now. "Yes. You did offer me marriage that one time. But why? Why did you do that?" she persisted.

He did not want to answer her; she could see that. "Tell me," she pressed him. "Tell me why."

"Because I loved you!"

Lightning could not have shattered the night more powerfully than those few angry words. He pulled away, raking agitated hands though his hair while Rhonwen reeled from the impact of his revelation. She'd wanted him to admit as much, yet she'd not anticipated the force those words wielded. She hugged her arms around herself, trying to control her trembling while a smile lit up her face.

"Could you love me again?" she asked. "If you knew that I loved you too, could you ever love me again?"

He froze with his hands upraised, and stared at her as if not completely certain what she had just said. A chill of uncertainty settled over her. What if his answer was no?

Then he lowered his hands and faced her, his body tense, his brow creased in doubt. "If I thought you loved me . . ." He took a harsh breath, and in his eyes she saw fear and longing, misery and hope. "Is that what you are saying, Rhonwen? That you love me?"

Slowly Rhonwen nodded; the emotions clogging her throat made it impossible to speak. An amazing joy. Utter happiness . . .

"I do love you," she murmured, closing the distance between them. "I do. I have for so long now."

"Could that be true?" he whispered in amazement. But then he raised a hand, holding her back, and wariness rose anew in his face. Wariness and agony. "Do you truly love me? Or is this just another way to save Rhys?"

"No, 'tis not that at all! I love you, Jasper. But . . . but I confess, I do wish to save Rhys. He does not deserve to rot in a faraway prison. Still—"

"Rand does not plan to punish him with a prolonged imprisonment."

"What?" She gaped at him, in astonishment. "He doesn't?"

"No." His face closed in a frown. "Does that change anything?"

Rhonwen let out a huge sigh. "Yes. No. I mean, it changes nothing of my love for you—" She broke off.

"Go on. You love me. But what of Rhys?"

She swallowed hard and knew it was time to let go of pride and fear. "It changes nothing of my love for you, Jasper. That is deep and abiding. But . . . but it does make it easier to accept your brother as my brother-by-marriage—that is, if you still wish to wed with me," she finished in a mere whisper.

"I do."

"You do?"

He took the final step to close the distance between them. Then he took her hands in his and lifted them both to his lips. A feather-light kiss to her knuckles, a silent pledge to her heart. Then Jasper lifted his head and their eyes met and held.

"I have had other women in my bed, Rhonwen. I'll not lie to you. But I have never wanted anything from them beyond a moment's pleasure. But you . . . from the moment I saw you beside the river, I wanted so much more. I need more from you. And I need to know I have your love."

Tears stung her eyes. Foolish, embarrassing tears of joy and amazement. "I do love you, Jasper." She laughed and drew his hands to her lips. "I did not want to love you, but love you I do."

Then she was in his arms, wrapped in his loving embrace, any pain in her side forgotten. They kissed, a long, sweet kiss promising an enduring love, that soon changed into the hot, violent kiss of urgent desire.

"Rhonwen . . . Rhonwen . . ." he murmured against her lips, her cheeks, her eyes.

"I love you, Jasper. I do."

"Then marry me tomorrow."

"Oh, yes."

"Tonight."

"I will."

Without warning he swept her up in his arms and, with compelling haste, carried her back toward the castle. The guards in the gatehouse began to laugh when they crossed the bridge. Isolde, loitering in the bailey, giggled and clapped her hands in glee.

Josselyn appeared from a shadow and, at her knowing smile, Rhonwen ducked her head against Jasper's shoulder, happy, embarrassed, and overflowing with emotion.

"Is there no privacy in this place?" Jasper grumbled.

"There will be time enough for privacy later," Josselyn informed him.

"We are to be wed," Rhonwen revealed. She pressed a kiss to Jasper's neck, smiling as she did.

"We know," Isolde and Josselyn chorused.

As they made their way across the bailey, they were joined by others: two maids, Osborn, and two of the knights. Gavin and Gwen. With an entourage of well-wishers they ascended the steps to the great hall, where Rand awaited them, grinning his pleasure. Rhonwen swept the bailey with her gaze, noting the stout, encircling walls, the lit gate tower, and neatly organized yard.

From the outside Rosecliffe appeared a cold and menacing fortress. Yet within it was a home, warm and welcoming and safe.

Unaccountably Newlin's words echoed in her mind. *The end of the world as you know it.*

Yes, her old world, her old life, was done. But the new one would be better. Love would make it so.

Epilogue

When you come home your men among,
You shall have revell, daunces and song.

—*anonymous medieval verse*

Rosecliffe Castle
June 1146

The chapel bells rang Sext, pealing across the country-side, summoning the people of both castle and village. Gavin and Gwen together yanked on the knotted bell cord, throwing their meager weights to the task, and flying off their feet amid great good humor.

"Come, come, children." Josselyn clapped her hands at them. "Enough giggling. A baptism is a solemn event." But her wide smile gave the lie to her words. She was so pleased to be named godmother to Rhonwen and Jasper's new son that nothing could ruin her mood. Not even her own noisy off-spring.

The priest waited in the bailey beside a stone font that had been carried out from the chapel. It was a glorious day, and Rhonwen had insisted the baptism be performed in God's greatest church, serenaded by the fresh breeze and freewheel-ing birds, with the bright sky arcing over all.

Rhonwen held the baby in her arms, with Jasper's arms circling about them both. She looked down into the dark un-blinking gaze of her precious son, then up into the gleaming eyes of his proud father. Though people crowded the court-yard, eager for the ceremony and the feasting to follow, for Rhonwen there was only Jasper and her sweet little Guy.

"I love you," Jasper whispered, smiling down at her.

She nodded, unable to speak, for unexpected emotion ha
caught in her throat. "I love you too," she finally manage
"And I love this wondrous child you have given me."

"That you have given me," he amended.

On impulse she offered the child to him and when he gladl
took his son into his arms, quick tears stung her eyes. Ho
could she have lived her whole life, never suspecting the hap
piness to be had merely from the sight of a beloved babe hel
so lovingly in the arms of his beloved father?

The priest began the ceremony. Guy suffered oil upon hi
brow well enough. He even smiled when Father Christophe
lifted the ewer of holy water to his head and poured.

"I baptize thee in the name of the Father and the Son an
the Holy Spirit," the priest intoned.

Then the bells began again to ring, and Guy jerked in hi
father's grasp. His tiny face screwed up in a frown. At th
first furious wail, Jasper gave Rhonwen a worried look.

"Just hold him close and comfort him," she said.

When he did that, however, the baby began to root greedil
against his chest. Jasper's eyebrows arched, the pries
coughed, and Josselyn and Rand began to laugh.

"He needs your sort of comfort," Jasper said. Then he gav
her a crooked grin and added in a lower voice. "And so d
I."

As she took Guy into her arms, Rhonwen smiled into he
husband's face. "Comfort, you say. Hmm. I believe . . . yes.
believe I can manage that."

A hot light leaped in Jasper's eyes, and she felt an answer
ing heat. Nearly three months they'd restrained themselves
but tonight would see an end to it.

"I love you." He mouthed the words and the bells of Rose
cliffe seemed to peal the message across the land. He love
her. She loved him.

Was ever a woman so blessed?

Barnard Castle, Northumbria
June 1146

The bells of St. Joseph's Abbey, not a league distant from Barnard Castle, rang. Prime and Terce, Vespers and Compline. Every three hours the monks of the abbey pulled and leaped, marking the passage of the hours and days and seasons of the year.

Those bells proscribed Rhys's life at Barnard Castle, as surely as did the unchanging rhythm of his arduous days. Two years and a month he'd been under Friar Guilliame's tutelage. It felt more like ten years since he'd been gone from Wales, and yet sometimes he felt as if he'd been ripped from his homeland but last week.

The pealing of the bells for Sext ended, and at once the three lads who labored beside him put down the horse brushes they'd wielded for the past several hours. Time to wash up and prepare for serving the good friar and the rest of the castle retainers.

Edward, a skinny fourteen-year-old, dashed off first. Of late he'd taken to mooning over Lady Barnard's silly little daughter, and he took great pains with his appearance. Philip and Kevin, twelve and nine, hooted with laughter at Edward's taste.

But Rhys frowned. He understood how a woman could overwhelm a man's senses, making him behave the fool. A woman could turn a smart man into a half-wit. She could make hardened one soft.

Hadn't Rhonwen done as much to him?

His jaw clenched in anger to remember how much he'd loved her—and how much he'd lost because of her. Barnard Castle was not a prison. He worked among the other squires, though he was of an age to be knighted. Not that he desired that self-congratulatory Norman title. But he was a man stuck among mere lads. He learned Latin and French and etiquette

among them. He served his English master at table, and some
times helped him with his dress and other personal matter.
All in all, better than the dungeon at Rosecliffe, though it ha
taken him a long time to admit as much, even to himself.

At first he'd fought every effort to conform to a life amon
the English. But he'd been beaten into submission enoug
times to know that rebellion did him no good. So he watche
and listened and learned, and he took advantage of all the
taught him. No doubt the FitzHugh brothers thought to indoc
trinate him to their English way of life. The more fools they
for Rhys would never abandon his loyalty to the land of hi
birth.

For now, however, Rhys was content to let them believ
they'd succeeded. But he was a Welshman. The blood of drag
ons ran in his veins. Neither manners nor dress nor close
cropped hair could alter that.

He'd learned to ride like an expert and to wield a swor
with cool-headed determination, using his mind as much a
the strength of his arm. He tilted better than most of th
knights at Barnard, and his archery skills were second to none
He answered to Friar Guilliame and Lady Barnard as he mus
and plotted revenge against Jasper and Rand FitzHugh the res
of the time.

Now he was the last to leave the stables, pouring a bucke
of fresh water into a water trough, then hooking the empt
bucket on its hook. He patted the massive bay destrier on i
heavily muscled rump, then stepped out of the stall and close
it. Outside the stables he saw the castle folk making their wa
to the hall for their midday dinner.

One of the dairy maids sent him a shy smile. He nodded
but he steeled himself not to smile in return. It was a woma
who'd brought him to this: exile in a foreign land among
foreign people.

He'd vowed long ago that he would never give a woma
that sort of power over him again.

Rosecliffe Village
June 1146

From behind her, Isolde heard the chapel bells ring Vespers. Though the sun yet showed in the summer sky, the hour grew late. Soon enough the castle gate would be lowered. If she was not home before then, her mother would raise a great hue and cry.

But Isolde was restless. Ever since Guy's baptism earlier in the day, she'd been possessed of a strange and yearning feeling, as if some great change were about to occur. So she'd gone into the village with her friend Edythe. Now she should be hurrying home, but instead she'd paused at the unfinished edge of the town wall, where the cliffs began their sharp drop to the sea.

She leaned against a pile of rough-hewn masonry blocks and stared past the wall that separated the town from the wild fields and hills, until a cramp in her stomach brought a grimace to her face. All morning her stomach had felt odd. Now it was beginning to hurt down low. She pressed her palms against the crampy area. Had she eaten something that had spoiled?

A raven glided over the top of the wall, startling her. She turned to go home, then gasped when she spied a figure in the shadows of the wall. "Newlin!" she exclaimed, her hand at her throat.

He smiled and his ancient face creased in odd folds and wrinkles. "You do not contemplate another adventure in the forest." A statement, not a question.

Isolde smoothed a loose tendril of hair from her eyes. "Of course not," she answered with as much dignity as she could muster.

"That is good," the old bard responded. "Your mother is calling for you," he added.

She let out an exasperated sigh. "Why does she persist in treating me like I'm still a baby?" She lifted her chin and squared her shoulders. "I'm eleven—almost twelve years old now—practically old enough to wed. I'm well able to see to my own welfare while I'm in town. Besides, ever since my father sent that villainous ogre Rhys ap Owain away, there's been nothing to fear."

Unfortunately her bravado was undermined by another sharp pang in her belly and she bent over in pain. When it eased she looked sheepishly at Newlin. "I think I may have eaten something that was spoiled."

He smiled and began to rock forward and back, just a tiny movement, but it was mesmerizing. "You are no longer a child," he said. "Go to your mother. She will assist you. She will be pleased to know her eldest child is become a woman this day."

"A woman?" Isolde echoed. She pressed her hands to her cramping stomach as understanding dawned. "A woman," she repeated, and her frown became a smile. She'd been waiting for this day for a long time, but now that it had come she was a little afraid. She wanted her mother.

"Yes, I had better be going," she said, giving him a hasty wave. Then she started at a fast trot up the hill toward the castle gate.

Newlin watched her until she reached the bridge. Then he closed his eyes and rubbed his fingers over the lids. It was growing harder and harder to focus his wayward eyes on a single object. His thoughts, too, seemed often to veer in two directions at once.

So too were they all torn. A young woman, English in many ways, but Welsh in her heart where she did not yet see. And across the miles, far from the lands of his birth, an angry young man clung to his Welsh ways even as he soaked up the sensibilities of the English.

Meanwhile another babe was born and christened, half-Welsh, half-English.

Then he opened his eyes and smiled and turned for the *domen.* Life changed. It struggled and twisted and reinvented itself constantly. But it always went on.

The following is an excerpt from
Rhys and Isolde's story, the final
book in the Rosecliffe Trilogy:
The Mistress of Rosecliffe
coming soon from
St. Martin's Paperbacks

Isolde had heard very little, a dull thump from far away, a hushed voice on the nearby wall walk. She strained to hear better. Was it an English voice or a Welsh one? She'd not been able to tell. So she had lain there in the dark, cursing Rhys ap Owain, beseeching God's help, and bemoaning her own stupidity.

How could she have been so blind? How could she not have seen the resemblance? The same black eyes. The same arrogant manner. She should have recognized him. She should have guessed.

She should have listened to Osborn.

He had not wanted to let the minstrel band inside the castle at all. But she'd been so sure of herself, so heady with her own power. Just look where it had brought her.

In the darkened chamber she silently raged and fought her bindings. But it was a futile battle, as futile as her vain attempt to put the worst of her many errors out of her mind. She'd given her innocence to a man she hated, one she'd loathed since she was but a child. Like the green girl she was, she'd been completely taken by him, besotted by his fine physique, his deep voice, and his intense gaze. And to think she'd been fool enough to believe he possessed the heart of a poet.

Once more she fought her bindings, chafing her already

scraped wrists and ankles. Tears stung her eyes and slipped down her cheeks. Had she truly been so stupid as to think love was a part of her feelings for him? She groaned in shame. Bad enough that he'd evoked those incredible feelings from her body, traitorous creature that it was. But for a few moments she'd actually thought she loved the odious wretch!

Outside a voice sounded and she went still. Laughter. Had Rosecliffe's guards foiled Rhys's plans? Had they captured him and cast him into the deepest hole in the *donjon*? She prayed it was so. She prayed desperately that it was so.

But then a voice came more clearly through the window, a jovial Welsh voice. "Ho, Tafydd. What a night, eh?"

Isolde's hopes died a swift, brutal death. He'd won!

She hardly had time to digest that awful fact when footsteps echoed in the stairwell, heavy footsteps rising nearer and nearer.

She twisted her head to see the door and shuddered when it opened, for the figure silhouetted there was tall and broad-shouldered. It was him. She knew it though he did not speak.

He closed the door and moved deeper into the room. Metal struck against flint, and each time she jumped. Once. Twice. The third time a tiny spark caught the bit of charred cloth in the bowl beside the bed, and with that he lit a fresh candle.

But as light filled the chamber, as he lit two more candles and stood them in the candelabra, it was a different man who turned to face her. He'd abandoned his rough tunic for a warrior's leather hauberk, and his worn brogans for tall boots. A sword hung at his side, heavy and ominous, and a thin dagger dangled at his hip.

This was a man of war, not a minstrel. How had she not seen that before? Those thickly muscled arms came from wielding a sword, not a gittern. The wide shoulders and thick chest were built through years of battle and exercise, not through strumming and singing.

Then he raised the candles higher and she saw his face and gasped. Gone were the long wild hair and woolly beard. In their stead appeared a face she would have known. He was ten years older—and ten years harder—but he was the same

Rhys ap Owain who'd kidnapped her so long ago. He was her enemy no matter how comely his features and how manly his form. That his teeth were straight and his lips well formed only drove home to her the depths of her terrible mistake. He could have the face of an angel, yet still he was the devil's spawn.

Isolde's chest hurt, her heart pounded so violently. She should have been more wary. She should not have been so smug. She should have done as her father wanted and agreed to a marriage with Mortimer Halyard. Because of her vanity and stupidity, she'd been ruined, and had also opened the door to her family's ruin.

As if he guessed her thoughts, he grinned down at her, the awful, beautiful grin of a predator who toys with his victim knowing full well she has no escape. He crossed to the bed then set the brace of candles on a table near her head.

" 'Tis a great day at Rosecliffe, Isolde. The Welsh have regained what was stolen from them."

She closed her eyes against the wolfish triumph in his face then jerked them open again when he sat beside her on the bed. "I am victorious," he continued in a huskier tone. "And you know what is said of the victor. To him go all the spoils . . ."

Survey

TELL US WHAT YOU THINK AND YOU COULD WIN
A YEAR OF ROMANCE!
(That's 12 books!)

Fill out the survey below, send it back to us, and you'll be eligible to win a year's worth of romance novels. That's one book a month for a year—from St. Martin's Paperbacks.

Name _____

Street Address _____

City, State, Zip Code _____

Email address _____

1. How many romance books have you bought in the last year?
    (Check one.)
    __0-3
    __4-7
    __8-12
    __13-20
    __20 or more

2. Where do you MOST often buy books? *(limit to two choices)*
    __Independent bookstore
    __Chain stores *(Please specify)*
        __Barnes and Noble
        __B. Dalton
        __Books-a-Million
        __Borders
        __Crown
        __Lauriat's
        __Media Play
        __Waldenbooks
    __Supermarket
    __Department store *(Please specify)*
        __Caldor
        __Target
        __Kmart
        __Walmart
    __Pharmacy/Drug store
    __Warehouse Club
    __Airport

3. Which of the following promotions would MOST influence your decision to purchase a ROMANCE paperback? *(Check one.)*
        __Discount coupon

__Free preview of the first chapter
__Second book at half price
__Contribution to charity
__Sweepstakes or contest

4. Which promotions would LEAST influence your decision to purchase a ROMANCE book? (Check one.)
    __Discount coupon
    __Free preview of the first chapter
    __Second book at half price
    __Contribution to charity
    __Sweepstakes or contest

5. When a new ROMANCE paperback is released, what is MOST influential in your finding out about the book and in helping you to decide to buy the book? (Check one.)
    __TV advertisement
    __Radio advertisement
    __Print advertising in newspaper or magazine
    __Book review in newspaper or magazine
    __Author interview in newspaper or magazine
    __Author interview on radio
    __Author appearance on TV
    __Personal appearance by author at bookstore
    __In-store publicity (poster, flyer, floor display, etc.)
    __Online promotion (author feature, banner advertising, giveaway)
    __Word of Mouth
    __Other (please specify)_____

6. Have you ever purchased a book online?
    __Yes
    __No

7. Have you visited our website?
    __Yes
    __No

8. Would you visit our website in the future to find out about new releases or author interviews?
    __Yes
    __No

9. What publication do you read most?
    __Newspapers *(check one)*
      __*USA Today*
      __*New York Times*
      __Your local newspaper
    __Magazines *(check one)*

　　　　　__*People*
　　　　　__*Entertainment Weekly*
　　　　　__Women's magazine *(Please specify:_____)*
　　　　　__*Romantic Times*
　　　　　__Romance newsletters

10. What type of TV program do you watch most? *(Check one.)*
　　　　__Morning News Programs (ie. "Today Show")
　　　　　(Please specify:_____)
　　　　__Afternoon Talk Shows (ie. "Oprah")
　　　　　(Please specify: _____)
　　　　__All news (such as CNN)
　　　　__Soap operas　　*(Please specify: _____)*
　　　　__Lifetime cable station
　　　　__E! cable station
　　　　__Evening magazine programs (ie. "Entertainment Tonight")
　　　　　(Please specify: _____)
　　　　__Your local news

11. What radio stations do you listen to most? *(Check one.)*
　　　　　__Talk Radio
　　　　　__Easy Listening/Classical
　　　　　__Top 40
　　　　　__Country
　　　　　__Rock
　　　　　__Lite rock/Adult contemporary
　　　　　__CBS radio network
　　　　　__National Public Radio
　　　　　__WESTWOOD ONE radio network

12. What time of day do you listen to the radio MOST?
　　　　__6am-10am
　　　　__10am-noon
　　　　__Noon-4pm
　　　　__4pm-7pm
　　　　__7pm-10pm
　　　　__10pm-midnight
　　　　__Midnight-6am

13. Would you like to receive email announcing new releases and special promotions?
　　　　　__Yes
　　　　　__No

14. Would you like to receive postcards announcing new releases and special promotions?
　　　　　__Yes
　　　　　__No

15. Who is your favorite romance author? _____

WIN A YEAR OF ROMANCE FROM SMP
(That's 12 Books!)
No Purchase Necessary

OFFICIAL RULES

1. To Enter: Complete the Official Entry Form and Survey and mail it to: Win a Year of Romance from SMP Sweepstakes, c/o St. Martin's Paperbacks, 175 Fifth Avenue, Suite 1615, New York, NY 10010-7848, Attention JP. For a copy of the Official Entry Form and Survey, send a self-addressed, stamped envelope to: Entry Form/Survey, c/o St. Martin's Paperbacks at the address stated above. Entries with the completed surveys must be received by February 1, 2000 (February 22, 2000 for entry forms requested by mail). Limit one entry per person. No mechanically reproduced or illegible entries accepted. Not responsible for lost, misdirected, mutilated or late entries.

2. Random Drawing. Winner will be determined in a random drawing to be held on or about March 1, 2000 from all eligible entries received. Odds of winning depend on the number of eligible entries received. Potential winner will be notified by mail on or about March 22, 2000 and will be asked to execute and return an Affidavit of Eligibility/Release/Prize Acceptance Form within fourteen (14) days of attempted notification. Non-compliance within this time may result in disqualification and the selection of an alternate winner. Return of any prize/prize notification as undeliverable will result in disqualification and an alternate winner will be selected.

3. Prize and approximate Retail Value: Winner will receive a copy of a different romance novel each month from April 2000 through March 2001. Approximate retail value $84.00 (U.S. dollars).

4. Eligibility. Open to U.S. and Canadian residents (excluding residents of the province of Quebec) who are 18 at the time of entry. Employees of St. Martin's and its parent, affiliates and subsidiaries, its and their directors, officers and agents, and their immediate families or those living in the same household, are ineligible to enter. Potential Canadian winners will be required to correctly answer a time-limited arithmetic skill question by mail. Void in Puerto Rico and wherever else prohibited by law.

5. General Conditions: Winner is responsible for all federal, state and local taxes. No substitution or cash redemption of prize permitted by winner. Prize is not transferable. Acceptance of prize constitutes permission to use the winner's name, photograph and likeness for purposes of advertising and promotion without additional compensation or permission, unless prohibited by law.

6. All entries become the property of sponsor, and will not be returned. By participating in this sweepstakes, entrants agree to be bound by these official rules and the decision of the judges, which are final in all respects.

7. For the name of the winner, available after March 22, 2000, send by May 1, 2000 a stamped, self-addressed envelope to Winner's List, Win a Year of Romance from SMP Sweepstakes, St. Martin's Paperbacks, 175 Fifth Avenue, Suite 1615, New York, NY 10010-7848, Attention JP.